TITLES BY ALEX BERENSON

THE
COUNTERFEIT AGENT

ALEX BERENSON

J

JOVE BOOKS | NEW YORK

THE BERKLEY PUBLISHING GROUP
Published by the Penguin Group
Penguin Group (USA) LLC
375 Hudson Street, New York, New York 10014

USA • Canada • UK • Ireland • Australia • New Zealand • India • South Africa • China

penguin.com

A Penguin Random House Company

THE COUNTERFEIT AGENT

A Jove Book / published by arrangement with the author

Jove Books are published by The Berkley Publishing Group.
JOVE® is a registered trademark of Penguin Group (USA) LLC.
The "J" design is a trademark of Penguin Group (USA) LLC.
The Edgar® name is a registered service mark of Mystery Writers of America, Inc.

For information, address: The Berkley Publishing Group,
a division of Penguin Group (USA) LLC,
375 Hudson Street, New York, New York 10014.

ISBN: 978-0-515-15510-5

PUBLISHING HISTORY
G. P. Putnam's Sons hardcover edition / February 2014
Jove premium edition / February 2015

PRINTED IN THE UNITED STATES OF AMERICA

10 9 8 7 6 5 4 3 2 1

Cover art: "flag" © Danita Delimont / Gallo Images / Getty Images;
"Istanbul scene" © Murat Taner / Photographers Choice / Getty Images.
Cover design by Richard Hasselberger.

PROLOGUE

All private planes were not created equal. The woman who called herself Salome usually rode a Gulfstream G550, a jet that could jump nonstop from Zurich to Johannesburg. But her boss had commandeered the 550 a week earlier. *Busy month. Take the IV.* The G-IV was a fine aircraft, but it would have run out of fuel over the jungles of Congo.

And the meeting could not be postponed.

So Salome made a virtue of necessity, overnighting in Nairobi. She added a pistol and extra ammunition to the deposit box at the Standard Chartered. She checked the alarm in the safe house in Westlands. True, she had nothing planned in Kenya. But better to have and not need . . .

Salome was pretty, when she wanted to be. Not exactly beautiful, but outright beauty was not an asset in her line of work. Beautiful women were memorable. She preferred to be forgotten. She was in her thirties, slim, with shoulder-length hair, light brown eyes. Her least attractive feature was her nose, which seemed imported from a bigger face. She could have been Spanish or Italian, but she wasn't. Her English was flawless, but she wasn't American or British. She wore a simple gold band on her ring finger, but she wasn't married. Men paid much less attention to married women.

To say she *called* herself Salome was not exactly correct. None of her passports used the name. She rarely spoke it aloud. More accurate to say she *thought* of herself as Salome. Lately the name had become more real than the one her mother and father had given her. Salome, who danced for Herod and demanded the head of John the Baptist as her reward. A biblical vixen up there with her better-known cousins, Jezebel and Delilah. A stagy name. Spoken too often, it might sound foolish. Yet she couldn't deny its power over her.

So. Salome.

The jet left Wilson Airport in Nairobi a few minutes after sunrise, following a grimy Cessna that Salome suspected was CIA. She restrained the urge to wave. The G-IV was too showy for this airport. The 550 would have been worse. Something to remember for her next visit. She closed her eyes and counted to ten. At six she was asleep.

She woke only when the flight attendant touched her shoulder.

"Ms. Kerr? We land in ten minutes."

She was Helen Kerr today, according to her passport—which happened to be Kenyan. The choice wasn't as odd as it first seemed. Thousands of British colonists and their families had kept their Kenyan citizenship. Plus South Africa didn't require a visa for Kenyans, making it a good place to use the passport. Salome rotated her identities carefully. Airports were tricky places for her, surveillance funnels that tightened each year. Entry and exit records were permanently saved, passports checked against transnational databases. Some countries now took digital head shots of every arriving passenger. The National Security Agency had access, overt or covert, to every record.

Fortunately, most countries did not routinely fingerprint passengers. Not yet. When that day came, Salome's trips would become even more complicated. Fewer private jets. More border runs, train rides, and chartered ships. She would become a smuggler, with herself as her only cargo. She didn't look forward to the change.

Today, though, the immigration agent barely glanced at her photo. "Purpose of trip?"

"Safari."

"You don't safari in Kenya?"

"I hear Kruger is better. Wanted to see for myself."

The agent smiled. "Length of stay?"

"Three days."

That quickly he stamped her passport, nodded her along. As she walked through the nothing-to-declare line at customs, she felt the familiar relief that came with escaping the funnel. She could never be sure. She didn't underestimate the NSA's abilities. Their computers could trace a signal through a trillion bits of noise. But they needed a place to start. Helen Kerr's safari wasn't it.

She emerged from the terminal at eleven a.m. and blinked her eyes against the bright sun. Winter in the northern hemisphere, summer in the south. A perk of this trip. Her driver, Jan, stood beside a Land Cruiser, holding a sign with her name. He was a white man, thickly muscled.

"Ms. Kerr. Pleasure to meet you." He had a strong South African accent, the words spoken slowly, the syllables mashed together. *Plea-shuh.* He grunted a little as he lifted her bag into the Toyota. "Heavy." He didn't dare ask what was inside.

She ignored him, ignored him again when he asked if her flight had been smooth. Best if he knew nothing about her. Not even her accent. For two hours they drove west on a divided highway filled with square Mercedes trucks and pickups overloaded with furniture. South Africans loved auto racing. The drivers on this highway seemed to think they were auditioning for Formula One. They sped, tailgated, sliced between lanes without signaling— sometimes all three at once.

Finally, a sign proclaimed the Free State province, featuring the suitably Orwellian motto *Success Through Unity.* After another hour Jan steered the Toyota north onto a rutted two-lane road that cut through rich farmland, sunflower and wheat fields. "Another forty, forty-five minutes." Nothing more. *Good boy,* she almost said. *You're learning.*

During apartheid, this province had been among the

most racist areas in South Africa. Blacks without the proper pass cards had a nasty habit of disappearing, their bodies turning up months later. Of course, apartheid had ended decades before. Blacks could live wherever they chose in South Africa. Yet many avoided the Free State. Because of men like the one Salome had flown five thousand miles to see.

His estate was small and manicured. Two gray mares grazed behind a low brick wall topped with a wire fence. Every few meters, pictographs of a lightning bolt hung from its mesh. To warn off anyone who couldn't read "Danger: Electricity," Salome supposed. The entry gate was eight feet of wrought iron watched by twin security cameras. Behind it Salome glimpsed a handsome brick house with a columned front porch. "Witwans Manor," a bronze plaque proclaimed. Rand Witwans had stolen even more money than Salome had imagined. Or his wife had been an heiress. Or both.

The gate swung open as the Land Cruiser arrived. They were expected. The Toyota rolled up the gravel driveway as a German shepherd trotted alongside. Like everything else here, the shepherd was a model of the breed, tall and imposing, with dark, broody eyes: *That bite hurt me more than it hurt you.* Salome preferred cats to dogs. Cats were more subtle. Deadlier, too. The average house cat killed hundreds of birds and mice every year if its owners were kind or foolish enough to allow it outside. Though Salome had neither cat nor dog. Nor husband nor child. Years before, she'd imagined she would. No longer. This project had become her life.

As the Cruiser stopped in front of the house, the shepherd barked an urgent warning. In a window on the second floor, a steel-gray Great Dane looked down on them, jowls quivering. A thief who feared dogs had best find another house.

The front door swung open. A tall man wearing a blue blazer and khakis stepped onto the porch. Rand Witwans. In his mid-seventies, he still aspired to be an English country gentleman. He had most of his hair, but the wattles of his neck betrayed his age.

"Natalie," he shouted. "So nice to see you again."

Her name wasn't Natalie, either.

The shepherd stepped close to the Toyota. He bared his teeth and gave a guttural growl, low and carnivorous. A knife being whetted. Witwans whistled. The shepherd turned and trotted inside the house.

Jan stepped around the Cruiser to open her door. "I'll be here. Call if you need me. Though you seem very"—he paused—"self-sufficient."

The screened back porch overlooked a swimming pool whose water was a shocking electric blue. Salome and Witwans sat side by side in wicker chairs, like an old married couple. Close up he smelled of expensive scotch and cheap aftershave. The blood vessels in his nose and cheeks were cracked. The shepherd lay in a corner. A bookcase beside Witwans's chair was piled high with articles about Oscar

Pistorius, the amputee Olympian accused of killing his girlfriend.

"Last year's news," Salome said.

"I know his family. He's a good boy. He was framed, you know. The regime, they couldn't accept that the most famous South African was *white*. No more Mandela; everyone loves Oscar. Any excuse to string him up."

Salome had promised herself that she wouldn't debate politics or anything else with Witwans. But she couldn't help herself. "You also think HIV doesn't cause AIDS?"

"Don't confuse me with the blacks, Natalie. I understand science." Blacks sounded like *bliks*, a single short syllable. No doubt Witwans said the word a hundred times a day. Just as Communists were inevitably obsessed with money, Afrikaaners focused incessantly on race.

"He admitted shooting her."

He wagged a finger. "What they did to Oscar, they could do to any of us." Witwans reached for a bell on the bookcase. A trim black man in his late fifties appeared even before its ringing stopped. "Sir."

"Glenlivet for me. Neat."

"Double, sir?"

"Yes, double, Martin. Unless I say otherwise, always double. How many times must I tell you?"

"Pleasure, sir." He smiled. Salome imagined him smiling that way as he squeezed a dropper of poison into the scotch. *Mixed this one special for you. No need to thank me. Not that you would. Pleashuh, suh.*

"And the lady?"

"Just water, thank you."

"At least a glass of wine," Witwans said.

"Too tired for wine."

"My cook makes a first-rate cappuccino."

"Cappuccino, then. But no strychnine."

"Strychnine?"

"Ignore her, Martin. She's being foolish."

Martin disappeared.

"My staff depend on me," Witwans said. "Martin's mother died when he was two. He's lived here his whole life."

"Then he knows how he'd redecorate if you had a tragic accident."

"Joke if you like, but the blacks need us. We're the reason South Africa hasn't gone the way of Zimbabwe. And the price of gold."

For a half hour Salome listened to Witwans rant about the failings of the black-run government. At least the cappuccino was tasty. Finally, Witwans finished his Glenlivet. He reached for the bell, but she laid a hand on his arm.

"Don't you have something to show me?"

"There's no hurry."

"I'm flying out this evening."

She was lying. As she'd promised the immigration agent, she wasn't leaving South Africa right away. The all-seeing NSA might flag a shorter trip, since Johannesburg was so far from anywhere. *Don't give them anything to notice and they won't notice anything.* But she couldn't sleep in this man's house.

His scotch-wet lips drooped. She felt almost sorry for him. His wife was dead. His children and grandchildren lived as far away as they could manage. On most days, his only companions must be the servants he regarded as not quite human. They surely felt the same about him. The loneliness of the master race.

"To business, then."

In the kitchen, he unlocked a door to reveal a wooden staircase that led into a lightless basement. Despite herself, Salome felt a visceral dread, the product of a hundred horror movies. *Don't go down there. He'll chop you up.* But the fear was absurd. Witwans was harmless. Her true anxiety was that Witwans didn't have what he claimed. That she'd wasted a year searching.

"Ready to go down, Natalie?"

He winked, his eyelid as thick as a lizard's. She wondered if he was playing the fool to overcompensate for the loneliness he'd revealed, or if the scotch had hit him. He flicked on the lights, stepped uncertainly along the bare wood staircase. She hoped he didn't slip, break his neck. She wouldn't appreciate the irony.

The staircase descended five meters into a concrete-walled room filled with glass-fronted wine cabinets. A dozen vents were cut into the ceiling, keeping the air cool and fresh.

"I have one of the best collections in all the Free State."

"Congratulations."

"Sarcasm doesn't suit you, Natalie. Now help me."

Witwans grunted as they pulled an empty cabinet from the room's back wall. He flipped up an electrical outlet to expose a keypad, punched in a ten-digit code, touched a green button. They stood in silence as—

Nothing happened.

"A moment." He tried again. This time, a low grinding sound came from inside the wall. But the wall itself remained unbroken.

"Plastered over," Witwans said. "A thin layer, but we'll need to smash it." He pulled two rubber mallets out of another cabinet.

"Why would you—"

"Extra protection. A little extra protection never hurts, Natalie."

Now he raised his eyebrows. Maybe she was wrong to imagine him lonely. Maybe he was a horny old goat importing the local talent from Bloemfontein once a week. She grabbed a mallet to distract herself from the image of him rutting away. Worst of all, she couldn't guess what color he preferred for his *amours*. He would hardly be the first racist whose loins had their own ideas.

"Stick to the area directly behind the cabinet," Witwans said. "If you hit the wall itself, you'll get a nasty shock."

The advice came just as she cracked her mallet into the wall. Pain surged up her arms. She didn't drop the handle. She wouldn't give him the satisfaction.

After ten minutes, plaster shards covered the floor and they'd opened a hole big enough to squeeze through. Salome couldn't feel her hands. "If this isn't what you say, Rand, I'm going to put a bullet in you."

He handed her a flashlight and led her into a dark room about three meters square, its ceiling as high as the wine cellar. Her light played across stacks of canned food, cases of bottled water. Two shotguns, boxes of shells. Dog food.

Gas masks. Gloves. Tucked in a corner, three boxes of Trojans. Ribbed, for her pleasure.

"Why the condoms, Rand? Won't you want to repopulate?"

He tugged out a metal strongbox, led her back into the wine cellar. He huffed and puffed and sat on the stairs, the box in his lap. His hair was matted to his head, his cheeks the bright red of a stop sign. She wondered if he was having a heart attack. He handed her the strongbox, a simple steel cube. After all the security, the case had no lock, just a latch. She flipped it open.

Inside, a cylinder of dull yellow metal smaller than a soda can, its surface flat and smooth. She had never seen anything so perfectly machined. Her mouth went dry. Her heart jumped in her chest. The room seemed ten degrees warmer. She would need to test it, of course, but she *knew*. Witwans had told the truth.

She reached inside the box—

"There are gloves in the safe room," Witwans said. "This close, there is some radioactivity. At my age it doesn't matter, but for you it might."

She'd come this far. She could wait a few more seconds. She found the gloves.

She knew uranium was very dense, but even so, the cylinder's weight surprised her when she lifted it from the box.

"Beautiful, isn't it?" Witwans said.

From her bag, she pulled out what looked like a steel cube with one wall missing and a flat-panel screen on the side. She touched the screen. It came to life, blinked *0.000. Ready.*

"What is that?"

She put the cylinder into the cube, pushed the button. The LED screen went dark for a few seconds. Then it flashed red: *93.82 U-235. 1296.14 g.*

The last piece of the puzzle. Salome didn't think of herself as a religious woman, but at this moment, she felt God touch her. The air itself vibrated. *This was meant to be.*

"I told you." Witwans had to spoil the moment. "One-point-three kilos HEU."

During the apartheid era, Witwans had worked on and eventually run South Africa's nuclear weapons program. The government in Pretoria shared the cost of research and development with Israel. Two pariah nations teaming up. The Israelis ultimately built more than one hundred nuclear weapons. But South Africa never went past enrichment.

"All that talk about how you would never give the *bliks* power, and then you chickened out."

"I wanted to build. But it wasn't my choice, and in the end I'm glad we didn't. Apartheid would still have ended. We couldn't live with the sanctions, the world sneering. At least now the ANC doesn't have it."

"No one noticed you stealing a slug of HEU?"

"By the time we called off the project, we had fifteen kilos. It sat in a safe for a decade. By 1990, everyone knew the regime wouldn't survive. The stuff had to disappear. But no one would touch it. They thought the ANC would want revenge for anyone who was involved because it was under the same department as the chemical and biological programs. I knew they were wrong. We never made any weapons, so why would the blacks care? I said I would handle it. I asked the Israelis if they wanted it. Of course. I left our labs with 15.3 kilos of HEU. I passed the Israelis 14 kilos. Then I destroyed the records. No one I worked with ever asked me what had happened, and the new regime never knew."

"That simple."

"I know it must seem strange that I kept it. Not enough to make a bomb. I don't suppose you'll tell me what you want it for."

"I'm glad to tell you, if you don't mind my cutting out your tongue after."

"I built the cellar, and all these years I've left it here. Maybe I knew that someone like you would come along."

"Lucky it was me. Someone else would have taken it for nothing."

"Five million dollars is a bargain."

She knew he was right. "I have the million in cash in the car. I'll make a phone call and the rest will be in your accounts in a few minutes."

He stood, turned up the stairs. "Let's celebrate, then."

She grabbed his arm, wrenched it behind his back, pushed him down. His legs folded easily. He sat down hard, his mouth forming a surprised *O*.

"You'll get your drink. First you listen. Tell anyone I've been here—"

"Natalie, don't be ridiculous. What would I say? That I sold a kilo of bomb-grade uranium that I stole twenty years ago?"

"*Listen.* Maybe you get drunk. Brag to one of your

whores. I promise. I'll come back. I'll shoot your servants and your dogs. I'll cut off your shriveled cock and your tiny old-man balls, stuff them in your mouth. Then I'll tie you to a chair, set the place on fire, burn you alive."

As she spoke, she saw the flames licking at the house, the blood pooling beneath Witwans's chair. She knew he believed her, that he saw the truth of the words in the set of her mouth.

"I've kept my secret all these years. I'll keep yours." He reached for the banister, pulled himself up, his arms shaking.

"Let's celebrate, then."

"The offer's rescinded. Make your call, I'll check the accounts, then you can go."

She wanted to be sorry for him. But she felt only triumph.

Twenty minutes later, she stepped into the Toyota, the steel box cradled in her arms, the afternoon sun gentle on her skin. Witwans stood on the edge of the porch, the German shepherd beside him. Salome knew he would close his gates tight and hope never to see her again.

He needn't worry. As long as he stayed quiet she wouldn't hurt him. Let him live out his country squire's life. If he died violently, intelligence agencies might wonder why the former head of South Africa's nuclear program had been murdered. Alive, he was no one.

"Back to Johannesburg?" Jan said. She had a safe house there. In the morning she would drive to Kruger, South

Africa's giant national park. A two-day safari. Stick to her cover story.

She closed her eyes, let herself drift. She'd spent years building her team, finding everything she needed. The uranium was the last piece, and the most important. By itself, it was a piece of metal. As Witwans had said, 1.3 kilograms of uranium wasn't nearly enough for a bomb. But if she did her job, it would be more than enough. She couldn't help but feel that providence had guided her during the last few years. She didn't always believe in God. But God seemed to believe in her, to have chosen her as the agent of this plan.

Salome closed her eyes and dreamed of war. In black and white, like a newsreel from World War II. Silver-bodied propeller planes dropping strings of bombs as flak exploded around them. Tanks rolling through rubble, crunching shapeless bits of metal and concrete. Soldiers shouting, raising their rifles, running through a thick forest, dying one by one.

But nothing she saw frightened her, and when the Land Cruiser reached the Johannesburg suburbs and stopped beside her safe house, she felt relaxed, almost tranquil.

If she brought war, then let war come.

PART

ONE

1

The *Norwegian Epic* had everything.

Not just cruise-ship necessities like a casino, pools, and an all-you-can-eat buffet. Two bowling alleys. A seven-hundred-seat theater. A gym with rows of gleaming and rarely used treadmills.

After six days, John Wells couldn't wait to leave. On the cruise's final afternoon, he and Anne sat on their balcony as the *Epic* chased the sun toward Miami. The sky was a bright subtropical blue, marred only by the diesel exhaust unfurling from the *Epic*'s smokestacks. Like the ship was giving the ocean an inky middle finger. The *Epic* was as big as a skyscraper, a thousand feet long, with four thousand passengers and two thousand crew. It was the third-largest cruise ship ever built. Wells couldn't imagine numbers one and two.

Anne, Wells's girlfriend, had proposed the trip weeks before. The New Hampshire winter had been crueler than usual. Snow poured down by the foot. Drifts piled above the windowsills of their farmhouse in North Conway. Even Wells's dog, Tonka, a shepherd mutt who usually liked cold weather, went outside only long enough to take care of necessities.

Wells spent hours every day tending the fireplaces. He carried armfuls of wood from the garage, layered on logs until he'd built blue-flame blazes hot enough to warp steel screens. He watched as the hearths filled with glowing red coals that inevitably turned to gray-black soot. *Ashes to ashes and dust to dust* . . . the keeping of fires touched a chord in him primitive and true.

Anne spent her days on patrol in North Conway, waiting to join the New Hampshire state police. They'd offered her a job, but the state had a hiring freeze as deep as the winter. Wells found himself inward-turned, dreaming of the heat and dust of East Africa. One morning he woke to find Anne sitting beside him, her laptop open. "What we need."

"Summer."

"A cruise." She tilted the screen toward him. A gleaming white ship passed—barely—under a giant gray bridge.

"How does that thing even float?"

"There are last-minute sales."

"This is new."

"John, I know you think you don't belong on a cruise ship. Trained killer, savior of the unknowing masses, blah, blah, blah. It'll be fun."

She had him. If he complained, he'd sound self-satisfied and ridiculous.

"And I don't want to hear about carbon. You've put half the trees in this state up the chimney this month."

She had him there, too.

"Maybe terrorists will take it over. Like *Speed 2*."

"There was a *Speed 2*?"

"An excuse to relax. Besides, I'd like to have sex on a ship. Bet it's like a giant waterbed." She stroked his neck.

"That supposed to work? Throwing sex around as a treat so I'll do what you want?"

"Yeah."

He pushed the laptop aside and grabbed her. "It does."

So they went. Despite himself, Wells enjoyed the first couple days, if only for the sunshine. But as the cruise continued, he found its wastefulness gross. The way the crew scraped before passengers also bothered Wells. No doubt many sailors were desperately poor and glad to make five hundred dollars a month for twelve-hour days polishing and mopping. No doubt the cruise was a hard-earned luxury for many people on board, a vacation they had saved for years to enjoy. Still, Wells started to see the *Epic* as something like a floating plantation.

Anne wouldn't admit she felt the same, but she and Wells spent most of the cruise's last two days sunning on their balcony, avoiding the rest of the ship. Now, with Miami hours away, Wells had a decision to make. A big one. He wondered if he should take a walk on the decks. He had developed a hint of flab this winter. After a week of all-you-can-eat meals, the hint had become a suggestion. An insistent suggestion.

Anne leaned over. "You've had enough of this."

"David Foster Wallace was right." Before setting sail, they had both read Wallace's 1996 article about his miserable week aboard a cruise ship. Now Wells was rereading Wallace's book *A Supposedly Fun Thing I'll Never Do Again*, which contained the piece.

"No more David Foster Wallace for you. He's a depressing depressive. Was."

Wells clutched the book to his chest, an exaggerated gesture.

"I agree it's all a little much," she said.

"Everest is a little hill." Wells raised his sunglasses, wraparound Oakleys that had replaced the vintage Ray-Bans she'd given him. He'd lost those in Somalia. He was still sorry to have given them up, though he'd had no choice.

"Don't pretend you haven't enjoyed parts of this. I saw you scarfing down ice cream at the buffet like a *Lifetime* special on bulimia."

In retrospect, Wells had gotten excited at the sundae bar. He poked at his stomach. "It's going to take about a million hours of running to lose this. Past forty, it doesn't come off so easy."

She cuffed his cheek, peaceably. "The world doesn't know it, Mr. Wells, but you're as vain as a supermodel."

"I have practical reasons. The life you save may be your own."

"If an inch around your waist is enough to get you killed, you've pushed your luck way too far."

"Look tough enough and maybe you won't have to fight at all."

"You boys check out each other's abs before you get to it?"

"On occasion." Wells knew that when he got home, he would lose the pounds he'd gained, no matter how many hours it took. But he was more aware than ever that time was the ultimate victor. He had once been gifted with the coordination and hand speed of a professional baseball player. Now his reflexes had slowed. He'd gone to a batting range a few weeks before for his usual once-a-year test, found himself swiping hopelessly at fastballs he'd once crushed. He was still strong, but close-quarters combat was more about quickness. To compensate, he worked his shooting, putting in an hour a day at the local range. More than a year had passed since East Africa. Too long. He needed to get back in the field.

"Have you thought any more about the training thing?" Anne had suggested he approach the agency about working at Camp Peary, known to the world as The Farm, where the agency taught new recruits.

Wells had no intention of begging the CIA for something to do. "They come to me, I'll think about it." He went back to the Wallace book. After a minute, she walked into their stateroom. Wells watched her go. She had a sturdy New England body, not fat but solid, with supple legs, muscled arms.

A few minutes later, she emerged wearing a solid black one-piece swimsuit that favored her and carrying a pitcher of iced tea. "Put on some trunks. One last trip to the pool."

He held up the book.

"You'll regret it when we're back at the North Pole."

"I'll find you there."

"Want tea?"

"Sure." She poured him a glass. He reached for it and she grabbed the book. She cocked her arm, tossed the book off the balcony. They watched in silence as it tumbled end over end into the water. It must have splashed, but from this height Wells couldn't tell.

"Unnecessary."

"I'm not looking to that guy to tell me how to live my life."

"He was right. Cruises are the ultimate sign of late capitalism."

"You want the ultimate sign of late capitalism? Deciding you're too tortured to work. Too much of a genius. Then ditching your wife and everyone who loves you and hanging yourself." As Wallace had done.

"He was depressed."

She sat on the lounge chair beside him, rested a hand on his forearm. "People fight like hell to stay alive, John. No one knows that better than you."

At that moment Wells knew he had been right to bring the ring. He pushed himself up.

"Are we going?"

"Don't move."

He found the box at the bottom of his suitcase. Inside, a simple white-gold ring set with a diamond, not huge, but flawless. Only a connoisseur would know how much it had cost. A foolish luxury, but Wells had little use for money. He'd seen what it could not buy. He'd ordered the ring months before, after realizing how happy he was every afternoon to see Anne. How his days didn't begin until she walked into the kitchen and put her arms around him and mocked his half-assed cooking.

He pulled off his Oakleys, hid the box in his hand, walked back onto the deck.

"Take off your glasses."

"I'll go blind."

She took them off. Wells dropped to one knee. He felt like he was going into combat, all his senses heightened. The sun scoured his skin. A warm breeze roughed his eyes. Before Wells could lose his nerve, he opened his hand and lifted the box toward her. "I know I should have done this years ago, but I wanted to be sure. About me, not you. I've always been sure about you. You're smart and funny and gorgeous. I'm happy to fall asleep next to you and happier to wake up. You're right about everything except this cruise, and I even forgive you for that. I love you and I want us to be together for the rest of our lives. Marry me, Anne."

She was crying when he finished. He knew the tears weren't joy even before she shook her head.

"John." She took the box from him, opened it. "That is some diamond." She flipped it shut. "Like staring into the sun."

He couldn't pretend this was the lowest moment of his life. Waiting in the hospital to learn if Exley would die had been worse. But he wasn't sure he'd ever felt more shocked. He hadn't imagined she would say no.

He'd underestimated her.

"Throw it over, I'm going to be pissed. It cost a few bucks more than the book." He was croaking. His voice hardly worked, but he had to say something. She gave the box back to him.

"That's no, then?"

"It's not yes. I know you enjoy my company, John. I know you care about me. But I'm not sure you love me. I'm sure you want to love me, but I'm not sure you *can*. I'm not sure you don't still love Jennifer—" This was Exley, his former fiancée, his former handler at the agency.

"I love you."

"Let's say you do. I hope it's true. Because I *do* love you, and I want more than anything for it to be mutual. But you love your missions more. More than any of us. Even Exley. Wasn't that why she left?"

Wells didn't answer. To hear Anne dissecting him, so coolly, so accurately, made him wonder how long she'd waited to give this speech. How much hurt she'd swallowed on the way.

"So I would marry you, and I'd hope everything you say is true. Or might come true eventually. But I want kids, John. I'm closer to thirty-five than thirty now, and you may have noticed North Conway isn't long on marriageable prospects. I can't have kids with a man who's waiting for his next big chance to get killed."

"You want me to retire?"

"There are risks and *risks*, John. I'm not saying you want to die. But when you're on a mission, I'm not sure you care."

"I don't want to die."

"You know why I wanted us to take this cruise?"

She looked at him until he got it.

"You made me go on the *Norwegian Epic* planning to dump me when we got home?" Wells pulled himself up, turned away. He stared at the ocean, fighting the foolish urge to toss the ring. He wasn't sure if he was angry with her or himself. He'd never felt more foolish. Or less perceptive. He'd brought an engagement ring to a good-bye party.

"I wanted to remember you lying out in the sun, getting good and brown."

He turned toward her, flipped her the box. She caught it, pure reflex.

"I don't want to die," he said again.

"But do you want to be a father? A real father this time, present."

He didn't trust himself to speak. He nodded.

"Enough to walk away from an operation that's too dangerous."

He nodded again. Though he wasn't sure he knew what those words meant.

"I don't believe you. But okay." She set down the box. "I'll give you thirty days. If you truly believe you're ready to be a father, you come back to me with this."

"You'll say yes?"

"If I believe you."

So he stowed the diamond in his suitcase and they went for a swim. Neither of them wanted to be in the suite anymore.

2

They'd warned him.

His friends. His advisors. Even the *Post* reporter who covered the CIA. Every last one told Vinny Duto that he held far more power as Director of Central Intelligence than he would as a new senator. That he'd be at the bottom of a deeply hierarchical institution. That his clout would vanish so quickly that he would wonder whether it had ever existed.

Still he'd left the seventh floor to run for the Senate. He knew something they didn't. The President was tired of him, the way he controlled Langley. The slights piled up slowly. His meetings with the big man started late, ended early. A budget request that should have been waved through instead took months of meetings. The National Security Advisor demanded preapproval for all drone strikes.

Duto decided to jump before the slow leaks started and

he read about the agency's failures on the front page of the *Times*. He could have hung on for another year or two, but ultimately he would have lost. He might be the most successful DCI ever, but he was no match for the President.

He didn't discourage the inside-the-Beltway pundits, who said he was making a Senate run to position himself for his own grab at the White House. If not in the next election, then the one after that. He'd still be young enough to be a credible candidate. Younger than Reagan. And in the back of his mind, Duto hoped the conventional wisdom was right. But he didn't delude himself about the odds. He wasn't a natural campaigner. In Pennsylvania, he could run as a relatively conservative Democrat, but he wouldn't have that option in a national primary. No matter. He had years to decide. Meantime, he was glad to leave on what seemed to be his own terms.

He'd won easily. But he hadn't realized that life as a senator would be so mind-numbingly boring. As DCI, he'd regularly faced life-or-death decisions. *Four senior AQAP operatives are meeting at a madrassa in Yemen. Can we waste them without blowing up a room full of kids?*

Now, instead of ordering drone strikes, he listened to lobbyists and his fellow lawmakers drone on. Worst of all were constituent meetings. The Commonwealth of Pennsylvania had thirteen million residents. Sometimes Duto thought every one of them was lined up in his office foyer, waiting for a handout. The Harrisburg mayor begged for $27 million for a highway extension—and reminded Duto that Harrisburg had gone 70-30 for him. The president of Penn State hoped for an $11 million earmark for a new dairy-science building, and wondered if Duto wanted tickets to his box at Beaver Stadium. A roomful of wig-wearing cancer patients from Philly asked for an increase in the National Institutes of Health budget. In that case, Duto sympathized.

His chief of staff, Roy Baumann, insisted that he press the flesh. Baumann was firmly in the all-politics-is-local camp: *People don't know how you voted on specific bills, much less care. They care whether the turnpike's safe and the economy's decent. They know you can't do much about any of it, but they want to think you're trying. And you're not like ninety percent of these gasbags. People want to meet you, hear your stories. Nothing important. Like, did Osama bin Laden really have porn in his safe house, or did we just put that out to discredit him? After a year or two you can disengage. I don't recommend it, but I can't stop you. But for now you say yes. Yes?*

Thus Duto had said yes to lunch with the head of the Philadelphia hospital workers' union, Steve Little. Duto didn't like Little. Little had endorsed his opponent in the primary. *I'll remind him of that,* Baumann said. *This lunch is peaches and cream. Best friendsies.* Little was a trim black man with a perfectly tailored suit and shoes a Wall Street banker would have envied. Duto wondered if Little charged his clothes to the union. Probably—

"Senator."

"Yes?"

Little was shaking his head. "I lose you there? On the

Medicare HMO issue? You looked glazed. I know it's esoteric, but these are huge numbers."

Duto's phone buzzed. A number he'd never seen before. A 502-2 prefix. Guatemala City. He sent it to voice mail. The phone buzzed again. Some instinct left from Langley told him to take it. "I'm sorry. Excuse me, Steve."

He walked outside. "Hello."

"Remember me, *comandante*?"

Only one man had called him that. *"Diecisiete?"* The man's name was Juan Pablo Montoya, but Duto would always think of him as Seventeen.

"None other. Did you miss me?"

"No."

"Tenemos que hablar."

"Can we do it in English? It's been a while."

"If you must. I promise you'll want to hear this."

"One hour."

"Una hora, comandante."

3

Brian Taylor stood by the window in room 1509 of the InterContinental Hotel in Istanbul, looking at the dark water of the Bosphorus down the hill to the east. In twelve years at the agency, he had never been so excited.

Taylor was the CIA's deputy chief of base for Istanbul. His dream job, his dream city. He'd fallen for it backpacking across Europe at the end of the nineties. The last flash of American innocence, when taking a summer to drink cheap wine and run with the bulls still seemed adventurous. Taylor followed the usual route. He saw the sun rise over Montmartre, jumped off the rocks in Cinque Terre. He met his share of women. Always Americans. He never cracked European girls. Maybe if he hadn't tried so hard . . . He had fun. Yet he felt he'd arrived a couple generations late. The cities were open-air museums. Even the beautiful couples walking along the Seine seemed to hold hands almost ironically. Like they were reenacting movies about Paris instead of living there.

Then he found Istanbul. Its history stretched millennia, and it was as picturesque as anyplace he'd ever seen. Its giant mosques loomed over the Bosphorus, the mile-wide waterway that separated Asia and Europe. Yet it wasn't a museum. It teemed with life. Shopkeepers and students hustled along its hilly streets. Gleaming white yachts sped past packed ferries and rusted container ships. The Turks were hardworking and silver-tongued, loud and showy. Taylor had grown up in a stuffy town outside Boston. He liked them immediately. He even developed a soft spot for the devious shopkeepers in the Grand Bazaar. Those guys weren't exactly *trying* to take advantage, he decided. They wanted to deal. They wanted drama. Any tourist who didn't understand the game—which every guidebook explained in detail—deserved to be fleeced.

Taylor expected to be in the city three days. He stayed three weeks, flying home the afternoon before fall term started. He knew his sudden ardor was silly, but was falling for a city more absurd than falling for a woman? Both required a willingness to suspend disbelief. Anyway, now he had what every college student wanted. A goal, and a path to reach it. He would learn Turkish, move to Istanbul after graduation. Turkey had eighty million people and a fast-growing economy. Big companies needed Americans who spoke the language. And the University of Massachusetts shared an excellent Turkish program with other colleges around Amherst. He expected his parents to push back. They didn't. Dad: *It'll make you a lot more hirable than a history degree.* Mom: *I always wanted to live some-where exotic.* Turkish was tough, but Taylor worked hard. By the start of senior year, he was nearly fluent.

Then al-Qaeda attacked the United States.

Like his friends, Taylor was terrified and enraged and wanted revenge. Unlike them, he could help. Turkey shared borders with Iraq and Iran. The FSB, Mossad, and Revolutionary Guard all ran major stations in Istanbul. The CIA was badly outgunned. Just four agency officers spoke Turkish. By November, the agency had contacted language programs all over the country in search of candidates. With his 3.8 GPA and spotless background, Taylor jumped out. A recruiter invited him to Boston for a meet-and-greet. The remains of the World Trade Center were still smoldering. He never considered saying no.

And he had never regretted his decision—not even during his ten-month posting to Iraq, when he'd left the Green Zone only four times. He'd spent most of his career at CIA stations in Istanbul and Ankara, the Turkish capital. Taylor knew he wasn't a star case officer. The stars worked in Beijing or Kabul or Moscow. But he was reliable, dedicated, and a good fit for Turkey. Though he had joined after September 11, Taylor was something of a throwback. He disliked drones, preferred old-school spying, the careful recruitment of agents from government and business. Guys who lived in mansions, not mud huts. His best sources were mid-level officers in the Turkish army, bureaucrats in the Ministry of Finance.

So Taylor's career progressed, and his social life, too. He made a habit of American twenty-somethings who came to town on two-year stints for multinationals. He replaced them easily enough. His years with the agency had given him an appealing air of mystery. His apartment had a killer view of the Bosphorus. Plus he knew every restaurant in town, and he always picked up the check. Case officers had practically unlimited expense accounts. No accountant at Langley would question a two-hundred-dollar dinner for "recruiting."

The CIA promoted Taylor to deputy chief of base in Istanbul on the eleventh anniversary of his hiring. He planned to stay three years, then head back to the United States. He was ready to settle down, have a family. He didn't think he would ever be a chief. Taylor still believed in the mission, that in some small way he protected the United States. But he supposed that he'd become a careerist. September 11 had faded in his memory, along with everyone else's.

Then the letter arrived.

Almost half a year later, its details were etched in his mind. Noon on a Friday in early September. The consulate mostly empty as the long Labor Day weekend approached. Istanbul stuck in a heat wave, smoking like a kebab on a spit. Taylor's office was air-conditioned, of course, but through its narrow bulletproof windows the men on the streets looked sullen and irritable.

A knock on his door. His secretary, Alison. She carried

an envelope, holding it by her fingertips. Like it was con-
taminated. Though the consulate scanned local mail for
anthrax and other nasties. She handed it to him without a
word.

It was addressed to Nelson Drew, Associate Director for
Citizen Services, United States Consulate, Istanbul. Taylor's cover name and job. Inside, a single page of staccato
laser-printed sentences.

> *"Nelson." You are spy. CIA. Real name Brian*
> *Taylor. Speak Turk/Farsi. I am Rev. Guard Colonel.*
> *"Reza." I need to meet.*
> *Grand Bazaar 6 Sep 3 p.m. Ethcon Carpet.*

Taylor felt like he'd gone to the doctor for a routine physical and been told he had an inoperable brain tumor. Impossible. The letter's plain white paper burned his fingers.
You are spy . . . He couldn't be blown like this. But wishing
wouldn't erase the words.

He handed the letter and envelope back to Alison.
"Make a copy for me, one for Martha." Martha Hunt, the
chief of base. "Bag the original and the envelope. Try not
to touch them, in case there're fingerprints."

Though he didn't expect forensic evidence. Whoever
had sent this was smart. And knew much too much about
him. That he worked for the agency. His real name. Even
that he knew Farsi. He'd learned the language working
with Iranian exile groups in Ankara. He hadn't liked the
exiles. Most just wanted to hang out in Turkey on the CIA's

dime. They found excuses whenever Taylor proposed operations that would send them back into Iran. Still, every so often one had decent intel, so the agency tolerated them.

Now that work had bitten him. As he'd assumed, some exiles were double agents spying for Iran. Still, he couldn't imagine how they'd found his real name. He'd been careful. But he'd been stationed in Turkey for a long time. Probably the Guard had put the pieces together bit by bit. Finding the answer would be impossible. He'd left Ankara four years before. The exiles had scattered. What mattered was that his cover was blown. What if the Guard knew where he lived? Part of him wanted to get on the first flight home.

But he knew he had to stay. The man who'd written this letter could be an enormously valuable source. The United States was desperate to stop Iran's nuclear program. Washington had imposed sanctions and attacked the program covertly. Still, the Iranians hadn't quit. Policymakers badly needed to know how close Iran was to a bomb. But the United States had few agents anywhere in the Iranian government, and none in the Revolutionary Guard. Instead, the CIA and National Security Agency relied on their usual technical wizardry. But Iran had buried its enrichment facilities to keep them from satellites, drones, and radiological sniffers. Following a joint American and Israeli attack on their computer systems in 2009, Iran's scientists had removed the computers from their labs. They solved equations with calculators now, used plaster to model bomb designs. Still, they were making progress. After all, the American scientists at Los Alamos had designed the first bomb in the 1940s with slide rules and hand-drawn blue-prints.

Without hard evidence, the United States could only speculate at Iran's capabilities and intentions. Some analysts thought Iran would finish its first bomb in less than a year. Others said five years was more likely. This Revolutionary Guard colonel might have the answers.

If he was real. And not luring Taylor into a trap.

Martha Hunt was named Istanbul station chief four months after Taylor became deputy. She was two years younger than Taylor and didn't speak Turkish. But he didn't begrudge her the job. She had served three years in Kabul, two in Islamabad. When they disagreed, she was usually right. The fact that she was shockingly good-looking, tall and slim, with killer blue eyes, didn't hurt. He'd never hit on her. He knew his league. She wasn't in it.

They met in the safe room beside her office. It had no windows and was swept weekly for bugs.

"I don't like it, either," she said, as soon as he closed the door.

"Hello, Martha."

"For all the obvious reasons. Who sets a meet in the Grand Bazaar? Must be five thousand security cams in there. But you've got to go." She didn't wait for him to agree. "We've got a week. Let's use it. Get a camera to put eyes on the door. He's dressed wrong, looks like he's hiding a vest, you abort. He wants to blow himself up, not your problem. Meanwhile, you want to stay in the safe house until this is done, I'm fine with that."

"I'll stay put. Can't give up that view." No way would he let Hunt think he was scared.

"You have a view? I hadn't heard." A joke. Taylor's apartment was a minor legend.

"Come on over sometime, see for yourself." He snorted, so she'd know he was kidding. Though he wasn't.

"Tell you what. Get us inside the Iranian nuclear program and I will." She smiled a smile he'd never seen before.

He spent twelve hours wondering if she was flirting. Until he realized what she'd done. She'd given him a tiny ambiguous signal to chew over. To take his mind off the letter. Taylor had heard some men weren't suckers for beautiful women. He'd never met one.

The week dragged. Taylor looked over his files from Ankara, but nobody jumped out as a possible double agent. The station's tech-support team—two chubby guys named Dominick and Ronaldo—placed a thumbnail camera to watch the front door of the carpet store. The same night a cleaning crew threw it away. Hunt and Taylor decided not to risk placing another.

Two days before the meeting, Taylor checked out the shop himself. It occupied expensive space a few feet from the domed square where the bazaar had begun five centuries before. Rather than traditional patterned carpets, it specialized in modern, brightly colored rugs. Under other circumstances, Taylor might have bought one. Instead, he wandered into a pipe store and watched Ethcon's entrance as he pretended interest in an overpriced meerschaum.

He'd come early. The bazaar was almost empty. After a few minutes, the Ethcon clerk poked his head out to talk to his counterpart across the corridor. Taylor recognized his accent as from southeastern Turkey, near Iran. Probably a coincidence. Hundreds of thousands of the region's villagers had migrated to Istanbul. The letter writer had likely chosen Ethcon at random. The company didn't show up on agency databases, and when Taylor had checked its Turkish records he'd found nothing suspicious. Taylor eavesdropped as the clerk talked about very little. Finally, he handed back the meerschaum and left, ignoring the curses the pipe store owner tossed at his back.

He spent that night staring at the Bosphorus. He hated the way this meeting had come together. Simply by showing up, he was confirming his identity to whoever had sent the letter. Plenty of terrorists, from al-Qaeda to Greek anarchists, would gladly take a CIA scalp.

"Good night's sleep," Hunt said the next morning.

"We don't all have your cheekbones."

"Why don't you take the day off, practice your shooting."

The agency had a deal with the Turkish army to let officers use a range at a base near Istanbul. As usual, she was ahead of him. Taylor hadn't fired his pistol in a year. A day shooting would help him relax and might save his life. "I'll see you tomorrow."

The bazaar stretched across a dozen blocks in Sultanahmet, the heart of Istanbul's Old City. On Friday afternoon, Taylor sat at a nearby McDonald's, watching tourists and Turks slurp down Cokes against the late-summer heat. He wore a tiny receiver in his right ear for updates from the surveillance team, a baggy T-shirt to hide the pistol in his waistband. At 2:44, his receiver buzzed.

"Pico One. Possible Gamma sighting. In the forest now." Taylor could no longer bear the plastic friendliness of the McDonald's. He shouldered his way to the bazaar's southeast entrance. Two minutes later, his earpiece buzzed again. "Pico One. False alarm on that Gamma, unless he has three kids." Finally: "Pico Two. Empty forest. No Gamma, no X-rays." Picos One and Two were the CIA team around the store. Gamma was the letter writer, whoever he was. X-rays were a potential enemy team. X-rays almost certainly meant a trap. Reza would arrive alone if he was genuine.

At 2:55, Taylor entered the bazaar. Six minutes later, he reached the store. Pico One was gone, but Two stood down the corridor. He wore his Real Madrid cap backward, signaling to Taylor that the store was empty except for the clerk. Reza hadn't shown. Unless the clerk himself was Reza, a long shot.

Taylor walked inside. The Ethcon clerk was dark for a Turk, with oily black hair. He wore a T-shirt and jeans, both too tight to conceal a bomb. "You are Mr. Nelson?" Taylor controlled his surprise. The store was a single room, its only entrance the front door. Rugs were piled high along the walls. Nowhere for anyone to hide. Taylor took the bait. "Nelson Drew, yes."

The clerk picked an envelope off his desk. "Boy come yesterday, say you come to store today, I give you this. He say you want many rugs."

"How old?"

"Our rugs are new—"

"The *boy*. How old was the boy?"

"Ten years, maybe."

"Iranian?"

"Turk."

Reza had figured the agency would be watching the store. He had used a runner to get a letter into the store safely. Basic tradecraft. The clerk handed Taylor the envelope. *NELSON* was printed across the flap in black letters. Taylor tore it open, found a single sheet.

> *Tram to Cevizlibağ. Down stairs to gas station.*
> *Arrive by 3:30. ALONE. Other Wise I will go and*
> *never contact you again.* "Reza"

On his way out of the bazaar, he called Hunt, read her the note.

"As a meet, it makes sense," she said.

"It's no fun at all."

"No cameras, we can't box him. When he's done, he gets back on the tram or finds a cab and disappears onto the highway. I think this increases the odds he's real."

"You're not the one with no backup."

"It's nice and public. Nobody's gonna touch you there. Just don't go further. He tries to get you into a vehicle, tell him no."

"What if he says I can have a puppy?"

He hung up, dodged through a busload of Chinese tourists blocking the bazaar's main entrance.

The tram stop was close to the bazaar. Istanbul had lousy public transportation—the city had promised a subway line under the Bosphorus for decades. But the trams came often and were the fastest way around the Old City. Taylor waved his pass at the entrance gate's scanner and joined the Turks crowding the platform. A tram was just arriving. He pushed his way on. The car was packed, and he wedged his hands against his sides. The butt of his Sig bulged under his T-shirt. A woman stared until Taylor shook the shirt loose to hide the pistol.

The stink of onion and garlic and summer sweat overwhelmed the tram. Many older Turkish men still preferred traditional baths to everyday showering. Taylor fleetingly wondered if Hunt had given him this mission as a prank. Maybe she thought his life of expense-account dinners was too comfortable.

The tram chugged along, passing cars that were barely moving on either side. At 3:26, a cheery automated voice announced Cevizlibağ. Taylor shoved himself out. Sweat coursed down his chest. He unzipped his jacket, fought the urge to draw his Sig.

The gas station lay below the tram platform, beside the highway, an eight-lane monster that connected the airport with central Istanbul. Taylor joined a line of men walking down the spindly steel stairs and looked for his contact. *There*. A man leaned against the concrete retaining wall that supported the tram tracks. He had brown Persian skin. He wore wide mirrored sunglasses and jeans and dragged on a cigarette. His T-shirt and jeans were too tight to hide a bomb.

Taylor stopped halfway down, checked out the lot. Dozens of pumps and a busy minimarket. Lots of gas being sold, no sign of a kill or kidnap team. Men pushed past him, annoyed that he'd blocked their path. The guy in the sunglasses stepped toward the stairs. Taylor had reached the point of no return. Choose or lose.

He walked down.

Up close the man was older than Taylor expected, early forties, though Iranians could be tough to judge. He wore blue jeans and knockoff Doc Martens. He was tall and handsome, with salt-and-pepper hair. "I'm glad you came," he said. In Farsi. He sounded native, as best Taylor could judge.

"What about the store?"

"This is better." He led Taylor to the retaining wall, took a final drag on his smoke, and scuffed it under his shoes. His first mistake. Taylor would grab the butt after he left. The agency would test any fingerprints and DNA against its databases.

"What's your real name, Reza?"

"Cigarette?" He offered Taylor the red pack of L&Ms.

Taylor shook his head. "You know my name, I don't know yours."

"You have a weapon, I do not." He lifted his arms over his head, made a single slow twirl so Taylor could see the truth of his words. Like a middle-aged Iranian ballerina.

"Playing the fool, drawing attention to yourself."

"If someone has followed me here, I'm dead already."

"How does the Guard know my real name?"

"They don't. Only me."

"How's that?" In Ankara, Taylor had used a different cover identity.

"We have a photo of you from Ankara in our files. Nobody ever bothered with it. I saw it a few months ago, I had an idea. Our man said you spoke excellent Turkish—"

"Who was the man?"

"He called himself Hussein al-Ghazi when he was in Ankara. A nobody. Back in Tehran."

Taylor didn't remember the guy. But the Ankara exile groups had hundreds of members. "And this man Ghazi gave me up?"

"All he said was that you spoke good Turkish—"

"Excellent."

"Excellent, yes. Shall I explain, so we can put this behind us, I can tell you why I'm here? We don't have long."

Taylor nodded.

"I guessed your age and found all the Turkish-studies programs in America and looked up the graduates on the Internet. You don't look Turkish, so I imagined you must learn at a university."

"What if I knew the language because I had some family connection to Turkey instead?"

"Then I wouldn't find you. A small risk. All I would lose is time."

"Every program?"

"They're not large, and most students are Turkish. All the way from 1995 until 2000 I saw only about three hundred Americans. I checked yearbook photos until I found your real name. It took less than a month from beginning to end."

Taylor was speechless. A monstrous security flaw, one he'd never considered before.

"Then I looked at our photos of American consular and embassy officers. We take those as a matter of course. I was fortunate you were still in Turkey, under official cover. And that you'd been here long enough for us to have your official name and title so I could know where to address the letter. I imagined if I'd guessed correctly, you would come. As you have."

"But no one else in the Guard—"

"Correct. Only me. And I don't intend to tell anyone."

The words Taylor had hoped to hear. If they were true. "You want to work for us, Reza? A man in your position must have valuable information."

"I'm not here to sell out my country."

If a decade as a case officer had taught Taylor anything, it was that agents always said that before they sold out their countries. The Iranian lit another cigarette, dragged deep.

"Our leaders, they've swallowed their own poison. They believe this bomb will make them safe. They hate you and the Jews for trying to stop them."

"How close is it?"

"I don't know exactly. I have a friend in the program, he tells me very close. Though our engineers have been too optimistic before. But what your country needs to understand, it is already affecting our policies. Sometime next week, we will bomb two Israeli embassies."

The surprises kept coming. "Where?"

"One Africa, one Asia. There was supposed to be a third, in Bulgaria, but it got pulled. Security was too tight. That's how I know."

"This is Hezbollah or the Guard?" Iran used Hezbollah, a Lebanese militia, for most of its attacks on Israel.

"Hezbollah. But we're helping even more than usual. It's complicated. Two simultaneous bombs, two continents. Also they're very focused on Syria right now."

"Why not delay, then?"

"If we had any choice, we would, but the orders come from the top. A message to the Israelis, stop shooting our scientists."

"Which embassies?"

"I don't know."

"Bombs? Does that mean truck bombs, suicide bombs?"

"Bulgarian was truck. I think the others, too."

"This is confirmed? Two embassies?"

Reza turned to Taylor, raised his sunglasses so they were eye-to-eye. "I don't have much respect for your agency. Technology, yes. Officers, no. You, you speak Turkish, your Farsi isn't bad, so I hope you're not stupid. Then you ask questions like this. Yes, it's confirmed." Reza took a last drag of the L&M, crunched it under his heel. "I must go."

"Reza, I need to know more about you. *We* need to know more. Why you're offering this information—"

"I'm sick of these fanatics who run my country. I don't like the idea of a nuclear war. You need more reasons?"

"If you have them."

"A friend of mine, the Basij-e beat his cousin to death during the Green protests." Following a disputed election in the summer of 2010, college students and other young Iranians filled Tehran with anti-government protests that became known as the Green Wave. The regime struck back with paramilitary gangs called the Basij-e Mostaz'afin—the name meant Mobilization of the Oppressed. The Basij-e were poor and devout and hated the protesters, who were wealthier and less religious. They attacked viciously, killing dozens and wounding hundreds more. The police didn't stop the violence. Sometimes they even worked with the Basij-e.

"At least tell me your name."

"I've told you the truth. You don't believe me, watch the news next week. See that bag behind that piece of concrete." Taylor followed Reza's gaze to a brown paper bag. "A phone for you. I'll call when I have something. It may be a while."

"I can't—"

"It's not a bomb. Just a phone I bought today. Still in the package."

"I need a way to reach you."

"I don't want you to reach me. Or pay me. Or take my photo. Or put my DNA in a file." Reza picked up his crushed cigarette butts, tucked them in his pocket. "The

Guard have a prison near Qom, underground. They keep rabid dogs. They take off your clothes, handcuff you to a post, open the cage. They tell about the rabies so you'll know what happens after the bite."

"We can't protect you if we don't know who you are."

Reza pushed his sunglasses down. "Tell the Israelis. The end."

Three pumps down, a taxi had just finished filling up. Reza strode to it, spoke to the cabbie. He slid inside and didn't look back as the taxi rolled off.

Taylor squatted down beside the paper bag. He couldn't see what was inside. Anyway, what was he expecting? That it would be ticking? He unrolled the top, nudged it over with his sneaker. A little mobile slid out in a clamshell case. Taylor decided to take a cab back to the consulate, just in case. If the phone blew up, there'd be less collateral damage.

When the Marines at the consulate's front gate scanned the phone for explosives, it came back clean. Taylor left it with the station's techs. "Make sure it's not bugged."

"Can I take it apart?" Ronaldo said.

"Do what you want, long as you don't break it. You break it, I break you."

Hunt waited in the conference room, two digital tape recorders on the table. "Tell me just as it happened. No opinions. Facts, as you recall them. I want every detail while it's fresh."

For a half hour, he recounted the meeting. "You did well," she said when he finished.

"Thank you."

"Did you get the cab's plate?"

His elation vanished. "No, it was too far—"

"Forget it. I think you handled it about as well as anyone could have. But I have to know one thing. Don't hesitate. Just yes or no, from the gut. Is he real?"

"Yes."

"Because?"

"His anger at the regime felt real. His Farsi sounded native. Even the way he described the op, that it's in trouble but the top guys are pushing. Whichever team you play for, we've all had that. And it doesn't make sense otherwise. He gave us a very specific tip. We'll know in a week if he's lying. If the point was to set me up, why not shoot me today? We both know I couldn't have done much."

"Write up your report, I'll cable the desk."

"I wish I'd gotten a picture somehow."

"Maybe we can convince the agency to put a sketch artist on a plane tonight before your memory fogs."

"You think he's real, Martha?"

"I trust you."

An answer that wasn't exactly yes. And, more important, left the judgment squarely on him. He was disappointed in her—and in himself for letting her beauty fool him. She was chief of base. He was deputy. Ever thus.

Taylor spent the next two days on conference calls with Langley, answering the same questions again and again. How the letter had come in. What had happened at the carpet store. Finally, he reached Bart Regina, an assistant deputy director. "You know no Rev Guard officer has ever defected? Not one. Ever."

Taylor didn't bother to answer.

"If we pass this warning to the Mossad and we're wrong, we will look *muy* foolish. But you think we should go ahead."

Hunt scribbled on a piece of paper and flashed the words at Taylor. *Decision made, ass covering.* So this call was pro forma. Regina wanted to hear that Taylor believed. Then the backsplatter wouldn't touch Regina if the tip didn't pan out. If it did, no one would care that Regina had raised an alarm. The seventh floor would be too thrilled with its new source.

These internal games were the reason Taylor liked having a quiet career. Bigger stakes, bigger politics. Now he stretched out his neck, put it on the block. "Sir, if you're asking me whether Reza was genuine, I believe so. If for no other reason than he got my name from *somewhere*. The story he told makes sense. Believe me, I know we'd rather have his real name. But given the risks he faces, I'm not surprised he kept it to himself."

Despite the second-guessing—or maybe because of it— Taylor increasingly believed that Reza was who he claimed to be. Not just because being wrong would end his career. Taylor wanted everyone to have to admit he was right. *Everyone* included Martha Hunt.

"Good," Regina said. "We'll let the Israelis know. Classify it as single-source, probability four." The scale ran from one to ten, one completely reliable and ten wild rumor.

Considering that the agency had only Taylor's gut as a data point, four was a vote of confidence. The line went dead.

"Nice guy," Hunt said.

"Just covering his ass. Like a certain station chief I know."

To his surprise, she smiled. "Guess I deserve that."

"Should have put your chips next to mine, Martha."

Four days later, in Luanda, Angola, a Nissan van accelerated down Rua Rainha Ginga and rammed through the outer gate of the Israeli embassy, a small two-story building. As the Nissan approached the inner gate, its guards opened up with their AKs. The driver lost control. The van slammed into a concrete chicane that the Israelis had hastily put up after the American warning. The driver ran to a motorcycle and escaped.

Thirty seconds later, the van exploded. Two guards were killed, three others wounded. Six embassy employees were also hurt. An Israeli investigative team later found the van had held three hundred kilograms of fertilizer and fuel oil, enough to have taken down the embassy if it had reached the building.

Six thousand miles away, a taxi stopped at the rear entrance to the Israeli embassy in Bangkok. Neither driver nor passenger had an entry permit, so the local guards wouldn't raise the gate. After a fifteen-second standoff, the taxi's passenger shot the driver in the head and ran.

Forty-five seconds later, the taxi blew up. The driver and one guard were killed, two others badly injured. The passenger escaped. Thai police estimated that eighty pounds of a military-grade explosive called Semtex had been placed in the taxi's trunk.

The Israeli prime minister called the President to thank him for the warning. The President called his new DCI, Scott Hebley, a Marine four-star who had replaced Duto. Hebley called Taylor. Langley sent a surveillance team to Istanbul to help the station trace Reza. NSA cloned the phone that Reza had given Taylor so it would ring on a dedicated line in the Counterterrorism Center. Taylor kept the original. After all, Reza had chosen *him*. Despite the risk, he badly wanted Reza to call again. He expected to hear within a few days. Surely the Iranian would want credit for the tip, if nothing else.

Weeks passed. The agency checked its sketch of Reza against its databases, along with those from the FBI, Interpol, and the MIT, the Turkish intelligence service. No matches. The surveillance team went home. In Angola and Thailand, the attack investigations stalled. The van had been stolen. The cabbie in Bangkok appeared unconnected to terrorism. He'd done nothing more than pick up the wrong fare. The Semtex was traced to a Czech factory that supplied half the world. Neither Hezbollah nor Iran took credit for the bombings, but their silence wasn't a surprise. They rarely broadcast their involvement.

September became October. Still Reza stayed away.

Taylor found himself depressed, strangely jealous, a lover spurned after a one-night stand. *Why doesn't he call? What did I do?* He asked NSA to double-check that the phone was working. He changed ringtones, went back to the original. He put off his other agents, ignored calls, canceled appointments. For four straight Fridays in November, he reenacted every detail of the meeting. After the fourth, he found Hunt outside his office. "Have a drink with me," she said.

He knew he wouldn't like what she was going to tell him. He also knew he needed to hear it. In her office, she pulled a bottle of Laphroaig and two glasses from her bottom drawer and poured for them both.

"Most likely he's not in Istanbul anymore. They probably found him."

They both knew that if the Guard had discovered that Reza was a traitor, it would have arrested and tortured him. In that case, Taylor's cover was blown. He should transfer out of Istanbul. He wanted to stay. He wanted to be around when Reza called again.

"They're not on him. He's careful."

"Don't be irrational."

"That tip saved lives."

"Three months ago."

"You're jealous because you didn't buy in."

She sipped her scotch. "Plenty of glory to go round. Only one squandering it is you. You got PTSD from a single successful meet. First time in history."

He wanted to argue with her, but he knew she was right.

"That phone rings, we'll be ready. Meantime, be a man. Get back to work. Let it go."

"You be a man." He wanted to be funny, but even to his ears the words sounded petulant.

"*Salud*, Brian." She raised her glass and downed the whiskey in one gulp.

Fall ended. Christmas became New Year's Eve and Taylor invited Hunt to his annual party. She didn't come. Turkey entered its short, sharp winter, an unpleasant surprise for out-of-season tourists. Snow on the Bosphorus sounded picturesque, but Istanbul wasn't built for cold. Winds whipped off the Sea of Marmara. Sleet frosted the sidewalks. The Turks hurried along in their too-thin coats, trying not to fall on patches of black ice.

Taylor felt almost relieved to be back to his everyday work. Still, he made sure the magic phone was always fully charged, always within arm's reach. It rang at ten p.m. on a Friday night. For a few seconds, Taylor didn't quite believe his ears. Then he grabbed for it. The screen reported the incoming number as the 123456 of a Skype call. He clicked on.

"Mr. Nelson."

Taylor knew Reza's voice instantly. "Yes."

"InterContinental Hotel. Envelope at front desk. Pick it up, come to room 1509. Alone." *Click.*

Taylor messaged Hunt: *R called. Activating team.* Each month, Hunt chose two officers to stand by in case Taylor needed backup. Basically the assignment meant, *Be ready to drop whatever you're doing if Brian needs you. Make sure your phone is charged, and don't get too drunk.* Dominick and Ronaldo were part of the team, too, though their job was only to get a picture. They weren't trained in active surveillance.

They'd planned for a no-notice call like this. They wouldn't have time to set a trap. The tech guys would park near the hotel. One officer would wait in the lobby, the other outside. They'd all seen the sketch. They wouldn't follow Reza. Taylor and Hunt agreed a tail would be a mistake. Based on how cautious he'd been during the first meeting, Reza could probably make a two-man tail. If he did, he would be furious. He might break contact forever. So the station would settle for a photograph of him, and to see if anyone was with him or watching him at the hotel.

Taylor's apartment was a little more than a mile south of the InterContinental. He dressed, strapped on his holster, made his way into the misty Istanbul night. He walked northeast as texts lit up his phone, the team reporting in. Dominick and Ronaldo lived together a few miles north of downtown. Taylor had never understood whether they were roommates or lovers. Either way, they promised to reach the hotel in thirty minutes. One of the live surveillance officers said he could arrive in twenty. The second didn't respond. The guy was single. He could be in a loud bar and have missed the text. A bad break. But Taylor knew the truth. He would have gone in with no backup for the chance to meet Reza again.

The envelope the concierge passed him was nearly weight-less. Taylor tore it open in the elevator, found only a hotel key card. He turned it in his hands and knew Reza wouldn't be waiting.

He stood outside the room and listened. Nothing. Knocked. No answer. He drew his Sig, held it at his side, pushed the key card into the slot. He shoved the door open as the lock beeped green. He hid at the edge of the door frame and waited. No footsteps scuffling inside, no whispered voices. He pushed inside, put the key into the slot by the door so the lights would pop on.

The room was empty, the bed unmussed. In the marble bathroom, the soaps and shampoos and bottled water were untouched. Taylor had brought a radio-frequency sniffer that would find basic bugs. He scanned the room. Nothing. He didn't think Reza had been here. The agency would check the name on the reservation. But Reza had no doubt used a runner again, paid some lucky Turk a few hundred dollars to book the room. Taylor sat on the bed and scrolled through pay-per-view movies while he waited for the call.

Twenty minutes later, the phone rang.

"I said no surveillance. Did you think I wouldn't see those fat men in the van?"

Taylor knew why Reza wanted to keep his name secret. He understood why the Iranian had brought him here. Reza knew NSA had tapped the phone he gave Taylor. The room phone was clean. So Reza didn't have to worry about an immediate trace.

Still, the gamesmanship grated on Taylor. Agents and case officers had tricky relationships. To defuse their fears, some agents needed to prove they were smarter than their handlers. If Reza and Taylor were going to work together long-term, the Iranian's attitude needed to change. For the moment, Reza held the cards. Taylor couldn't risk driving him off.

"It's natural we're anxious to have a photo of you."

"I'm anxious that you don't."

"That's also natural."

"Will you give me your word that the next time we meet, there won't be surveillance?"

"I give you my word that next time you won't see it."

Reza laughed. *We are both men of the world*, the laugh said. *We understand each other. I don't hold the surveillance against you. You play your part as I play mine.* A knot in Taylor's stomach eased. Reza would cooperate today.

"Did you think I would call sooner?"

"I thought you would call when you had something to say."

"I told you, smarter than the average CIA. We are planning to assassinate a station chief."

Martha? Taylor almost said. He bit back her name in time. "Here?"

"Too close to home. Not Europe, either. The police, too good. I'm not involved directly, but I am told we're choosing from one in Asia, one in Africa."

"Hezbollah?"

"Too tricky for them. The Guard itself."

"That's like declaring war."

"No one asks my opinion. But we won't take responsibility, you can't prove it. Maybe we blame someone else. Al-Qaeda."

"When?"

"This one, it could still be called off. But I believe the approval's coming. Within the next ten days. The planning is done."

"A sniper, a bomb, poison?"

"I don't know."

"Give me *something*, Reza. We can't lock down the whole world."

"Of course, Brian. I will call General Moghrabi, demand he tell me. When he asks why, I'll say my friend at the CIA needs to know."

The phone went dead. Taylor listened to the dial tone until it turned into a fast, angry beep. The most important agent he'd ever had, and Taylor had treated him like a thousand-dollar-a-month file clerk. He stood by the window, looking at the Bosphorus. The windows were undoubtedly too thick to break. Lucky him.

The phone rang. Taylor dove for it. Actually dove across the room, grabbed the handset, sprawled on the bed. Not cool, but no one was watching.

"Next time I don't call back."

"I'm sorry."

"The risks."

"You could have had a team waiting to drop me, Reza. I came."

"You have men."

"Downstairs. What good are they when I open this

door?" Taylor counted to five in his head. *Slow it down. Calm him down.* "We're in this together."

"Then let me do what I can. Don't ask for information you know I don't have. If I get what you need—"

Taylor suddenly knew what to do. "I'll set an account for you. At UBS. Monday."

"An excuse to get my name."

"No safe-deposit box. No keys. No nonsense. It'll be online, under the name Reza Istanbul. You'll have the account number. Real money, not a promise. Take it out, transfer it, whatever."

"It's not necessary."

"Two hundred thousand to start. If you defect—"

"I won't."

You might, Taylor thought. But even if he never touched the money, Reza would like having it. Two hundred thousand dollars was a small price to build loyalty from an agent like this.

"Next time we talk, will you tell me more about your biography? How old you are, where you grew up, when you entered the Guard, your life."

"Why would I do that?"

"So we can understand each other better."

"Good night, Brian."

Taylor reached for a Heineken from the minifridge, then reconsidered and grabbed a Coke. He had a long night ahead. He would have to send a CRITIC-coded cable reporting the threat. Since Reza had been right about the embassies, the agency would put out an immediate world-wide alert, which would cause an immediate worldwide mess. The more cautious station chiefs would turtle up. The cowboys would figure this warning didn't tell them anything they didn't know, that they were always at risk, and without a specific threat the tip was useless. They were right, and wrong. Reza might not know how the Guard intended to pull this off. But if he said the planning was done, Taylor believed him.

He popped open his Coke and stood by the window, looking out at the dark water of the Bosphorus, the shining city around it. Waiting for his stomach to settle.

It didn't.

4

Anne and Wells shuffled down the gangway with their heads down, like earthquake survivors waiting for aftershocks. Wells wanted to grab her, beg her to reconsider. But she'd said no for the right reasons. In thirty days, he would give up the job or walk away from her forever. He couldn't imagine either one. Or maybe he could. Maybe he already knew exactly what he would do, and he wouldn't admit the truth to himself.

They'd just slid into a cab when his phone interrupted his uncheery thoughts.

"Where to?"

"Miami International." Wells rejected the call, sight unseen. A minute later, the phone rang again. This time he checked the screen. *VD*. Duto. He again sent the call to voice mail, switched the phone to vibrate. Within seconds, it began to buzz. Despite himself, Wells felt his interest stirring. If Duto needed him enough to call three times, Duto had a problem.

"Do what you have to do," Anne said.

Wells clicked on. "Senator."

"Any chance you could meet me tonight?"

"Any chance you could tell me why?"

"Not on an open line."

"Then no."

"Ellis will be there."

If Ellis Shafer was going, then Wells was going. Pointless to pretend otherwise. Though they'd fought some ugly battles in the years since Wells returned from Afghanistan, Shafer was now Wells's closest friend inside the CIA, or anywhere else. He was part boss, part confidant, part fixer, and he had pulled strings to save Wells's life more than once. But Shafer was now past the CIA's retirement age, and with Duto gone, Wells knew that Shafer was on borrowed time at the agency. He didn't want to think about what either of them would do when Shafer finally was shown the door.

"We meeting in D.C.?" Wells said.

"Philly. Can you get to my office by ten?"

"Thought you slept in a coffin."

"I'll text you the address." He was gone.

Wells tucked away the phone, looked at Anne. Started to reach for her. Stopped. "I—"

"Go. I'll take care of Tonka."

"I've still got the thirty days, right?"

"Don't, John. Just don't."

The condo towers loomed over Biscayne Bay like fifty-story mirages.

His flight was late. Philly matched his mood. Cold and wet. He didn't reach Duto's offices until almost midnight. He followed a plainclothes police officer down a hallway covered with maps of Pennsylvania and photos of the Liberty Bell. Duto and Shafer sat watching ESPN, drinking Budweisers from a twelve-pack on the couch between them, resting their feet on a coffee table. Sixty-something fratboys.

"John." Shafer raised a can of Bud in greeting. "Get off those dogs, have a beer."

"When did you two turn into such good buddies?"

Duto lurched up, extended a hand. "John Wells. My heart flutters. Together again, we three amigos."

"We were never three anythings." Wells ignored Duto's outstretched palm until Duto sat back down.

"Nice tan," Shafer said.

"Must be living right," Duto said.

"He went on a cruise."

"Ellis," Wells said.

"If you were stuck watching TV with him, you'd drink, too," Shafer said.

"This job," Duto said. "The people *this*, the people *that*—"

"Why am I here?"

"Old times' sake."

Wells stepped toward the door.

"Let's say you're here to repay a favor." The drunken playfulness had left Duto's voice.

"How's that?"

"Really? After I sent that drone to save your ass."

Wells eyed Shafer. Shafer lifted his old-man shoulders a half inch. So he agreed.

"We both know without that, you weren't getting out—"

"All right."

"Take a seat, John."

Wells pushed their feet aside, sat on the coffee table.

"Your attention, please." Duto turned off the television. "Juan Pablo Montoya called me today."

"Should I know that name?"

"He was an agent of mine in Colombia. An army officer. We've stayed in touch. He wasn't all that nice, but he had his uses."

"This ring a bell?" Wells said to Shafer. Shafer shook his head.

"He lives in Guatemala now. Retired, or so he claims. He wanted to pass along a tip. A friend of his is part of a team that plans to assassinate a station chief. Weird part is that a CIA officer is supposedly running the op."

"A case officer trying to kill a COS? He lose out on a promotion?"

"I know it sounds weird, but Juan Pablo's not into bullshit. If he's calling, it's true. Or at least he thinks it is. Before you ask, he doesn't know the station."

"But his friend does."

"Correct. He'll give us the friend's name for one hundred

thousand dollars. Plus I have to go to Guatemala City to meet him in person. I'm sure you can see that wouldn't be a good idea. Which is why I'm deputizing you in my stead."

"You don't need to say *deputizing* and *in my stead*, Vinny," Shafer said. "Either will do. More important, this afternoon we got a report that Iran is planning to kill a COS, name and location unknown."

Duto's eyebrows nearly came off his skull. The surprise looked real to Wells.

All three men fell silent. Wells spoke first.

"Let me make sure I have this. In the last day, both Vinny and the agency itself have been warned about a plot against a station chief. Vinny's info comes from a guy in Guatemala who used to be an asset. He says that a case officer is running the plot. Meanwhile, the agency's report comes from—"

"Turkey," Shafer said.

"Human, ELINT, third-party—"

"Closely guarded."

"You don't know."

Shafer shook his head.

"Anyway, whoever it is, this source says that Iran is behind the assassination. Rev Guard or Hezbollah like Buckley?" Hezbollah had killed William Buckley, the station chief for Lebanon, after kidnapping him. The agency had always believed Hezbollah wouldn't act so provocatively without at least informing Iran of its plans.

"No, the Guard itself."

"So two very different reports. And the only thing they have in common—"

"Is that a COS is getting . . ." Duto made a pistol with his fingers and pulled the trigger.

"A station chief hasn't been killed in twenty years," Shafer said. "Since Freddie Woodruff."

Woodruff, the chief in the former Soviet republic of Georgia, had died in 1993 under circumstances that remained murky even now. Woodruff, a hard-partying Oklahoman, had come to Georgia just after the collapse of the Soviet Union. At the time, Moscow hadn't fully reconciled itself to the loss of its satellite states. Woodruff was riding with his security guard in a jeep when a single bullet hit him in the head. He died before reaching a hospital.

The police arrested a former Georgian soldier, claiming he had taken a single blind shot from the side of the road. The soldier's car had run out of gas, and he was angry the jeep hadn't stopped to help him, the police said. After days of beatings, the soldier confessed. But the forensic evidence didn't match the police theory. The FBI and CIA picked up rumors that Russian spies had shot Woodruff to warn the United States against encroaching on Moscow's turf. But after a short trial, the Georgians convicted the former soldier. The FBI had reinvestigated the shooting without success. The only certainty was that Freddie Woodruff was buried in Arlington National Cemetery.

Buckley's kidnapping and Woodruff's murder had led the agency to tighten security around station chiefs. None had been killed since, though they were top targets for al-Qaeda.

"A few choices," Duto said. "One, Montoya is lying, looking for a hundred K. And he's the luckiest scammer in the world because he picked up the phone the same day this other plot came in. Two, it's open season on station chiefs and these plots happen to be unrolling at the same time. Three, Iran has hired one of our case officers to kill one of our station chiefs. Am I missing anything?"

"Heart, soul, conscience," Shafer said. "But in this case, no."

"So call the seventh floor, tell them about Juan Pablo," Wells said. "Let them figure it out."

"Too squishy. It'll look like I'm interfering. Like I can't back off, let Hebley do his job."

"Talk to Montoya yourself, then."

"I'm scheduled for like the next three weeks. Plus this isn't a guy I want to be seen with. He's not senatorial. For lack of a better word."

"But you're okay sending John?" Shafer said.

"John's a big boy. He'll be fine."

Wells wondered how dangerous Juan Pablo Montoya really was. No matter. As Duto's emissary, Wells should be safe. Anyway, the trip would take his mind off Anne. "You sure you want to waste your favor on this? Using me as a messenger boy for some two-bit narco."

Duto nodded.

"Then Guatemala City it is."

So: a new assignment. He wouldn't be going back to New Hampshire.

Wells wanted to pretend he felt something other than relief. He couldn't.

5

The United 737 came into La Aurora International from the south, so close to the concrete rooftops that Wells could count clotheslines. Even before the jet stopped rolling, Wells lit up his phone. No messages. Not from Duto or Shafer. And not from Anne. He wished she hadn't given him a month. Without it, they might have made a clean break. He was thinking about her more than ever. Or maybe she'd intended that.

He needed to put her aside. Drugs, gangs, and poverty made Guatemala one of the world's most dangerous countries. Wells was unarmed. Naturally, he hadn't taken any weapons on the cruise. Not even a knife.

Just the ring.

The sun was low in the sky as Wells stepped out of the airport. He called Montoya, but no one answered. At his hotel, he channeled his frustrations into a monster workout. Two hours of cardio, another of lifting. The exercise exhausted him, but still he slept poorly. He dreamed that Anne stood on the front of the *Titanic*, her arm cocked back. He yelled to her. She ignored him and flung the ring into the ocean.

When he woke, he found himself annoyed by his lack of imagination. His unconscious was stealing from movies now? He should have dreamed . . . he didn't know what. Of his parents, maybe. Their house in Hamilton. Something that connected past and future.

But thinking about the past meant thinking about the men he'd killed. He'd walled himself off. Now he saw that imagination was memory's twin. His forced amnesia gave him movies for dreams. He closed his eyes, saw himself hiking on a ridgeline, sheer thousand-foot cliffs on either side, an army of the dead behind him, wool-thick fog rolling toward him. *The only way out is through.*

He showered, shaved, called Montoya.

"Buenos días."

"And good morning to you." Wells wished he spoke Spanish. He'd always enjoyed its smoothness.

"Who is this?"

"John Wells. I work with Vinny Duto."

"You are in Guatemala, Señor Wells." The guy spoke the last two words like a Telemundo villain. A joke, Wells figured.

"Sí."

"I told the *comandante* I'd meet him. Not an errand boy."

"Never been called that before."

"Do you have my money, errand boy?"

"We can discuss that in person."

"So you don't."

Wells was tired of this Latin braggadocio. "You think a United States senator jumps on a plane because you say so, you've sampled too much of your product. I promise you'll get paid. Assuming this story isn't complete caca."

Montoya laughed. "Be at the Parque Central at five p.m. No, six."

"Why don't you just tell me where you live? Or are you being difficult because you're annoyed Vinny's not here?"

"My men will pick you up. No weapons, please."

Words that made Wells want a pistol more than ever. He hung up, called the front desk. "Can you call me a cab to the nearest Walmart?"

"You're sure you want a Walmart, sir? We have excellent shopping nearby."

"I'm on a budget."

Officially called the Plaza de la Constitución, the Parque Central had once been Guatemala's government and religious center. Now the president worked elsewhere, and the palace on the park's northern end served as an art museum. But the cathedral on the east side, which had survived multiple earthquakes, remained home to Guatemala City's archbishop.

"Don't go after dark," the desk clerk said, when Wells asked about it. "Better to stay in the Zona Viva. Here, it's patrolled."

"Even around the palace?"

"Especially there. They look for tourists." *I know you won't listen,* the clerk's face said. *You want to find out for yourself. The foolish privilege of the foolish privileged.*

Wells stowed his wallet and passport and ring in the room safe and left the hotel at 5:30, the winter sky nearly dark. Even in the patrolled area, the Zona Viva, the streets were nearly deserted. The cab turned onto Avenida 7A and rolled north past long, low concrete blocks, pockmarked and covered with graffiti. Guatemala City reminded Wells of a boxer, a lightweight with a losing record and prison tats that didn't quite cover his acne scars. The cab stopped for a light beside a drugstore marked with a green neon cross. A chubby man in a white coat pulled down a steel gate as two guards flanked him. They were armed like a police tac team, shotguns and bullet-resistant vests.

"*Farmacias,* many robberies," the cabbie said.

Ten minutes later, the cabbie turned left through an archway and stopped outside a squat stone building topped by two low bell towers. "Cathedral. Parque Central." The square was smaller than Wells expected, with a dry fountain in the center protected by a low wall. A grove of trees shaded the southern side. The final strips of daylight were fleeing the sky. A dozen teenage boys sat on the wall beside the fountain. Others squatted on their heels around the plaza. Two leaned against the cathedral, chins lolled to their chests, tongues dangling.

"They take glue," the cabbie said. Liquid cement was the drug of choice for the poorest kids in Latin America. Glue was a strange drug. It didn't bring the euphoria of heroin or the stimulation of cocaine. It made time vanish and obliterated the mind. Huffers rarely lasted much past their teens. The freefall wasn't a side effect, Wells figured. It was the point.

He reached for his door, found it locked.

"You see, now back to hotel, yes?"

"I'm meeting someone. Can you wait?"

"Too many gangs."

"How about at the corner of Calle Ocho, Avenida Cinco?" Two blocks away.

"How long?"

"Half hour." Wells passed the cabbie two twenty-dollar bills, way more than the fare. "I'll give you one hundred U.S."

"Fifty now. You come by six-thirty, hundred fifty more. Otherwise I leave."

Wells handed over fifty dollars from the loose cash he was carrying in his baggy black Walmart sweatpants. The real prizes from his shopping trip were hidden under the sweats. Wells had taped a metal flashlight to his right calf, sheathed a four-inch knife to his left. He would have preferred a pistol, of course, but the knife and light were the best he could do on a few hours' notice.

In movies, no one ever had a problem getting weapons. In the real world, people who tried to buy guns illegally were apt to be arrested, or worse. A would-be buyer had to find someone who already had a firearm—while advertising that he had money but no weapon of his own. A more obvious prescription to be robbed was hard to imagine.

The urchins stared as Wells stepped onto the plaza. The nearest were forty feet away, three kids squatting side by side by side. The one in the middle pointed a finger pistol at Wells and said something under his breath. The other boys laughed. The plaza reminded Wells of the sunbaked plains of Kenya. The boys were the hyenas, Wells the lion. In a one-on-one fight, he would dominate. But hyenas ran in packs. And in packs they had been known to run lions off, or even kill them. Already the three kids in the middle were pushing themselves to their feet, looking around for friends.

Wells decided to bring the fight to them, send the others running. Even if the tactic worked, it would buy him only a few minutes. Then whoever controlled this plaza would hear what had happened. The guys with the AKs would show up. He had to assume Montoya's men would pick him up before then. If Montoya wanted to get Wells killed, he would have insisted Wells go into a hillside slum at midnight. Instead, Montoya was testing him. Taunting him. *Gringo, are you man enough to be my man?* A stupid game.

Wells strode toward the three boys. The only real risk was that their leader might have a .22. But these kids looked too broke to own even the cheapest pistols. Their jeans and T-shirts were more holes than fabric. Plus Wells had never seen anyone who was holding make a finger pistol. Wells put them on box cutters, homemade shivs, butterfly knives.

He was making a lot of assumptions. Wrong one way, he would wind up with a dime-sized slug in his chest.

Wrong the other, he would worsen the misery of a bunch of pathetic street kids. He would go with the flashlight first in a fight. Better to break bones than leave these kids bleeding to death. He had no choice but to get in close and let the question answer itself. His biggest advantage was that kids weren't expecting *him*.

The boys muttered as he closed the gap. Most of the plaza's streetlamps had burned out. In the light that remained, Wells saw that the boy in the middle wore a filthy yellow soccer jersey. It hung long and loose over the kid's jeans, plenty of room to hide a pistol.

Wells walked straight to him. The kid was both more pathetic and more dangerous up close. In another life he would have been handsome, with brown eyes and jet-black hair and an angular face. But sores marred his lips, and a long white scar crossed his forehead. His head barely reached Wells's sternum, but he looked up without fear.

"American?" The word was a curse.

"Guilty." Wells waited. Not his normal move. He had stayed alive all these years by striking first. But he had to give this fourteen-year-old a chance to walk away.

"Want drugs? *Chinga?*"

The kid's right hand had been flat on his leg, resting on his jeans. Now he moved it up, slid his index and middle fingers under the edge of the soccer shirt. The kid had a gun tucked into his jeans.

"Money." The kid slipped his hand under his shirt—

Wells shoved the boy backward, his hands side by side on the boy's chest like a close-grip bench press. Wells had the weight and the leverage. The kid had no chance. He stumbled back and Wells stepped forward with him, pushing him down like an offensive tackle pancaking a linebacker. The boy pulled his hands out and away to brace his fall. The pistol rattled against the cobblestones as he landed on his ass with Wells on top of him.

The kid tried to reach underneath himself for the gun, but Wells raised his right elbow, cracked it into the boy's temple. The kid grunted and crumpled against the plaza's paving stones. Wells flipped him over, pushed up the soccer shirt, found a tiny black pistol—

As he did, he felt motion from the right. Another boy was coming, right arm cocked, a tiny blade gleaming in his hand, two steps away and closing. Wells was on all fours, no time to get to his feet, no time to shoot, and he wouldn't have shot this kid anyway—

Wells pushed himself off the plaza's stones and drew his right shoulder down and in, launching himself into a roll *at* the boy. The squats he forced himself to do every day paid off now. He knew the kid couldn't adjust in time. He felt the knife swipe over him as the boy stabbed downward and found air. He rolled into the boy's legs, a vicious chop block that would have earned him a fifteen-yard penalty if a ref had been watching. He weighed twice as much as the kid. The collision instantly reversed the boy's direction, flipped him backward onto the stones. Wells heard the sharp crack of bone as the kid landed, followed by a low moan. Probably an elbow. Wrist fractures didn't hurt very much, but broken elbows were nasty.

Wells used his momentum to push himself up. The boy lay on his back, his right arm twisted. He was channeling the pain by tearing at his lip with a proud pair of buckteeth. His switchblade lay useless on his chest.

Two street urchins, disarmed. American might at its finest. The third boy hadn't moved. "Some friend you are." Wells stepped toward him and he took off. Wells went back to the kid in the soccer shirt, the one who'd started the trouble, reached down, grabbed a skinny biceps, and picked him up. The boy was so light. Not even skin and bones. Skin and air.

"Puta."

Wells pulled two twenty-dollar bills from his pocket, pressed the kid's hand around them.

"Cash for guns." He didn't know what a Saturday-night special went for in Guatemala City, but forty bucks seemed fair.

"Chinga tu madre."

Wells flung the kid away. He stumbled a half-dozen steps, gained his balance, raised an invisible assault rifle. *"Rat-tat-tat—"* He backed away, turned, ran. The other boys on the plaza followed, all but the one with the broken elbow. He walked slowly, keeping his right arm steady and pressed against his side. Wells reached into his pocket for the rest of his money, six hundred dollars. The boy shirked away. Wells folded the cash into a tight roll and stuffed it into the boy's left hand. "Yours. Get your arm fixed." The boy didn't say a word.

"John Wells!"

The voice came from a minivan stopped beside the

cathedral. A man stepped out, holding a pistol. Not a .22. A grown-up gun with a five-inch barrel. Probably a .45. Wells didn't like pistols that big. They looked mean, but they were impossible to hide, slow to draw, and tough to aim because they kicked so hard. Even so, the guy was barely fifty feet away, close enough to put a hole in him.

"Hope you guys enjoyed the show."

"Drop your gun."

"I paid forty bucks for this thing."

The guy raised his pistol. "Drop it."

Wells skittered the gun along the cobblestones.

"Front seat," the guy said. Wells took his place in the passenger seat. Two guys in back, plus the driver. No one searched him. They must have figured that if he hadn't pulled on the kid, he was unarmed. Dumb, but Wells wasn't complaining.

Montoya lived in the wealthy southern suburbs, past the airport. Guatemala was even poorer than the rest of Central America. But its ruling class lived well, behind electrified fences and armed guards. The minivan turned into a cul-de-sac and parked in front of a property that appeared relatively unprotected, just a spiked fence. Then the lights flicked on, revealing the real security system. Four Dobermans stood on their hind legs in their eagerness to get at the intruders. Wells loved most dogs, but Dobermans were twitchy and short-tempered. He hoped Montoya didn't have kids.

The house behind the fence was built in classic Spanish

adobe style, white with a flat roof and red-brown ceramic tiles. A handsome man a little older than Wells waited at the front gate. Wells opened his door without being told and jogged to him. The guards hurried after him, shouting in Spanish.

"Juan Pablo—" Wells sensed a guard behind him, too close. He half turned, tried to get his arm up, but he was leaning forward, his weight going the wrong way. Metal cracked into the side of his head. A web of pain ran in every direction around the world. Wells blinked, but when he tried to open his eyes he couldn't. *No*, he said, or tried to say—

His legs went and he fell to his knees and the black swallowed him.

6

Most of his life he'd had a different name. A different face. He'd grown up in Ontario, California. East of Los Angeles, west of Death Valley. Caught between hell and the desert, his dad said. His mom taught third-graders, his dad managed a dry cleaner. They weren't rich, but they did fine. His mom always used exactly those words, *We aren't rich, but we do fine.*

He remembered perfectly the moment he left them behind. Disney World. Not Disneyland, Disney World. They'd scrimped for a year to fly across the country and ride the exact same rides that they rode in Anaheim. He was on Space Mountain with his dad, second time that day. Suddenly he caught himself thinking, *I will not be these people. I will not be ordinary.* He was twelve. He felt something like shock. *You look green,* his mom said when they got off the coaster. *Too many Cokes?*

Through junior high, he waited for the feeling to wane. Instead, it put vines in him. Only one problem. He had no idea how he would make his mark. The obvious routes to fame and fortune were out. He was five-ten, one-sixty, no athlete. He couldn't act or play guitar. He was average-looking, with dark hair and brown eyes that were a little too small. He was smart, but plenty of kids were smarter.

What, then? Finally, he saw that he did have one exceptional quality, an uncanny ability to blend in. He was at home with the jocks, the theater geeks, the UN club. The teachers liked him, too. He simply shut his mouth. Everyone in the world wanted to talk. He listened. He let an endless stream of words flow over him, offered the right answers at the right moments. Over time, he grew to see conversations almost as a game. How little could he say? He never passed on the gossip he heard. X had cheated on her boyfriend? Y was cutting school to smoke pot? So what? Once he'd learned a secret, he no longer cared.

He's so mature, the teachers told his parents. *So empathetic.* In fact, he was the opposite. The right test would have revealed that he was close to a psychopath. But he wasn't conventionally dangerous. He had no interest in hurting anyone. Not back then.

In eleventh grade, he took a modern history class whose syllabus included *The Spy Who Came in from the Cold.* When he read it, he knew. He belonged with these men who lied to one another and everyone else, who stood outside the world's laws.

Finding a way into their world was straightforward. The era of Ivy League shoulder taps had ended decades before.

He studied Spanish and international relations at UC San Diego. After graduation, he became an analyst at the RAND Institute in Los Angeles. RAND was federally backed, thick with former intelligence officers, a clear path to Langley. The agency called three years later. *You can't tell anyone*, the recruiters told him. *Not your friends. Not your family.* The most thrilling words of his life.

He aced training and was sent to Peru. With the Cold War over, Congress was cutting the agency's budget. But the news hadn't gotten to Latin America, the last refuge for cowboy case officers who ran their own foreign policy with duffel bags of cash. For a while, he loved the job. Especially the tradecraft. Countersurveillance runs through the slums on his way to meetings. Growing into his cover as an engineer for a mining company prospecting around Machu Picchu. Helicoptering into the Andes with a briefcase full of cash handcuffed to his wrist.

After a year, the thrills began to fade. Slowly. Like a song he'd heard too many times. He realized the agency was a bureaucracy like any other, driven by its own perverse internal incentives. The CIA's primary mission in Lima was helping the Peruvian army fight leftist guerrillas who called themselves the Shining Path. By the mid-1990s, the Path was unraveling. Its violence had alienated the peasants who formed its core. The CIA could have encouraged the army to stand aside, let the Path commit suicide. Instead, it kept paying for ops that mostly killed civilians. *Anybody ever think about dialing things back?* he once asked his station chief. A casual question over beers.

We have a budget. Budget means ops. Don't get any points for saving it. We don't spend it, they don't give it to us next year.

A few weeks later, he fell in love.

He'd never been in love. Never even had a girlfriend, though he'd slept with scores of women in California. The girls were usually a little overweight, a little older. They were needy and unhappy, and they always told him what a good listener he was. After he moved to Los Angeles to work for RAND, he began to dream about hurting them, dreams that always ended the same way, him taping their mouths shut.

What the hell? He wasn't a killer. He'd become a vegetarian in college because he couldn't abide the taste of dead flesh. He stopped going to bars. Maybe his brain wasn't wired for love. But he resolved to stop the listening game, look for a real relationship. To his surprise, he found one.

Julia was a Peruvian who worked as a translator and reporter for the Associated Press. She was small, almost scrawny. She wore her hair long and had deep brown eyes, the most beautiful he'd ever seen. He met her at the ambassador's Fourth of July barbecue, a cheap way for the embassy to build goodwill with reporters in Lima. She filled her plate like she was training for an eating contest. In forty-five minutes she plowed through two hamburgers, two ears of corn, a plate of ribs. She didn't make a mess, but she left nothing behind.

"They must not pay you enough."

"They don't." She said the words without heat.

"I'm Ron—" His cover name.

"Julia."

He waited for her to talk. People always spoke; they couldn't bear silence. Their voices relieved them. Once they started, they never stopped.

But she didn't start. After a minute, she walked to the pie table, the highlight of the afternoon, a half-dozen varieties, plus cans of Reddi-wip flown in by the case from Houston. She came back with wide slices of lemon, apple, and pecan. She ate carefully, relentlessly. He felt her responding to his stare. Maybe even putting on a show for him. All this in silence.

She finished, reached into her pocket, slid a card across the picnic table to him. "Call me sometime." She walked away.

He looked at the card—*Julia Espada, Associated Press*—and wondered if he could fall in love with someone over the way she ate.

The fact that her English wasn't great helped. He didn't always understand her. She had to repeat herself. The irony did not escape him. But mostly they didn't talk. Translating tired her tongue, she told him. The quiet relaxed her. They sat together, reading and companionable. Drove along the coast road as Pacific waves crashed into the rocks. Cooked in his apartment, the kitchen hushed as an operating room in the middle of tricky surgery.

They saw each other two and three times a week, but she wouldn't sleep with him. He should have been frustrated. In truth, he respected her for her restraint, so unlike the women at home. After two months, she offered herself to him with no false ceremony. *Tonight I'm staying over. I hope you have condoms.* The word sounded small in her mouth, the syllables precise and separate. *Con. Doms.*

Their sex was quiet, too. In California, he'd learned not to believe the screamers, who were mostly parroting the porn that guys made them watch. But Julia was nearly silent. *Is something wrong?* he finally asked. She told him not to worry.

Later he would wish he had.

She moved in eight months after they met. Per agency regs, he reported the relationship to his boss. The station found no red flags in her background. Her father was dead, her mother a secretary at Peru's national electric company. He assumed she knew what he did. But she never asked. In turn, he didn't press her for information about the stories she was working on. He didn't want her to wonder whether he was with her because he saw her as a potential source.

Caring about her made him a better case officer. He spent less time at the station, but he had more energy, worked harder. His doubts about strategy quit bothering him. He began to see what he was doing as a job. A job that came with a diplomatic passport, a fake name, and an apartment with blast-resistant windows, but a job nonetheless. His tradecraft improved with experience, and so did his evaluations. *A talented case officer who has recently grown into his work,* his station chief wrote in his annual evaluation.

If he'd been writing his own evaluation, it would have been far simpler: *For the first time I can remember, maybe the first in my life, I feel like a human being.*

Then James Veder showed up.

Veder came to Lima on TDY, temporary assignment, from Bogotá. He was hot shit, as he would be the first to explain, a throwback to the agency's OSS roots. He drank and smoked and screwed anything that wasn't nailed down. He had once expensed a Harley to the agency. Somehow the report went through.

Julia met Veder two years to the day after she'd met him, the same Fourth of July barbecue. She still ate like she was starving. *That guy's such a jerk,* she said afterward. *Do you work together?* She had never asked about another case officer before. *I don't even know him,* he told her. The truth.

Two months later, he scheduled an overnight trip to Iquitos, the northeast corner of Peru. He was recruiting an engineer for Chevron. *See you tomorrow,* Julia said. By then he was thinking about an engagement ring, wondering if she might want an emerald, something nontraditional.

He arrived in Iquitos to discover that the engineer had a 104-degree fever. He decided to catch the afternoon flight home. Didn't call. Figured he'd surprise her.

He heard her moaning even before he opened their apartment door. Sounds she'd never made with him. He hoped he was caught in a bad dream. But he knew her voice. He let himself in quietly. The bedroom door was open. He

watched Veder's head between her legs, her hands squeez-
ing his shoulders. When she saw him, she pushed Veder
away and yelped and covered herself in sheets that until a
few moments before he had thought of as theirs.

He expected to find shame in her eyes. Remorse. He
saw pity instead.

Veder grabbed his boxers. He wiped the back of his hand
over his mouth with the relish of a kid who'd just eaten a
chocolate bar. "She said you guys were breaking up."

"Out, Jimmy."

"Don't hurt her, man. She's not worth it."

Veder's words broke his anger. He didn't know what
he'd been planning. Bloodying Julia's nose, breaking her
teeth. Replacing what he'd seen with an image that at least
was under his control.

He shoved her at Veder. "Both of you. Now."

"Don't do this," Julia said. But she almost sounded
relieved.

"Thirty seconds, then I get my gun."

Veder grabbed for his Levi's, tugged them on both legs
at once, like he'd been through this drill before. "Let's go,
babe."

The man watched his future pull on sweatpants and an
Associated Press T-shirt. "Ten seconds." She grabbed her
passport from the nightstand. He wondered what she really
thought of him. What clues he must have missed.

"*Vámonos,*" Veder said.

"You don't even know her name, do you?"

"Come on, Julia."

He wished he hadn't asked. His wall safe was hidden

behind a poster of *The Kiss*, the Gustav Klimt painting. The irony was so cheap that he wanted to cry. Then he did cry. He turned to the wall to hide the tears creasing his cheeks. The safe was an old-school model with a dial, not a keypad. *Left three times to 22 . . .* He gripped the knob in his fingertips. Too tight. He lost track of how many times he'd spun the dial and had to start over. He heard the apartment door close as the tumblers clicked.

Inside, a 9-millimeter Sig. He didn't reach for it. If he reached for it, he would pick it up. If he picked it up he would open his lips and put it in his mouth. If he put it in his mouth he would pull the trigger. Simple as dominoes falling.

He shut the safe, set to work cleaning the apartment, removing all trace of her.

Maybe they would have reconciled. Maybe he would have quit the agency. Maybe he would have drunk himself into a suicidal stupor, put the Sig in his mouth after all. Maybe he would have figured out what had gone wrong and why he hadn't noticed. Maybe he would have punched out Veder at a Christmas party and they would have wound up buddies. A long shot, but maybe.

But none of those things had the chance to happen. He walked in on them on a Monday. Monday, September 10, 2001.

The attack made his private grief small and self-indulgent. No one knew what might happen next. Every station went to war. Through the fall, he worked twelve-hour days, seven-day weeks. As the immediate crisis abated, the agency began planning for the Iraq invasion. He volunteered to return to Langley for training in Arabic. He left Peru without speaking to Julia.

He arrived in Baghdad in June 2003. Within months, he realized that the agency was making the same mistakes he'd seen in Peru, focusing on its own priorities rather than the reality around it. Only this time, the stakes were far higher. Senior officers spent their time scheming with Ahmed Chalabi. Chalabi wanted to run Iraq, but he was a pretender who had fled the country a generation before. Meanwhile, no one seemed to notice the worsening chaos. Even after the insurgency erupted, the agency and its Green Zone overlords blamed al-Qaeda. They never acknowledged the truth. The occupation had made life miserable for ordinary Iraqis. Their children risked kidnapping whenever they left home. Each night they went to bed hungry, frightened, and waiting for civil war. Each morning more of them condemned the United States.

He couldn't tell whether his fellow officers couldn't see the truth, or whether political pressure from the White House had overwhelmed them. He found himself profoundly disappointed, in them and himself. He'd wanted to live an unusual life. He supposed in a way he'd succeeded. He worked for a bureaucracy as allergic to reality as any in corporate America. His home was a trailer on a fortified base in a country whose people hated him. He had no chance to use the tradecraft he'd honed in Peru. And he had no family and no prospects for one.

So he stayed. If he couldn't win the war, at least he could

lose himself in it. Most case officers left Iraq after a few months. He spent more than three years in Baghdad. For eighteen months, he worked as an analyst for the agency/ military task force that targeted top terrorists. With phone intercepts and interrogation reports, he pieced together networks in villages that he'd never seen. He felt like a kid who'd been given a jigsaw puzzle that had a trillion pieces and no edges. But at least the task forces had a clear mission, unlike everyone else in the Green Zone. And though he was under no illusion that killing Abu al-Zarqawi's jihadis would turn the tide of the war, he wanted them to die. He'd seen enough of their videos to know that they gloried in torture and murder.

He worked himself beyond exhaustion. In October 2006, he was caught sleepwalking while holding a loaded pistol. *Time to get out,* his boss said. He was so deep inside the war that he couldn't imagine leaving. *You punched your ticket. You know that, right? You've got one assignment until February, a paid vacation. And figure out where you want to go next. I mean anywhere. You're at the top of the list.* Sir— *Don't argue. You've earned it. Just thank me and pack.*

He went home. He hoped Ontario would seem more real to him than it had as a teenager. He imagined he'd take care of his parents, bond with them in their slow decline. Love, one emptied bedpan at a time. Mom and Dad had other ideas. She was sixty; he was sixty-two. Their years of saving had paid off. They weren't interested in bedpans. They'd bought an RV for an Alaska-to-Florida road trip.

They loved him, but dimly, almost abstractly. They called him a hero, a meaningless word meant to free him of responsibility for the choices he'd made. They saw his sadness, but they knew they couldn't help. They looked at him in a kindly, puzzled way, like dog owners who wished their Maltese would stop peeing on the floor.

He left after ten days, lonelier than ever. He rented a room at the W Hotel in Westwood and made up for his years of celibacy. The women in L.A. were even easier to take home than they'd been a decade before. Internet dating and drunk texting had erased the last vestiges of shame from one-night stands. Then he had a torture dream, more vivid than he remembered, amplified by what he'd seen in Iraq. He knew that these cruelties were real. He feared what that knowledge might allow him to do.

He quit the bars, wondered if he should try to find Julia. But that wound was both too raw for him to touch and too callused for him to care. His time in Baghdad had destroyed every instinct except survival, every memory except yesterday.

Yet his puzzlement and anger at her infidelity remained. He still didn't know why she'd slept with Veder. Had he seduced her, or the reverse? Had that afternoon in the apartment been their first time together? He'd imagined she loved him. Why hadn't she told him when she felt herself slipping away? The questions gnawed, but he would never ask her for the answers. Not after the way she'd walked out. Not after what he'd seen.

He wished he'd killed Veder.

He left California, spent the rest of his time off traveling, a month in Africa, then Thailand, the land of misfit toys. He drank himself stupid in Bangkok and Phuket and watched the low comedy play out each night, lonely *farang*s fulfilling their fantasies on the cheap. The men all had sob stories about women back home, who were too fat or cared too much about money or thought they were too good to do the dishes. Every tale finished with some version of *These girls here, maybe they don't understand English, but they understand* me. *They love me. They see me for who I* am.

Yeah, right. For the first time, he joined the world's talkers, knowing the men around him would love every miserable detail of what Julia had done. Sometimes he even embellished—

I had the ring in my pocket and I wanted to surprise her—

Don't say it, man—

I walked in—I couldn't even see his face, do you understand what I'm saying?

I would have killed 'em both. Let's get another, my friend. That calls for another.

He wondered if he should quit, but he had nowhere to go. He considered asking to be posted to Bangkok, but he feared he would become one of the whoremongers he despised. He chose Hong Kong. The city was the opposite of Baghdad in every way, glamor and neon, filled with hundred-story skyscrapers. Aside from the occasional gang fight, it was basically nonviolent. Money was its sole religion.

He was pleasantly surprised when the agency kept its

word. He waited a few months in Langley for a spot to open, but by fall 2007, he was living in an apartment in Kowloon and studying Cantonese. A year passed. His station chief was pleasant enough and kept a respectful distance. His work in Baghdad had bought him credibility. *Take as much time as you need to learn the language, and when you're ready to get back into the field, let me know.*

Day by day, Hong Kong's energy flowed into him, sweeping aside his memories like a flood cleaning out a polluted canal. He felt almost lucky. Like he'd been given one more chance. Then fate intervened, in the form of a BP tanker truck speeding west on a two-lane highway outside Fairbanks, as his parents' Winnebago headed east. A state police lieutenant politely encouraged him to save himself the flight to Anchorage. The remains were unidentifiable.

We aren't rich, but we do fine . . . But they were rich after all. The lawyer back home told him that between their estate and BP's settlement offer, he would wind up with more than two million dollars. His catastrophe was complete.

Gambling is deeply ingrained in Chinese culture, but Hong Kong has no legal casinos. Bettors ride ferries forty miles west over the gray waters of the Pearl River Delta to Macao. For centuries, Macao was Hong Kong's ugly cousin, a corrupt, dingy Portuguese colony known mostly for gang wars. But in 1999, China took control of Macao. The People's Republic invited major casino companies to set up shop—and allowed millions of its own citizens over the border as customers. In a few years, Macao became the world's largest gambling center, far bigger than the Las Vegas Strip. The action centered on an artificial island called Cotai, a postapocalyptic place where fifty-story temples of misery loomed above eerily empty avenues.

In his first year in Hong Kong, he'd gone to Macao three times, lost a few hundred dollars playing blackjack and craps. No big deal. Everything changed when the wire transfer from his parents' estate hit his HSBC account. His new balance: $2,452,187.19. He knew how casinos treated high rollers. If he lost a couple thousand dollars playing blackjack, he'd get a free room, a five-star meal. At ten thousand, he'd rate a private helicopter flight from Hong Kong, no need to share a hydrofoil with the commoners. Another level up, women and drugs would find their way to his suite without his having to ask.

He held out for three weeks. Then he took one hundred thousand Hong Kong dollars, about $13,000, to the newest, shiniest casino in Macao, the 88 Gamma. The Gamma was a sci-fi-themed palace, sleek and edgy. It had an oxygen bar and a shark-filled aquarium that encircled the casino floor. He sat at a blackjack table and watched the faces around him shrink into themselves as the night passed and the house edge triumphed over prayers and promises. Yet no one cared. They went to the ATM and returned with bundles of fresh cash.

He was lucky that night. He broke even. He forced himself to leave the casino at dawn. On the ferry to Kowloon, he closed his eyes against the screaming sun and dreamed of blackjack. He was back the next weekend, and every weekend after that. He didn't need a shrink to tell him what he was doing. He believed that losing his parents' estate would bring them back. He'd have another chance with them, a chance to replay his whole life.

But gambling gained its own power over him. He craved the anesthesia of the table, those rare nights when the chips piled up. Beating the house meant beating death itself, reversing time and entropy. He knew he was succumbing to the ultimate fallacy, that hot streaks were a function of probability just like cold. But at five a.m., as he looked at a ten and a six and curled his fingers forward and watched the dealer slide a five from the shoe, the truth meant less than nothing.

The girls were another kind of anesthesia. They were young and desperate and did whatever he wanted, to him and to one another.

In a year, he lost everything. More than everything. He was $550,000 in debt by the time Gamma cut him off. He had lost an even three million dollars. And he had missed so many workdays that the head of security for Hong Kong insisted he take a polygraph. He failed it and the drug test that followed. The agency fired him.

Only then did reality strike him. He had *nothing*. He couldn't even go back to the Gamma. Gambling took money, and he didn't have any. He begged the agency for another chance, but no one in Hong Kong knew him well enough to stand up for him. He was written off, another promising case officer ruined by Iraq.

The end.

His depression resolved into simple self-loathing. He had squandered three million dollars. He was worse than a fool. The money had vanished as completely as his parents. He debated killing himself. The act seemed like a rational response to the mess he'd made. He imagined diving off the Star Ferry into the murky waters of Hong Kong Bay. But as deeply as he hated himself, he didn't want to die. He didn't see heaven in his future, which left hell and oblivion as his only options. Neither appealed.

His limbo lasted three months.

The knock came at eight a.m. on a Saturday. Light but insistent. A woman.

He lay in bed, nestled beside a three-quarters-empty bottle of Johnnie Walker Black. He tried to imagine who might want to talk to him. No one came to mind. He wondered if he might be dreaming, but the pain behind his eyes convinced him otherwise.

"Mr. Mason? Glenn Mason?"

An unfamiliar voice, but a familiar name. His. His real name. His California name. He sat up, too quickly. "Hello?" His voice scratched like a garage-sale LP. His balance was all wrong. His brain seemed to have been doused in gasoline and set afire. The Johnnie Walker bottle had been full the afternoon before.

More knocking. He pulled on a T-shirt and boxers, staggered to the door. He dropped the chain, opened up. Lousy tradecraft, but at this point anyone who wanted him could have him.

The woman outside was medium height, mid-thirties.

She had short brown hair, Mediterranean skin. She wore jeans and a khaki jacket that were expensive enough to get her into a three-star restaurant, anonymous enough not to be noticed. She pushed into his living room.

"You look awful." She wasn't American, but he couldn't place her accent.

"Who are you?"

"I'm here to save your life."

She bought two large coffees, led him to the little park on the harbor by the Star Ferry terminal. "We could go for a ride, but you'd mess up my shoes." They sat close on a bench. Anyone watching would have thought them lovers. "Are you ready to get back to work?"

"You seem to think I'm someone I'm not."

"Don't be stupid. I know your name. Shall I tell you your résumé, too?" She wrinkled her nose at the whiskey pouring off him. "If I had a match, I could set you on fire. Maybe I was wrong. Maybe you're too far gone for this."

"I don't even know what *this* is."

"I'm looking for an experienced case officer. The pay is fifty thousand dollars a month. American, not HK."

The pain in his head was so steep that he could hardly focus. He wondered if he was hallucinating. "If you don't mind my asking, what's your name?"

"You can call me Salome."

She had to be joking. Yet she seemed serious. He waited. He still knew how to listen.

"You'll work directly for me. I need an operations officer."

"This is a private security agency, like Blackwater."

"Nothing like Blackwater. We're not in the profit-making business. We're not for hire."

"Is this an off-the-books agency op?"

"You know better than that."

He was glad she'd said no. Otherwise he would have had to write her off as a liar. The CIA didn't run secret ops outside its network of stations. It happily broke laws all over the world, but it didn't violate its own bureaucratic rules.

"But you have funding. From somewhere."

"Unlimited. You can work in your accustomed manner."

"Meaning a lot of memos from human resources that no one ever reads."

For the first time that morning, she smiled. She had small, perfect teeth. "Safe houses, secure coms. Tech. Whatever you need."

"Is this one mission, or several?"

"It has an indefinite time frame. First I need a team. And that starts with you."

"And you plan to operate in a—an extralegal manner."

She sidled closer. "We're on the side of the angels. This is about nuclear nonproliferation. By any means necessary."

"I never would have guessed you liked Malcolm X."

"Who?"

He couldn't tell if she was joking.

"Assassinations. Industrial sabotage. Things America should be doing but isn't."

He wondered if she worked for Israel. But the Mossad was already running these operations against Iran, and it would never have trusted such sensitive missions to non-Jews.

"But you need to understand. That grand machine you worked for all those years, it won't be happy with this. I doubt you can ever go back to the United States."

"Lucky for both of us I don't much care." Despite himself, he began to be impressed. Every intelligence officer dreamed of this, a black network unbound by rules and bureaucracy. "The CIA or Mossad will destroy you. Even if they agree with what you're doing."

"Not if they don't know we exist. Not if they can't find us, don't have anywhere to look. And you're right, the Mossad will take the blame for a lot of what we do. The more they deny it, the less anyone will believe them."

"One example. You give me a new name, new passport. Even if it's perfect, NSA will eventually run a face scan, compare the passport photo to its database. They'll match my new name with my old face. They won't understand why. They'll decide they'd better find out. They'll look for me. And when they look, they find."

"Plastic surgery. We'll send you to Thailand. There are ways to change your facial features and beat the software without making you look too strange."

He wanted to believe that she'd come to him because he had some special skill. But he knew the truth. She'd stumbled across him somehow, realized he was desperate enough to say yes.

"I can't betray my country. If you're working for Russia, some enemy of the United States, tell me now so I can walk away."

She shook her head. "It's not an enemy. All I can tell you. You want to be reassured like a child, find another job. Or drink yourself to death. It's no concern to me."

He closed his eyes, wondered if she'd still be real when he opened them.

She was. "All right."

She extended a hand. He took it. The gesture somehow felt both absurd and necessary. "You'll need a new name."

"Duke. Abraham Duke."

7

Pain and consciousness crossed the line nose-to-nose, too close to call. Wells awoke with the uncanny feeling that someone was vacuuming his brain through his right ear. The vacuum quieted to a steady buzz, a Harley engine on a distant highway, and Wells remembered. The gate. The guard. *Montoya*.

Wells collected himself. He'd never entirely understood the expression before. Putting together body and mind, making sure every part still worked. No broken bones, though his right hand seemed stuck. He tilted his head slowly down. His forearm was cuffed to the chair where he sat. He had been parked at a long wooden table in the house's formal dining room. A painting of Montoya and a younger woman filled one wall, a lusty Old Master knock-off. The couple wore modern clothes, a suit and dress, but they bore the self-satisfied smiles of seventeenth-century royalty.

Wells wondered if he ought to tip the chair over, try to free himself, but he had no next move. Better to stay upright. He reached behind his head with his left hand, touched fingertips to skull. Lightly. Blood seeped from his torn scalp. A swollen ridge of bone ran along the side of his head like an old-style three-dimensional plastic topographic map. But no fracture. He had a couple rough days ahead, but unless he had a brain bleed, he'd be fine.

Wells reached down for his knife and flashlight. Both gone. Montoya hadn't survived so long by making stupid mistakes. Wells wished he understood why the Colombian was treating him this way. He wanted to consider the possibilities, but the buzzing in his ear crowded his thoughts. After a minute, he gave up, closed his eyes.

A creaking door woke him. He turned. His brain wasn't ready for rapid movements. Bile filled his mouth. He choked it down before it seeped from his lips.

"Mr. Wells." The ceiling lights flicked on. A dog's nails scrabbled across the floor. Montoya came around, took the chair next to Wells. A Doberman followed, sat at his feet. Montoya carried a plastic gallon jug of water and two cups. He had changed his clothes. Now he wore a polo shirt, jeans, buttery brown loafers. Like an investment banker on Saturday. Wells had seen this stylishness before in men of extreme violence. He disliked it. It was an affectation that didn't make the torture or murder less real.

Montoya splashed water into the cups, gave Wells one,

drank from the other. A simple way of proving the liquid wasn't drugged. Wells sipped cautiously, knowing he'd vomit if he drank too fast. Head injuries went better on empty stomachs.

"None of this is necessary," he said. "I'm only here because you called Vinny."

"The Parque was my little joke. I know who you are, I knew you would have no trouble with those boys. This"—Montoya tapped his head—"I didn't intend. Pedro, my guard, he saw you come to the gate, he overreacted."

Wells closed his eyes and marveled at the world's stupidity. And his own. If he'd only listened to the guards when they told him to wait. But his adrenaline had been shouting too loudly. Or maybe Montoya was lying. Maybe that little love tap had been his way of showing Wells he was in charge. "He didn't see you reaching to shake my hand?"

"It seems not. No matter. You're here now." Montoya's English carried only a trace of an accent. He must have had a tutor growing up. He pulled a penlight from his pocket. "Open your eyes wide." He shined the light into Wells's eyes. The glare was agony, but Wells was glad for the field medicine.

"Your pupils are normal." Meaning that Wells wasn't hemorrhaging. "I'm going to uncuff you. I understand if you're upset, but you should know that Mickey is very loyal." The dog grunted in agreement as Montoya popped the cuff. "May I tell you why you're here?"

"Tell me whatever you like." Wells poured himself a fresh

glass of water. He wanted this foolishness over, so he could go back to his hotel and sleep, if the buzz in his ears would let him.

"Your former director and I knew each other in Bogotá. This was late eighties, early nineties. When he was kidnapped." Duto had been taken hostage for two months while he served as a case officer in Colombia, a fact almost no one outside the agency knew.

"He said you were one of his agents."

"I was in the army. We traded information about the FARC. I called him *comandante* as a joke. He didn't run me any more than I ran him. In fact, I helped find him when he was taken."

"Thought that was an SF job."

"Without us, they'd never have found him."

A bit of revisionist history that might even be true. "What about you?" Though Wells hardly needed to ask. Montoya's smooth English and white skin marked him as Colombian aristocracy.

"I grew up in Bogotá. All I wanted to do my whole life was fight the scum."

"The guerrillas trying to keep their families alive, you mean."

"Communist filth who think stealing is easier than working."

Mickey the Doberman sensed his master's irritation and growled. Time to move to safer conversational ground. In truth, Wells knew little about the Colombian civil war.

"How long were you in the army?"

"I resigned in '93. Not my choice."

"You have aspirin, Juan Pablo? Advil?"

Montoya rose. Mickey stood to follow, but Montoya grunted in Spanish, and the dog sat down. No wonder Montoya hadn't worried about taking off the handcuffs. Wells was a prisoner here with or without them. He stared at the painting of Montoya until the man himself came back. "Ibuprofen or Vicodin?" Montoya rattled the pills like a game-show host offering a deal.

Wells dry-swallowed four Advil. "You were telling me why you called Duto."

"I was telling you about 1993. My nickname." Montoya didn't wait for an answer. "*Diecisiete*. Means seventeen. I was leading a company, chasing a FARC platoon that had hit one of our patrols. The village was called Buenaventura. The peasants there, they sympathized with the scum. Wouldn't tell us anything. I knew they were lying, but I decided not to hurt them."

Wells held his head very still.

"A kilometer after we left, an ambush. Bombs, sniper, multiple fields of fire. Very professional. They knew we were coming. No question they set up while we were inside the village. It took three hours to run them off. I lost four men, five more wounded, eight minor injuries. Seventeen. I turned around, brought my company back to Buenaventura."

Montoya poured himself a glass of water. Wells saw that he'd told this story before. That he enjoyed it, wanted Wells to ask questions, play a role. Wells didn't speak. Finally, Montoya drank his water and went on.

"This was about ten p.m. We went into seventeen houses, told the fathers, you or your oldest son. Only one tried to give us his son. Of course, we didn't take the boy. I lined those seventeen lying bastards up in the square, the middle of town. The plaza. I brought out the whole village. I told them, these soldiers are my family. My family dies, your families die. At midnight we lined them up, shot them all. Except the one coward. Him I beat to death myself. He cried for mercy all the way down."

"You showed him."

"Word got out and the human-rights *coños* made a fuss. They called me *Diecisiete*. My colonel made me resign. I was kind. I should have burned the whole village. They set us up, they knew it."

"I hope you don't stay up late waiting for your Peace Prize."

"Afterwards, a friend of a friend came calling. From Medellín. He told me he wanted me to work for him, he needed men like me. I decided if the army wouldn't have me, I might as well. This was before the Mexicans got in the way, all the money came to Colombia. You can't imagine. This man had a room in his basement filled with pallets of bills. Waist-high, hundreds of millions of dollars waiting to be laundered."

Again Montoya stopped, waiting for Wells to ask about the life. Give him a chance to brag about the hookers, the cars, the parties, Pablo Escobar.

"Then the Mexicans took over. Meth got popular—they didn't need us for that, they made it themselves in the desert. Plus we made a mistake and let them into our networks. Another mistake, we paid with product rather than cash. And, the truth, they were harder than we were. For us, the violence was part of business. The Mexicans liked killing. I saw the future. In 1999 I hooked up with the Sinaloas."

"And stayed in touch with Vinny."

"Every so often, he had a question for me. Mainly political. Which generals were the greediest, which ones we couldn't buy. After September eleventh, he asked me to tell him if the Muslims paid the cartels to sneak anyone over the border. Though the cartels would never have agreed. They had way more money than those crazy Arabs, and they didn't want war with the United States."

"In return."

"Three times the narcos came close, three times Vinny made sure I knew."

An answer that explained why Wells was here. Montoya wasn't just another agent whom Duto had run twenty years before. He was a contract killer whom Duto had kept as an off-the-books source. And Duto had blown three federal drug investigations to protect him.

Inside Langley, no one cared about the drug war. It was viewed as a nuisance at best, a threat to regional stability at worst. But senators couldn't work with cocaine traffickers. Montoya was a piece of Duto's past, and Duto had expected he'd stay there. His phone call had no doubt come as an unpleasant surprise. Duto needed to know what Montoya wanted, whether he was trying a backdoor blackmail scheme, but he couldn't meet Montoya in person. Thus Wells was beating up kids in Guatemala City.

"When was the last time you talked to Duto?"

"Two thousand seven. By then, the Zetas had taken over.

The worst of all. Near the border, they had ranches where they dissolved corpses in acid. Not always corpses, either. Sometimes the men were still alive."

Listening to Montoya, Wells felt like a coral reef in a befouled sea, the world's ugliness covering him, seeping through him. "So you ran."

"The Zetas told us, disappear or die. The men I worked for had no choice. They had nowhere to go, and they were too proud anyway. I had money, a passport. I didn't care about a narco ballad for my glorious death. I went to Cuba, ended up here."

"You're not on anybody's list?"

"Everyone I worked for is dead. I didn't snitch and I didn't kill anyone's family, except once. Maybe one day someone's cousin will come for me. We're only two hundred kilometers from Mexico. Meantime, I enjoy my life. I have a new wife." He nodded at the painting. "We just found out she's pregnant. Twins."

"Congratulations." Wells almost envied Montoya his psychopathy. The Colombian had tossed his crimes aside as easily as a bag of garbage. Or leftover bones. Wells wondered if Montoya's dreams were as pallid as Wells's own. He wouldn't ask. He wanted nothing in common with this man. "So you hadn't talked to Duto in all these years—why call him now?"

"In Mexico, I worked with a man named Eduardo Nuñez. Peruvian. When I left, he decided to disappear also. We only saw each other once more. But we trusted each other. We stayed in touch, knew how to find each other. A while ago, he told me he had something. That an American named Hank had put a group together, and Eduardo had told him about me. I wasn't interested, but I wanted to see this guy, if he was any threat. I said okay, if he comes to Guatemala we can meet. A couple weeks later, he called me."

"You make him go to the Parque Central?"

Montoya smiled. "He was smarter than you. We met in the Radisson. He was in his early forties, I think. Medium height, medium weight. Horn-rim glasses and a baseball cap. Nothing in his face to remember."

"A good spy."

"We met in his suite. Straightaway he showed me two passports, U.S. and Australian. He wanted me to see the quality. They were good. Better than any I'd seen. *The people I work for make your friends in Mexico look poor. I need professionals for a professional operation, and I'd like you involved.*"

"He said *people*? Not agency, not government, *people*." The choice of word didn't necessarily mean anything, but Wells wanted to be sure.

"Yes. *People*. I asked for specifics. He said we could talk about money, but that he couldn't tell me about his group. Not who was financing it. Not who or what they might be targeting, not unless I agreed."

"Timing?"

"He was vague. Said they'd been running for a while, but now they were shifting gears. I asked if it would be one operation. He said no, several, different levels of complexity. I asked him what he wanted me to do and he said the work would be familiar. I told him I couldn't do anything in Mexico or Central America or Colombia, I was too well known, and he said that wouldn't be a problem."

"But no hint to the targets. Or type of ops."

Montoya shook his head. "I'll admit, I was intrigued."

"Assuming it was real."

"Eduardo had known Hank before, and he wasn't the type to fall for a scam. And Hank looked real to me. Agency or ex. I saw case officers in Colombia, not just Duto, and he had the same air."

"Which is what, in your opinion? Like he was dangerous?"

"No. In my experience, very few CIA are personally dangerous. Or brave. The *comandante* was an exception. He went on raids with us, and after the Special Forces rescued him, the first thing he said to them was—"

"What took you pricks so long?" Shafer had told Wells the story.

Montoya smiled, his first real smile of the night. "*Sí.* No, what all CIA have in common is this attitude that you're in control. You make me an offer, you don't care whether I take it. I don't, someone else will. And if it all blows up in the end, you go to another city, at another station. It's my life, my country. For you, it's a game, a job."

The description had been more true before September 11, Wells thought. The stakes were higher now, and case officers faced more personal danger. But let Montoya think what he liked. "That's how this man Hank came across?"

"Yes. One more reason I didn't think he was faking. The simplest of all. He had to know that if he tried to take advantage of me, I'd make him pay. I told him I'd think it over, the next day I told him I wasn't interested. That was it. He didn't push. Never contacted me again. Then, two weeks ago, Eduardo called. He said, Juan Pablo, you won't believe this. The American wants us to kill a station chief. I said, *Don't. If you do this, the CIA, they chase you forever*. He wanted to talk about it. I told him not over the phone. He was supposed to come to Guatemala last week. He didn't show up, didn't call. I don't know if he's dead, or still on the operation, or he ran."

"He didn't give you details. Not the country or the time or anything else."

"I wouldn't let him. Face-to-face only for something like that."

"Let's go through it one more time. Some guy whose name you don't know tried to hire you for a superelite hit squad. Which is now going after a station chief. Whose name you also don't know."

"The senator will tell you I've never lied to him, Señor Wells. Why now?"

"A hundred thousand dollars."

Montoya swept his arm in a vague oval: *Look around. You think I need a hundred thousand dollars?* "What I want, truly, is for the *comandante* to talk to INS. A visa. My name is on the restricted list. My wife and I are overdue to visit New York. A shopping trip."

One that ends with her giving birth in a hospital in Manhattan so your twins are American citizens. "Not sure he has that pull anymore."

"If I'd wanted to blackmail, I would have called sooner. I'm giving him this, a favor."

"Tell me about Eduardo."

"Mid-thirties. He moved to Panama City after Mexico."

"Eduardo was his real name?"

"The only one I ever knew him by."

"How did he know Hank?"

"Peru. Eduardo was in the army there."

"Don't suppose you have a picture of them."

"I have a phone for Hank that doesn't work anymore and two numbers and an email for Eduardo. You can have them all." Montoya walked out. Wells was glad to be alone. The Advil had lightened the pressure in his skull, but overwhelming fatigue had taken its place.

He closed his eyes for a few seconds, woke to find Mickey the Doberman nuzzling his crotch. "Mickey—"

Behind him, Montoya yelled in Spanish. The dog trotted out, leaving Wells with a trail of slobber across his sweatpants. "He gets excited."

"I'm just glad he likes me."

Montoya handed Wells a paper, three phone numbers and an email address, written in an elegant script. Wells wondered if he should tip the possible Iranian connection, decided to take the risk. "Did Hank or Eduardo ever mention Iran?"

Montoya shook his head.

"The Revolutionary Guard? Hezbollah?"

"Nothing."

Wells pushed himself up. A wave of dizziness nearly pulled him down, but he braced his hands against the table until it passed.

"Stay the night if you wish." Montoya put a hand on his

arm. Wells shook him off. He wouldn't become beholden to this man for even a few hours of rest. He wouldn't give Montoya the pleasure of thinking they were brothers-in-arms.

At the hotel, Wells drew the blackout shades and slept. Shafer could wait. He woke once but couldn't remember his dreams. Or even if he'd had any. In the morning, his headache had diffused like a stain down his neck. A sign of healing. He hoped. Twenty-seven days left before Anne's deadline. Or was it twenty-six? His phone vibrated. Shafer.

"This is not the *Jewish Weekly*."

"What does that even mean, Ellis?"

"You got to Guatemala City a day and a half ago."

"Talked to him last night."

"And?"

"I don't want to talk too much on an open line, but it's weird. He's got almost no details, and the ones he has are bizarre. A supersecret organization with untold wealth. But he's convinced it's real. And Vinny's right, he's a serious guy. A snake, but serious."

"Snake."

"This little trip was good for me. Reminded me how dirty Vinny can play when he sets his mind to it."

"You forgot?"

Like Shafer hadn't been in that office two nights before, telling Wells he owed Duto a favor. "Point is, I'm half convinced, too. He gave me three phone numbers and an email address. I'll send them. Anything new up there?"

"Nobody talks to me anymore."

"Poor Ellis. The guy who connected him to the case officer has a girlfriend in Panama City. I'll go down there while you run the numbers."

"Extending your vacation."

"Always wanted to see the Canal Zone. Call me if anything hits." Wells hung up. He wasn't sure he believed Montoya's story, but it was too good not to chase.

8

Soon as the plastic surgery healed, Duke went recruiting. Agents he'd run in Lima. Mercenaries he'd met in Baghdad. An ex–FSB officer from the bars in Phuket. The game was tricky. He needed guys as desperate as he'd been. But not so desperate that they would trade him to the police or the agency to solve their problems. Guys who saw a couple moves ahead, saw he was serious and the money was real.

He found them. Three South Africans for security and skull cracking. A Peruvian and a Mexican, left over from the cartel wars. Brothers from Beirut who'd lost their parents to a Hezbollah bomb and thought the idea of coming back at Iran was just peachy.

As Salome had promised, technical support was no problem. She handled the back end. She had a houseful of hackers and document forgers somewhere in Eastern

Europe. Safe houses all over the world. Private planes. Duke didn't see the budget, but they were spending at least a hundred million dollars a year. Government-sized money, though he couldn't figure which government.

Nine months after their first meeting in Hong Kong, Salome ordered him to Rome. She gave him two photographs of trim middle-aged white men in sweaters and slacks. He knew they were German even before she told him. Only Germans wore mustaches so proudly.

"Herrs Schneider *und* Wolff run a steel company in Munich. Sudmetallfabrik A.G. They're selling ultra-high-strength steel to Iran for centrifuge parts. The export papers say it's for a gas pipeline in Indonesia, but it's being diverted in Dubai. They know. They're charging double the usual price."

He asked a few questions. She had the answers. He didn't doubt her intel. These guys weren't exactly the top of the food chain, but he supposed that was the point. *Even if no one's heard of you, if you're helping the Iranian nuclear program, you're at risk.* Plus they'd be light on security. If his guys couldn't handle this job, they'd have no chance with harder targets.

"No warnings."

She shook her head. He ought to have been horrified. They were about to kill two men for selling steel. But he felt the same cool excitement that came at the blackjack table when the cards fell his way. His whole life had brought him here. He was through swimming against the devil's tide.

Besides, slowing down the Iranian nuclear program wasn't the world's worst idea.

"When?"

"Soon. Our backers have been patient, but they'd like to see some return on their investment. Beyond that, the operational details are up to you."

He wished he had something smart to say, something to immortalize the moment. "Done and done." The words didn't sound as cool out loud as he had hoped. She handed him the file with their photos and nodded: *dismissed*.

He wanted to kill them together. Separate simultaneous assassinations meant keeping two teams in constant contact. Using a single team for two jobs was even riskier. Too much could go wrong in even a five-minute window. Best to shoot them at work, be gone before anyone called the police.

Sudmetallfabrik operated from a two-story factory in a middle-income neighborhood in northwest Munich. Two weeks of surveillance revealed that Schneider and Wolff followed a simple, rigid schedule. No surprise. They were German. Schneider, the company's Geschäftsführer, arrived each morning at 7:30 a.m. Wolff, his deputy, came in ten minutes later. Both men drove gunmetal-gray BMW sedans. Schneider left between 5:45 and 6:00 p.m. Wolff stayed another half hour.

The factory had a single guard at its front gatehouse and was ringed by a low fence with no barbed wire. But it had cameras watching the entrance, and one hundred and fifty workers inside. Not ideal.

Fortunately, Schneider and Wolff made a habit of having lunch outside the factory. On the first four days of the workweek, Schneider's BMW rolled off the lot at noon. It returned an hour later, plus or minus five minutes for traffic. The men went to a different restaurant each day. On Friday, they stayed in. Duke figured they ate with their managers on Fridays.

They followed the same restaurant schedule both weeks. Monday was Alter Wirt day, traditional Bavarian. Duke planned to hit them on their way out of the restaurant's parking lot. They'd be more relaxed. They might even have had a beer or two.

He put Eduardo Nuñez and Rodrigo Salazar on the hit. His cartel vets. Nuñez was almost Duke's age. They'd worked together in Lima. Salazar was a few years younger, and Duke knew him only through Nuñez. They were used to narcos who traveled in armored convoys. He doubted they'd ever had a job this easy.

The day dawned bright, clear, unseasonably warm for fall in Munich. Schneider and Wolff rolled off the lot at 12:01 p.m. Five minutes later, they reached the Alter Wirt. Duke trailed in a Passat, with Nuñez in the passenger seat. He wanted to be sure they had the right targets. Killing two random Germans would be an unpromising start to his new career. He drove slowly past the parking lot as the BMW's doors swung open.

"Yes?" Nuñez said.

He watched Schneider and Wolff step out. "Yes."

Ten minutes later, he dropped Nuñez off at a bus stop that had no surveillance cameras. After that, the job belonged to Nuñez and Salazar.

At 12:57, Schneider and Wolff left the Alter Wirt. They were eager to get back to work. Sudmetallfabrik was bidding for an order from a natural-gas plant in Qatar. The BMW's keyless entry system unlocked the car as Schneider approached. The men slid in, buckled up. Schneider put the sedan in reverse—and the rear camera warning beeped. A black motorcycle filled the screen in the BMW's center console.

Schneider wondered where the bike had come from. He hadn't seen it in the lot as they walked out of the restaurant. Nonetheless, there it was. A sportbike with rider and passenger, both wearing black helmets, tinted faceplates.

The passenger stepped off, walked around the side of the BMW. Schneider wondered if the man was upset that he'd backed up. Schneider hadn't hit him, or even come close. But these younger bikers were fanatical about their motos. Schneider himself rode, though only on weekends.

The man knocked on Schneider's window. A foolish interruption. Now he was simply wasting time. Schneider lowered the window a few inches. The man reached behind his jacket, came out with a *pistol*, a heavy black pistol—

Schneider had no time to hit the gas, no time to duck, no time for anything but—

Nuñez shot the driver four times, though one would have done the trick. The passenger scrabbled for his door handle, but he had less than no chance. Nuñez went to one knee and popped him four times, too. He liked symmetry in his hits.

The shooting took six seconds. The pistol was unregistered, untraceable. Nuñez dropped it in the driver's lap, walked calmly back to the bike, took his place behind Salazar. They were gone before anyone even pulled a phone to call the police. Salazar turned right out of the lot, rode hard for thirty seconds, then made a left and slowed to a more deliberate pace. Eight minutes later, he ditched the bike behind a grocery store in Dachau. They switched to a gray Opel Astra, the most forgettable car in existence. They drove north for a half hour, parked the Astra in an Ikea lot. Across the lot was another Opel, this one white. Duke sat in the driver's seat.

"Next time give us a harder one," Salazar said.

"Be careful what you wish for."

The killings generated headlines across Germany, especially when newspapers in Munich and Berlin received documents showing the company's connection to Iran. Munich police acknowledged asking the BND, the German intelligence service, for help in the investigation. A left-wing Munich paper reported that the BND was examining if the Mossad was involved. The article prompted angry denials from Jerusalem, silence from Berlin.

By then, Duke and his team were on their next job, two Iranian nuclear scientists at a conference in Belgrade. This one was trickier, but still easy enough. The scientists traveled under false names, but they didn't have bodyguards. For twelve thousand five hundred euros, a Serbian police colonel on the conference security team gave up their hotel and room. Nuñez shot them in an elevator on the conference's second morning. He was fifteen kilometers outside Belgrade before the police put up their first roadblock. Duke never found out if the colonel had thrown in the delay as a freebie.

Over the next eighteen months, they poisoned three rocket engineers in Kiev, garroted a banker in Madrid. Finally, in Singapore, they shot the president of a company that supplied radar for the antiaircraft batteries that surrounded Iran's nuclear facilities. *Mossad Widens Front in Secret War Against Iran*, reported the London *Times*. Israel's denials were ignored. Duke found himself inside the life that he'd imagined growing up, the life that neither the CIA nor gambling had delivered.

Between missions, he lived in a house he rented in Thailand, on an island near Phuket. He'd been back from the Singapore operation for three weeks when Salome called. *Tomorrow*, she said. An address in Bangkok's eastern suburbs. He expected another target. They'd seen each other only once since that first mission.

He arrived the next morning to find Salome curled on

an expensive leather couch, her hands loose. She reminded him of nothing so much as a hungry cat. He could guess at the mouse.

"This isn't working, Glenn."

The name stung. He couldn't remember when last he'd heard it. Even in his dreams he was Duke. Worse, he didn't know what he'd done wrong.

"Are my old friends on us?"

"Why would they bother? We've done *nothing*. Newest NIE"—National Intelligence Estimate—"says that by 2015, 2016, Iran will have a bomb, 2017 at the outside."

Her casual reference to the estimate confirmed what he'd always believed, that she or her bosses had Washington connections. National Intelligence Estimates were offered to the President as the best guess of the CIA and the rest of the American intel community. A report on Iran would have been classified at the highest level.

"The Iranians built their program to survive a full-scale attack from Israel. A mercenary team isn't taking it down. Not without capes and superpowers." His voice was tender and low in his throat. He feared she'd dismiss him, send him back to the empty place that he'd lived.

"We need a new course."

He remembered the magic moment in blackjack when the dealer pulled a card, slid it across the smooth green baize. His fate determined, yet still hidden.

"Only the Americans can do it," she said. "But they won't risk war. We have to make them see Iran as a direct threat." She spoke patiently, as if only an idiot couldn't follow the logic. *Only the American military can stop Iran; therefore, we'll trick it into an attack. Q.E.D.*

"That's impossible."

"Not necessarily." She told him how. "So? What do you think?"

What he thought was *treason*. He could justify what he'd done so far. The people they'd killed were helping Iran build nuclear weapons. Now they were talking about killing Americans. He would be a traitor. Worthy of the needle. But he no longer cared.

"You have someone who can play this role? Speaks perfect Farsi? Native Iranian?"

She nodded.

"Even so. My professional opinion. First thing CIA will wonder is whether the Iranians are running a false flag. Everyone remembers 2002, how we got used to push the Iraq invasion. That's deep institutional memory."

"Of course." She smiled, those clean white vampire teeth.

"Our guy can't give them too much, either. Or everything at once. Has to be multiple ops, several months, and the intel has to be fragmentary. Make it too easy, spoon-feed it, they won't believe that, either. He needs enough details to make himself credible, without giving up anything that the agency can verify inside Iran. He needs what a comic-book writer would call an origin story—"

"What is that?"

"A reason that he's picked this specific case officer. He needs to seem jittery, but not so scared he lacks credibility.

The more serious this gets, the worse they'll want to debrief him. That can never happen. His legend won't hold. So there will be tension between the value of the intel he's giving them and the fact they don't know who he is. They'll hate it. We have to give them something they can't ignore, no matter how much they want to."

"Such as?"

Killing the President was impossible. Killing a cabinet member or senator was easier, but getting away clean would be tricky. Anyway, killing a station chief was already part of the plan. Another assassination would merely repeat the pattern. They needed something different.

"Bomb-grade uranium. If our guy turned up with an ingot, it would stampede them."

"HEU."

"I have no idea where you can get it. Half the people who say they have the stuff are lying. The other half are FBI agents looking for terrorists dumb enough to think they could buy it on eBay. I wouldn't even mention it as a possibility, but you seem to have a few connections."

She ignored the not-so-subtle question: *And who are they?*

"How much?"

"Not necessarily a whole bomb's worth, but at least a couple hundred grams."

She shook her head. He expected her to object that he might as well ask her to deliver a unicorn horn. Her complaint was different, though equally valid. "That doesn't make sense. Why would he have it? How could he have gotten it out of Iran?"

"Maybe he stole it—"

"That's ridiculous. Foolish. Even if he's a high-level Revolutionary Guard officer, they're not going to let him walk into an enrichment plant and leave with HEU."

She was right. They needed a very good reason for their plant to have the stuff.

And then Duke knew. He explained.

"Might work," she said when he was done.

"If you can get it. The depots are the most tightly guarded buildings in the world."

"Let me think about it."

So she had a source in mind, or at least a thread to one.

"Come up with that, then maybe we can make this happen. Move slow setting up the contact, then fast, so they get caught up in the momentum."

The plan—crazy as it was—had one crucial factor on its side. Unlike the Iraqis, the Iranians really *did* have a nuclear program, and no one knew what they would do with a bomb.

"Tell your men we're suspending everything," Salome said. "We'll keep paying them, but there's no point in risking them on little jobs. Also, think about a case officer for the approach. Someone smart, not too smart."

"Lots of those. Where?"

"Istanbul, ideally."

He liked the location. Close to Iran, a natural place for a Rev Guard source to pop up. "You think you can find HEU?"

"You hoping I can or I can't?"

He told his guys they'd hit the lottery, they'd be paid half their salaries not to work, for a few months at least. They'd get the other half when he called them back. They promised to return when he asked, and he sensed they would.

For a year, he scouted targets, moved money and weapons, added extra safe houses and cars in Turkey. He chose Angola and Thailand for the Israeli embassy bombs. He emailed Salome brief coded notes once a month, filling her in on his progress. She trained the Iranian herself. His name for the operation was Reza. She didn't tell Duke where she'd gotten him, and he didn't ask.

Everything was in place, but they didn't have the uranium. He moved back to Thailand. The call came on a Sunday morning in May, the rainy season just starting. "Time to get the team together."

"You have it?"

"I'm close. May take a couple more months. The owner's skittish."

"It would be ironic if the Iranians finish before we do."

"Call your guys."

He met them in Cyprus, a hotel near the airport. He explained they had changed their strategy, and their next hit would be on two Israeli embassies. The change obviously puzzled them, but they weren't the type to argue, not as long as they were getting paid.

For the pigeon, Duke chose a case officer in Istanbul named Brian Taylor. They'd met in Iraq. At the time, Taylor struck Duke as naïve but decent. One of those guys who'd joined in a flush of patriotism after September 11 without knowing what he was getting into.

Years later, as Duke neared the end of his disastrous run in Hong Kong, Taylor had visited the city on vacation. They'd had dinner at an overpriced Indian restaurant in Kowloon. With his mind on cards, Duke talked even less than usual. Taylor filled the silences. He'd finished a stint in Ankara and was headed back to Istanbul. He had a strange hard-on for the city. Duke remembered enough details from the meal to concoct a plausible cover story for Reza to contact Taylor.

Reza didn't have the usual cover details. No bank account, driver's license, or passport. NSA would tear them apart. He would present himself as a ghost of a ghost, a man who didn't trust the CIA with even the briefest facts of his life. In place of papers, Reza had only himself, his certainty that he was the man he pretended to be. He traveled to Bulgaria to scout the Israeli embassy for an attack. *Part of a worldwide operation,* his bosses at the Guard told him. Or would have, if they'd been real. He rented a van and garage in Sofia, bought a hundred plastic jerricans, the core of a crude fuel-oil bomb. Then the generals canceled the operation. Security in Bulgaria was too tight. Reza told them he was sorry to lose the chance to bomb the Jews. In reality, he felt only relief. He had to stop his country before it pushed the world into nuclear war. Through his own hard work, he had found a CIA case officer in Istanbul. Brian Taylor, alias Nelson Drew. He wrote Taylor to ask for a meeting.

The embassy bombings went as planned, a few unlucky guards dead, no real damage. The Israelis would thank Langley for the warning, and be ready to listen the next time Taylor's mysterious source appeared.

Duke told his guys to be ready to move to Manila. Veder was chief of station there. He'd finally have his revenge. Strange but true: for years, Duke had hardly thought of the man. Yet now that Veder had left the on-deck circle and was on his way to the plate, Duke's anger was rising. If Veder hadn't come to Lima, maybe Julia wouldn't have cheated. Maybe he'd still be Glenn Mason, married to her, with a couple rugrats.

Maybe not.

Day after day, his impatience rose. Only one problem. Fall came and went, and Salome still couldn't lock down the HEU. In December she ordered him to Jakarta. They met in yet another safe house, the kind Duke had grown to expect over his years working for her. A three-bedroom house in a gated community in a suburb that catered to expats. A cursory look at the place revealed its essential emptiness. Generic posters in the bedrooms, bookcases filled with unopened novels, an oven without even a trace of grease.

The houses were owned by local law firms that specialized in buying property for multinational companies that didn't want their names on the deeds. The lawyers usually didn't have to disclose their clients. If they did, they listed local shell companies controlled by corporations registered in the Cayman Islands. Salome—or whoever was behind her—had no doubt created so many interlocking shell companies in so many countries that unknotting them would take the CIA years, even with subpoenas.

Another way of saying that Duke still had no idea who was behind this operation.

In Jakarta, he found Salome in the kitchen. He reached into the refrigerator, found a cold bottle of Perrier. In every country, the safe houses had Perrier.

"Almost four years, Salome, I don't know a thing about you. I'm not talking about anything important like your real name. I mean the food you like. If you've ever been bungee jumping. If your parents are alive. If you even like Perrier." He hesitated. "Don't even know if you like boys or girls."

"He's agreed to sell it. More than a kilo."

"There goes our little chat."

So she would have her chance at a war. And he would have his chance at Veder.

"Enriched to ninety-plus."

"Don't suppose you want to tell me who he is?"

"I had to convince him it's not a trap. And I couldn't just take it. Better to buy it, keep him quiet."

"If you say so."

"We'll spend today talking through Manila. Tomorrow, what comes after. Because we need to be ready. Next time I see you will be Istanbul."

Duke met his men in Manila three days later. Big teams came with their own problems. They couldn't use the Manila safe house. Even a half-blind neighbor would notice eight military-age men moving in. They rented four apartments, all in a five-block radius in Quiapo, a dingy neighborhood near the port that had more than its share of bucket-of-blood karaoke parlors. Karaoke was a violent sport in the Philippines. Fights over songs were common, shootings not unheard of.

Still Salome wasn't ready. Duke used the time to have his men look around, check out Manila's rhythms for themselves. Twelve million people lived in metropolitan Manila. Google maps and satellite photos were no substitute for on-the-ground experience: How quickly did the cops answer alarms? Which intersections had surveillance cams? What back streets and alleys would help them shuck pursuers?

After a week, he called a meeting at his apartment. He couldn't wait longer. They needed to know the target was a CIA station chief.

Nuñez and Salazar sat on the floor. Everyone else piled onto his couches. The room stank of cheap tobacco, cheap plumbing, cheap curry from the Indian restaurant on the building's first floor.

"I want to be sure before we go any further that everyone's on board," Duke said. "This is an American target. Government. You're not cool with that, no problem. Get up, walk out."

"Like you'd let us," Bram said. Bram Moritz was one of his South Africans. Six feet tall, 215 pounds, not an ounce of fat. He had the tiniest ears Duke had ever seen. Duke wondered if they signaled mental retardation, because Bram was as lethal and stupid as a canyon fire. Back when they were still trying to stop the Iranians directly, Bram had killed the Madrid banker, taken his head half off.

"I would. None of you know who's paying for all this, and I can disappear, too." He was lying. The roach-motel rules ended only when the job was done. If ever. Quitters would find their life expectancy measured in hours. But Duke didn't expect anyone to get up. No one did.

"Good. The target." He brought a whiteboard and a corkboard out of his bedroom. Intentionally low-tech, a way to remind the guys of their outsider status. He'd push-pinned photos of Veder onto the corkboard, along with the American embassy and Veder's house, both massively pro-tected. And maps detailing Veder's routes to and from work.

"Chief of station for Manila. James Veder. Nasty bugger."

Duke knew they wouldn't care. These men had no love for the agency. The South Africans blamed it for using mercenaries like them in Iraq for risky jobs—and then refusing to help if they were captured or injured. Leonid, the Russian, hated the United States so much that he'd nearly refused to work for Duke.

Even so, the room briefly went silent as the guys looked at the photos. The lethality of the CIA's drone campaign and the success of its hunt for bin Laden had erased its failures in Iraq. Not since the 1950s had the agency's mys-tique been so overwhelming.

"You didn't think we were paying all this money to kill Spanish bankers. So this will be like the embassy. We'll let them know in advance that a station chief is the mark—"

"But this time we don't miss," Leonid said.

"That's right. Make them wish they had listened to our source."

"Goes back to the larger scheme you can't tell us about."

"Any particular reason we pick him?" Nuñez said.

Duke wondered if Nuñez knew about him and Veder and Julia. "Manila's a good place to operate. I knew him back in the day, but it's not personal."

Duke waited for Nuñez to say something more, but the Peruvian merely nodded.

Duke spent an hour outlining the security they could expect. Veder would ride in an armored SUV, inch-thick glass, steel-sided doors. Maybe steel plating underneath. At least two bodyguards, probably ex-Rangers. Pistols on their hips, M-4s close by. Veder would have a pistol, too. All three men would probably wear vests, thin ones like those police officers wore.

"No Kevlar?" Bram said.

"Far as they're concerned, anonymity is their best defense. Hard to stay low-profile in tac plates. This one won't be easy. Especially since they'll know we're coming."

"Are we telling them we're hitting this station?"

"No. Not even going to give them a continent. Otherwise they can focus security too tight. But they can look at a map, see Manila's not far from Bangkok. They'll figure this is a potential target."

They strategized the rest of the afternoon. Duke felt like a football coach, diagramming X's and O's on the whiteboard, language itself bending to depersonalize the targets. He dismissed his guys around six. The dinner rush was starting downstairs. The smell of curry hung in the air so powerfully it was almost visible, mouth-watering and stomach-churning at once. The men walked out quickly. Except Nuñez, who hung back until they were alone.

"You okay, Eddie?"

"This mission, I have concerns." Nuñez got formal when he was anxious. He'd killed guys on four continents. Shooting strangers didn't trouble him. Standing up to Duke did.

He was a trim man, wiry and handsome, with a square Incan face and long Spanish fingers. He'd once shown Duke a laminated business card of a woman holding a guitar. His girlfriend, he said. She was a singer. As far as Duke could tell, he neither liked nor disliked the job he'd chosen, killing other human beings.

Why did you go to Mexico? Duke had asked him years before.

The money. No other reason.

"Want a Coke?" Duke didn't wait for an answer but pulled out two lukewarm bottles of Coke. The fridge barely worked. Luckily, Coke tasted decent at sixty degrees.

"What you said, it's true. We do this, they look for us forever."

"We'll do it right. They won't find us."

"But this time, there's a connection. You, Veder, the woman. That's why you chose him, yes?"

So he knew. "No. It was a long time ago. Julia"—the sting of her name in his mouth surprised him—"it's not like we were married. The agency will be thinking terrorists all the way. They can't find us if they're not looking for us." Salome's favorite line. Duke believed her.

"Sooner or later, somebody will think of you."

"I'm a ghost."

"Strange. Because I feel like I'm looking at you right now. And you tell me this has nothing to do with you walking in on Veder and your girlfriend?"

"Getting scared, Eddie?"

"I respected you. I came to you privately."

And signed your death warrant. Duke knew he ought to thank Nuñez for taking this to him one-on-one instead. But the humiliation was too intense. Instead, he found a way to be angry for what Nuñez had done. Obviously the man wasn't frightened of him. Otherwise he wouldn't have challenged Duke face-to-face. He would have disappeared. Now Duke would have to kill him. Too bad. Nuñez was the best hitter on the team, and Duke liked him. But he couldn't risk Nuñez talking. For now he needed to smooth the situation over, figure a clean way to get rid of Nuñez.

Aloud, he said, "I'll think it over for a couple days. Maybe we go somewhere else. All I ask in return is that you do the same. I want you on the team. I want you in."

"Yes."

"You need to get out, we'll cut you loose. You promise to be quiet, I trust you."

Nuñez left. Duke gave him a half hour, then texted Salome from a burner, a blank message with the subject heading "5to1." Odds meant an emergency.

She called four minutes later. "Yes?"

"Dennis has a cold." *D* for Dennis, since Nuñez had been the fourth man to join the team.

"He always seemed hearty to me. Any reason in particular?"

Duke didn't plan to tell Salome that his history with Veder had spooked Nuñez. "He's run-down. It happens."

"He contagious?"

"That's always a risk." Duke paused. "We can play without him."

"I'm not thrilled, but I'll defer to you. If you're sure."

Was he sure? He would be killing one of his own men. Not to defend himself. Not even from lust or anger. Simply to smooth the path for yet another murder. "I'm sure. What about on your end? Are you close?"

She hung up.

Now Duke just had to get rid of a trained assassin. Duke would have one chance at him. If he missed, he could be sure Nuñez wouldn't.

Duke spent the night drinking cold coffee, considering plays. First he leaned toward sending Nuñez to do a job outside Manila. Hong Kong, say. Split him from the team. Ask Salome to hire guys to kill Nuñez there, make the body disappear. No doubt she had connections in Hong Kong. She'd found Duke there easily enough.

But the play was way too obvious. *Hong Kong? Why me? Why now?* Nuñez would take off. Before he did, he would tell the rest of the team that Duke was after him, and why.

Duke could also try to arrange something sly in Manila. A hit-and-run. A botched mugging. But even if Nuñez survived for only a few hours, he would tell the police what he knew. And nobody would believe Nuñez had died in an accident, no matter how well Duke sold it.

As dawn approached, he fell asleep. When he woke, he saw a third way. The more he considered it, the better he liked it. He called Salome, explained what he needed.

"You're sure this is best?"

"Yes."

"All right. You'll have it tomorrow."

She hung up. If she could get him everything that fast, she must have a second team running surveillance on him and his guys. She was even more paranoid than he'd imagined.

The package came the next afternoon. Thinner than he'd hoped. A dozen photos, bank statements, a flash drive with a few soundless video clips. The B-team must be just one or two men. Even Salome had limits. No matter. The "evidence" would be enough, if he presented it the right way. And to the right person.

He called Bram. "You alone?"

"Sure."

"*Roja*. Now." *Roja* was his apartment. "Come by yourself, don't tell anyone."

Bram arrived fifteen minutes later. With his short haircut and square face, he looked like what he was, dumb muscle. What Duke needed. Anyone else would have shredded the story he was about to spin.

"We have a problem. And you're the only one I trust enough to tell."

Duke laid the photos on a table. Long-lens surveillance

of Nuñez in Panama City, sitting with a fortyish man in a short-sleeve blue silk shirt and linen pants. Duke neither knew nor cared who the other man was.

"You know what you're seeing?"

"Eddie."

"And a guy he owes a million dollars. Named Carlo."

"Huh."

"Nuñez told me he was clear of the cartels. He didn't tell me he had to buy his way out. He borrowed money from this guy. Four hundred thousand at two and a half points a month plus a buck a year. You know how that works?"

Bram shook his head.

"Costs him ten thousand a month, every month. Then, if he doesn't pay the whole nut back by the end of the year, they add another hundred thousand."

"Ten thousand dollars a month? That's crazy."

Duke nodded. *Poor Eddie.* "He's stuck now close to a million."

"Eddie can take care of himself. I'd take odds on him over this guy."

"Maybe one-on-one. But they're looking at his family, too. Eddie's got one move left. Tell Carlo what he's been doing with us."

"But we have nothing to do with Panama."

Trust Bram to raise the one objection Duke could answer. "Our activities are of interest to various intelligence services, Bram. Which makes information about them valuable." Duke made sure to lay the sarcasm so thickly that even Bram would understand the sneer in his voice. *Don't argue. Trust me and do what I say.* "Long story short, Eddie came to me, said if I don't get him square he'll have no choice but to try to settle this on his own. Which means giving us up."

"Eddie always seemed straight to me."

"This kind of hole, you can't know what someone will do."

Bram's eyes backed into his head until they were as small and dull as jellybeans.

"You want me to show you how we know he's paying Carlo?" Duke grabbed a marker, started drawing boxes on the whiteboard, throwing in names of banks at random. Boxes and lines always intimidated.

"It's all right, then. I get it."

"I knew you would."

"Now what?"

"We deal with it. It's my fault. I never should have brought him in."

"Eddie?" Bram scratched his chin, a parody of deep thought.

"It's my call." An old trick. Take away the subordinate's authority, and with it the moral responsibility. *My decision. I'll face the consequences.* Duke waited for a final nod from Bram. "Good. We need to move tonight—"

"But—"

Duke steamrolled the objection. "Call Nuñez. Tell him you're worried about him. You want to meet him somewhere no one will suspect. A karaoke club. Tonight. Late. Suggest the Lucky Jack."

"Is that around here?"

"Santa Mesa. I'll give you the address." Santa Mesa was a dingy neighborhood east of Quiapo. Duke had scouted clubs there the day before, looking for a place that had private rooms and no security cameras.

"He'll go for it?"

"Don't overthink it, Bram."

"What if he wants to meet somewhere else?"

"Has to be there. Somewhere no one will see you."

Bram called Nuñez, repeated Duke's lines word for word. Nuñez seemed hesitant but eventually agreed. Probably he viewed Bram as too dumb to fear.

Across the street from the Lucky Jack Karaoke Special Club was a run-down six-story building filled with massage parlors that made no effort to hide their real business as brothels. At nine p.m. Duke entered the chipped concrete lobby, made the mistake of riding the elevator up. The cab stopped twice without explanation. *On the way down, I'll take the stairs.*

After a three-minute, sixty-foot ride, the doors opened onto a weirdly well-lit corridor. Duke walked inside the Little Flower Massage Spa, explained he wanted overnight use of a room with a window that overlooked the street.

"All night? Big man." The madam was a stout unpleasant woman who wore cat-eye contact lenses. She led him into a room directly across from the entrance to the club.

"Perfect."

"One girl, two girls?"

"No girls. No sex."

"No sex, still pay. Three hundred U.S."

He handed over fifteen twenty-dollar bills. She counted them twice, held them close to her nose like they might be fake. "Like to listen, huh?" He ignored her until she left. He set his phone alarm, turned out the light, lay on the floor. He wasn't taking a chance on the massage table. Probably bacteria from four continents in its seams.

His alarm woke him at eleven. He left the room dark, stood by the window. He should have been nervous. He'd never killed anyone. But he was ready. He saw now the devil didn't come shouting for your soul. He touched your shoulder and told jokes until you gave it to him on your own like a guy buying a friend a drink.

Fifteen minutes later, Nuñez showed. He wore a green windbreaker, three-quarters unzipped. Duke could just see the faint outline of the holster tucked inside his waistband. He looked around, walked inside the club. He emerged a few minutes later and stood outside, smoking. Nuñez didn't smoke. Basic countersurveillance. He looked around for about two minutes, then stubbed out the cigarette and disappeared into the club.

Bram showed up at one minute to midnight. As Duke had ordered, he wore a T-shirt and shorts, no place to hide a weapon. He walked into the club. Duke left the massage parlor, hustled down the fire stairs beside the elevator. He held a cheap nylon bag in his left hand. Inside the bag, a 9-millimeter Sig with suppressor already screwed to the barrel.

The emergency lights were burned out on the last two floors and he had to grope his way down the stairs. At the bottom, he grabbed the door handle. It refused to give in his hand. Locked. He should have checked after he decided not to take the elevator. Why hadn't he made sure? *Stupid.* He slammed it with his shoulder, but it stayed locked.

He grabbed the pistol from the bag, put the tip of the suppressor an inch from the door jamb, pulled the trigger twice. The suppressor quieted the shots to an asthmatic puff, an old man blowing out candles. Duke dropped the pistol back in the bag and turned the door handle again. This time it opened.

No biggie. He'd lost a minute or two. The delay might even work to his advantage. Bram and Nuñez were probably just sitting down in the private room. He walked across the street. The club had a front room twenty feet long. A bar ran along the side and an eight-foot-tall projection screen hung from the back. The private rooms lay along a corridor that ran from the back of the room to the rear of the building.

The club was mostly empty on this weekday night. Madonna strutted on the projection screen as a half-dozen drunk Filipino guys shouted lyrics: *When you call my name, it's like a little prayer, down on my knees . . .* Three transvestites watched from the corner, wearing long dresses, careful makeup. Demure. Behind the bar, a lighted board indicated which rooms were taken and which available. Perfect. Only three rooms were in use: 1, 6, and 8. "Ask hostess for room," a sign beside the board said in English and Tagalog. "CC required." The hostess sat beside the entrance to the corridor. She looked about fourteen. She reached for Duke as he walked by.

"I'm looking for my friends—"

"Price per person—"

"No worries. I'm not staying."

He brushed her hand aside, walked through a beaded screen. The corridor was blacklit. Ghostly white numbers hung above the rooms, five on each side. The doors had narrow glass slots so people walking by could peek inside. Duke didn't plan to press his face to the glass, an excellent way to get shot. He pulled open the door of room 1, found a transvestite and a Chinese man in a suit making out to the tune of "Rumour Has It."

In room 6, he found three women sitting side by side by side on the couch, eyes glazed, too drunk to sing. Which left room 8. He reached into the bag for the nine, pressed his finger against the trigger. Nuñez was a fast draw, but even John Wayne couldn't pull quicker than a guy with a pistol already in his hand.

The metal was cool against his finger. He stepped down the hall. No waiting. Aim and fire. He pulled open the door to 8—

Found himself looking at four uniformed Philippine National Police officers. Three hookers, too. The cops weren't happy to see him. Two yelled in Tagalog. The one nearest the door lurched up—

"Sorry, sorry—" Duke shut the door, turned away. Were Nuñez and Bram in the bathroom? In one of the supposedly empty rooms? He couldn't hang around to find out. The cops might not bother to come after him, but if they did, they'd find the pistol.

He'd thought his plan was solid. The karaoke noise

would hide the suppressed shot. He and Bram would take Nuñez's identification, shove him into a corner of the private room. By the time the waitress found the body, Duke and Bram would be gone. He'd tell the team that Nuñez had disappeared. Bram would keep his mouth shut, and in a few weeks Duke would deal with him, too.

Now he had trouble. He'd figured on shooting Nuñez soon after Bram showed. He hadn't given Bram a cover story for Nuñez, or warned Bram what Nuñez might say. Just: *Sit with him, I'll be right there.* Now, though . . . what was Nuñez saying? *Veder was screwing his old girlfriend in Lima, this is revenge, the agency will figure it out . . .* Even Bram would be able to see that Nuñez's story made more sense than Duke's half-baked lies about a Panamanian loan shark.

The hostess walked toward him. "Sir—"

"Coming, sure—" He looked in the men's room, the women's just in case. Empty.

"Now."

Duke doubted she would let Nuñez and Bram in a room without paying. By the book, this one. He followed her out. One of the transvestites was up, a surprisingly sweet rendition of Whitney Houston, *And ayyyyyy will always love youuu*, arms spread wide.

No Nuñez. No Bram.

They were gone. *How? Think.*

Nuñez waited up front. Bram came in, and Nuñez steered him away from the private rooms. *Let's walk. We can talk easier outside, this place gives me a headache, let's get some air.* Nuñez was a pro. Like a pro, he'd changed the terms, made sure he wasn't rat-cornered in a karaoke room with one door. He'd hustled Bram outside while Duke was stuck on the stairs.

"Sir." The hostess again. He wanted to set her on fire. "You stay, buy drink."

Duke turned to leave. Then realized. Nuñez wasn't caught in a dark room anymore. Duke was. His watch said 12:10. Bram and Nuñez had been gone for seven or eight minutes. Time for Nuñez to see Bram had set him up. Time for him to take Bram out. He was holding, Bram wasn't. Though Nuñez might let Bram live, figure that Duke used him.

Either way, Nuñez would want Duke. Duke could practically see him. Crouched low behind a car on the street. Standing in the alley around the side of the building, pistol low at his side. Expecting Duke to run out, looking for him and Bram. Patient. Quiet. He could wait all night. Duke wondered if he could convince the cops in room 8 to escort him out. Yeah, right. What would he tell them? *This man, he's an assassin that works for me, but I double-crossed him and he knows it* . . . They'd laugh. And drive him to the nearest mental hospital.

Panic poured into Duke's stomach like a spigot he couldn't shut off. He remembered his last night at the 88 Gamma. The floor manager had tapped his shoulder as he stared at a square mile of empty green felt. *No more chits, sir, we're sorry, no more.* He was a coward, he saw that now. He thought he was a killer, because he worked with killers. But he was a middle-aged bureaucrat named Glenn—

No. Glenn was gone. He was *Duke*. Duke had a pistol

just like Nuñez. Nuñez had ducked the snare, set a trap of his own? Fine. Duke would play right back. He walked to the bar, splayed twenty-dollar bills across it. "Drinks on me. For everyone. And I'll take a San Miguel."

He checked his watch. 12:12. An eternity in those two minutes. The bottle appeared in his hand, cool and covered in freezer dew, label already peeling. He drank half in one swallow. His first taste of alcohol in four years. Set it on the bar. *No more. Stay focused.*

The Whitney Houston song ended. The room briefly went silent as another song loaded. "Paradise City." An omen. "Gotta take a piss. Okay with you?" The hostess looked at the money on the bar and nodded. Duke walked through the beaded curtain and down the hall, praying for a fire exit.

Past rooms 9 and 10, the corridor turned right. He found himself at an American-style fire door with a panic bar. "EMERGENCY ONLY! ALARM!" was painted on the door. Duke didn't see an alarm box. He suspected the warning was for show, to keep people from letting friends into the private rooms. For a moment he wondered if Nuñez had set up outside this door instead of the front. Anticipating this move and playing back at Duke one more time. No. Nuñez was good, but he wasn't subtle.

Duke pulled his pistol from the nylon bag, pressed the panic bar.

No alarm.

The door angled open a few inches. Outside, a narrow alley, scattered with broken bricks and broken bottles. The night air moist, not quite warm. Winter in the subtropics.

Nuñez might be a hundred feet down, where the alley met the street. He'd be looking at the club's front door, wondering why Duke hadn't come out yet. Duke pushed the door a few inches more, hoping it wouldn't creak. He dropped the bag so he'd have both hands free. He stepped into the alley, turned so he faced the street.

Nuñez was at the end of the alley. Pistol in hand. Head cocked to peek at the entrance. As Duke had hoped. Duke stepped toward him. Music leaked out from the open door behind him. Not much, but enough to catch Nuñez's attention. If Nuñez turned, he could pin Duke in the alley.

Nuñez raised his head. Like a hunting dog catching a scent. He shifted his weight, swung his shoulders—

Duke lifted the Sig, a two-handed stance, weight slightly on the front foot, aimed center mass, fired twice. Missed. Close. Concrete flaked off the wall to the left of Nuñez. Duke expected Nuñez to dive for cover. Instead, Nuñez kept coming, reaching for his pistol, bringing his arm forward, pure intent. *This ends now.*

Neither man spoke, the song providing the alley's only noise—*the grass is green and the girls are*—

Duke stepped forward. All his senses on fire. He shifted his aim right, just a fraction, pulled the trigger. The shot struck Nuñez square and low in the gut, drove him back a step. Nuñez tried to raise his pistol, but Duke fired again. This time the blood jumped out of Nuñez's chest. The suppressor did its job. The alley swallowed up the shots.

Nuñez dropped his pistol, went to his knees. His head drooped, but he forced it up.

He mumbled something in Spanish. Duke didn't answer. Glass bits crunched under his feet. He walked briskly toward Nuñez, savoring every step. Nuñez's head wobbled on his neck like a cheap toy, but he looked at Duke without fear. Either he was too far gone to care or he had seen this ending long before.

Duke pushed the pistol into his temple and pulled the trigger. Nuñez's brains exploded against the wall. His body crunched face-first as his soul fled the scene. Duke expected fear. Instead, a neon sign flashed *pleasure pleasure* inside his skull. No drug on earth felt this good.

He peeked out of the alley. The street was empty. The massage-parlor building was dark. He reached for Nuñez's wallet and phone and pistol. He strode back down the alley. The emergency exit was still ajar. Duke half wanted the cops to have heard the commotion. Let them come. He'd kill them all. But the alley stayed empty. Duke picked up the nylon bag, tossed everything inside, walked on, Tagalog-accented Guns N' Roses fading behind him. *Oh won't you please take me home . . .*

Bram didn't show at Duke's apartment that night. The next morning the Philippine National Police reported two foreign nationals shot at close range in Manila, neither man carrying identification. "Detectives believe robbery to be the motive in both cases and will investigate with diligence," the two-paragraph statement read. "It is not yet known whether the shootings are connected."

By then Duke had wiped both pistols and dumped them and everything else into Manila Bay. He wasn't worried about an immediate knock on his door. Manila was among the most dangerous cities in East Asia. Unregistered pistols were common, the police understaffed. As a rule, police in poor countries had an all-or-nothing rule when foreign nationals died in bad neighborhoods. If family members made noise and tourism was at risk, the cops investigated seriously. Otherwise, they brushed off the deaths as drug- or sex-related. Neither Bram nor Nuñez was married. Duke didn't think anyone knew either man was in Manila. No one would call embassies to complain.

Even so, he thought he should get out of Manila soon. He'd pulled the trigger like a pro, but he'd blown the rest of the hit. Even the laziest detectives might wonder why no one inside the club had heard the shots. If they realized the killer had used a suppressor, they would investigate for real. When they did, they'd find half a mountain of evidence. Duke hadn't exactly gotten in and out quietly. The hostess and the bartender would remember him. So would the police officers in room 8. He'd left fingerprints all over. Across the street, the madam at Little Flower Massage would remember his three-hundred-dollar room rental. Little Flower might even have surveillance cams. He hadn't seen any, but they would be hidden. He had gone to incredible lengths in the last four years to make sure police and intelligence services took no notice of his remade face. Now he had to worry that someone in authority would see him.

Even so, he knew he couldn't leave Manila. If he fled under these circumstances, his team would implode. He would have to stay, hope that the Philippine National Police lived down to their reputation. By noon, less than twelve hours after he'd killed Nuñez, he realized he needed to admit his involvement to his guys. They wouldn't trust the police. They'd ask questions at the club themselves and figure out Duke had been there. Duke had to get in front.

With Nuñez and Bram dead, Duke could tell his men whatever he liked. But he'd get one chance. If he didn't sell his story he'd lose them. They wouldn't quit all at once. They'd disappear one by one, and one would take him out along the way. Only the truth would set him free.

The sort-of truth.

That night, he called his guys together. A two a.m. meeting. They arrived in a group, silent, grim. The room felt airless, even with the windows open. Leonid stood by the door, the butt of a pistol peeking from his jacket pocket. The threat didn't surprise Duke. Its openness did.

"You want to know what happened. So do I. What I can tell you—Bram came to me the day before yesterday, told me he had proof Nuñez was going to narc on us." A sublingual murmur of disbelief passed through the room. "Anybody know what Bram might have known, or suspected, or imagined?"

Silence.

"I don't, either. Bram wouldn't say. I told him he was crazy, that I knew Eddie way better than he did and Eddie was clean. I told him I was in charge, to listen to me. He wouldn't lay off. He told me to meet him at this karaoke club at midnight. He'd show with Eddie and prove it.

I went. I figured Eddie and I would talk some sense into him. And I—"

Duke broke off.

"Best tell us, *patrón*," Salazar said.

"I brought a Sig with a suppressor, because if we couldn't talk Bram down—"

"For Bram, this was? Not for Eddie."

Duke nodded.

"You call Eddie, tell him what was up?" Salazar said.

"I tried him, he didn't answer. Anybody see him after like seven or eight?"

Heads shaking.

"I get to the club at midnight, a minute or two late. They aren't there. I check the place out. I get spooked. Bram made a big deal out of it, be there at midnight. I go out the back. Soon as I do, I can't believe it, Eddie's there, waiting at the end of the alley. Watching. I walk toward him, say, *Eddie, come on, what's going on?* He turns toward me, not a word. He brings his gun up. I shot him. That was it. I figured him or me."

"Maybe he didn't see you," Salazar said.

"He saw me. Plenty of light."

"He didn't say nothing?"

"Nothing. Didn't tell me to stop, didn't ask me if I had a gun. I hadn't shot him, he would have killed me. I'm sure of it. Then I figured Bram was dead, Eddie killed him, so I grabbed Eddie's stuff and ran."

"*You* killed Eddie," Salazar said. "You *killed* Eddie." Like he'd believe it if he could just get the sound right.

"What about Bram?" This from Pieter de Velde, another South African, Bram's closest friend on the team.

"Never saw him. I hoped I was wrong about Eddie taking him down until the cops put out that statement this morning."

"We don't know who killed him," Salazar said. "Only thing we know is that you killed one of your own. Shot him in the street like a dog."

"You think I wanted this? The guys paying for this, I told them everything, and they're scrubbing Eddie now, looking for anything that might have made Bram think he was dirty. If they get anything, I will tell you."

"They won't get anything. This story is crap. Eddie told me two days ago you have your own agenda on this. That there's stuff you aren't telling us."

So Nuñez had walked up to the line, but he hadn't given away the secret. Duke had anticipated something like what Salazar had said. He was ready to deflect it. "He was right. There's a lot of moving parts on this. Mainly to do with the next job. Which is even bigger than this one. But Eddie shouldn't have known about that. I don't know what he saw or heard or thought he knew." Duke stepped forward now, raised his hands. "I don't get it, either. But everything I've told you is true. You want to cut me down, do it now."

Salazar was silent. Duke looked at the other men.

"Anybody want to ask anything? Do that now, too."

Leonid threw out a few Russian-accented questions: *How could you be sure he was drawing?* *What exactly did Bram say?* But Duke stuck to his story, and Leonid flamed out fast. In truth, none of these men knew Nuñez well enough to be sure he hadn't betrayed them. Not even Salazar.

"Anyone else?" Duke said. "Anything else?" No one spoke. One fine night at the 88 Gamma, Duke had lost nineteen hands in a row. The odds were a half million to one against a streak that bad. He changed his bet sizes, tipped the dealer. Nothing mattered. The dealer won every conceivable way, blackjacks, flat twenties, thirteen finding eight, even sixteen pulling five, the worst of all. Hand by hand, Duke watched his stacks evaporate, wondering what he had done to deserve such a beating, if he could possibly slide his chips forward to be taken again. Yet he did. He saw the same grim resignation on the faces of the men in this room.

"What now, Cap'n?" de Velde said. "We go our separate ways?"

"Until we hear different, the job's still on."

"You want us to attack a CIA station chief when we're already busted."

"Bram didn't say Nuñez had narced. He said Nuñez planned to."

"Next you'll be telling us you need to leave before the local cops find you. Walk away and leave us neck-deep. Just like Iraq."

"Up your ass. Even with the police on me, even knowing that any of you might wake up tomorrow and frag me, I'm seeing it through." *If Salome can ever get the HEU, that is.* "And I'm going to insist everybody gets a fifty-K bonus and fifty percent more from now on." Salome wouldn't argue, not once Duke told her they were an inch away from having no team at all. "You'll see the money in your accounts tomorrow."

"Double pay," Salazar said.

Good. They were haggling about price now. "I'll ask."

The men sat up straighter. They were insane to stay, of course. Either Nuñez had been about to give them up or Duke had killed him and lied about what had happened. But Duke knew the empty lives they faced on the outside.

"One last thing," de Velde said. "Time you tell us what this is all about."

"I can't. Not yet."

"Then I'm out." De Velde stepped to the apartment's front door.

Duke wondered how the truth would play. *We're trying to con the United States into a war.* These guys might even be impressed. But he couldn't tell, not without Salome's okay. "I'm sorry."

"Give me something. Some reason to trust you."

Then Duke knew. Some part of him must have known even before Nuñez came to him. Some part of him had wanted this chance. "Way we worked it, Eddie was going to do Veder, right? Now someone's gotta step up, take that spot. Be the hitter."

"Yeah, so—"

"I'll do it."

9

The flight from Guatemala took all of ninety minutes, but three messages waited on Wells's phone when his plane touched down in Panama. Shafer, Shafer, and Shafer. *Call me. Call me. You* still *on that plane? Call me.* Wells hadn't entirely shaken the headache from his foolishness at Montoya's mansion. He gritted his teeth and called.

"Good news, bad news."

"Good news first."

"One of those numbers from Montoya is a landline. Maybe the last in creation. Tracks to apartment 2106, Oro Blanco Tower, on Avenida Five-A Sur. A high-rise downtown."

"Sounds classy."

"Looks nice on the Google. The name in the records is Eduardo Nuñez, but there's a woman associated with the address, too. Sophia Ramos."

"You have a picture?"

"We have eight-point-three million. Hispanic names don't come much more common than Sophia Ramos. Database boys are looking for a date of birth to narrow it down. Get you a driver's license, bank, that fun stuff."

"Those crazy database boys. And the bad news?"

"There isn't any."

"You told me there was bad news when there wasn't."

"I wanted to give you a pleasant surprise."

As usual, Shafer's logic was equally bizarre and irrefutable.

Downtown Panama City proved to be half Miami, half Dubai, with the inevitable Trump-branded skyscraper and the inevitable absence of street life around in the high-rise district. Business seemed good, though. Either the real-estate bubble was already reflating, or it had never burst. Low taxes, bank secrecy laws, easy access to cocaine—what more could a hedge fund manager want?

The Oro Blanco was less impressive than its name. It stood twenty-five stories, a midrise by local standards, on a busy avenue three blocks from the harbor. Larger towers blocked its line of sight to the water. The apartments inside would have a view of a view. So close, yet so far. At street level, signs papered over empty storefronts, promising, in English and Spanish, "Oro Blanco, Your Golden Dream! Affordable Luxury! Financing Available! 65% Sold! Agent On-site!"

Wells parked outside and watched as a uniformed man opened the front door for a sixtyish woman whose neon-blue skirt barely covered her ass. Wells wanted to admire her courage for defying societal conventions. But the outfit belonged on a much younger woman, or maybe a cartoon character. Meanwhile, he needed a way upstairs. He wondered if a twenty to the doorman would do the trick. The security cameras behind the front desk suggested otherwise. "Agent On-site!" . . . He checked to be sure his clothes could pass for those of a potential purchaser, headed for the lobby.

The chill of its air-conditioning reached him while he was on the sidewalk. The Oro Blanco's developers apparently wanted to prove they could waste energy as aggressively as their more expensive neighbors. They'd splurged on the fixtures, too, spending money in an obvious way, marble and mirrors and polished brass.

"Señor?" the doorman said.

"Is the agent here today?" Wells was used to a different context for that word. "Sales agent." The doorman nodded to the back of the lobby. Gold letters proclaimed "Sales Office" on a frosted glass door.

Inside, the walls were covered with photos of couples smiling at each other and singles smiling to themselves in nicely furnished apartments. A pretty Panamanian woman in a black suit sat at a professionally clean desk. She gave him a smile that made Wells wonder why the building wasn't already sold out. "I'm Julianna. Pleased to meet you."

"Roger Bishop." The name on his passport, in case she checked.

"You're interested in the Oro Blanco?" Latin women could sound sultry saying anything.

"I'd love to see the model units."

"The office closes at two today. But may I take your information, schedule an appointment?"

Perfect. It was 1:40. "Julianna, I'm looking at several buildings—"

She raised a hand to her mouth, flirty mock horror.

"But you're first. If you could show me around, I promise to have you out in time."

"In that case. If I can make a copy of your passport for security purposes, Mr. Bishop."

And send me promotional mail until the end of time. Wells handed it over. "Call me Roger."

"Our model apartments are on twenty-three," she said, as he followed her into the elevator.

Good news for Wells. Not twenty-one, but close enough.

"Bet they get great light." Wells found himself falling into his role as Roger Bishop, apartment hunter. The elevators were slow. One demerit.

"Wonderful. And we have a great relationship with American banks. Of course, you're welcome to use your own financing."

"Based on the prices I've seen, I think cash."

She leaned toward him like a plant questing for the sun, and he knew he'd said the magic word. "If you don't mind my asking, how did you hear about us?"

"A friend."

"An owner in the building?"

"No, but he knows someone who is. I put in my twenty with the NYPD, now I'm looking to go someplace warm full-time. Get outta Dodge, if you know what I mean."

She didn't. "You'd like a one-bedroom? Two?"

"I want to see both."

"Are you married?" She gave him an almost-flirty smile.

My fiancée just gave me thirty days' notice. "Being a cop doesn't go great with marriage. I was. A long time ago."

True enough. And he had a son again. He and Evan had stayed in touch since Wells's trip to Dadaab. They talked once a week, mainly about Evan's struggles to get off the bench for the San Diego State basketball team, which had the politically dubious name the Aztecs. For the first time in his life, Evan was playing every night against guys quick enough to beat him off the dribble. He had a beautiful seventeen-foot jumper, but he needed to quicken his release and extend his range. Even then, he might never be more than a spot starter.

Wells encouraged him but didn't have great advice. He'd played football at Dartmouth, been a good linebacker by Ivy League standards. But football wasn't basketball. In college basketball, powerhouses and second-tier teams regularly played each other. In football, a team like Alabama would shred Dartmouth. Not just on the scoreboard. The ambulances would be full by halftime. So Wells had always been shielded from his limits as an athlete. He'd known them, but knowing wasn't the same as having them exposed on the field, grabbing at air when you were certain you were in place for the tackle. Sports were a cruel master. All the practice in the world couldn't replace raw talent.

Not that Wells planned to tell Evan any of this. The boy had plenty of time to learn it on his own. In truth, the conversations between father and son verged on banal. No matter. Wells counted the rebirth of his relationship with his son as a minor miracle, considering he'd missed the boy's entire childhood.

Julianna brought Wells into 2310, a two-bedroom. Over the next few minutes she pointed out the appliances— *all General Electric*—the master bathroom—*his-and-hers marble sinks*—and the price—*among the lowest per square meter in the center city*. She was charming without being pushy, pretty without being a distraction. Wells hoped she would find a job at a more expensive building. Her talents were wasted here. He asked enough questions to prove he was serious. Then they were done, and back in the lobby.

"You really can't stay?"

"I'm sorry. Believe it or not, I'm going surfing." She seemed embarrassed that she'd given him that personal detail and returned to the pitch: "But look around. I'll see you tomorrow. You won't find a better value than the Oro Blanco."

Wells shook her hand. Walked out. Drove off. Parked four blocks away. Waited forty-five minutes. Ran back to the building. Out of breath. Frazzled.

"Julianna here?"

The doorman shook his head.

"I left my phone upstairs. In one of the model apartments. Maybe the two-bedroom—2310, right? I know they're not locked. We just walked in."

"I'm sorry, sir. Only tenants and guests."

"Please, you just saw me. That phone has my whole life—if you can't let me up, can you go yourself?" Wells was betting the answer was no.

"I can't leave—"

"I had to sign in to take the tour. She's even got a copy of my passport."

"All right. But find it quick, okay? Don't be screwing around up there."

"You are a lifesaver." Wells rode to twenty-three, knowing the doorman would watch the elevator. The Oro had two sets of fire stairs, which offered access to every floor from the inside, according to Julianna. *Some people, they have friends a floor or two away, they like to take the stairs.* Wells ran two floors down. The twenty-first floor was identical to the twenty-third, down to the hallway paint, a muted subtropical orange.

Besides a standard lock, 2106 had a deadbolt plate. Wells put an ear to the door. Silence. Then a woman in the apartment across the hall. Wells wondered how to explain his presence. But she turned away, walked deeper into her apartment. Wells reached for his miniature electric pick set, a special CIA design. It popped the standard lock in two seconds, the deadbolt in seven.

Behind the door he found a clean living room, bare wood floors, cheap modern furniture. A black cloth sofa sat prayerfully close to a flat-panel television. Only an acoustic guitar case saved the room from complete abstrac-

tion. Wells headed for the kitchen. Tacked to the refrigerator, a sheet of black-and-white head shots of a woman with
tan skin, a crinkled, too-big nose, long ringlets that looked
almost silver. Two photos in the center were circled. They
had been lit to look more dramatic than the others. *My
voice will take you to a place of mystery. And I don't mean
the DMV.*

A desk was built under the kitchen cabinets. In the
center drawer, Wells found bills and a bank statement for
Sophia Ramos. Lots of small withdrawals, a mortgage
payment, and two seven-thousand-dollar wire-transfer deposits from a sender called the ABCD Exchange Center,
Georgetown, Barbados. Wells suspected that if he went
looking for it, he would find servers and fiber-optic cables
in place of an actual office.

Beside the bills, a rubber-banded stack of postcards.
Sophia walking on a beach, strumming her acoustic guitar.
Sophia Ramos: Escucha La Música! Wells took two. Now,
at least, he had her photo. He would look her up, see if she
had a regular gig. Nothing about the apartment screamed
brilliant singer, but then he was no expert on artistic tem-
perament. Maybe she saved her passion for the songs.

Underneath the postcards, he found a flowery Spanish
birthday card, the words inside printed in blocky semi-
literate handwriting: *MI AMOR SOPHIA, PIENSO QUE SIEMPRE—
EDUARDO.* On the facing page, the letters bleeding together
in an excess of emotion: *TU VOZ ES MÁGICA!!!* The card
seemed impossibly sad. Wells dropped it like it was on
fire.

At the back of the drawer, he found a photo of Ramos

and a Latin man on a beach, their arms around each other. The man was small and solidly built, with a cross tattooed on one pec, the angel of death on the other. She gave the posed smile of her publicity photos. On the back, the same shaky handwriting: *Eduardo y Sophia, Miraflores*. So this was Eduardo Nuñez. Wells had seen enough killers to know they came in all shapes and sizes, but the calm melancholy in Nuñez's eyes was disconcerting. Wells wondered if they'd ever meet.

He copied Ramos's bank and mobile account numbers, enough information for the NSA to trace her. Then he left. Sophia Ramos was a lead to a lead, not worth arousing the doorman's suspicions. In past years, Wells had pressed too hard too early on missions, forcing unnecessary violence. He'd already broken a street kid's elbow this weekend. He preferred to keep future civilian messes to a minimum.

"You find it?" the doorman said as Wells left.

He held up his phone. "Thanks."

After an Internet detour that led him to a strip joint in Panama City, Florida, a search for *Sophia Ramos Panama music* turned up a standing ten p.m. gig on Monday nights at a club called Cortes Frescos. Not exactly prime time, but a break for Wells. No waiting. He'd see her tonight.

The club was in Casco Viejo, one of the city's original neighborhoods, dating from the Spanish colonial era. Now the area was in mid-stage gentrification, art galleries and boutique hotels scattered among empty lots and worn buildings. Cortes Frescos—Fresh Cuts—was a converted butcher shop. Hooks hung from its ceiling. Its walls featured close-up high-gloss photos of T-bones and lamb chops. A painted sign behind the bar warned "No Yanquis," and the tatted bartender looked at Wells disdainfully. Wells wanted to ask for a Bud, just to see how the guy would react. He restrained himself and ordered a Balboa, which seemed to be the local beer.

Though he wasn't drinking these days. He'd decided a few months before that he needed to respect Islam's restrictions on alcohol and pork. He knew he wasn't so much recommitting fully to the religion as avoiding hard decisions. Giving up booze was easier than prostrating himself to Allah five times a day, seeking the submission that was Islam's very name. Not to mention trying to understand if he could consider himself part of the *umma*, the worldwide brotherhood, when he'd shed Muslim blood more times than he could remember.

Wells picked at the Balboa's label as he waited for Ramos. He didn't see how the moody singer he'd seen in the head shots would fit at this Panamanian version of New York's now-departed CBGB. Sure enough, he was one of only eight people in the place as she stepped to the stage. The acoustic guitar from her apartment was strapped around her neck. She took the microphone confidently, wearing jeans and a blue halter top that highlighted her best feature, her smooth brown arms.

"*Gracias a todos por venir.* Even Americanos who got lost looking for the Hard Rock Cafe." She stared at Wells.

He wondered if she'd made him somehow, then realized new faces might be rare at her shows. "And now I tell you, *escucha la música!* Listen to the music!"

Wells was glad Ramos spoke English. Less glad that he'd guessed right about her talent. She sang in Spanish, but he didn't need to understand the words to recognize that her voice was reed-thin. Wells and the other patrons shifted in their seats, avoided one another's eyes. After forty-five interminable minutes, Ramos finished with an instrumental number on the acoustic, her fingers working the strings. Her guitar playing was far stronger than her voice. Wells suspected Ramos couldn't admit that truth to herself. She would sing alone in empty clubs forever instead of joining someone else's band. Wells wondered how Eduardo Nuñez had come across her. The Peruvian assassin and the Panamanian songstress seemed an unlikely match.

She finished to relieved applause. "*Gracias.* Thank you. Come back next week—I'll be here, trying new material. *Escucha la música!*" Even before she stepped away from the microphone, the club's speakers returned to the Violent Femmes, picking up mid-chorus: *Two two two for my family and Three three three for my heartache* . . . Musical whiplash.

A tall man waited for Ramos at the bar, a Latin hipster in skinny jeans and thick black glasses. He tried to kiss her on the lips but she ducked him, gave him her cheek. Wells had hoped to approach quietly, put her at ease. But she wouldn't want to talk about Nuñez in front of this guy. Wells would have to pry her away. He moved to the bar.

"Sophia?"

She tilted her head, trying to place him.

"You were great. The guitar especially." He had to shout to be heard over the Femmes. "My name's Roger Bishop. I see you're busy. I just wanted to tell you, I'm"—Wells was about to say "an A&R guy," then realized he didn't know if they still existed—"with an Internet company, streaming radio."

"Pandora?"

"Yes. Exactly. Pandora. Always looking for exclusive content. If you have a minute, I'd love to buy you a drink—"

"You have a card?"

"Just gave out my last."

Her friend frowned, whispered into Ramos's ear.

"Look, we can sit right there—" Wells nodded at a battered table in the corner.

"Long as you don't ask me to sign anything," Ramos said.

"Of course not."

They sat. Now Wells had to switch gears, hope she didn't toss her beer in his face. He nodded at the bar. "He's right."

She lapsed into Spanish. *"Qué?"*

"I lied. To get you away from him. I'm looking for your boyfriend."

She shook her head. "He's not my boyfriend."

"Eduardo Nuñez."

She pushed away from the table like Wells had told her he was carrying a deadly, highly contagious virus. "How did you find me?"

"A man named Juan Pablo Montoya. In Guatemala."

She leaned in, wrapped her fingers around his forearm. "Tell me who you are right now."

"I work for the CIA. Montoya told me Eduardo's involved with an American who calls himself Hank. That Eduardo—"

"Call him Eddie. His name's Eddie."

"That Eddie called him, said Hank was planning to kill a CIA officer. They were supposed to talk more, but Eddie never called back."

She tilted her head back, looked at the ceiling. Wells noticed for the first time that it was covered with decals of cows.

"I want to find him before something bad happens."

"You know what Eddie did in Mexico."

Wells nodded.

"Don't you think something bad has already happened?" Her voice was a sneer. She raised her arms Superman-style. "Here you come to save the day."

"I want to help."

"Of course you do. Come back here tomorrow, ten p.m. I'll tell you what I know."

Wells wondered why she'd changed her mind so abruptly. "Thank you."

"And you'll bring one hundred thousand dollars in cash."

A hundred thousand seemed to be the going rate. Wells was about to argue. But they both knew she'd probably seen the last of those handy deposits from ABCD Exchange. She was a lousy singer, but she wasn't dumb. Anyway, he didn't mind spending Duto's money. "Fine." Wells decided a warning would serve them both. "But under-stand, the money won't be all I'm carrying. Try to take it for nothing, I'll be upset."

She nodded.

"And so we're clear, you can tell me where to find Eddie."

"Yes." Her eyes slid sideways with the lie. "Yes." More conviction this time.

Wells figured she had a lead, a phone number or a plane ticket. Not the whole picture. He'd find out soon enough. "See you tomorrow."

She nodded, went back to the bar without a second glance.

At his hotel, Wells called Shafer.

"Hundred thousand seems steep."

"Foreign aid."

"She can get us to him?"

"She has a lead. A good one." An exaggeration.

"I'll tell our friend. He may want to talk to you about it."

"Tough." Wells was still angry that Duto hadn't told him how dirty Montoya was. He was done with Duto. For now.

"I'll tell him that, too."

In the morning, Wells found a text: *Kibble in your bowl by noon. Delicious kibble.* He imagined Shafer smirking as he sent the message. At 12:10, Wells saw the extra money in his account. A Web search revealed several Chase branches in Panama City. By 12:30, he had presented his passport to a polite assistant manager and in turn received ten slim packets of hundred-dollar bills. The manager showed a discreet disinterest in Wells's desire for hard currency.

Even so, Wells took a cab to the Trump Ocean Club instead of his hotel, in case someone at the branch had tipped off friends. An American carrying a hundred grand made an easy target. The real problem was once again his lack of a firearm. Wells hung out for ten minutes in the Ocean Club's lobby before hailing a cab to a Walmart in the suburban sprawl west of the city. He bought an aluminum bat and an ugly knife. He'd have happily traded the metal for a rusty .22 like the one he'd grabbed at the Parque Central. If Ramos didn't think she had enough information to sell, she might try to take the money preemptively.

Still only 4:15 as he approached his hotel. *When in doubt, move first.* The wisdom of Guy Raviv, the best trainer Wells had ever had. Lung cancer had galloped Raviv to the grave, but Wells still heard his rusted-out smoker's voice every so often. *Why give her time to set a trap?* Wells nodded to himself and Raviv, headed for the Oro Blanco.

Julianna mustered a dim smile as he walked into the sales office. "Señor Bishop. Your appointment was for ten-thirty. Six hours ago."

"It was unavoidable." A formulation that left open the question of what exactly *it* was. Wells spread his hands wide. "I'm sorry, Julianna. But am I lucky? Are you free now?"

"Between appointments, yes."

"Listen, I asked my friend the name of his friend here. Sophia Ramos, in 2106. I'd love to talk to her."

"Why not just ask her, then?"

"I don't know her well enough. I thought we could both go up together."

She shook her head. He could almost hear her thoughts: *A jerk for sure, but still a potential buyer . . . I hope.* He opened the packet from Chase, showed her the money inside. "I brought my down payment."

She ran a hand through her hair. "You want to talk to Ms. Ramos—" Her voice was perplexed.

"See what she likes, if there's anything I should know about the building—"

"And you want me to come up?"

"At least see me to her door." He saw she wanted to say no. But the money was a powerful lure.

"All right. If she's home and doesn't mind."

She led him to the doorman's station.

"Miguel. Call 2106."

The doorman buzzed, handed Julianna the phone. After a rapid-fire Spanish conversation: "She asks, can you turn to the camera so she can see you?"

Wells did. He was giving Ramos a choice. He'd proven he could find her at home. She could see him under these relatively controlled conditions, or send him away and risk that he wouldn't be so polite the next time he wanted to meet.

He took the phone. "I brought my down payment." He held up the open envelope so she could see the money inside. "A hundred thousand."

"This wasn't what we agreed to."

"No, this place is perfect." Wells gave Julianna a thumbs-up. "I'd really like to talk. I'm giving you back to Julianna now. Just let her know it's okay."

Wells rode the elevator alone. He had to admit he was pleased. In Guatemala, Montoya had treated him like a fool. Here he'd forced a meeting on his terms.

He was lucky the elevator was slow. Around twelve, he wondered why Ramos had agreed so readily. Why she hadn't asked Julianna to come up, too, if only to have a second set of eyes on him?

He heard Raviv in his head again. *Never trust it when it's too easy.* He jabbed at the button for twenty, stepped off, flipped the fire alarm to freeze the elevator. Wells ran for the fire stairs as the alarm bell shrieked. If she had a pistol and was waiting in the corridor when the elevator doors opened, he had no play.

Wells vaulted up the stairs to twenty-one, opened the door a crack. Ramos stood outside the elevator bank, a pistol in her hands. So much for forcing the meeting on his terms. He wondered if she was any kind of shot. She was holding the gun too hard, her arms rigid. On the other hand, she was barely fifty feet away. Even someone who'd never pulled a trigger before could get lucky that close. Only one choice left. He opened the door.

"Sophia." She looked to him. He raised his hands. "Do not put a hole in me."

"*Qué?*"

"Don't shoot. Please."

She swung toward him. Even from fifty feet, he saw the pistol barrel shaking.

"Leave me alone."

"Let's go inside. Talk."

"Eddie said someone like you would be coming."

He feared if he took even a single step, she'd start shooting.

"Think it through. If I'd wanted to hurt you, I wouldn't come in such an obvious way. With the doorman and Julianna knowing I'm here. And I wouldn't have brought the money." He raised the envelope.

Her arms sagged, like the pistol weighed a hundred pounds. The strain would rise in her until she surrendered or pulled the trigger.

"We were supposed to meet tonight."

He didn't answer. Inch by inch, the pistol drooped, until finally the barrel was vertical. The elevator alarm still rang crazily a floor below.

"I don't want you in my apartment."

Too late. "There's a pool on the roof, right? Put away the gun, we'll go up, talk there."

"Not the roof."

"The gym?" Julianna would have been pleased: All the Oro Blanco's amenities were making an appearance.

The developers had skimped on the gym. Behind the frosted glass double doors of the Oro Blanco Fitness Center were two small rooms of treadmills and Nautilus equipment.

Second-floor windows overlooked the street. Wells and Ramos sat side by side on a padded exercise bench.

"Let me see."

He handed the envelope to her. She thumbed through a packet of bills. Then she tucked the envelope at her feet and without further ado told him what he'd come to hear. "I met Eddie five years ago. I was working as a masseuse." She spat the word. "You understand?"

"I think so, yes." A prostitute.

"He came from Mexico a year or two before. He drank all day. But quietly. Rum and Diet Coke. He wasn't an angry drunk, a showy drunk like a lot of our men. This was to hide something very deep inside him. When I told him I was a singer, he came to hear me. After that, he decided to support me, get me out of the life."

"He believed in your music."

"Of course." Matter-of-factly, as though Nuñez was one of a legion of fans. "He kept drinking. I didn't try to stop him. We didn't get married or anything. I'm barren—" A word Wells couldn't imagine an American woman using. "I didn't used to be, but I had a bad abortion. I told him. He didn't care. He said he didn't want children, didn't deserve any."

"Did he tell you about Mexico?"

"Enough. He didn't seem like one of those men, but I never doubted him. Then—this must have been a year, a year and a half after we met—an American called him, came to meet him."

"You met this man?"

"No. And Eddie never told me his name. He said the

less I knew, the safer I would be. He said he'd known the man in Peru. Anyway, the man wanted to hire him."

"So this was more than three years ago?"

"Right. And Eddie didn't take long, he agreed. *I was born to be a mule,* he told me. *It's time for me to get back in the harness.* He stopped drinking. I didn't think he could, but he had three bad nights and then it was gone. Like he'd never touched the stuff."

"But he wasn't doing anything then. For this man."

"No, he was. That first year, he went away several times."

"He say where?"

"Europe. That was all. But I'm sure he was doing jobs."

"Three years ago." Wells couldn't understand how this group had operated so long without being noticed, much less caught. Either Nuñez hadn't been killing anyone back then, despite what Montoya and Ramos thought, or an intelligence agency was funding these guys and maybe helping with coms and transport.

"Three years, yes. He worked for more than a year. Then everything stopped. He was home several months. He bought this apartment. I thought it might be done, but Eddie said they were still paying him."

"All this time, he didn't tell you anything specific?"

"Nothing."

"I don't mean targets. What about how many men he worked with? Who was behind it? He never showed you a fake passport? Nothing?"

"You don't understand."

She was wrong. Wells had lived for seven years among al-Qaeda guerrillas who would have gutted him if he'd ever hinted at how he felt about them. He knew the value of silence.

"So he was—off duty, let's say—for a while. Then what?"

"Last May, he left again. Said he might not see me for a while. He came back for a few weeks in September and October. Then gone again. Finally, two weeks ago, he called me. He was angry."

"He said that?"

"No. But he spoke in a way I'd never heard before. *'This man wants revenge for something that happened a long time ago. A woman. It's a mistake.'* I told him, leave. He said he had never quit halfway through a job, that he would try to make Hank change his mind. He said he could handle Hank."

"He mention the CIA? A station chief?"

"No. Since then, nothing. No call, no email. Of course, he has disappeared before, but this is different. I think he's dead."

"I'm sorry to keep asking the same questions, but this American who hired him, all Eddie said about him was that they worked together a long time ago in Peru?"

She reached down, picked up the packet of money.

"That's right. I don't think I know anything more. But you could ask, if you like."

Wells had a thousand questions for the woman who sat beside him. How could she be so clear-eyed about Nuñez, who he was, what he'd done for her, the sadness of their partnership, yet so delusional about her ability as a singer? How had she wound up as a prostitute? Was she in on the joke at Cortes Frescos? Or did she think she was one song away from her big break? And, on a more personal note, how close had she come to pulling the trigger upstairs?

But a judge would strike them all as irrelevant, and potentially upsetting to the witness. Wells would carry only speculation in his baggage.

"Did Eddie ever mention Iran?"

Her face was a blank. "No."

"Revolutionary Guard? Hezbollah?"

"I never heard of those." She tucked the packet to her chest like she feared he might change his mind and take it. "*Gracias* for this."

"Can I call you if I have questions?"

"I'm going away from Panama City. I have family in Bogotá. No one can find me there. But I'll have my phone."

"If you have your phone, someone can find you. Leave it. Get a new one." He scribbled one of his email addresses on the envelope. "Set up a clean email account, send me your number at this address, and then never use that account again."

"It's like that."

"Yes."

At the door, she turned to him. "You think Eddie's alive?"

"I don't know."

"You're lying."

"He's a survivor type."

"Like you."

"*Sí.*"

"Remember this, then. When you remember me. Mr. Bishop or whatever your name is. Everyone dies. Even the survivor types."

He half expected her to pull a pistol and plug away. Instead, she pushed open the door and bowed her head as she walked off. He understood her not at all, but he was sure she'd told him the truth about Eddie.

Back at the hotel, he passed the word to Shafer.

"'Curiouser and curiouser,' cried Alice."

"Who's Alice?" Wells said.

"My sister-in-law. Got Alzheimer's. All she can remember are nursery rhymes. You went a long way for that story. Spent a lot of money."

"I believe you pointed out it wasn't ours. Anyway, we have a timeline now that dates back three-plus years."

"Which doesn't make sense."

"I know."

"So we're looking for an officer who was in Lima back in the day."

"And got into it with someone else—"

"Over a woman. To the extent that this officer holds a grudge a decade or more later."

"Sounds like someone should remember it," Wells said.

"So what's your next move?"

Wells found himself wanting to see Ramos settled to safety. He read the feeling as protective, not sexual. Her singing career seemed no less noble for its inevitable failure.

He wondered if she had touched a similar streak in Nuñez. "Lima, maybe?"

"Whole station's turned over two, three times since then. Anyway, we're low on time. Nuñez has been gone for a couple weeks. The Iranian warning came in last week. Assuming they're connected—"

"You think the Rev Guard would hire an American to put together a hit squad?"

"Not impossible. A few years back, the Iranians tried to hire a Mexican cartel to kill the Saudi ambassador to D.C. Lucky for the Saudis the guy they went to was a DEA agent. Check the court records if you don't believe me. Come on home, we can talk this through in person."

"Plus I'll have the joy of seeing you face-to-face."

"I thought that was understood."

10

White-knuckle night driving was another of aging's indignities. Oncoming traffic streaked blurrily by. The road itself seemed as narrow and slick as stones in a stream. Shafer kept his hands at ten and two, stayed below the speed limit. He'd never been much of a speed-limit guy. But then he'd never been old. Worse, he was sure the drivers stuck behind him were thinking *Outta my way, geezer.* He'd have thought the same, a few years back.

Fortunately, he hadn't misplaced his mind. Not yet. He hadn't visited Duto's house in years, but he knew every turn. He rolled up to find a black Chrysler 300 parked outside the front gate. He handed his license to the unsmiling man inside.

The guard looked it over, handed it back. "The senator's expecting you."

"You mean Vinny."

The guard ended the conversation by raising his window.

"Don't you need to frisk me?" Shafer knew he was acting up. The security annoyed him, though Duto needed it. Former agency directors made ripe terrorist targets, none more than Duto, who had run the CIA's drones as enthusiastically as a queen bee.

The Chrysler edged into the street and the gate swung open, revealing two more sentries in a black Chevy Tahoe. Shafer waved at them. They stared back like they were looking for an excuse to shoot.

The front door was unlocked. Shafer let himself in, found the man himself sitting on a rocking chair in his glass-walled back porch, sipping a glass of something brown. A cigar smoldered in an old-school black plastic ashtray at his feet. The *Post* and *Times* lay on the table at his elbow, alongside a BlackBerry and iPhone. Shafer had known Duto for decades. Even so, he couldn't be sure if he was watching a subtle self-parody: *I, Washington Insider.*

"Is Ward Just eavesdropping in the kitchen?"

"Ward who?" Duto reached down, came up with a square bottle. "Straight from Kentucky. Delicious. Have a splash, take your cares away."

"Have a *what*? When did you turn into Lyndon Johnson's love child?" Nonetheless, Shafer dribbled a finger of the stuff into his glass, took a sip. Duto was right. It was delicious. Too bad he couldn't drink more of it. Not until his car learned to drive itself.

"What do you think?"

"That it violates a gift limit. Can I tell you what Wells found or do I have to gaze with wonder at the backyard first? *I sho' do love yo' oak trees. Mulberries, too.*"

Duto exhaled a cloud of cigar smoke at Shafer for his insolence. "Go."

Three minutes later, Shafer was done.

"One hundred grand for that? Glad it wasn't my money."

"Whose, if you don't mind sharing?"

"Someone who's in my office a lot. Told him the truth. Not for me, not illegal, might mean a lot to the country. Two hours later, I had a cashier's check for ninety-nine thousand nine hundred ninety-nine dollars. At a hundred, he would have needed an extra signatory."

"You threw in the last dollar yourself? On a senator's measly salary? Charity lives."

"Let's assume the story's true. That the station chief who's been targeted misbehaved back in the day in Lima. Then what?"

"Any tales of one-sided wife-swapping make it over the Andes to your happy house in Bogotá?"

"Assuming we can trust the timeline, this happened right around 2000. I was gone."

"Beginning your climb up the skull ladder."

"Exactly."

"Would Cannon know?" John Cannon had followed Duto as Bogotá station chief.

"Too nose-in-the-air to care about who diddled who. Spencer might, but he hates me. Maybe Hatch—"

"Don't know that name."

"Chip Hatch. He was in Colombia for around five years about that time. At Lockheed now."

"Course he is. It's a wonderful world."

"There's a couple other guys, too. I'll make calls."

"They won't talk to me."

"Sadly, no."

The great irony. Shafer couldn't stand Duto, but he wished the man had never quit. Everyone senior at Langley had known that Duto used Shafer and Wells when he wanted to steer clear of agency rules. As long as Duto was DCI, Shafer had juice. Even when he wasn't working for Duto, people assumed he was.

Now Shafer needed to beg for even small favors. So far he'd worked mostly as a conduit on this mission. Not the way he hoped to end his career. He sucked down the last of his bourbon, hoping to anesthetize his self-pity. As soon as it hit his throat, he knew he'd made a mistake. The Honda would feel like an eighteen-wheeler on the way home.

"Care for a cigar?"

"Pass." Shafer's bones creaked like a bridge in a hurricane as he sat up. "I have to go."

"Call you if I hear something. Though I have to say if anybody but Wells came back with this, I would have laughed. If we had to worry about every ex–case officer with a grudge, we'd be in a world of hurt."

Every ex–case officer with a grudge. The words gave Shafer an idea. Sure, Duto had the money, the power, and maybe even the friends. But Shafer had the brains. The bourbon filled his stomach and warmed his heart. He upgraded his self-assessment. Not just brains. Genius.

The next morning, Shafer reached his desk before sunrise. He spent two hours concocting a realistic-sounding memo, printed it out, called Lucy Joyner. It was barely 7:30, but he wasn't surprised when she picked up.

"Lucy."

"Ellis." Which sounded like *A-lis*. Three decades in Washington hadn't touched Joyner's Texas accent. She used it as she did her bleached-blond hair, to hide a fierce intelligence and loyalty to the agency.

"We're overdue for dinner."

"How come you only call when you want something?"

"Who said I wanted something?"

Joyner didn't bother to answer.

"Let me explain in person. Five minutes. Ten at most."

"This going to be"—*gun be*—"ten minutes I regret? Had a few of those in my life."

"Maybe."

"Then get down here primo pronto. 'Fore my admin gets here and this becomes an official and scheduled visit."

During much of Duto's time as director, Joyner had served as the agency's inspector general, its second-worst job. When he left, her reward was a transfer to the worst job of all, director of human resources. A less committed employee would have taken the hint, retired, cashed her pension. But Joyner, who had never worked as a case officer, had deep and unrequited love for those who did. Shafer had seen the attitude in other support staffers. *I'm not worthy of front-line duty, but I will carry water as best I can. Abuse me. I deserve it.* In her twenty-ninth year at the CIA, Joyner still worked sixty hours a week.

Most officers and desk heads regarded the human resources department as useless at best, an impediment at worst. Joyner didn't try to change their minds. She focused on recruiting, where she did have leverage. After September 11, the agency had hired heavily from the armed forces. Veterans knew government bureaucracy, and many came prequalified with security clearances. But they inevitably contributed to the CIA's creeping militarization. Joyner was enlarging the pool of civilian candidates by recruiting older employees. She had increased the agency's presence at elite scientific universities like Caltech and at times pressed for hires with smudges on their background checks.

Shafer understood her goals, though he worried the experiment might end badly. The Snowden case proved the risks. If one of the new hires went wrong, the CIA's congressional overseers would howl, and Langley would wind up leaning even more heavily on the military than before.

Meantime, Joyner was one of the few people Shafer still trusted. Years before, she had seen Duto at his Machiavellian worst, using Wells and Shafer against the Director of National Intelligence. The episode had cemented her relationship with Shafer. They ate together every few months. Shafer was married, Joyner was divorced, but they had reached an age where they could have dinner without misunderstandings. At their last meal, Shafer had made the mistake of suggesting they might even have made a good couple once upon a time. Joyner chortled so loudly that even the waitresses looked at her.

"What?"

"My type's a little more—" She laughed again in big honking hoots. Finally, she broke off, rubbed her jaw. She was a solidly built woman, the type who turned almost masculine in late middle age. "I don't want to hurt your feelings. Let's just say cowboy."

Shafer took the cheapest shot he had. "Sure you don't mean cowgirl?"

"Completely."

Joyner leaned over her keyboard, editing a PowerPoint slide titled *Retention Rates at SIS-1 Level by Geography and Subspecialty.*

"Fascinating."

"We also serve. How you messing up my life today, Ellis?"

"As it happens, I also have an interest in retention. Specifically, case officers who served in South America, including TDYs, and who were fired or left under duress between four and twelve years ago."

From the timeline that Montoya and Ramos had given Wells, the rogue officer must have left at least four years before. The twelve-year outer limit was arbitrary, but Shafer was short on time and needed to shrink the pool of suspects. For the same reason, he had limited his search to officers who had been fired or forced out. Of course, the suspect might have nursed his grudge quietly, left the agency with a clean record. But the showiness of the planned attack struck Shafer as the work of someone who had flamed out spectacularly and wanted revenge.

He knew he faced long odds trying to find a traitor this way. The alternative was to sit in his office waiting for Duto to call.

"You want this why?"

He handed her the memo he'd concocted. "I want to look at station management techniques. This is the first step." The story was as far from the truth as possible without technically being a lie.

She read the top paragraph, pushed the memo back. "Wanna tell me what this really is?"

"Not a bit."

"All those personnel records are TS, and some are SCI, you know that."

He did. He also knew that Duto's departure had cost him his super-duper all-access backstage pass. Why he was reduced to these games. "I'm looking for a name. Someone with a grudge."

"And you can't tell me more—"

"Better if I don't."

"Define *left under duress*."

The fact that they were still talking gave him hope. "Resignation or retirement after a negative evaluation, a failed poly, referral for alcohol or substance use. Et cetera."

She sighed like the sweet San Antonio girl she'd once been. "May take a couple days."

"Too long."

"I'm liking this less and less."

"It's an active grudge."

"This is the only way?"

"Unless you want me to have to depend on Vinny Duto." The truth, though he knew she'd read the words as sarcasm.

"Your piece of short fiction, please."

He passed back the memo. She read the whole thing this time.

"Thinner than an oil slick. And twice as ugly. Let's hope nobody ever asks about it. Set up in there"—she nodded at her conference room—"so I can keep an eye on you. I'll have a tech bring in a laptop with the files. You take paper notes only, leave the laptop here whenever you leave. Call of nature, whatever. Everything stays in the room. I'll handle my assistant. She's a little bit nosy. Actually, a lot. In fact, it would be better if you just snuck back at lunch, stayed in there the rest of the day."

"Yes, ma'am."

"Don't screw me on this, Ellis. I still have some things I want to do at this place."

"I won't."

"And don't call me ma'am. You're even more decrepit than I am."

"No cowboy, either."

"For sure."

That afternoon Shafer hunched over a laptop, scanning personnel records for forty-two case officers. He wasn't expecting to find anything as obvious as a note explaining that an officer had lost his wife in an intramural three-legged race. He planned a process of elimination, looking for guys who had been thrown overboard in rough seas. He hoped to end the day with a few names worthy of further scrutiny. The agency didn't usually require ex-officers to register their addresses or new jobs. But the older targets should be trackable through their pensions. As for the rest, Shafer would have Social Security numbers and photos. They ought to be easy to find, unless they were hiding, which would be a red flag in and of itself.

He knocked out twenty-five names with little trouble. Fifteen had worked only in Argentina, Brazil, or Chile and couldn't have known Eduardo Nuñez. Ten more had resigned to join other government agencies and had no problems with their records. He assumed Joyner's staffer had included them by mistake. Seventeen officers were left, a manageable number.

He paged through, looking at all the ways a CIA career could implode. Seven officers had evaluations no worse than mediocre but had been transferred repeatedly to smaller and less prestigious stations, a sure sign that they had problems with senior officers. Eventually all seven had quit. Six others had resigned or retired after warnings about their failure to recruit agents or general lack of productivity.

Maybe one of those thirteen was angry enough to decide to assassinate a station chief years later. But none jumped at Shafer. They were second- and third-tier case officers who had been winnowed out. It happened.

The other four names on the list were more interesting.

Gabriel Lewis was sent to Johannesburg after a successful rotation in Bogotá. In South Africa, he spent thirty-two thousand dollars on a recruiting trip that turned out to be a ten-day vacation with his mistress. His station chief was angry enough to argue for referring the case for criminal prosecution, though Lewis was ultimately allowed to repay the money and resign. But Shafer saw one immediate problem with Lewis as a suspect. Based on his name, he was probably Jewish. An Iran connection was hard to imagine.

Ted Anderson had started in Lima and moved to Saudi Arabia, then Spain. In Madrid he flunked a routine five-year polygraph, registering as deceptive on a crucial question: *Have you ever had contact with a foreign national that you failed to reveal?* He denied committing espionage, and that answer registered as true. But when he was asked why the poly showed deception on the other questions, he didn't know. Three months later, he resigned.

The agency reviewed all his files, found no evidence that he'd given up classified information, and quietly closed the case. A one-page note at the end of the file revealed that Anderson now worked for a Geneva hedge fund that specialized in oil trading, which might explain his lie on the poly. Maybe he'd been selling information to the fund all along. Shafer viewed him as a long shot, too.

Fred Beck had served all over Latin America during the nineties, including temporary assignments to Lima and Bogotá. His career went sideways in 2002 in Nicaragua. Beck accused Steve Antoni, another officer in Managua, of lying about a car accident. Antoni said he'd been alone, but Beck claimed a "female host-country national" was involved.

Beck was probably right. No matter. Antoni was well connected, popular at the station. Beck wasn't. After a cursory investigation, Antoni received the mildest of wrist slaps, a loss of three vacation days for failing to report the accident promptly. Beck was snubbed as a troublemaker. *Has difficulty understanding the complex realities of re-*

cruitment, his station chief wrote the following year. *May be better suited as an analyst.* About the worst slur the clandestine service could offer.

Beck quit in 2004. On his way out, he wrote an angry letter to the inspector general's office about "the rancid cesspool of corruption in Managua—in fact, all over Latin America." The letter might have gotten more attention if the agency hadn't been desperately trying to fix Iraq. Of even more interest to Shafer, Antoni was now chief of station in Tunisia.

Glenn Mason, the fourth of Shafer's top suspects, had been a solid officer in his first posting in Lima. Then his career got interesting. From 2003 to 2006, he served with distinction in Baghdad. But in fall 2006, he came unhinged. He accused an Iraqi translator of being a double agent for al-Qaeda. A few weeks later, he was found outside his trailer, yelling incoherently and holding a pistol. He claimed not to remember the incident. An agency psychiatrist insisted he be transferred out. The agency gave him several months' leave and then moved him to Hong Kong, as he requested.

But his posting there started badly and ended in disaster. He was absent for days at a time. Because of his Iraq commendations, the chief of station was loath to challenge him. He was asked if he wanted to transfer to another station, and he refused. By the end of his second year, he'd used up any goodwill from his time in Baghdad. The station recorded his failures, building a case to fire him. He was written up for drinking at work, offered inpatient treatment for alcohol abuse. The files depicted him as curiously passive. Without ever having met Mason, Shafer could see him apologizing to his chief in a flat, dull voice, making promises he had no intention of keeping. Finally, the station's security officer insisted he take a poly. He failed questions about cocaine use, consented to a drug test, failed that, too. He was fired.

Shafer read the file twice. He found himself unsatisfied. Mason's instability disturbed him. The man had worked impossibly hard in Iraq, then thrown away his career. Why hadn't he tried to save himself, worked with the agency's clumsy efforts to help him? Was he a casualty of Iraq, or broken even before Baghdad?

By the time Shafer finished looking at the files, it was past midnight. Joyner had stayed until eight, then conceded defeat. "I'm trusting you."

"Scout's honor. Nanoo-nanoo."

Now Shafer looked at the pages of notes he'd compiled. He couldn't remember the last time he'd worked an eighteen-hour day, but he felt exhilarated. His next step would be seeing what Lewis, Beck, and Mason had been doing since they'd left.

Shafer had left his phone off all day aside from two short calls home. He turned it on now, found messages from Wells and Duto.

He called Duto first. "Where have you been all day?"

"Detecting. You have a name?"

"Hatch said he'd heard rumors of weirdness in Lima,

but he couldn't remember the details. I'm waiting on the other guys. You have to remember, Colombia back then was crazy. Then 9/11 happened. And this was all a long time ago."

"Call Hatch back, see if these names jog his memory." Shafer read them off.

"Why those guys?"

"Just do it, Vinny."

"Now? Past midnight?"

"You want me to read you the names again or can you remember them?"

Ten minutes later, Shafer's phone rang.

"How did you know, Ellis?"

Almost Retirees 1, All-Powerful Senators 0.

"Tell me how."

Shafer pressed his luck. "It was Mason, right?"

"Soon as I said it, he remembered. Mason walked in on another officer with his girlfriend, she was Peruvian, this was just before September eleventh, literally the day before, so it all got forgotten."

"Who was the other guy?"

"James Veder. He's—"

"Chief of station in Manila. It's real, Vinny. It's happening. Now we just have to make Hebley believe it."

"I'll call him."

Shafer still didn't understand how these pieces fit together. Was Mason working for the Iranians? What had he and everyone he'd hired been doing for the last three years? They would have time to answer those questions. Right now they had to make sure Veder knew he was at risk.

"We're a hundred percent sure this is real?" Duto said.

"You're the one who hooked Wells up with Montoya."

Duto was silent for a while. Then sighed. "I still have the emergency numbers for the stations. I'll call Veder, tell him to watch his back. I'll call Hebley tomorrow."

"Will he believe you?"

Duto hung up without answering, much less thanking Shafer. No matter. They both understood the truth. Duto would have come up with the name eventually. Someone would have remembered Mason and Veder. But Shafer's intuition and hard work had saved crucial hours, if not days.

Neither of them had any way to know that they were already too late.

||

Like other Pacific Rim megacities, Manila no longer had morning and evening rush hours. Traffic choked expressways and surface roads from dawn until midnight. Men wearing tissue-thin white masks waded between cars, hawking newspapers, water, and buckets of fried fish and rice.

To James Veder, the traffic was like Manila itself: maddening, though with a certain loopy charm. He almost never drove himself, so he could work or catch up on email. And every so often he saw something that made him wish he could lower his bullet-resistant windows and take pictures. A month before, a fiftyish woman in the next lane had given herself a haircut as she inched along. Not a trim, a full haircut. With shears. Even more amazing, her car was a subcompact. She could barely move her head. She positioned the blades with surgical precision before each cut.

Two days ago, Veder had caught a man in an early-eighties Michael Jackson outfit singing full throttle with his windows up. No doubt practicing for karaoke. Veder would never understand the Filipino obsession with karaoke. Even the smallest villages had at least one crude machine for everyone to share.

His tour here was nearly done. In six months, he'd be on to his next posting. He expected Mexico City, though the move hadn't been finalized yet. But he would miss the Philippines. The post had drawbacks, not least the twelve-hour time difference from Virginia. At least once a week someone at Langley woke him at three a.m. Still, Manila was a pleasure to run. He'd overseen a successful op aimed at the Chinese navy, which was encroaching on the Spratly island chain. He'd managed counterterror raids against the Islamists in Mindanao. He'd even helped the Pentagon track the pirates who popped up in the Celebes Sea. The Philippines were important enough to merit attention and resources, but not so vital that he had to endure endless visits from seventh-floor managers proving their importance.

Best of all, Filipino women had shucked their Roman Catholic scruples long ago. As a group, they were the filthiest bedmates Veder had known, and he had plenty of experience. Maybe after he retired, he'd publish his memoirs. He had the perfect title already. *Screwing the World: My Life with the CIA*. Too bad the censors wouldn't approve. He would sell a million copies.

Because of Manila's traffic, Veder preferred not to leave the embassy during the day. Today, though, he had no choice. He was lunching at a club outside the city with

Admiral Juan Fortuna Ocampo, vice chief of staff of the Philippine navy. The navy knew about the meeting, but not the nineteen thousand dollars Veder would leave in the admiral's golf bag. Veder wasn't sure the money bought anything that Ocampo wouldn't tell him for free. The Philippine government was close to the United States. But the CIA liked to pay sources. Friends could walk away. Co-conspirators couldn't. Analysts took purchased information more seriously than what was freely given. It was as if Langley didn't believe anyone would help the United States for any reason but money.

So Veder had a slim envelope filled with hundred-dollar bills in his briefcase. After all these years, Veder still got a charge from carrying cash. He knew some case officers didn't like the agency. They questioned the work, the bureaucracy, the morality, the drones, the blah, blah, blah. He never argued. Let them whine. But what he wanted to say was: *Shut up and man up. Being a case officer is the best job in the world. If you're too dumb to realize it, we don't need you. Go ahead and quit.*

Though no job was perfect. Now the agency was having one of its periodic panic attacks about what the security guys called TTP, threats to personnel. The Revolutionary Guard had jerked the agency's chain with a mysteriously vague threat against a station chief. Veder would bet every dollar he was carrying that the source for this so-called plot was an Iranian plant. Iran had enough problems keeping its own scientists alive. No way would the Guard come head-on at the agency. Instead, it had invented this little threat to gum up ops all over the world.

Veder wanted to give the Iranians credit for the ingenuity, but he was angry that his security chief had made him give up his predawn jogs in Rizal Park. He was traveling with a second bodyguard now, too, and switching vehicles every day. He regarded the exercise as silly. No matter. In a couple weeks, the threat would fade, and he could get back to running.

Motorcycles were the best way to beat Manila's traffic jams, at least during the dry season. So Veder wasn't surprised when one rolled slowly past his window, a big bike. The driver and passenger were dressed identically in full leather and black helmets with mirrored visors.

The bike stopped beside the driver's window, rose on its springs as the driver dropped his feet to the cracked asphalt. The passenger reached into his messenger bag and pulled out a piece of steel almost three feet long. He slapped it against the Suburban's front and back driver's-side doors so that it extended about a foot on either side of the seam between them. Isaiah Thorpe, Veder's driver, popped the door locks, tried to shove open the door. Thorpe was too late. The rod was attached magnetically to both doors, jamming them in place.

Veder banged against his door, trying to force it open, doing nothing but bruising his shoulder. No. He needed to go the other way, out the opposite door. And even as he processed this thought, the motorcycle passenger reached again into his bag and came out with another piece of metal. This one about the size of a dinner plate, perfectly circular, at least an inch thick. He ripped off a thin plastic backing and pressed it against the window.

"Oh, shit—" Thorpe said. He was a wiry, tough-as-nails ex-Ranger from south Alabama. Veder had never heard him curse before. A single word rang in Veder's mind. *Away.* He swung his legs, kicked himself off the window like a swimmer making a turn. On the other side of the glass, the motorcycle rolled off, accelerating through traffic. Neither the driver nor the passenger had raised their visors or spoken a word. Not *Allahu Akbar*, not *Die CIA*, nothing. Not a single wasted moment. The rod had locked them in, and the plate would blow them up.

Thorpe worked to pull his carbine with his right hand while frantically trying to lower the window with his left. But the plate was attached firmly and its bulk kept the window jammed closed. "Shoot across me," Thorpe yelled to Steve Clark, the second guard in the Tahoe. "Shoot!" But Clark was leaning away from Thorpe, opening his door—

Veder scrabbled across the backseat, reaching for the passenger door, trying to get out or at least get the bulk of the SUV between him and the bomb. Too late.

An avalanche caught Veder, doubled him up, threw him down a rabbit hole covered in the softest white fur he could imagine. He wasn't unconscious, but he wasn't conscious, either, and though he couldn't remember what had happened, he knew what would happen next. Like time was running backward. Then the avalanche ended and he landed in the backseat. The rabbit fur was gone and the pain seeped in, not all at once, but steadily rising.

He couldn't hear anything, not even a hum. A thousand colors clouded his vision, a cable feed that had gone funny. Somehow he pulled himself up, looked at the driver's seat. Thorpe didn't have a head anymore, it was gone, replaced with a smear of brain and blood on the windshield like half-mixed baby food. Weirdly enough, the rest of his corpse was still vertical in his seat, apparently undamaged from the neck down.

Veder looked for Clark, but Clark wasn't moving, either; he was slumped against the front passenger door with a metal arrowhead spiking from his temple. *No*, Veder said, or thought he did; he wasn't sure if he could speak anymore.

But he was still alive. He knew that. He didn't know why the men had put the bomb on the front window instead of his own, but they had. So he was still alive. Dense white smoke filled the passenger compartment. He was sure he was coughing, though he couldn't hear himself. *Out*. Before the Suburban burned up. Then the rear passenger door swung open. A hand reached down, looped under his shoulder, pulled until his head and neck were free. A miracle. Life.

Thank you, Veder tried to say, wanted to say. Then the man stopped pulling and Veder could see he was wearing a motorcycle jacket and a helmet with a mirrored visor. The miracle was no miracle at all. The man reached under his jacket, came out with a pistol. Veder tried to pull himself away, but he had no strength left, not even to beg—

The man leaned in close so only Veder could see him and lifted his visor. And Veder saw himself looking at a familiar face, but he couldn't think of the name. He wanted so much to remember. If he could only think of it, he was sure he could connect with this man, an American, not just an American, *a case officer*. Veder's mind circled the name, another moment or two and he'd have it, he could change the man's mind—

Veder felt the touch of steel against his temple—

South America—

He remembered all at once, that apartment in Lima on the day before the World Trade Center burned, *Glenn, Glenn Mason*—

He thought he'd spoken aloud. But the man shook his head, a single firm shake. Veder felt overwhelming regret. He'd been so sure—

He knew his last hope had vanished into the unsmiling face above. Veder could argue no more with his death. He closed his eyes even before his killer pulled the trigger.

PART

TWO

12

This time Duto's guard waved Shafer through, no ID check. Inside, Duto had dropped his great man posturing. He sat at his kitchen table, bathrobe loose on his shoulders over a thready V-neck T-shirt. Instead of whiskey, he sipped milk from a half-gallon jug. Shafer wondered if Duto had an ulcer. For the first time, he seemed *old* to Shafer. Shafer hated thinking of him that way. Duto was younger than he was. If Duto was old, what was Shafer?

He was pleased to see Duto put down the milk, sit up straight, slip on his commander's mask. "Where's your buddy?" On cue, the front door creaked open. Twelve quiet seconds later, Wells joined them. His hands were loose at his sides and he looked curiously around Duto's kitchen like he'd never seen appliances before. Tactical readiness. Or maybe just looking for a glass. He opened a cupboard, found one, swiped for the jug.

"Careful," Shafer said. "Vinny drinks straight from it."

"Whatever he has, I'm sure we've already caught." Wells poured himself a glass. "What happened?"

"All I know, the alert came through about fifteen minutes after I got off the phone with him." Shafer looked at Duto. "Attack in Manila. Worldwide lockdown."

"I called the station. Veder's office. Nobody answered."

"I think it was already done. The alert said forty minutes prior. Bomb in his SUV."

"Guards, too?"

"Dead at the scene. I checked at the TOC"—the Tactical Operations Center—"before I left. No new cables, but local TV in Manila had live feeds. The SUV was shredded. Witnesses saying two motorcycles, each with a rider and passenger. Whole show over in less than thirty seconds. Somebody had a cell-phone video, but all it showed was a motorcycle cutting through stopped cars. Back of a rider in a leather jacket. They'll get other video, but I don't think it'll show much. A pro job."

"By definition, anybody who kills a station chief and two bodyguards is a professional," Wells said.

"Nobody's taken responsibility yet."

"What are we doing?" Duto said.

"FBI is waking a forensic team up. They'll be in the air before dawn. And we're moving a SOG team from Mindanao to Manila." SOG stood for Special Operations Group, the CIA's paramilitary arm, mostly ex–Special Forces soldiers.

"There's going to be Olympian-quality ass-covering on this one. Why didn't we take the warning more seriously, et cetera. Tricky part is, what does Hebley tell the FBI?"

"Maybe he keeps it inside the tent, claims that disclosing it would jeopardize an ongoing op," Shafer said.

Duto shook his head at the suggestion. "Too many people know already. They can't make it disappear. So they admit it, but they emphasize it was vague, unspecific, untraceable."

"That's what you would do."

"Yes."

"Love that three of our guys aren't even cold and you're more worried about where the blame is going than finding out who killed them."

"I am telling you that Hebley will smell the reputational risk and act accordingly. You can choose to pretend otherwise and blunder into some avoidable political trap. Like you've done your whole career. Only now you don't have me to bail you out, Ellis."

Shafer couldn't believe that a couple minutes before he'd felt sympathy for Duto. "James Veder would still be alive if you'd pushed your guys harder yesterday. If you'd gotten us a name."

Duto shrugged: *I tried*.

"This make sense to either of you?" Wells said. "If the Iranians are really so close to a bomb, why poke us now? Why not keep their heads down until it's done?"

"They don't know they have a leak," Duto said. "They don't know we know they're behind this—"

"If they're behind this—" Shafer said.

"And maybe they're done already. Maybe they've got a nuke on a shelf in a cave somewhere."

Shafer wanted to believe Duto was wrong. CIA, DIA, MI6, the counterproliferation guys at the International Atomic Energy Agency, everybody said the Iranians were years from a bomb. But the estimates could be wrong both ways. The agency might have been so worried about giving Iran's scientists too much credit that it hadn't given them enough.

"And this is their coming-out party?" Wells said. "Prod us, dare us to respond?"

"Not like they're going to take out an ad on *Jazeera*."

"A giant mushroom cloud," Shafer said. "We're in the club. But they haven't run a test." Meaning an underground nuclear test. The United States had installed sensors in Afghanistan, Turkey, and Iraq to detect the shock waves an explosion would produce.

"Can they be confused with earthquakes?" Wells said.

"I don't think so. It's a very distinct signature. I'll check in the morning."

"Maybe they're so confident—" Duto said.

"I don't care how confident they are. They need to be sure, and that means a test."

"What are the other options? False flag is the most obvious." Meaning that another intelligence service had both invented the Revolutionary Guard double agent and carried out Veder's assassination, with the aim of making the United States blame Iran.

"From who? Who gains if we attack Iran?" The crucial question. But none of the answers made sense.

"The Israelis," Duto said. "And they love motorcycle bombs."

"Can't see them bombing two of their own embassies to build this guy's legend."

"They didn't exactly level them."

"And kill a station chief. We've had their back for fifty years. They wouldn't risk that. Especially since they know they might convince us to attack Iran anyway."

"Who, then?"

"The Russians or the Chinese might kill a station chief if they thought they could get away with it—"

"That's a stretch—"

"I *know* it's a stretch, Vinny. But, again, why? Moscow, Beijing, they don't mind an Iranian nuke. They can manage Iran easier than we can. At least they think so."

"Maybe they changed their minds. Maybe they've decided they can't trust Iran."

"Then why not just come on board with sanctions, help us put pressure on Tehran?"

"So as not to piss the Iranians off," Duto said. "Look publicly like they've abandoned their ally."

"They could whisper to the White House, *Go ahead, do what you have to do, we won't stop you—in fact, we'll help you target.* Much easier than taking the risk of killing one of our station chiefs. No."

"No," Duto said. "I don't suppose we think MI6 or any of the Europeans are possible."

"What about the Saudis," Wells said. "They'd love to see us hit Iran, and I can't see them shedding too many tears over one station chief."

"But they're like Israel. They wouldn't risk the blowback if we found out."

"We keep tripping over the same rock," Shafer said. "Allies don't kill allies. Let's go the other way. From the bottom. Glenn Mason."

"Somebody—Iran, for the sake of argument—hires him," Wells said. "He puts together a team. Attacks two Israeli embassies. Then settles his score with Veder. On the Rev Guard dime. And Iranians didn't mind?"

"Maybe it was part of the deal. They wanted to kill a station chief, he wouldn't work for them unless they let him pick the target."

"Okay, but what's he been doing the last three years?" Wells said. "The Iranians were so sure they'd have a bomb by now that they decided to hire Mason back then?"

In the dining room, Duto's grandfather clock chimed three times, sweet and sober.

"We can't solve this in your kitchen," Shafer said. "Too many moving parts. The seventh floor needs to know this is more than chasing down some Iranian cell. They need Mason's name so they can focus on him. Where he's been. Where he's getting his money."

"And if you're telling them that—" Duto said.

"We tell them how we got onto this. You, your buddy Juan Pablo Montoya."

"Enjoying this, Ellis? You wonder why people don't like you—"

"I know why people don't like me. I just don't care. I don't draw my entire identity from a crowd of ass-kissers."

"Do what you have to do." Duto smiled. "You may not get the reaction you expect." He turned to Wells. "What about you? You going in, too? They'll love to see you."

"If we can find her name, I'm going to look for the woman."

"What woman?" Duto and Shafer said simultaneously.

"The one who caused the trouble between Mason and Veder."

At home, Shafer found his wife asleep, snoring lightly, a new habit. She used old-style face cream, the gloppy white stuff, masking her cheeks. Not that she needed it, as far as Shafer was concerned. The mirror gave him no relief. But when he looked at her, he saw her true youth smiling under her skin. He kissed her ear and she sighed in her sleep. He lay on the covers beside her and waited for the morning.

He arrived at Langley at seven a.m. The bad news had spread overnight. Three dead, no suspects, the threat still out there. In the elevators, men and women nodded grimly at one another, no easy greetings today.

Shafer's phone rang as he reached his desk. Lucy Joyner. "What did you get me into?"

"We almost saved him. Truth."

"I'm making those files go away. And your note."

"Before you do, one more favor."

"Ellis—"

"It'll only take a second. Please."

She didn't answer.

"I need the SUFC reports for Glenn Mason from '98 through 2001." Case officers had to report what the agency inelegantly called *serious unauthorized foreign contacts*, a term that essentially translated into relationships with foreign nationals. Mason had almost certainly filed an SUFC on the Peruvian woman he'd dated.

"They weren't digitized in his personnel file?"

"Didn't see them."

"I'll take a look."

"You're the best." Shafer hung up before she could change her mind. He tried not to notice the tremble in his fingers as he punched in his next call.

"General Hebley's office." A woman's voice, calm, efficient, slightly cold. A nurse who specialized in blood draws.

"It's Ellis Shafer. I need to talk to the director. It's urgent. About today's attack."

"Ellis who?"

"Special Assistant Deputy Director Ellis Shafer." Duto had given him the title just before he left. Shafer had figured out the acronym, decided to let Duto have his little joke. He wished he hadn't.

"Spell your last name?"

"S-H-A-F-E-R." He resisted the urge to throw in a *T* after the *F*. In the background, he heard a man say, *"Kyra!"*

"I'll get him the message."

"Thanks—"

She was gone. Shafer waited an hour before calling again. This time she was curt. "I have passed along the message—"

"Please tell him it's time-sensitive—"

"Yes, Mr. Shafer."

Shafer knew he couldn't call again. While he waited, he read up on the Revolutionary Guard and the Iranian nuclear program. The idea that the Guard would have used Glenn Mason was not as odd as it first seemed. The Guard's Quds Force, which handled foreign espionage and operations, had a history of using non-Iranians for politically sensitive jobs. As far back as 1984, Iran had used the Lebanese Shiite guerrilla group Hezbollah to bomb the American embassy in Beirut. If Mason had somehow come to the Guard's attention, its commanders might have seen him as a perfect way to attack the agency. *We'll use this traitor, show you that you're rotten from the inside out.*

Shafer's phone rang, a blocked inside number. He grabbed for it.

"General—"

"This is Jess Bunshaft. I understand you have some information for us."

Bunshaft was one of Hebley's mid-level assistants.

"I can come up—"

"That won't be necessary. I'll be in your office in five minutes."

Click. The seventh floor was making a habit of hanging up on him.

Five minutes became forty-five by the time Bunshaft showed. He was a small man with a big gym-grown neck, a receding hairline, and a neatly groomed goatee. He was half Shafer's age. Or less. Like most of the world. He reached out a stubby-fingered hand.

"Jess Bunshaft. Sorry I'm late. It's a pleasure to meet you." Bunshaft showed Shafer a mouthful of perfect white Chiclets. Everyone under forty seemed to have teeth meant for high-definition television. "You're a living legend."

"Which translates as *won't retire though I desperately should*."

Bunshaft made a sound that could have been a laugh. He sat on the edge of Shafer's couch and reached into his jacket for a reporter's notebook and pen. He broadcast eagerness, but not to hear what Shafer had to say. To be done with this chore, so he could get back to more productive tasks.

"Ever heard of Glenn Mason?"

Bunshaft shook his head.

"He was a case officer for more than a decade. Lima, Baghdad, Hong Kong. Resigned a few years back."

"Got it, got it, Lima, Baghdad—" Bunshaft scribbled in his notebook, the kind of active listening that wasn't listening at all but a parody.

"Put the notebook down for a second and *pay attention*." Shafer hated sounding like a cranky old man, but he had to get through.

Bunshaft smiled. "Sure." He placed the notebook and pen on the couch, patting them carefully, *Like you asked, Gramps*.

"Glenn Mason ran the cell that killed Veder."

"Our source says—"

"I know what the intel says about Iran. I don't know

whether the Rev Guard brought Mason in to do the job or whether this is some false flag meant to get us at Iran's throat, but Mason's the guy. Mason has a personal beef with Veder that goes back to Lima. In 2001, Veder stole his girlfriend there."

Bunshaft stopped pretending to listen, started listening for real. "You think this is about a woman? In *2001*?"

"I don't think. I know."

Shafer explained. Duto, Wells, Montoya, Nuñez, Ramos. The whole story, aside from yesterday's research in Joyner's office. Bunshaft took careful notes.

After twenty minutes, Shafer wound up. "That's it. I thought you'd want to know." Despite everything, he vaguely hoped that Bunshaft would extend a hand, invite him up to seven. *Great work. Now I see why Duto kept you around*.

"You didn't think you should tell us about this earlier?" Bunshaft said.

"I called the seventh floor as soon as I got in—"

"Yesterday, I mean. Last week. When it could have done some good."

Now Shafer understood the note-taking. Bunshaft had wanted to be sure of every detail so he could use them all for the prosecution, like a detective listening to a husband offering a half-assed alibi for the night his wife was killed.

Duto had warned him, but he'd refused to listen. Now Shafer was a convenient scapegoat if the congressional investigators came calling. *We could have stopped the attack if these guys had told us instead of freelancing*.

"This has all come together in the last three, four days. Duto only called me and Wells last week. We had to have the name. Imagine I'd come to you with a story about a disgruntled case officer whose name we didn't even know."

"Do you know when the Colombian—"

"Montoya—"

"When Montoya initially called the senator?"

Shafer shook his head.

"So, just so I have this timeline right, John Wells informed you on Monday about the possibility there might be a personal motive for an attack on a station chief—"

"Right, Monday. I told Duto. He said he'd call some of the guys he'd worked with. Came back to me with a name last night."

"What time?"

"Right around midnight. I think he was maybe ten minutes too late."

"If you're playing some other angle on this, tell me now."

"My angle is to get you to find Glenn Mason."

"And the senator and Mr. Wells will confirm what you've told me."

"Of course."

Bunshaft stood. At the door, he stopped. "Stick around this afternoon, okay? Carcetti may want to talk to you." Max Carcetti was Hebley's chief of staff and enforcer. Hearing his name didn't inspire confidence.

"I'll be here."

He called Wells and Duto, told them to expect questions from Bunshaft. Then Joyner called. "What you want is a paper file, hasn't been scanned."

"I thought everything from the late nineties was scanned—"

"Not everything, not for officers who have departed the agency. Those are in the files downstairs. You want it, go get it yourself. I'd do it sooner rather than later because suddenly the PTB"—a Joyner expression, *powers that be*—"seem interested in your man."

"Will the records guys let me in?"

"I'll tell them. This is the last favor, Ellis. I mean it."

The personnel records unit was on the second floor of the Old Headquarters Building, shrinking steadily as files were digitized and archived to cold storage in the West Virginia mountains. In twenty-five minutes, Shafer had the forms. In 1999 and 2000, Glenn Mason reported a relationship with Julia Espada, a reporter and translator for the Associated Press in Lima. His report for 2001 didn't mention her. The name was common, but Shafer figured tracking down an AP reporter, or ex–AP reporter, should be easy enough.

Back in his office, he turned up Espada after ninety minutes of searching, mostly on public databases. She was an American citizen now, lived in Houston. He called Wells to pass along her name and address.

"I'll go to Houston tonight."

"Try not to scare her."

Wells hung up.

Shafer spent the rest of the day talking to the U.S.

Geological Survey and the Comprehensive Nuclear-Test-Ban Treaty Organization, confirming that Iran could not have conducted an underground test without being caught. He knew he could have answered the question in a few minutes on Wikipedia, but he preferred to distract himself from the seventh floor's silence.

The sun had set and he was reading the latest updates from Manila when his phone rang. Bunshaft. Shafer snatched the phone.

"Mind coming upstairs?"

It wasn't a question.

"Of course."

"I'll meet you at the elevator."

And there Bunshaft was, waiting for him like an old friend, leading him past the guard station that protected the suite where the director and his deputies worked. Bunshaft made a right, then a left. Suddenly Shafer knew where they were heading, a windowless conference room sometimes called SIS Jail, because it could be locked from outside. He'd seen it with Wells, years before. It wasn't exactly Guantánamo. It had phones, a couch, a private bathroom. Mainly it was used to intimidate officers suspected of mid-level misbehavior like expense account fraud or leaking to the press.

So he was in worse trouble than he expected. He stopped. Bunshaft waved him on like they were headed for Hebley's suite.

"Don't bullshit me. I know this floor better than you."

Bunshaft's fake smile disappeared, then came back stronger. "Come on, Ellis. It's just for a couple hours. Didn't want you to get bored and go home."

Arguing would be pointless. Shafer followed Bunshaft into the conference room, which was as studiously neutral as he remembered. He settled himself on the couch, pretending not to hear the click of the lock as Bunshaft left. A laptop and phone on the table, twin honeypots. Shafer wished he could warn Wells and Duto. But every call and every keystroke from these rooms was monitored in real time. He dialed his wife instead.

"Ellis."

"Hi, babe." In almost forty years of marriage, he had never called her that. He knew she'd understand.

"How was your day?" She coughed, trying to force the word out. *"Babe."*

"Not bad. I'm stuck in a meeting. John might come by looking for me. If he does, just tell him you don't know when I'll be back." The listeners could guess what he was doing, but he'd gotten the message out with enough deniability not to worsen his position, whatever his position was.

"Will do. Love you, Ellis. Hope you get home soon."

"Me, too. I love you, babe."

"Don't push it."

He watched the seconds slip into minutes and then hours. He closed his eyes, tried to meditate. But he'd never been much for meditation. He kept trying to calculate how many hours he had left. Life expectancy for a man his age couldn't be more than twenty years. Twenty years, seventy-three hundred days, one hundred seventy-five thousand hours. Give or take. Sounded like a lot, but Shafer knew better. Like sands through the hourglass, et cetera, et cetera. Cheery thoughts. Maybe he ought to concentrate on the practical. He wondered if they'd keep him overnight. He'd sleep on the floor. His back couldn't tolerate the couch.

Around eleven, the lock clicked open and Bunshaft walked into the room, followed by a tall man with a high-and-tight haircut, broad shoulders, and a perfectly round paunch. Like he'd swallowed a bowling ball. This was Max Carcetti, Hebley's chief of staff. Hebley had been Carcetti's patron in the Marines. They'd risen together until Hebley had four stars on his collar and Carcetti three of his own. Now Carcetti was the aide Hebley trusted most, the one who made problems disappear. Almost everyone at the top had someone like Carcetti. Except for guys like Duto, who preferred to play the role themselves.

Shafer stood. "General."

Carcetti crossed the room in two big steps, put out a hand, crushed his bones in a Marine grip. "Ellis Shafer. Myth and legend. Sorry to meet you under these circumstances."

If Carcetti was being polite, Shafer was in even more trouble than he thought. Carcetti and Bunshaft sat side by side across the table from Shafer. "Tell me what you told him," Carcetti said. "Not the highlights. The whole thing."

Shafer repeated the story that had led him and Wells to Glenn Mason.

"Ever met Mason?" Carcetti said when Shafer was done.

"No."

"What about Veder?"

Shafer tried to remember. "Not that I recall."

"Because, I have to say, the story is compelling. There's only one problem."

"Sir?" Shafer wasn't in the habit of calling anyone *sir*, but the expression on Carcetti's face suggested he ought to make the effort.

"Glenn Mason is dead. He's been dead more than three years."

13

ISTANBUL

To the reporters of AL JAZEERA and the others, the americans who died in the bombing in Manila are crusader spies. We have punished them for their crimes against the soldiers of ALLAH and the Prophet Muhammad, Peace Be Upon Him. the true name of "william hansborough" is james Nicholas veder. he is Station chief of the Philippines for the central intelligence agency. The other two were his puppet-guards. All suffered the wrath of the righteous.

Do not let this knowledge go silent. Tell the people all over, the believers and the unbelievers also. The court of the Islamic Army of Mecca and Medina has sentenced to death the spies of the c.i.a. Each and every one. Under Sharia. With the approval of all those who bow their heads before ALLAH. Death for the cruel attacks in Afghanistan and Iraq. For their Cowardly drone bombings. There is no escape. THERE IS NO GOD BUT ALLAH AND MUHAMMAD IS HIS PROPHET

Abu Bakr and the true Sunni Warriors of
THE ISLAMIC ARMY OF MECCA AND MEDINA

Salome sat in the back of a Nissan sedan, reading the email on a two-year-old Dell laptop. She'd written it the afternoon before, when Duke called to confirm that the job was done. His men had stowed their motorcycles in an old cargo van, ditched the van in a long-term lot near the international airport in Manila. They would leave the Philippines one by one, by sea and air, for Hong Kong and Bangkok and Dubai. As always, time and planning were the best defense against surveillance. CIA, NSA, and the Philippine National Police would watch the airport and the international ferries. But hundreds of thousands of men entered and left the Philippines each week. Without a tip, the pool of possible suspects was too large to track.

A day had passed since the attack. It was nearly noon in Manila, morning in Istanbul, the sun still hidden behind the city's eastern hills. Salome was about to send her email to reporters around the world. She would cc a copy to Veder's CIA account, too, to be sure that the agency saw it immediately. She had intentionally written the email to appear over-the-top. Its real audience was the CIA, not the media. And the CIA already knew that the claim of responsibility was fake, that the Army of Mecca and Medina didn't exist. After all, Reza had told Brian Taylor that Iran planned to invent a Sunni terrorist group to take credit for the assassination.

The Nissan stopped at a light on Tarlabaşı, a wide, grimy avenue that traced a scar through central Istanbul. Salome handed the Dell across the backseat to Vassily, a twenty-two-year-old Bulgarian who was her best hacker. Vassily had a rash of pimples on his chin and the pale doughy skin

222 | ALEX BERENSON

of a man who spent his life in basement rooms lit only by computer screens. He could easily be a virgin. He was at least half in love with Salome. She wondered if she should sleep with him, guarantee his loyalty forever. But the experience would be too much for him. He'd wind up obsessed. Anyway, he was already loyal. Let him enjoy his suffering. In her experience, Eastern European men were either sadists or masochists, and Vassily was no sadist.

"Send it."

Vassily clicked open a map studded with green and yellow icons. "There's an unlocked Wi-Fi three hundred meters down."

The Nissan's driver raised his eyes to her to show her he'd heard. He was a tall, slim man in his late thirties. He almost always wore a suit and almost never spoke. He was a former soldier who had nearly died in a motorcycle crash a decade before. The accident tore most of the skin from his legs, crushed his nose and chin. Then he had fallen into the trembling hands of an alcoholic surgeon whose repair efforts nearly killed him. Ultimately, another set of doctors repaired much of the damage, though up close the soldier's cheeks and nose glowed with an unnatural shine.

He and Salome had lived two houses apart growing up. He was two years older than she, and they'd had their share of teenage fumblings. Nothing serious, but enough to give them reason to keep in touch, see each other on those rare occasions when both were home. In another life, she might have married him. After his accident, she visited him in the hospital a dozen times. She asked him once how he'd managed the pain. His eyes went flat. *Every day I prayed for the world to end*, he said. *Not just to die, for the whole world to end.*

I understand, she said. And she did. As a child, a teenager, she'd thought of herself as happy. But at twenty-two, she'd plunged into a depression so black that she couldn't leave her room, couldn't eat. Couldn't even sleep. She lay on her floor, eyes open, waiting to die, *hoping* to die, knowing she wouldn't. Worst of all, she had no idea what had triggered her pain. She was getting ready for her first year of law school. She had plenty of friends. No one in her family had died. She just . . . disappeared.

After nearly a month, her roommate insisted on taking her to a local infirmary. She was so terrified of being locked up that somehow she faked her way through a ten-minute interview with the doctor on duty. She walked out with an appointment with a psychiatrist and a prescription for Prozac. *This may take a few weeks to work*, he said.

But he was wrong. She could have been an advertisement for Eli Lilly. After a week, the clouds over the world had turned from black to gray. She could pretend to be human again. After a second week, she wasn't pretending. Yet the experience profoundly unsettled her. She had lost her balance so easily, fallen so far so fast, that she could no longer trust herself, much less the rest of the world.

She couldn't directly connect that episode to the choices she'd made in the years that followed, much less to the mission she'd chosen for herself. Yet she knew the link was real.

She wasn't sure how much her driver knew about that lost month. He'd been serving at the time, and a few months later he'd crashed his bike. By the time the reconstructions were done, so was his military career. He disappeared to Africa, worked as a soldier of fortune and bodyguard. When she decided to devote her existence to this mission, she knew she would need one person she could trust absolutely. The list was short. He was at the top.

He agreed without hesitation. He had served as her driver and bodyguard ever since. He kept an eye on Vassily and the other bright boys when she couldn't. But he wasn't exactly her lieutenant. He'd never volunteered an opinion on what they were doing, whether it was moral, whether it even made sense. And she'd never asked.

Vassily ran a finger across the Dell's battered black case, as close as he came to a sensual gesture. "After we send the email, you destroy this. Safest way, use it once and never again. Throw it in the Bosphorus, set it on fire, I don't care. I have a hundred more."

"I'm aware. You buy them with my money."

Vassily picked up used laptops at flea markets in Belgrade and Sofia, wiped their hard drives, installed Linux or pirated copies of Windows as operating systems. Intel, AMD, and the other chip makers all embedded unique serial numbers in each processor they created, the computer equivalent of a vehicle identification number. But buying used laptops for cash broke the chain of custody and stopped everyone, including the NSA, from linking the chip serial numbers to the new owner.

Along with new operating systems, Vassily installed special antisurveillance software to block bugs, location finders, or keystroke capture programs. His programs were far more aggressive than the commercial antispyware that companies like Norton sold. They would wipe the entire hard drive if they discovered any suspicious program.

Salome's email would be double-bagged, in hacker jargon, routed through an anonymizing server in Denmark, then a second in Iceland. Vassily had assured Salome that the NSA would need weeks to trace it to Istanbul, much less this wireless connection, which was an unlocked router that couldn't be connected to them anyway. Even so, he had insisted that they use the laptop only once. *For a message this important, it's the only safe way. They track everything on the Internet. And it's like a thread—once they start to pull it, no one can stop them. They make connections between an email you sent today, a phone call you made two years ago, a text message I sent from another phone that wasn't even to you. You know the difference between God and the NSA?*

The NSA doesn't wish it was God.

"The router. Pull over." The Nissan stopped. "No surveillance, clear signal. At your word."

"Send it."

Vassily typed, lifted his hands from the keyboard with a flourish. "All systems go, as the Americans say." In the rearview mirror, the driver caught Salome's eye: *Must he prattle so?*

The sedan rolled on. Salome stowed the laptop on the floor, rested a hand on Vassily's arm. He sighed like a dog whose master had just scratched his belly. "You've done well. We'll drop you at the Galata." The sigh turned to a grunt, but he didn't argue.

Ten minutes later, the Nissan pulled over. "Remember what I said about this." He tapped the laptop. His hand was the color of an egg-white omelet and not much firmer.

"Go," Salome said.

The Galata Bridge was a wide, low span that crossed the eastern edge of the Golden Horn, a narrow channel that stretched west off the Bosphorus. To the north, a hilly neighborhood called Karaköy offered some of Istanbul's best views. The plaza at the bridge's southern end functioned as Istanbul's Times Square, a transportation hub for locals and tourists alike. The bridge itself provided a close-up look at the never-ending parade of freighters, ferries, yachts, and cruise ships that made the Bosphorus one of the world's most vital waterways.

On this morning, commuter traffic choked the Galata, though the sun had just appeared over the mosques and apartments on the eastern side of the Bosphorus. Winter clouds reflected the city's lights onto the strait's black waves, creasing it with streaks of orange and yellow. Finally, the Nissan crawled off the southern end of the bridge. It turned left onto a wide boulevard that circled the edge of the Eminönü peninsula, the end of Europe. The high walls of the Topkapi Palace loomed atop the hill above this road. For centuries, the Topkapi had been home to the sultans of the Ottoman Empire. Now it was a museum for tourists.

Salome looked at the high brick walls of the palace. She saw Langley, and Fort Meade, and all the other high-security campuses that had sprouted in the forests around

Washington. The Ottoman sultans had openly disdained their subjects. The DCI and the rest of America's modern princes claimed to serve the people outside their walls. Maybe they even believed their speeches. But they had more in common with the Ottomans than they knew. Walls offered security, but at a price. They blinded those inside to the world around them. Salome was rescuing the princes from their insularity, forcing them to recognize a threat they should have already seen. For this heroism they would call her a traitor, if she was fool enough to let them discover her.

The Nissan pulled over. Salome handed her driver the laptop. He would make sure it was clean of fingerprints and leave it in an alley to be scavenged and resold. Salome preferred anonymous disposal to destruction. In the unlikely event that the Americans could track it based on a single email, they would be chasing a false trail.

"One hour."

"One hour."

She walked to the terminals that served the Bosphorus commuter ferries. Every hour, dozens of ships docked around the bridge. Thousands of men and women were now hurrying through the plaza on their way to work. A brisk ten-minute walk brought her west of the bridge, to the terminal for the busiest ferry of all, a short route that ran almost straight across the Bosphorus. The man who called himself Reza waited near a ticket booth. He smoked a cigarette and wore a shapeless windbreaker with a nylon hood that shadowed his head. A baseball cap and heavy plastic glasses further hid his face.

As Salome approached, he took a final drag on his cigarette and tossed it to his left. Left signaled that he had not been followed and could call Brian Taylor. Salome gave no sign that she'd noticed him. She kept walking. She was looking for surveillance overt or covert, Turkish police or plainclothes officers, anything out of the ordinary in the morning scrum. She didn't expect anything. In the aftermath of Veder's killing, the CIA would be desperate to talk to Reza, but it had no way of finding him. Still, she'd decided to check the plaza herself. She had to meet Reza after the call anyway.

She took one more look. The plaza was the usual perfect mess of confusion, nothing more or less. She joined the crowd heading south, her wordless signal that she agreed he was clean. The moment was his.

Reza smoked one more cigarette. Then he pulled out a new, unused mobile phone that he'd bought for cash near the Grand Bazaar a couple weeks earlier. Nothing in the world was untraceable anymore, but Salome and Reza and Duke were trying. They knew NSA and CIA would try to pinpoint a call to Taylor's phone even before Taylor picked up. The Turks might even be helping, though the CIA wouldn't ask for local aid on a job this sensitive unless it saw no alternative.

Even NSA's newest software couldn't find a call from a prepaid handset instantaneously. In middle- and high-income countries, big telcos tolerated prepaids as a way to reach poorer customers. But they designed call-routing software to prioritize monthly subscribers. They were also very concerned with making sure that hackers didn't find ways to beat their tolling systems and get free airtime. What all this interference meant in practice was that the NSA needed at least ninety seconds to lock down new prepaid phones.

Reza hoped to finish his call by then. But even if he went long, NSA would have no way to pick him out from every other commuter holding a phone. Surveillance cameras had become all but inescapable in major cities. The key to beating them was not hiding from them but confounding them with crowds.

Reza murmured in Farsi, amping himself up, getting into character. *You warned this CIA officer. Told him an attack was coming. He didn't listen. The blood of these men in Manila, it's on his hands. Not yours.* He looked around for his Revolutionary Guard minders, the men who would torture him and his family in Tehran if they knew he was making this call. Did they exist? Of course they existed. If they didn't exist, he couldn't betray them. Were they in this plaza even now, watching him?

No. He was clear.

Taylor answered on two rings. "Yes?" In Farsi. "Reza? Is that you?"

"I warned you. And now it's happened."

"We didn't have enough specifics—"

"You blame *me* for this?"

"That's not what I meant—" Taylor sounded panicked.

Reza wondered how many people were listening from the American side. Ten? Twenty? Whispering in Taylor's ear, *Don't lose him*—

"Help us. Help us catch them."

"I don't even know why they chose Manila."

"Come in for a debrief, Reza. We can talk somewhere safe."

"How many times must I tell you? I am not your agent."

"I don't even know your real name, that's the problem—"

"Not a problem. My protection, my only protection."

Reza checked his watch. Sixty seconds already. He turned east, surfing along the commuters pushing south. Not too fast. He wanted the whole call to route through a single tower, give the Americans as few clues as possible.

"At least help me understand what happened. We don't *get* this."

"I don't, either." Reza couldn't hide his frustration. He was a proud Rev Guard officer. Admitting ignorance to an American embarrassed him. "What's happening in Tehran, who's making these choices, I don't know. I'm not at that level. They give me orders, I follow. Ask your other sources." *Like you have any.*

"We're trying. What about tactically, are you planning more attacks?"

"I haven't been told."

"I know you don't care about money—"

"If you know I don't care about money, why do you insult me by talking about it?"

Silence.

"Can we meet face-to-face—"

"Again?"

"Not a debrief. Just you and me."

"Lie."

"No. Your terms, you set the time and place. You're doing this for all the right reasons, Reza"—the words too obvious, his wheedling tone pathetic—"but it'll be helpful for us both."

"I'll consider it. I have something to tell you anyway."

Reza hung up, looked at his watch. One hundred fifty-six seconds. Too long. The phone buzzed in his hand. Taylor, calling back like a woman. He powered down the phone, joined the commuters headed up into Sultanahmet.

The street was just wide enough for a line of parked cars and a single traffic lane. On both sides were tiny stores stuffed with sewing machines and bolts of cloth. Twenty years of growth had given Istanbul massive suburban-style malls on its edges and ultra-luxury stores in the ritzy neighborhoods northeast of Karaköy. But in the Middle East tradition, the city still had clusters of tiny specialty shops that all seemed to offer identical products at identical prices. A woman peered in the window of a store that hadn't yet opened for the day. Salome. She turned and followed as he walked past. This street had no cameras. They'd checked. He extracted the SIM card from his phone, crushed it in the gutter. The phone itself was useless now, and untraceable. He'd wipe it down and dump it in a trash can.

"So?"

Reza told her.

"Did he believe you?"

"I think so." He tapped the pockets of his windbreaker until he found his cigarettes. He held the pack to her. Pro forma. He'd never seen her smoke. But today she took one. She must be pleased. He lit hers, then his.

"Good. Now we make him suffer," she said. She dragged deep, blew a perfect smoke ring into the gray morning air. She wasn't short on tricks. They both watched in silence until it dissolved away. "We make him wait."

his pension for almost four years. Thing's building up in an HSBC account at the rate of eight hundred forty American dollars every two weeks. Okay, fine, I know what Ellis *Shafer* will say if I tell him that, he'll say that's just what Mason would do if he's gone undercover to work for the Revolutionary Guard. Of course, dumb Marine like me, I would think that if Mason was working against the United States, he'd be sure to draw that money down so it wouldn't be obvious, in case anyone ever went looking for him. But fine, I'm trying to think like Ellis *Shafer* would—"

Each time, *Shayy-fur*, Carcetti drawing out Shafer's name, ridiculing it. Mockery was among the oldest interrogation tricks around, and the most effective.

"So I tell Jess, check Glenn's passport, and wouldn't you know, that hasn't been used in close to four years, not since he entered Bangkok on a tourist visa. Not a peep. And so I myself call our COS in Bangkok this afternoon. He's none too happy to hear from me, what with the time difference, but he picks up like a good soldier. I ask him if come the morning he won't try to help us find Mr. Mason. Turns out he doesn't have to. Because before he does, he checks the embassy's records for reports of Americans who have died in Thailand in the last five years. In those files is the sad tale of an American citizen named Glenn Mason, who drowned in a boat accident off the coast of Phuket. Three weeks after his arrival in Thailand. Mr. Mason was unmarried and without siblings or parents—in fact, without anyone who merited notification. So he was cremated and presumably turned into landfill, or whatever the Thais do with the ashes of Americans that no one wants—"

Shafer had to say *something*, if only to stop the flood from Carcetti. "When the report came in, nobody at the embassy realized that he was a former case officer?"

"Why would they, Ellis?" This question delivered reasonably enough. Shafer had no answer. American men died regularly in Thailand. Of alcohol poisoning, heroin overdoses, and, yes, drownings. Mason's name wouldn't have stood out to the overworked State Department officer who happened to see it.

"So he drowned. And I think to myself, what might Ellis *Shafer* say to this sad story? He might argue that Mr. Mason had gone to Thailand to assume a new identity for his work as a double agent for the Islamic Republic of Iran. Never mind the incredible implausibility that Iran would recruit him in the first place. Or that he would agree to such recruitment. This afternoon, yours truly asked NSA for a priority search, has anyone whose photo matches Mr. Mason traveled under *any* name with *any* nation's passport in the last four years? Would you like to guess what the search found, Ellis?"

"You're grinning like a monkey that hijacked a Chiquita truck, so I'm going to say nothing."

"Correct. By the way, NSA checked to see if his email accounts had been active since the accident, cell phone, et cetera. Nothing."

Carcetti spread his arms, turned up his hands like a scale. "The evidence Glenn Mason is dead." He lowered his right hand to just above the table. "The evidence he's alive at all, much less running a worldwide plot on behalf of Quds Force or anyone else in the Rev Guard." He lifted his left hand over his head. "Since even you would have to agree he couldn't do that without leaving some electronic trace."

Earlier in his career, Shafer would have argued. Age had not exactly brought him wisdom, but it had slowed him down. On the one hand, he could take his spanking like a good boy and move on. On the other, having his objections noted for the record might help him later. He decided on the second course. Carefully. Carcetti looked to be about a half inch from sending him home for an internal review that would last long enough to tip Shafer into retirement.

"Jess, did you call anybody who worked with Mason to find out for yourself if he'd fought with James Veder over a woman in Lima? Did you talk to Wells?"

"I—"

"He didn't have to do any of that," Carcetti said. "Unless Glenn Mason can kill from the afterlife."

"Do you think I came up with Mason on my own? Or was I duped? Me, Duto, and Wells, why would we stick ourselves in this briar patch?"

"If I had to guess, I'd guess that you are desperately trying to prove yourself relevant. So you took a half-assed theory and ran with it."

"Anyone from the embassy see Glenn Mason's body before it was cremated?"

"Why would they?"

"And the station hasn't gotten the original police report yet."

"So the Thai police are in on the conspiracy, too?"

Faking a death for an offshore accident wouldn't require

anything like a conspiracy. Rent a small boat, fail to return it, let it be found empty a day or two later. Arranging for a body would be the only tricky part, the only part that might require the cooperation of a helpful police officer. Or maybe not. Neither salt water nor the creatures of the sea were kind to human flesh. After a few days in the ocean, corpses were indistinguishable.

But Carcetti had made up his mind. He'd made up his mind even before he told Bunshaft to check the records. He or his bosses had decided that Glenn Mason could not be working for Iran, that the idea was idiotic. His certainty told Shafer something else—that the seventh floor had locked on to the theory that Iran was responsible for Veder's killing. Believing Mason might be involved was easier if there was a possibility that someone other than the Revolutionary Guard had hired him.

"You aren't interested in talking to John. Vinny. Even Montoya."

"I am interested in making this whole sorry episode disappear so we can figure out who shot Veder and what to do about it."

Shafer decided to make one last play. He knew he'd fail, but maybe he could provoke Carcetti into telling him more about the Rev Guard tipster.

"Our source for these plots."

"Yes."

"I've seen some cables—"

"We're going to want to tighten that list." Carcetti wasn't smiling.

"My understanding, this is humint, one source, same guy who gave us the Israeli embassy bombings a few months ago. And my understanding, he's new. Very new."

Carcetti looked at his watch. "Much as I love chatting with you, Ellis, I have to be up in five hours. The director doesn't like it if I'm late for our morning run. So, the point, please—"

"Guy comes out of nowhere. Suddenly he's giving us grade-A intel on the Guard. Better than we've ever had. How much do we know about him? Do we even know his real name?"

Carcetti didn't answer, and Shafer knew he'd scored.

"We know everything he's told us has checked out."

"Doesn't that seem awfully convenient?"

"I'm just a big dumb Marine, Ellis. But I have a different word for that kind of intel. I call it actionable. I call it a godsend."

"What if he's fake?"

"You think you're the first person with that theory? What's the logic, that the Iranians are intentionally tipping their own attacks? That some other service is running a false flag, killed Veder and bombed those embassies to get us to attack Iran? All right, fine. Tell me who. Make it convincing, I'll drive you to Hebley's house myself."

For the first time since Bunshaft had brought him to this room, Shafer felt something like hope. Carcetti meant to be sarcastic, but his words betrayed a faint uncertainty. He might listen to an alternate theory. Too bad Shafer didn't have one. "If I can prove that Mason is still alive—"

"No one up here is interested in letting you freelance.

We can't control your buddy John, but you still work for us."

A nicely tricky formulation. Shafer wondered if Carcetti was subtler than he looked. Maybe he was inviting Shafer and Wells to keep investigating, just in case. Or maybe he was sure Shafer and Wells were wrong but didn't mind watching them put their necks in the guillotine. Either way, he'd offered Shafer the tiniest of openings.

Carcetti pushed back from the table. "Do we understand each other?"

"Yes, sir."

"Good. Know if I ever bring you up here again, your resignation letter will be waiting."

"Great to meet you, too, General."

15

Julia Espada lived in a one-story ranch east of downtown Houston's skyscrapers, an iffy neighborhood. A battered swing set occupied most of her narrow front yard, under a big porch light for security.

Avis had stuck Wells with a neon green Jeep Patriot, gaudy and underpowered. The worst possible car for a spy, or anyone else. He eased it into her driveway behind a decade-old Explorer. Inside the house, a dog yammered. A big dog. Wells wondered if he should wait for morning. She hadn't answered his calls. She was divorced, looking after two kids. She might not take kindly to an intrusion at this hour. But Shafer was in a mess at Langley, and the time they had wasted over the weekend had probably gotten James Veder killed. Wells stepped out of his car. "Hello!"

A lamp clicked in the living room. Wells saw a Rottweiler standing on a couch, scraping at the window. A Lab would have been too easy.

The door opened a notch. "What do you want?" Shouting over Rottie the Rott. Not exactly *How are you this evening?* but better than *Get off my property* or *I have a gun.*

"My name's John. Here about Glenn Mason."

To his surprise, she didn't say *Glenn who?* or stall for time. She said something in Spanish to the dog. He whimpered and sat. The door opened. "Come."

Inside, Wells found sagging furniture and a thready blue rug with a pattern too faded to make out. He perched awkwardly on a recliner as she sat on a couch. The dog circled the coffee table, allowing Wells to see that he was unneutered. Very unneutered. Finally, he took his place at Julia's feet. He looked up balefully at Wells, awaiting orders.

"This is Pedro."

"Bet he makes the other dogs in the neighborhood jealous."

She laughed like a mountain stream high with snowmelt. Her hands were thick and tired and her hair was short, more gray than black. But when she laughed, Wells could imagine men fighting over her. "You came all the way from Langley to see me in the middle of the night."

"I tried to call."

"Lots of break-ins in this neighborhood. You're lucky my children are with their father this week or I might have let Pedro take a closer look at you."

The Rottweiler wagged his stumpy tail in a way that managed to menace. "I don't exactly work for Langley." Wells explained who he was, what he wanted.

"You can't make me talk, then."

"Older I get, the more I realize I can't make anyone do anything."

"You only help people do what they wanted to already."

"That's me. Next best thing to a shrink. You don't seem surprised to see me."

She leaned back, settled herself against the couch. Like he really was a psychiatrist and she had a dream to tell. Wells had caught a break, a witness who wanted to talk.

"I could tell you all about myself, how I don't work for the AP anymore, I was laid off two years ago, now I translate for legal aid groups, public defenders. But you're not here for that."

She pointed to a framed photo: her, two kids, and a middle-aged white man with the start of a potbelly. "My ex. I met him in Lima. He was a project manager for Habitat for Humanity down there. Good man. Boring. I'll let you in on a secret, Mr. I Don't Exactly Work for Langley. I married him for the *permiso de residencia*, the green card. Don't tell INS." Her voice had an easy Spanish lilt. She turned out the lamp, left the room in what passed for dark in central Houston.

Wells went with the vibe, closed his eyes. "Did he know?"

"A very good question. Either way, he deserved better. But I wanted the card, and I wanted boring after James and Glenn. Such strange men. Especially Glenn. Sometimes when we were home, hours went by without him speaking. Latin men, they talk like women, more. I liked the silence."

"Until it got strange."

"Yes. And he made me, frightened isn't the word, but he was dark. The stray dogs in Lima live in the hills, come down to scavenge after dark. One night we were on the highway and one came across, a big one with a limp. It turned, looked right at us. Glenn didn't slow down until I screamed. He pretended he hadn't seen, but I knew he had. He wanted to hit it. Feel the bones crack against the bumper. That was the beginning of the end for us, I think." She went silent. Wells waited. "Maybe I'm making him sound worse than he was. He loved me, I think, as much as he could. He wanted to marry me. I didn't know how to break it off—"

"Did you know he worked for the agency?"

"Of course I knew. By the third time you go to the embassy, it's obvious who is and who isn't. He didn't really hide it. Most of them don't."

"That didn't bother you? Peru, the late nineties—"

"I didn't love Shining Path, either. So, no, that didn't bother me. But when the end came, I should have known better, told him it's over. And I probably would have, but James got there first, and he was a—"

She sighed, a lover's light sigh.

"Must have been good, you remember him that way after all these years."

"I know it's foolish, but yes. He had the confidence. And with reason. *Cojones* like Pedro." She laughed. "All the tricks, too. I can't explain, when I met him I couldn't stand him, I knew what he was, Mr. James Veder, CIA from Colombia, a real dirty war going on up there. But he had something."

"Charisma."

"I knew I was going to be his conquest of the month. I didn't care."

"Until Glenn walked in on you."

The light snapped on. Wells opened his eyes to see her sitting up. Relaxed no more.

"Why do you come here if you know the whole story?"

"I don't."

"James came to see me at Glenn's. The first time for us there. Glenn was supposed to be away overnight. Something happened, he flew back. Me and James, we didn't even have time to cover ourselves when he walked in—"

"That bad."

"He threatened to kill us. Of course I wanted to live, but part of me understood. How he must have felt. But he didn't do anything. The next day was September eleventh, and that made it worse. I knew I'd never talk to him again, we would be stuck in—you know, like a fly in the yellow stone—"

"Amber."

"*Sí*. Set in amber."

"And did you? Speak to him?"

"Never. Neither him nor James. James went back to Colombia in October. I don't know when Glenn left, but a while later someone told me he was gone. I wish I could have said good-bye."

"You never spoke to Mason again." Wells couldn't hide his disappointment. She'd been their best chance.

"Yes and no." She paused. "This might sound odd.

About three months ago, someone called me, here. Maybe eight-thirty in the morning, the bus just come for my kids. I hear breathing, music in the background. No words. I say *Hola. Who's there?* No answer. I hang up. No caller ID, it was the landline, so I star-sixty-nine it, but it's a weird number. Okay, no problem. A minute later, it rings again. This time the music is louder. That song by Phil Collins, the one from *Miami Vice*—"

"'In the Air Tonight'?"

"*Sí.* Glenn loved the show. The song also. The DVD for it just came out back when I knew him and he was so excited. He had someone buy it, send it to him."

Growing up in western Montana, four hundred miles from the nearest major city, Wells hadn't paid much attention to pop culture. And the culture itself was different then. Less enveloping, less self-aware. People could watch television shows without having a *position* on them, reading plot summaries of every episode. Still, *Miami Vice* was burned into his memory. Every teenage boy in America wanted to be Don Johnson or Philip Michael Thomas back in 1984. They were that cool. Mason must have felt the same.

Hard to believe Crockett and Tubbs would be old enough to collect Social Security now.

"So when you heard the song—"

"I wanted to hang up, but I didn't. I must have been figuring it out; after a few seconds something clicked in my mind. I knew. Not just the song, but the way he was so silent, that was just like him. I said, *Glenn, is that you? I'm sorry we never talked. I should have called you.* He didn't say

anything, but that made me even more sure, because anybody else would have hung up, I mean, I wasn't shouting
or anything, if this was a, a *broma*—"

"A prank—"

"Yes, a prank, then I wasn't doing what he wanted. I
said, *I'm glad to talk about it if you want.* He hung up. I
don't know what he wanted me to say, but he never called
back."

"Three months ago, this was."

"About then. I don't have the exact date."

"Did you write down the number you star-sixty-nined?"
Another blast from the past.

"I did, but I don't know where I put it. I must have lost
it. But it started with a one and then six-six. I remember I
Googled it. The country code for Thailand. Does that make
sense?"

"Maybe." Not even twenty-four hours had passed since
Duto and Shafer fingered Mason. Wells knew the outlines
of Mason's career but not the details. Shafer might have
found more since Wells had left for Houston, but Shafer
wasn't answering his phone. And his wife had left a five-
word message on Wells's voice mail: *Ellis is in trouble
upstairs.*

"You never talked to Veder again, either."

"No. He was embarrassed. He liked the game, but he
didn't want to get caught. I think he regretted going after
another officer's girlfriend. Is he in Thailand?"

"He was chief of station in the Philippines until about
twenty-four hours ago. Someone blew up his car. Killed
him, two guards."

Her mouth opened in a silent *O*. She walked out of the room. Pedro followed her to the doorway and blocked it, daring Wells to follow. Wells didn't move, and after five minutes Julia came back.

"You think Glenn did this."

"What do *you* think? It was a long time ago, what happened. A long time for a grudge."

She twisted her hands.

"I can imagine it. Even the way he made love."

"He was angry—"

"Not angry. I don't think you can understand unless you're a woman, but sometimes I felt he wasn't touching me at all. That I wasn't a person, just a hole he was trying to rip wider. I mean, every man has some of that in him, but he had a lot."

Wells tried not to wonder what his exes would say about him. He scribbled his number and email on a paper from the reporter's notebook he carried.

"You think of anything else, he calls you—"

She nodded.

"Anytime."

"Be careful, Mr. Wells. I think he called because he wanted me to know that whatever was in him back then has come out."

Wells headed north on 45. He wanted to be on the first plane to Los Angeles in the morning. Then Bangkok. He wasn't sure how he would narrow down his search once he arrived in Thailand, but maybe Shafer would have ideas.

As much as he hated the Jeep, driving in Texas was a joy. Average left-lane speed was low eighties, and the cops just watched. The more gasoline burned, the better. Wells watched enviously as a bright yellow motorcycle blew by like the Patriot wasn't even moving. After a couple minutes, his backup burner phone buzzed. Only Shafer had the number. "Ellis."

"You found her?"

"She said he called three months ago. From Bangkok. Where I'm going."

Wells was modestly surprised that the answer elicited a stream of low-grade profanity. "What's wrong with Bangkok?"

"These pricks up here, they think he's dead."

A long honk alerted Wells to the fact that he was drifting between lanes. The Patriot definitely did not drive itself. "Hold on. One minute." He found an exit, pulled into an off-brand gas station with big signs demanding "Pay INSIDE Only: Cash AND Credit." Despite its arc lamps and surveillance cams, the place looked as though it got robbed at least once a month.

"Tell me."

Shafer explained what Carcetti had told him.

"He's stayed off the grid for four years?" After what Julia had told him, Wells had no doubt Mason was alive. Beating the NSA that long was impressive. Maybe he was running the operation through a courier, bin Laden–style. But Wells thought Mason would have wanted to get his revenge against Veder firsthand.

"Not just off the grid. They ran a face-recog search and

it came up blank. So he hasn't traveled, either, unless he's so connected that someone's getting him around passport control."

"No." Sovereign countries watched their borders. The President didn't need a passport. Everybody else followed the rules. Diplomats and celebrities might be taken through secret lines so no one bothered them at Heathrow or JFK, but they still got stamped and photographed.

"I don't get it, either, but they're convinced back here. They don't want to hear about Mason at all. Plus the momentum to blame Iran is building. It might not matter, but will this woman testify that she talked to him?"

"She didn't exactly *talk* to him," Wells explained.

"She knew it was him because she heard the *Miami Vice* theme song?"

Wells riffed off the drum solo that was the song's signature.

"No you don't fool me, the hurt doesn't show, but the pain still grows—"

"None other. I can actually see them flashing across Biscayne Bay in a speedboat. Pastel jackets. Three-day beards."

"Tell me you're joking, John."

"Nope."

"Then I'm going to keep this little tidbit to myself, so the new director doesn't laugh me all the way into retirement. But at least it fits with what Carcetti told me about the drowning. For whatever reason, Mason based himself in Thailand. Find a bar in Phuket with a *Miami Vice* fetish."

"Can you check her phone records? NSA's got to have

that call somewhere. At least the metadata." Meaning the incoming number, if not the call itself.

"May take a couple days. If I haven't made it clear already, the ice up here is about a half-inch thick. Ever think you'd miss Vinny, John?"

Wells hung up.

Insult to injury, the hotels near the airport were sold out. Wells backtracked halfway to downtown before he found an empty room. Flight schedules showed the shortest route to Phuket was almost thirty hours. If the hunch was wrong, he'd lose another thirty getting back.

But Phuket was their only lead. So Wells booked the ticket: Korean Air, Houston-L.A.-Seoul. Then a small break, straight to Phuket without a stop in Bangkok. It was three a.m. when he closed his eyes, a wake-up call not even four hours away.

He thought of Anne. At this point, he wasn't sure how many days were left in her countdown. Twenty-four? Whatever the answer, his uncertainty was not promising. Was she sleeping now in their bed, Tonka beside her, the two of them snoring? Anne didn't believe him when he told her she snored. But she did, especially after a long day at work. Or maybe she was awake, staring at the ceiling, wondering what Wells would do.

No. He'd vote for sleep. She had written him off already. She'd given him the thirty days to come to terms with the truth. But he wasn't ready for the truth yet. Maybe he'd walk away. Maybe this would be his last ride before he sailed off with Crockett and Tubbs into the sunset . . . His consciousness was dissolving sweet as sugar in water . . . an ageless retirement . . .

Ageless?

Wells sat up. Reached for his phone. Changed his mind, decided to let Shafer sleep. Then changed it again. Shafer had woken him enough times. He was almost disappointed when Shafer picked up on the second ring.

"Better be important."

"I wake you?"

"Dummy. My wife."

"Sorry. I know why the NSA recognition software can't find him. And why he went to Thailand."

"Do tell."

"Plastic surgery."

Facial-recognition software didn't exactly *look* at faces, as a person would. It compared the dimensions of various facial features that conventional disguise could not change. Those included the eye sockets, the jawline, the distance between the bottom of the nose and the upper lip. At any time, NSA looked for a few hundred people around the world, and pulled down tens of billions of digital images each day. Not just from obvious places like cameras on federal buildings and airport immigration control. From pictures uploaded to Facebook, Instagram, Flickr, and other photo-sharing sites. Feeds from satellites and drones.

The matching required massive processing power. The images came in every conceivable size, shape, and resolution. Some included a single face, others had dozens or hundreds. Some shots were head-on, others angled. As a first step, the agency's software digitally rewrote them to approximate a standard passport photo, the base-case image. The process was known as rendering, but many photos couldn't be rendered. Their resolution was too poor, or they didn't contain anything that the software recognized as a face. Those were thrown into the digital equivalent of cold storage, though no photo was discarded for at least six months.

After the rendering process was complete, another software program examined the images to determine the dimensions of the "unique signifiers"—the facial features that determined identity. It matched those against the targets in its database. Billions of images, dozens of parameters, and hundreds of targets translated into trillions of comparisons a day. Adding to the complexity of the problem, the matching software needed to account for the errors that rendering inevitably introduced. Comparing two original passport photos was easy enough. Those were taken in standard sizes everywhere in the world, precisely to make identifications easy. Matching a man wearing a hat in a crowd in Times Square to a cell-phone shot taken covertly at a madrassa was far harder. But the software got more sophisticated every year.

If enough variables matched, the software alerted a human analyst. It sent him the surveillance images, the original image or images of the suspect, and the rendered standardized versions. The analyst looked over the photos himself to decide if the software had found a true match.

Most of the time, it hadn't. And because the software compared so many images, NSA had to calibrate the parameters for a match carefully. Allowing too wide a margin of error would waste analysts' time. Setting it too tight might miss a match.

After a back-and-forth that reached the agency's highest levels, NSA kept the criteria strict. The agency considered the possibility that a high-level terrorist might have plastic surgery to remake his face but dismissed it as impractical. An operation would require tens of thousands of dollars and weeks of recovery time. In the four-thousand-mile hot belt that stretched from Algeria to Pakistan, only a handful of hospitals and surgeons had the skills to handle such a makeover, mainly in Saudi Arabia and Dubai. The *mukhabarat* in those countries had already told those doctors that if anyone . . . problematic . . . appeared at their clinics they should inform the authorities. Otherwise they would risk being considered supporters of terrorism, with tragic consequences. The warnings seemed to settle the issue.

No one had considered that a terrorist might have surgery *before* he was a target, to give himself a new identity in this age of surveillance.

"Plastic surgery," Shafer said now. "Like that movie with Travolta and Nicolas Cage."

"If he had his cheeks and eyes and nose and chin done—"

"It would hurt. Cutting open his cheekbones and all

the rest. And he'd look weird. Like one of those actresses who seems younger at fifty than thirty."

"But it would work."

"I'll talk to people who know how the algorithms work. But I suppose."

"For the right price, he could find a clinic that would do anything he wanted—"

"I get it."

"Being a jerk because you're sorry you didn't think of it." Wells hung up. He tried to sleep but couldn't. Instead, he spent the hours until morning trawling the Internet for Thai plastic-surgery clinics. He had close to a hundred names by the time he was finished, and no idea how he would convince their doctors to talk. Still, at least he had a theory now, a lead to chase. He was smiling as he boarded his flight to Los Angeles.

16

The first cable reporting the attack arrived at 8:34 a.m. local time, as Brian Taylor sat down at his desk with his morning coffee. Within an hour, the calls from Langley started. Taylor spent the next twenty-one hours sitting beside Martha Hunt in the station's coms room, answering questions about Reza from the many desks that could stake a claim to handling the Iranian.

Near East had geographical standing, along with a list of twenty-two questions for Taylor to run by Reza about the structure of the Revolutionary Guard and the Quds Force. Counterterror had a say because of the Hezbollah connection, and fourteen questions of its own. Counterintelligence insisted that Taylor *at least get his real name*, those last six words spoken in incredulity. Like Taylor hadn't realized the man's identity might matter. Special Operations Group made a pitch to snatch Reza. *Guy popped up months ago. Time to resolve the uncertainty, debrief him whether he likes it or not.* Taylor and Hunt pointed out that kidnapping an agent wouldn't do much to help his loyalty, and for now that plan was off the table. *I'll talk to him,* Taylor said.

Too bad he couldn't. Not unless Reza called. Standard rules of tradecraft simply did not apply in this case. Reza was the worst agent Taylor had ever run, and the best. He wondered if Reza might be a Revolutionary Guard plant. After all, Reza had given up just enough details about the attack on Veder to prove his bona fides, but not enough to stop it. But why would Iran risk the anger of the United States by killing a station chief and then leaking its responsibility? An Iranian exile group was another possibility, but Taylor didn't believe any of them had the skill for an operation this large and complex.

So when the section chiefs asked Taylor what he thought, he told them the truth. He believed in Reza. Even the holes in his story could be viewed as proof of his authenticity. If the Revolutionary Guard were dangling Reza as a provocation, he would have handled himself more slickly, given Taylor enough details for the agency to confirm his identity. On the other hand, if Reza had chosen to betray a brutal regime . . . and was paranoid by nature and training . . . and was operating alone . . . he might well choose to keep his identity secret even from his case officer. For a while, anyway.

At 5:30 a.m. the morning after the attack, Hunt told the masters at Langley that she and Taylor needed to sleep. *We still have questions,* one of the suits said. Hunt nodded, turned off the screen.

"Let's go home."

"You're tops. I think I'm in love."

Hunt opened the soundproof steel door that separated the coms room from the rest of the station. "Take a nap, a shower. I'll see you at nine." Taylor staggered up, trailed after her.

In the hallway outside, she turned. "Do you believe in him, or have you just argued yourself into it?"

His head felt like it weighed five hundred pounds. "He's told us about two different attacks."

"You've met him once."

She was right. He didn't have enough evidence to judge Reza either way.

"You need to see him again."

"Think I don't know that?"

Two hours later, Reza called.

Over the next two days, Taylor reviewed surveillance footage from the dozens of cameras around the Galata Bridge plaza. But the cams had poor resolution in the weak morning light. Taylor spotted a man who might have been Reza, but the Iranian's disguise of hood, cap, and glasses was surprisingly effective. The photos were of little use.

Reza's parting words to Taylor, the promise of more information, sent the agency into a fever. SOG moved a six-man team from Warsaw to Istanbul, with orders to stay as long as necessary to get photos of Reza—though history suggested he might not pop up for months. The team was very experienced, all ex–Special Forces, two Deltas and four

Rangers. Unfortunately, their experience had come in Afghanistan, Iraq, and more recently Yemen. None spoke Turkish. In fact, only one had ever visited Istanbul. Taylor feared that they wanted an excuse to snatch Reza, though SOG had promised that they were tasked with surveillance only.

To balance out the paramilitaries, Near East desk moved two case officers from Langley. They spoke Turkish and had worked Istanbul before. With the entire Istanbul station, plus the two backups, plus the SOG team ready to scramble, Taylor figured they would get at least a clear photo of him next time he made contact.

He was wrong.

The call came on his landline around two a.m. on a Monday morning, eleven days after the hit on Veder. Taylor was stretched on his couch. He didn't remember falling asleep. He sat up, rubbed his eyes, wondered who at Langley had a question that couldn't wait.

"Good evening." In Farsi.

"Reza?"

"I'm outside."

They hadn't figured Reza would call on Taylor's Turkish landline. It was taped but not monitored in real time like the mobile. No doubt NSA would fix that oversight tomorrow. Meantime, Reza had again outsmarted Taylor and everyone else. Or else someone inside was helping him. Taylor knew he was getting paranoid, but the guy never made a mistake. Nobody was that lucky.

"How did you get my number?" Stalling. Taylor's phone sat on the kitchen counter. He needed to grab it, text his backup.

"Be downstairs in two minutes. No surveillance. Leave your phone. If you try to have me followed—"

"You'll disappear and I'll never see you again." When Langley reviewed the call, his petulance wouldn't earn high marks, but getting outplayed over and over was grating.

"Walk south on Türkgücü. And wear heavy shoes."

"How will I—"

"It'll be obvious. Ninety seconds left." *Click.*

Heavy shoes? Taylor shrugged on a pair of jeans and a sweatshirt. He couldn't find boots, pulled on a pair of loafers instead. He reached for his phone and then gave up. The SOG guys were at a hotel north of Taksim. Close but not close enough. No way could they scramble in time. And they couldn't trace him anyway. He couldn't risk carrying his phone. It was big enough to be obvious even in a routine pat-down. He would be meeting Reza naked. Again.

He was on the street in just over two minutes. He jogged south. The night was cold and slick. He skidded on a patch of wet sidewalk, windmilled his arms, barely staying upright. He wished he'd taken a few extra seconds to find the boots. Would Reza have ditched him?

Maybe.

Two blocks south he saw the motorcycle, a sleek black Suzuki. The rider wore a helmet with a mirrored faceplate. Taylor was sure it was Reza. He ought to have been nervous, considering that motorcyclists had killed Veder.

Instead he felt the same stupid excitement he'd had when he saw Daniel Craig at a restaurant in New York.

Reza flipped up his face shield. "You bring your phone, anything that can track us?"

"No."

"All right. I will trust you."

Words that made Taylor wish he'd texted his backups, brought the phone. "Of course."

A helmet lay under elastic netting on the seat behind Reza. He offered it to Taylor. "You know how?"

Taylor hadn't ridden a motorcycle since senior year at UMass, when a friend insisted on taking out his old Honda Nighthawk 750, skidded off a curve on Route 22, and cut himself in half on a speed limit sign. He searched for an objection that wouldn't sound too lame.

"My shoes."

That wasn't it. Soon as the words left his mouth, Taylor wanted to smack himself in the forehead with the heel of his hand *Three Stooges*–style. *Nyuk, nyuk, nyuk*. When he wrote up this meeting for Langley, he wouldn't be mentioning footwear of any kind.

Five minutes later, they were on the O-2 expressway, which functioned as the city's ring road. Reza rode expertly, ignoring the rain-slick pavement, cutting through the light late-night traffic like a garrote wire. Taylor wondered if they were headed for the Sultan Mehmet Bridge and the Asian side of the Bosphorus. But Reza turned off well before. He piloted the bike northwest, into the heavily wooded hills that began almost at the outer edge of the expressway. The forest preserves stretched to the Black Sea, an abrupt and surprising contrast to the city's concrete.

A few minutes later, Reza turned in to an unpaved parking area whose sign warned in Turkish and English: "No Overnight Parking." At the edge of the forest, he cut the engine. Taylor pulled off his helmet, stood beside the bike. The night was silent aside from the spatter of rain on the motorcycle's gas tank and a distant rush of expressway traffic. Taylor was suddenly very aware that he hadn't brought his Sig. Reza could have planned an ambush with his Rev Guard comrades. They'd shoot him, drag him into the trees. His body might not be found for weeks.

Yet he didn't feel frightened. He didn't completely trust Reza, but he didn't see the Iranian as violent. Sly, maddening, not a killer.

Reza nestled his helmet against his lap.

"Where'd you learn to ride like that?"

"I know Allah will protect me."

The answer surprised Taylor. They'd never talked about religion, but he had assumed Reza wasn't observant.

After a beat, Reza laughed.

"You should see your face. You think I believe that nonsense? Like some taxi driver with a sticker on his bumper? I have as much use for Allah as He has for me."

"You enjoy making a fool of me." Taylor needed to put himself in charge, but he had no idea how.

"You don't like me, Mr. Brian."

"I like you fine."

"Maybe you want to *hit* me."

"I need your name. You have no idea of the pressure I'm under, Reza." *No.* Spies begged case officers, not the other way around.

"This way is safer for both of us."

Taylor tried another tack. "Did you check your bank account?"

"I tell you this isn't about money for me."

"We can't trust you if you don't agree to a real debrief."

"It's your choice, whether you trust me. I don't trust *you.* Every time I look around, you have another leak. Manning, Snowden."

"That was the Army, NSA—"

"You think your place doesn't?"

"Are you saying what I think you're saying, Reza?"

"What I say is, tell everyone I will not come in, I will not tell you my name. The end. Twice now I have given you enough to leave me hanging from a rope. That's enough."

"Maybe you still work for the Guard, Reza. Maybe they tell you what to say."

"Insult me this way." Reza started the Suzuki's engine, rolled off.

Taylor ran after him, yelling *Stop, stop,* like a lovesick teenager who'd just been dumped. Reza turned onto the road, still helmetless. Taylor couldn't do anything except watch him go. He didn't even have a phone. His feet were raw in his loafers.

A few seconds later, the motorcycle turned around, puttered back into the lot. The most humiliating moment of

Taylor's career. Turned out this wouldn't be the meeting where he established the proper officer-agent relationship.

Reza cut the engine. "I should have left, but I must tell you two things."

"I'm listening." Taylor said the words with all the dignity he could muster. Which wasn't much.

"We've put a package on a ship to the United States."

"A bomb?"

"Not bomb. Radioactive material. It's a practice."

"A test run."

"Yes."

"For what?"

"Three weeks ago, I went over the mountains, back to Tehran. A friend of mine, good friend, engineer in the program, he says we've made enough uranium for ten bombs, and more every day."

If what Reza said was true, he had just delivered a world-changing piece of intelligence. *Iran planned to smuggle a nuclear weapon into the United States.*

"When you say 'uranium'—"

"I mean what the scientists call *H-E-U*." Reza sounded out each letter. "My friend told me that this has happened in only the last few months, they worked out some technical problem I couldn't understand, now they make two, three kilos of it every day. He said they have so much that they don't even keep it in the gas form anymore, they turn it into the metal. I don't know what that means."

"I don't, either." But Counterproliferation would. "So they've built a bomb."

"Not yet. It's a matter of the engineering, making the

pieces fit. He thinks that's still two or three months away, but he isn't sure. That happens somewhere else."

"Can we talk to him?"

"Not unless you get someone into Tehran, maybe not even then. They hardly let the scientists off the bases anymore. Never out of the country. Both so they don't defect and the Israelis don't kill them. Plus he has his own special problems with them."

Then Taylor understood. Reza's hatred of the regime. His obsession with secrecy. Even what he'd said a few minutes before, *I have as much use for Allah as He has for me.* "This friend of yours, this good friend—"

"What about him?"

Taylor knew that if he was wrong, or if Reza's pride and whatever was left of his Muslim identity wouldn't allow him to admit his sexuality, taking this route would infuriate him. In an ordinary recruitment, Taylor would work up to this moment over years. But he didn't have months, much less years.

He decided to make the play. Obliquely.

"Is he married, this man? Does he have a family?"

"Why does that matter?"

"You tell me, Reza."

"You're a fool." Reza couldn't meet Taylor's eyes.

"If his heart is in the West, if he'd like to leave the regime behind, come to a place where he can live more freely, even get married, maybe we can get him out."

"It's impossible." Reza's voice was low and angry, the sound of a man who hated himself for his own hope.

"Nothing's impossible. Of course, for that we'd need his real name. And yours."

"I will ask. Now leave it alone, Mr. Case Officer." He thumbed the starter. The Suzuki came to life.

Taylor knew he'd pushed Reza to the limit. "Wait."

"What now?"

"In all this you haven't given me the details on the ship. Do you have a name?"

"No. I know it left Dubai seven or eight days ago."

"What flag?"

"Pakistan. It started in Karachi. Bound for the East Coast. I don't know where exactly. Not New York. The security there is stricter."

"Who knows about the package?"

"Probably only the captain, but I don't think he knows what it is. They bribed him. Probably he thinks it's drugs."

"Is this like the size of a container? A trunk?"

"Smaller. A small suitcase, a backpack. Lightly radioactive, maybe shielded."

"If it's out of Dubai, not your operation, how do you know any of this?"

"We had two choices, Dubai or Istanbul. They decided to use Dubai the first time. I don't know why, but they said they will come back to Istanbul soon. It's a test run, like I told you."

"Just so there's no mistake. You're telling me that Iran plans to bring highly enriched uranium into the United States?"

"There's no mistake." Now that the conversation had moved off his personal life, Reza had his sneer back. "Smuggle the components one by one, build the bombs in America."

"Bombs."

"Did you think we needed ten bombs for Tel Aviv?"

They stood side by side. An oddly powerful desire to kiss Reza swept over Taylor. He had never wanted to lock lips with another man before, so he could only assume that he was grateful to the Iranian for revealing that the United States faced nuclear blackmail, or worse. Fortunately, the feeling passed quickly.

"These bombs. Does Iran plan to use them?"

"I don't think so. My guess, we see them as a way to make sure you never invade. Put a few in different cities, tell your President. You attack us, we attack you."

"Don't they understand we'll see it as war?"

"Look at it as they do. You invade Iraq. Hang Saddam. Bomb people everywhere with drones. The mullahs expect you'll kill them, too, if you can. This way, they have an answer."

"We'll find those bombs and then we'll destroy the people who put them there. Not regime change. Regime erase." Taylor knew he sounded like a parody. He was trying to reassure himself.

"The bombs, imagine, they hide them in those lockers you have all over—"

"Self-storage."

"Yes. They don't even have to have anyone watching them, they can have remote triggers, mobile phones. Say you find three, or four. Can you know you've found them all?"

The nightmare scenario.

"Reza, you have to come in."

"Find the boat."

"We'll get your friend for you. Whatever it takes."

Reza grabbed Taylor's motorcycle helmet, stuffed it between his legs. "I told you not to say anything more about that." Before Taylor could protest, he rolled off.

Taylor could only watch as the motorcycle swung onto the road, disappeared into the night.

Best agent ever. And worst.

17

The voice in Wells's ear was manicured as a polo lawn. *Thank you for calling the Aesthetic Beauty Centre. To proceed in English, press one. Arabic, press two. Chinese—*

Wells pressed one.

You have reached the Aesthetic Beauty Centre, located near Bangkok, Thailand. Our surgeons and staff are renowned for discretion, skill, and service. As a reminder, all new clients must have referrals from existing customers. Please leave your name and telephone number and someone will call you back. You may also email us at concierge @abcbeautiful.com—

Wells clicked off, called back, pressed two when the language options came up. The message was the same in Arabic. "*Asalaam aleikum.* My name is Jalal. I am calling for Dr. Rajiv Singh about a possible surgery for my daughter. The matter is urgent. Please call me on my mobile."

All this in Arabic. Wells left a number with a Saudi prefix, 966, and hung up.

Finding Aesthetic Beauty had taken Wells ten days. Halfway through his flight to Seoul, he realized his plan to try to find Mason through plastic surgeons was worse than a long shot. No doctor would tell a random stranger about his patients. Wells was left with his original idea, casing bars and nightclubs in Phuket, looking for a bouncer or bar girl who knew Mason.

But Phuket took longer to search than he'd expected. The island had six hundred thousand residents scattered across dozens of villages and towns. Its tourist offerings ranged from high-end gated resorts for wealthy families to the infamous Patong Beach. Patong's sex trade wasn't confined to a few alleys. Its red-light district stretched along a four-lane road for what felt like miles. Every night, the sun dipped into the sea. Neon signs for Singha and Heineken flickered on. Cover bands struck their first chords. And swarms of sunburned *farang*s poured from hostels and hotels, ready to feed.

During the day, the bars were empty, leaving Wells no choice but to join the herd. He handed out photocopied pictures of Mason to hundreds of bartenders, bouncers, madams, and prostitutes. He expected sharp questions—*Why are you looking for this man*? Instead, the Thais he asked seemed to see the search as a joke. They gave him answers straight from *The Hangover Part II*. The movie

270 | ALEX BERENSON

was hugely popular in Thailand. *Check the elevator! Come back with Alan, I tell you! Where you monkey?* When Wells pressed on: *He steal your money? Screw wife?*

The whores ignored his questions entirely: *Phuket no place for trouble. Worry tomorrow, come with me tonight.* From one bar girl whose head barely reached Wells's chest: *Big handsome, I give half-price, then we do twice!*

By the end of his second night, Wells realized he should just call himself a private investigator. Insurance companies and divorce lawyers regularly sent detectives to Phuket after disability claimants and badly behaved husbands. The locals were happy to cooperate, for the right price. Wells made more photocopies, this time with "REWARD: $2,500" above Mason's forehead. He would have made the figure higher, but he didn't want the search to stand out to the police officers who sometimes appeared at the bars.

After an exhausting week, Wells had visited every club and disco on Phuket. He heard "In the Air Tonight" at least twice a night—not surprising, given the demographics of the men around him. Phuket had lost its status as a destination for hip young backpackers decades before. The bars were filled with guys in their thirties and forties, many past fifty. They were mostly European and Russian, not American, but it seemed *Miami Vice* had been a global phenomenon after all.

Wells found the bars grim and unsexy, even when the girls were beautiful. Especially when they were beautiful. *Farang*s in Thailand offered a long list of self-serving excuses for what they were doing. Among the most popular were that Thai men also frequented prostitutes and that

Buddhism didn't frown on prostitution. The arguments weren't entirely wrong. Compared to the hard-edged desperation of red-light districts in European cities like Amsterdam, the sex trade in Phuket wasn't hopeless. Its ubiquity lessened its stigma. Prostitutes here didn't view themselves as fallen women, and they were much less likely to be abused or murdered than American streetwalkers. They earned decent livings, and they did sometimes escape the bars entirely by marrying their clients. But the *farang*s ignored the incredible imbalance in wealth that drove the trade. No Thai teenager dreamed of moving to Phuket to sell herself to men two or three times her age. The women came from poor villages in northern Thailand, hoping to make enough money to support their families. They had only a few years to do so before younger girls replaced them. And though they were encouraged to use condoms and regularly tested for HIV, about one in fifty still became infected. Many more wound up with other sexually transmitted diseases. Once they aged out of the bars, they had little chance for marriage or legitimate jobs.

Wells returned to his hotel each night exhausted and depressed. No matter what time he got home, he set his alarm to wake him for the *fajr*, the first of the day's five Muslim prayers. He turned west toward Mecca, closed his eyes, murmured the Arabic phrases that had comforted him since those first days in Afghanistan when he'd learned about Islam. When he was done with his own devotions, he prayed for the whores, that Allah grant them the most important of all His gifts, the ability to endure.

As for the men, Wells tried to ignore them. He wanted

272 | **ALEX BERENSON**

to feel sorry for them, especially the ones who believed they could buy something more than sex, who had flown halfway around the world chasing a cheap replica of love. But even the least of them were predators. On his fifth night, at one of Patong's sleaziest bars, Wells saw two fortysomething men standing at a cocktail table with a Thai girl who was seventeen at most. One of the guys was skinny, with greasy skin and a slicked-back widow's peak. His buddy was stout, a rugby player gone to seed. The girl wore a neon-green dress. When she stepped away to get them fresh beers, Wells saw her clubfoot limp.

Wells had finished handing out photocopies and turned to leave when the music cut out and he overheard the fat one say, *Every hole and back again, Spence. One last night 'fore we go home to those frigid bitches.*

The big guy raised a hand and the two men fist-pumped over the table. Wells knew that changing their minds would be a long shot at best. Still he bought three shots of vodka, settled himself between them. "Gentlemen. How are you this fine night?"

The greaser's eyes were loose, floating on a sea of alcohol. The fat one had the satisfied dull face of a Soviet commissar presiding at a mock trial. Even before they replied, Wells realized he had no chance. However long they'd been here, they'd seen and done too much. Pingpong shows. Flaming banana shows. Live couple shows. One girl, two girls, three girls. Maybe even a boy or two. A lifetime of depravity in a few days. They'd drained the sensation from every act. Except pain.

"Not bad," the big one said. "Not at all." His accent was English.

He grinned. His teeth belonged on a more handsome face. Cosmetic dentistry had arrived in the United Kingdom. Better late than never.

"Couldn't help hearing your plans for this young lady."

"When we've done with her, she won't limp no more."

The words tore at Wells. He knew he should walk away. He knew he wouldn't.

"Humanitarians." He slid each man a shot glass. "I like that."

"Looking to watch, then?" The chubby one leaned toward his friend. "What do you think?"

"Wants to pay for it, why not, then—"

The music came up. They leaned in close to hear each other. *Perfect.*

"Drink to it." The fat one reached for a shot.

"Hold off. Those are for the headache." Wells put his arms around the men's shoulders.

"No touching, aye—"

"What headache?"

Wells snaked his hands into their hair and crushed their foreheads together like a cymbalist trying to impress the hottest cheerleader in school. Strength declined more slowly than reflex speed. Even now, Wells benched three hundred pounds, curled seventy-five. He had the advantage of surprise. They had the disadvantage of alcohol. They hardly flinched as their skulls crunched, the sound dull and dangerous as brick hitting pavement. The skinny one buckled to the floor, no muscle tone. The rugby player was tougher. His eyes rolled half into his head as he slumped onto the table.

"That headache."

The guy tried to stand. Failed. He swiped at the table, toppled down. The girl stared at Wells, lips parted. He pressed baht notes into her hand. She reached for him, but he shook his head, walked into the humid night.

By his ninth night in Phuket, Wells decided he was wasting time. The search was breathtakingly inefficient. He needed more clues, or FBI task-force-sized help, or both. He'd called Shafer twice for advice, ways to narrow the search. But Shafer had nothing to offer. When Wells asked how the investigation in Manila was going, Shafer answered. *They've got me so deep in the meat locker I think I've frozen solid.* He sounded terrible, like a losing coach just waiting for the season to end.

Wells decided to give himself one more night and then try something new. Maybe Hong Kong, chase what had happened to Mason on that last tour. But a little after midnight, at a narrow bar in an alley off Patpong, his persistence paid off. A bartender looked over the sheet, touched a finger to Mason's photocopied face. "I know."

"He's here?"

The bartender shook his head. "Other side of bay. Has house." He was twenty-five or so, with full hips and wide lips that gave him an oddly froglike look.

"You're sure?"

"I from there."

"Tell me how to find it, the reward's yours."

"Too busy now. Come back tomorrow. Noon." Before Wells could argue, the man turned away to pour shots for five ghost-pale Russians.

Wells worried the bartender wouldn't show. But when Wells arrived a half hour before noon, he was waiting. He led Wells past lumps of vomit congealing in the sun to an Internet café.

"I'm John."

"Prateep. You American."

"Yes. New Hampshire." The words made Wells think of Anne. He'd missed her the last few days, wondered what she would make of this awful scene.

"Like Phuket?"

"It's all right."

"Other islands better. Phuket good for money, no more."

The world's epitaph. Wells slid pictures of Mason across the table. Prateep held them close, like he was failing an eye exam. "Last night look more like him."

Wells understood. In the bar's low light, Prateep had focused on the contours of Mason's face. Now the details confused him. "That's an old picture. He had surgery for his eyes, nose. Everything."

Prateep stacked the photos on the tabletop, pushed them to Wells. "What his name?"

"His real name is Glenn Mason. I think he has a new name now."

"Call himself Duke."

"Duck?"

"*D-U-K-E*. Rent house on my island. Quiet. No trouble."

"When was the last time you saw him?"

"Six months, maybe. How you know him?"

"Friend of a friend."

"This man, he never let anyone take his picture. Don't bother anyone. Quiet. Why you want him?"

"Just to talk."

Prateep leaned back, receded into himself as big men sometimes did. Wells didn't press.

"Ten thousand, I tell you how to find him."

"Too much."

Prateep's face hardened. Ten thousand dollars was cheap if the guy really knew where Mason lived. "Twenty-five hundred now, rest after I get back."

"All now."

"How about I show you the cash, prove I have it? You come to the island, show me where he lives, you can have it all at once."

Four hours later, an open-canopied speedboat stopped beside a crude wooden dock that extended off a narrow white beach.

"Koh Pu," the pilot said.

He wore a floppy hat and the biggest sunglasses Wells had ever seen, almost goggles. They didn't affect his navigational skills. He had steered them expertly from the port town of Krabi, ten miles north.

Wells handed him one hundred dollars. "Until five-thirty." Two hours.

"You not here then, I come back tomorrow. Too much coral here. Dangerous in the dark."

Koh Pu was only thirty miles east of Phuket across the waters of Phang Nga Bay. But reaching it required a hundred-mile drive around the bay followed by a boat ride. After spending days on planes to get to Phuket, most Western tourists had no appetite for more travel. As a result, Koh Pu had no condo complexes or concrete-walled fortresses, and certainly no neon-signed brothels. Lushly forested hills rose into a perfect blue sky. A warm breeze ran off the bay's emerald waters. For the first time since landing in Thailand, Wells could imagine why backpackers a generation ago had seen these beaches as heaven on earth. *Call someplace paradise, kiss it good-bye . . .* At this moment, a developer was no doubt considering how many hotels he could build here, how much a hydrofoil from Phuket would cost.

Prateep stepped onto the sand. "Beautiful, yes?"

On the trip from Phuket, Prateep had explained that Koh Pu had two small resorts with barely a dozen beds each, along with a handful of villas owned by wealthy Thais from Bangkok and several hundred permanent residents. The island's isolation was curse as well as blessing. During the rainy season, few tourists came. Residents survived through fishing and rubber farming. Prateep's family owned the island's only bar outside the resorts. Prateep had worked there before plunging into Phuket's lucrative muck.

Fifty meters up, they reached the island's main road, a single lane of packed dirt. Prateep turned north.

They walked past tin-roofed houses with goat pens and fenced vegetable gardens. After a few hundred meters, Prateep turned east onto a narrow side road that rose up a steep hill. His feet sank into the loose red dirt. With each step he puffed heavily, a truck in low gear. The breeze turned, coming from the north, bringing with it a low sweet scent of a flower Wells didn't recognize. They passed two tin-roofed homes on garage-sized plots cut from the forest.

After a couple hundred meters they crested the hill. The road swung hard right, south. Past a thatch of trees, it dead-ended at a plot with a view of the bay and a low cement-and-glass box that looked like it had been airlifted from the Hollywood hills. Without ever having met Mason, Wells could imagine him here. The house was beautiful and strange. Its front side was a wall of glass, split by widely spaced support pillars. Thick black curtains hid the inside. It appeared to have been empty for some time. Cobwebs hung from the roof pillars. Still, someone was keeping an eye on the place, or at least weeding the gravel path that led around the front right corner to a brushed steel door.

"Know who takes care of it? When they come?" Though Wells figured the odds were against anyone paying a visit.

Prateep shook his head. "Bring money to bar."

"Take it now." Wells fished a stack of hundred-dollar bills from his pack. "Thank you."

Prateep reached for the money. His eyes were flat as stones, his big lips pressed together. Wells knew the look.

He'd seen it from more people in more countries than he could remember. *You thought you could buy me. And you were right.*

Prateep's steps faded, leaving only the mad songs of birds hidden in the undergrowth. Wells walked slowly around the house. It was a single story, fifty feet long, thirty-five wide. Only the front wall was glass. The others were concrete. Up close they were cracked and stained. No surprise. Thai rainy seasons wouldn't be kind to this design. And the concrete was probably less than skyscraper-quality. Just getting the sand and cement here must have taken half the men on the island.

Koh Pu had nothing resembling a police department, so Wells didn't expect an alarm. He didn't find one. Nor cameras. Nor trip wires. Mason must have decided that his face-altering surgery and faked death were protection enough.

Wells finished his loop and reached for his electronic pick. The house seemed to exhale when he opened the front door, as if no one had entered for months. He walked into a long living room with a wide-planked blond-wood floor that continued the California theme. He half expected a longboard hanging from the ceiling.

Despite the big west-facing windows, the curtains kept the room black. When Wells closed the door he'd be in darkness. He flicked the light switch beside the door, but nothing happened. Prateep had said the island had a central power grid. Either this house had been disconnected or its lights were burned out. Wells wanted to pull the curtains, but he couldn't risk announcing his presence if someone came up. He pulled the headlamp from his backpack. It looked silly, but it kept his hands free. He strapped it around his head, clicked it on.

The headlamp threw out a narrow cone of light, a horror-movie view. With the door shut, the house smelled heavy. Like the concrete had not completely dried from the rainy season. Wells scanned the room left to right— and saw, almost too late, a spider the size of a child's fist scuttling at him. He stomped it. The creature exploded with the wet gasp of an egg breaking. Wells was glad he'd chosen thick-soled boots despite the heat. Beneath his jeans, he'd hidden a knife.

He turned his attention to the floor. Was the spider Mason's version of a security system? Doubtful. More likely a local stopping by for a visit. Wells needed more light. He reached for the door—and heard a motorbike rumbling up the track toward the house. He waited for the bike to stop at one of the huts. It didn't.

Maybe Prateep had planned to set Wells up all along. More likely, the bartender bumped into the house's care-taker on the road and slyly suggested a visit. *Thanks for paying me early, dummy.* Or maybe the visit was just bad luck. Either way, Wells didn't think the good folk of Koh Pu would appreciate a *farang* breaking and entering. He would face an uncomfortable night or two in whatever closet passed for the island's jail. Worse, the caretaker no doubt had orders to call Mason if he caught anyone at the house.

The motorbike topped the hill. Wells stepped deeper inside. Most likely the guy would just peek inside the front door. Wells would stow himself in a closet, hope the spiders weren't biting. *The spider.* If the caretaker saw it, he would surely wonder who had stomped it. Wells peeled the corpse off the floor, tossed it in a corner. Then wished he hadn't. Spider bits were everywhere. A massacre.

The engine grew louder as Wells hustled across the living room, pretending not to notice a second spider scuttling by, this one bigger than the first. He opened the bedroom door, stepped inside, saw a third spider against the closet wall to his right, much larger than the first two. It was black, furry, with an oversized sac at one end. Not a spider. A tarantula.

Thailand had tarantulas?

For the second straight mission, Wells found himself in an episode of *Man vs. Wild.* He'd much rather be looking at a guy with a knife. The tarantula provoked a sickly adrenaline rush rather than the calm of combat. Okay. He'd be honest. It creeped him out.

He pulled his knife as it scuttled toward a crack in the closet door, like it was deciding what to wear for the evening. *You'll need four pairs of shoes, buddy. Must be expensive.* Hardee-har-har. It disappeared into the crack. Then it re-emerged, came at him, moving quicker than he expected. It escaped the cone of his headlamp. He ducked his head to follow it. Three feet away, two—

He raised his right foot to stomp it. But the closer it came, the faster it moved. It cut to his left as smoothly as an eight-legged running back and crawled onto his left boot. His jeans were loose around the leather uppers of the boots. Wells looked down as the tarantula scuttled around the back of his boot, like it was searching for a way in. Was the warmth of his skin drawing it? He cursed in the dark as it crawled up the boot. With the knife in his right hand, he couldn't get a clean swipe. He switched the blade to his left, jabbed downward at his calf with five inches of double-edged serrated steel. He aimed high, above the top of his boots. He was willing to cut his leg in order to get the thing off him. He wasn't sure if its venom could kill him, but he knew he didn't want to find out.

But he felt the blade slice through his jeans as the tarantula's front legs touched his skin. He drove the blade down into something soft. The tarantula hissed as it slid off his boot and landed on the floor with a wet plop. Now that he'd sliced it open, it seemed pathetically small. White fluid oozed from its belly as it writhed and tried to stand. It looked up at him and feebly waved its forelegs, its hiss fading. Wells crushed it under his boot.

The engine outside cut out. Wells heard a man walking around the front of the house. He would be stuck inside until the caretaker left. He closed the bedroom door, pressed himself against the wall. Above his breathing, he heard what sounded like another tarantula in the closet. Maybe the caretaker doubled as an exterminator.

He looked around the room, which took up most of the north wall of the house. A king-sized platform bed lay beside Wells, no sheets or pillows, merely a bare mattress.

A dresser rested against the wall opposite the bed. In keeping with the house's modernist theme, all the furniture was steel-cladded, vaguely aeronautical.

To his left was the windowed west wall. To his right, the tarantula closet and an open doorway. Through it, Wells glimpsed a bathroom mirror and sink. Based on its location, this bedroom was the master. The guest bedroom would be behind the bathroom, with no view.

Wells had hoped for a laptop, piles of credit card statements, maybe even a photo of Mason postsurgery. But Mason had been careful, even here. Nothing was out. If he had any personal stuff, he'd hidden it. Wells reached for the dresser. The top drawer held an astounding collection of sex toys. The middle was filled with T-shirts and underwear. And the bottom contained shorts and sweatshirts. Wells started to close it—then stopped. Under the sweatshirts lay a manila envelope thick with paper. A single word was printed neatly on it: *Records*. Wells tucked it in his backpack. He shut the drawer, waited in silence as the caretaker puttered around outside. He didn't care about the spiders anymore. He would hide in this room as long as necessary, until the caretaker left and Wells could make a clean exit. This envelope would lead him to Mason.

Then he heard the click of the front door swinging open. Seconds later, light streamed under the crack of the bedroom door. Wells had forgotten that the guy didn't need electricity to come inside. He just had to open the curtains.

Now Wells was trapped. Then he realized: the bathroom might offer a way out. He edged the door open, looked inside. As he'd hoped, the bathroom was what real estate agents called a Jack-and-Jill, two entrances. A door on the north wall led to the guest bedroom.

Wells stepped through the bathroom, into the second bedroom. Mason had used the space as an office. A desk nestled in the corner. Wells prowled through its drawers, saw a tiny flash drive. It was loose, didn't look like it had been deliberately hidden. Probably it was blank and Mason had left it accidentally. Even so, Wells scooped it into his pocket.

He heard the man in the living room humming to himself, apparently unaware that Wells was in the house. Wells moved to the office door in two careful steps. He waited as the man stepped into the master bedroom. Wells pulled open the office door and stepped down the hallway that connected the guest bedroom with the living room. As he did, he heard the caretaker walk into the bathroom. As Wells had hoped, the caretaker was following his loop. Wells strode across the living room—and heard yelling in Thai behind him.

Wells ran for the motorcycle. It was a tiny Honda dirt bike with a 150cc engine, barely big enough to hold him. The caretaker had left the key in the ignition. Why not, up here? Wells didn't pause to consider his good fortune, but slid onto the bike. He pressed the starter and the engine came alive. The house's door swung open, revealing a bantam of a man in mud-splattered jeans. Wells swung the bike around on the gravel path, easing back the throttle. These little engines could be fussy, and he couldn't risk a stall.

The man yelled in Thai and pitched his arm forward like

he was trying to lasso Wells with an invisible rope. Wells straightened out, gave the bike gas. He kicked up gravel as he gained speed. The man ran for the front of the house, trying to angle him off. But Wells beat him to the corner. He reached the dirt path that led to the main road and bounced down it, resisting the urge to gun the engine. The bike was skidding and yawing too much already, dragging on its shocks under his weight. Anyway, thirty miles an hour, even twenty, should be fine. He had less than a mile to ride.

Two and a half minutes later, he bounced up to the beach. The speedboat was still waiting. Wells dropped the bike's kickstand, turned off the engine. No thank-you note. He'd have to be impolite. With the engine silent, he heard shouting up the road. He strode down the dock, swung himself onto the speedboat.

The pilot spun in his chair, grinned under his ridiculous sunglasses at Wells. "Why so much a hurry?"

The shouts grew more distinct. Wells could guess what they were saying. "Two hundred dollars, you go right now."

"Five."

Wells nodded.

"Grab anchor."

Wells pulled the anchor, stowed it behind the seats. The pilot turned in his chair, started the engine. Then glanced back at Wells. "They telling me to keep you, you a thief."

"I haven't taken anything from them, I promise." An answer that was technically accurate. Wells had stolen only from Mason.

The pilot shoved the throttle forward. The boat skipped

ahead fifty yards. Then the pilot eased off and they drifted. "One thousand dollars."

If not for the coral, Wells might have tossed the pilot overboard and taken the helm himself. The caretaker ran onto the beach, shouting. All he needed was a pitchfork and a flaming torch. Wells half wished he'd knocked the guy out, tied him up.

"One thousand. But no more."

The pilot pushed the throttle and away they went. Wells would never have imagined he'd be so happy to leave paradise behind.

Four hours later, he sat on a lumpy twin bed in a Bangkok hotel that wouldn't be in any guidebooks this year or next. The place was on the edge of the city's red-light district, even bigger and nastier than Patong Beach. Through his dime-thin window, he heard the noises people made when they were trying to prove they were having a good time. Men shouting. Women squealing. Wells had chosen this place not for its creature comforts but because it took cash and wasn't concerned with his name.

The more he saw of Mason, the more dangerous the man seemed. He was covering his tracks with the care of a man who had no agency to protect him. Yet he spent money like he had a government-sized bank account. And he'd been working on this operation since the day he left the agency, if not before. Wells didn't know if Mason had access to NSA's databases. But he had decided to err on the side of caution and avoid leaving his own trail wherever he could.

The *Records* envelope and flash drive lay next to his laptop on the bed. He tried the drive first. His laptop reported it empty. He'd send it to Shafer, in the hope that the geeks at Langley could find something. Assuming they still answered Shafer's requests.

Inside the envelope, a sheaf of records from the Aesthetic Beauty Centre for Abraham Duke. The file began with a two-page letter from Dr. Rajiv Singh, director of the center, thanking Mason/Duke for his initial visit and putting the cost of his operations at $93,500. Plus an additional $24,300 for a thirty-day stay in a recovery suite. All payments up-front, cash or wire transfer only, cash preferred. Duke wanted a rhinoplasty, cheek augmentation, hair transplantation, and three other procedures whose names Wells didn't recognize. *By the time we have finished, your face will appear distinctly different, as discussed,* the letter explained. *Renderings attached—see your new look!* But Mason had destroyed the renderings, or hidden them somewhere else. They were gone.

The next letter thanked Duke for his payment and reminded him that the center offered three follow-up visits over the next eighteen months at no charge. The plastic surgery equivalent of free oil changes with a new car. Two dozen pages of medical records followed. Wells couldn't be sure, but the operations seemed to have gone smoothly. Finally, the packet included two pages of postoperative instructions and reports on follow-up visits. The last visit had come two years earlier. Duke reported no problems, and Singh pronounced him fully healed.

The records wouldn't convince the CIA to take another look at Mason, especially since his name was nowhere in them. Wells needed before-and-after photos. Maybe Mason had burned them. More likely he'd locked them away in his house and Wells had missed them. Koh Pu was now off-limits. Wells thought his best chance would be with the surgery center. But he needed a good reason to visit. He had checked online, found the place had a one-page website. The kind that was intentionally exclusive. *We don't need to look for business on the Internet.* Saying he was CIA or FBI chasing a terrorist wouldn't work. Singh would call the American embassy in Bangkok to check his bona fides.

Wells was exhausted. He tucked away the records, lay down, closed his eyes. The shouting outside melted into a prayer call in his mind and Wells knew what to do. He fell asleep anesthesia-quick and woke to a heavy knock.

"Yes?"

"Checkout eleven o'clock!" It was 11:05, according to the clock beside the bed. Service with a smile. Wells passed another day's rent through the door, took a lukewarm shower, and got to work.

Years before, Wells had worked for King Abdullah of Saudi Arabia to chase down a terrorist cell backed by other Saudi royals. Wells had killed the terrorists, but the mission remained unfinished in his mind. The princes who had financed the cell remained inside the Kingdom, where Wells couldn't touch them. He hoped that one day he'd have his chance.

Meantime, in the wake of the mission, Abdullah had promised Wells that if he needed the Kingdom's help, he need only ask. Wells had drawn from that favor bank once already. He was wary of relying too heavily on it. In this case, though, what he needed was simple: a phone, a passport, and someone to answer a call at the Saudi embassy in Bangkok.

The king's word was still good. By late afternoon, the embassy had arranged what he needed. Wells moved from his hotel to the other end of the luxury spectrum, the Four Seasons downtown. A thousand baht didn't even cover valet parking there. On the other hand, the Four Seasons garage was cleaner than his old room.

A Saudi-registered mobile phone waited in an envelope at the front desk, with the promise of a passport in the morning. On such short notice, it wouldn't be live, but Wells didn't need it to travel. He would use it only as proof of a fake identity.

From his room, he called the Aesthetic Beauty Centre and left his message as Jalal. He expected he'd have to wait until morning for a call, but his phone rang back within the hour.

"Asalaam aleikum."

"Aleikum salaam." A woman's voice.

"Is this Dr. Singh?" Wells said in Arabic. A Saudi would know his accent was wrong, but this woman's accent was even rougher than his.

"I'm Aisha. Dr. Singh doesn't speak Arabic. And you are Jalal?"

"Yes. Jalal bin Fahd." Wells was implicitly claiming to be a member of the royal family by naming his father so prominently.

"How may the Aesthetic Beauty Centre help you, sir?" Wells heard her try to smooth her accent at his hint of al-Saud blood.

"My daughter will be married in five weeks."

"Congratulations."

"There is a difficulty. I don't like to speak of it over the phone."

She coughed. "A riding accident?"

"Very much so." Meaning: Her hymen is broken. She needs it in one piece if she doesn't want the groom to beat her senseless, or worse, on their wedding night. "I know there isn't much time. She told me only last week."

"We've dealt with this before."

"Thanks be to Allah. I'd like to come in, discuss it further with Dr. Singh tomorrow."

"I must ask, sir. Do you have an existing customer as a reference?"

So the security precautions were real.

"I do, but I promised I wouldn't use her name." Wells could have mentioned Duke, but he wanted to surprise Singh with the name face-to-face.

"A moment, sir." Wells heard a whispered conversation. "If you fax us the identity page from your passport, we'll schedule a consultation. Is your daughter here?"

"I wanted to know you could help before I brought her."

"That's fine. She'll need time to heal, but a day or two shouldn't matter."

"Thank you, Aisha."

"Yes, sir. I'll text you our fax number. Dr. Singh looks forward to seeing you."

She hung up. Wells wished he had the passport already, but he supposed he could hold them off until morning by saying he'd made a mistake with the fax number. Saudi princes were not known for attention to detail.

The Aesthetic Beauty Centre rose out of farmland seventy miles west of Bangkok, halfway to the Burmese border. The complex consisted of a two-story office building and two small outbuildings, all clad in expensive-looking coppery glass. A low fence surrounded the grounds, with a guardhouse at the front gate. A small helicopter sat beside the main building, presumably for repeat clients. Wells rated only a chauffeured BMW.

The gate swung open as the sedan approached. A tall Indian woman waited for Wells. "*Asalaam aleikum*. I'm Aisha."

"*Aleikum salaam.*"

The building gleamed inside as well as out. Surgical suites occupied the right side, administration offices the left. An Indian man wearing a white doctor's jacket waited in a conference room.

"You speak English, doctor?" Wells expected he'd have an easier time if he and Singh were alone.

"Of course."

"So do I. I'd rather—" Wells nodded to Aisha.

"I assure you, you may trust Aisha."

Wells shook his head.

"Aisha—"

She left. Singh snapped open a calfskin briefcase, pulled out a legal pad and pen.

"Tell me about your daughter, Mr. bin Fahd."

"I'd like to hear more about the center."

"Of course. I trained at Harvard, medical school and residency. After graduating, I worked in Los Angeles. I then returned to my homeland for eight years to practice in Delhi. I can tell you that I was considered perhaps the top plastic surgeon in India. I had achieved everything I hoped." Singh spoke with complete confidence. Wells guessed he'd delivered this pitch hundreds of times.

"But you left."

"Six years ago, I decided that the world's elite deserved cosmetic and reconstructive surgery at the highest level. With absolute privacy. No center like that existed. So I built it. I am one of three full-time physicians here, along with another surgeon and an anesthesiologist. We're all U.S.-trained. We perform most surgeries ourselves, with arrangements to bring in specialists when necessary. We have eight nurses and a nutritionist. We never have more than five patients on-site, and they don't see one another unless they specifically request otherwise. We are expensive, but you—or your daughter, in this case—get what you pay for. Our clients are billionaires, politicians, celebrities. From all over. India, of course, but also China, Russia, the Arab world, and our reputation is spreading into Europe. The United States has been harder to crack, but it will come."

"Impressive."

"Thank you. Now, may we discuss your daughter?"

Singh radiated self-assurance. The only way to crack him wasn't to try to trick him but to come straight at him, all at once.

"My daughter doesn't exist. And my name's not Jalal bin Fahd."

"Is this a joke?" Singh swept up his briefcase, stood, headed toward the door.

"Sit down."

Singh looked at Wells and sat.

"I work for the Saudi government. Chasing a man you operated on about four years ago. He went by the name Abraham Duke. His real name is Glenn Mason. Do you know who I mean?"

Singh shook his head.

"You're lying. He had several surgeries. He paid you more than one hundred thousand dollars. You changed the look of his face. His case would have been memorable."

"I never discuss my patients."

"I have his records, Dr. Singh. And I can tell you that the Kingdom of Saudi Arabia believes that Mr. Mason was involved in a plot against His Majesty. You cannot imagine how seriously the Kingdom takes that threat."

"This is silly. An effort to intimidate me into talking about a person who may or may not have been a patient. Whatever you're doing, it's time for you to leave, Mr. bin Fahd. Or whoever you really are."

Wells reached into his pocket, slid a folded piece of paper across the table to Singh. The doctor unfolded it hesitantly. "What is this?"

"The number for the Saudi embassy in Bangkok. Call them, ask for the diplomatic secretary. He'll confirm what I've said, who I am."

"You expect me to believe this is the real number?" But Singh didn't throw the number away.

"I expect you to check it and find out it is. I'll wait."

Fifteen minutes later, Singh returned.

"What do you want from me?"

"Very little. Then I'll leave and you can get back to putting new faces on drug lords." Wells handed over one of Mason's preoperative photos. "Remember him now?"

"I told you, I can't talk about my patients."

"If you think making an enemy of the Kingdom is bad, wait until the Interior Ministry tells the CIA that you refused to help capture a terrorist. Who happens to be an ex–CIA case officer."

"I don't know what you're talking about." For the first time, Singh's voice wavered. "We never ask our clients why they're here."

"That's fine. All I need is postop photos."

Singh laughed. "Look around, sir." Contempt replaced the doubt in his voice. "Do you imagine the patients who come here want us to keep before-and-after snaps? For our website, perhaps?"

"What about renderings? Your letter to him mentions renderings."

"We delete those at the final postop visit, assuming the

THE COUNTERFEIT AGENT | 295

healing has gone normally." Singh pressed his advantage. "I'm afraid I can't help you. Now, if you don't mind—"

"What if the healing doesn't go normally?"

"You say you've seen Mr. Duke's records—"

"But if there's a product recall, an emergency, even years later. You must be able to reach your patients. A phone number, an email."

Singh shook his head.

"Choice A: Give me those, I'm gone. Never bother you again. And he'll never know how I got them. Choice B: You get put on a whole bunch of lists you don't want to be on."

"I've done nothing wrong—"

"Even so. You think business will improve if the *New York Times* writes an article about a secret plastic surgery center in Thailand? That the kind of publicity your clients want?"

Singh picked up his briefcase, stalked out of the room. Wells wasn't sure who he would see next. The center's guards? The Thai police? Five minutes later, Aisha walked in.

"Dr. Singh said you'd asked for this."

She gave Wells an envelope. Inside, a single piece of paper with a Thai phone number and an email address.

"Sorry we couldn't help you today. Your car is waiting."

Wells made the call as soon as they cleared the front gate. Two a.m. in Virginia, but no matter.

"John?" He didn't even sound groggy.

"I have something for you."

"Pictures."

"No. The guy's a ghost."

"Shame to spend all that money on surgery and none of your friends can see it."

"Isn't it? But I have an email and phone. Not sure when he's used them, but they should be live. Are you still in purgatory or can you get them run?"

"I'll do my best."

Wells read them off.

"I'll see if I can't get it in before the morning rush." Meaning sneak the request through now, when a tired sys admin might not question it, or Shafer.

Back to Bangkok. Shafer didn't get back to him that night. Or the next morning. Even at NSA, where some of Shafer's best friends had worked, his juice seemed to be drying up. Wells wondered if he should go to Duto for help. Finally, just before midnight, thirty hours–plus after he'd passed Shafer the number, his phone buzzed.

"More to come," Shafer said. "But it's not too early to book your next flight."

"Where?"

"You have to ask?"

"Istanbul?"

"Where else?"

18

The United States spent sixty billion dollars a year to spy on friends and enemies, tap phones, intercept emails, peek through windows. It spent six hundred billion more to maintain an arsenal that ranged from insect-sized drones to aircraft carriers. The system had deep flaws. It was secretive, duplicative, inefficient. Yet its sheer size and power guaranteed its effectiveness. No country with a choice would go to war with the United States.

That was the theory, anyway.

For years, the intelligence community had promised the President that Iran's nuclear program represented only a minor threat to the American homeland. CIA, the Defense Intelligence Agency, the State Department's Bureau of Intelligence and Research, and the best independent think tanks all reached the same conclusion. Tehran wanted nuclear weapons for three reasons. First, to deter an American invasion. Second, to cement Iran's position as the strongest power in the Gulf, dominating Iraq and Saudi Arabia. Third, to menace Israel. Being able to threaten the Jewish state with extinction would make Iran's leaders more popular with their own citizens and their Sunni neighbors.

But the analysts put the odds that Iran would use a bomb against Israel as very low, and against the United States as vanishingly small. Israel had more than a hundred nuclear warheads of its own and wouldn't hesitate to annihilate Iran in a counterattack. History offered some reassurance. Despite Iran's bluster, its army had never joined any of the Arab wars against Israel.

Iran had even less appetite for war with the Great Satan. Tehran had used the Revolutionary Guard's Quds Force to bleed the United States military in Iraq and Afghanistan. But since the eighties, Iran had refrained from attacking American civilians directly or even through Hezbollah. The mullahs knew that the United States was too powerful to fight. A nuclear weapon, even a dozen weapons, would not change their calculus.

The consensus was not universal. Hawks in Congress argued that the United States simply could not trust Iran with a bomb. Even if it didn't attack America directly, it might use the weapon against Israel and suck the United States into a regional nuclear war. But the United States had just escaped Iraq and Afghanistan, two of the most frustrating conflicts in its history. The President had no appetite for another.

But at breakfast this morning, he had gotten a call from his National Security Advisor, Donna Green, that made him wonder whether the Chicken Littles were right after all.

He was digging into his scrambled eggs when his steward appeared with his encrypted iPhone. One of the peculiarities of being President was that he never carried anything. Not even a phone. The Secret Service offered a half-dozen reasons for the policy. He knew the truth. They were afraid of the security risk if he lost it. Not to mention the worldwide embarrassment.

"Mr. President. Ms. Green asks if you have a moment."

Green knew his schedule, and she was too smart to bother him without good reason. He reached for the phone. "Donna."

"Sorry to interrupt you, sir. Scott Hebley just called. He's asking for a Four-H today."

The term had nothing to do with state fairs or prize watermelons. It translated to an Oval Office meeting with the DCI, the Chairman of the Joint Chiefs of Staff, the Secretary of Defense, and the Director of National Intelligence—the Four Horsemen of the Apocalypse.

"He explain why?" No mobile phone was as secure as the hardline network that connected the White House with Langley, the Pentagon, and Fort Meade. Still, they could speak relatively freely. A 4096-bit encryption key protected this conversation. At current processor speeds, a hundred supercomputers would need a hundred years to crack the call.

"Iran. Beyond that, he said he'd rather discuss it with everyone in person, sir."

"Bit dramatic."

From anyone else, the President would have demanded a pre-meeting report. But he trusted Hebley, who had wound down the war in Afghanistan with a minimum of fuss. The President would never believe he fully controlled Langley, but at least he could count on Hebley to follow orders. Unlike the previous director. Vinny Duto had been a creature of the National Clandestine Service from the top of his lying head to the tips of his lying toes. The President had looked forward to the day when his spokesman would thank Duto for his service and announce his resignation as DCI. But Duto had seen the end coming, beaten him to the door. He was the Senate's problem now.

"Call Cindy. She should be able to open up a block around noon." Cynthia Stone was the President's chief scheduler, a hugely important position, given the value of his time.

"And the Veep?"

"We'll hook him in after." The Vice President liked the sound of his own voice too much for the President's taste. When he and the President were alone, he kept himself in check, but in bigger groups he couldn't help himself.

Stone moved one meeting, lopped fifteen minutes off another, and at 12:03 p.m., Green led the Four Horsemen into the Oval Office. They arranged themselves on the pale yellow couches that faced each other in the center of the room, perpendicular to the President's desk. The President himself remained seated. These military men had been trained to respect authority, and he liked to remind them of his status as Commander-in-Chief.

"General Hebley. You asked for this meeting. The floor is yours."

"Thank you, Mr. President. A little less than twenty-four hours ago, a case officer in Istanbul was contacted by a source we call Mathers. Mathers is our Revolutionary Guard walk-in, the same man who correctly informed us that Iran was targeting a station chief. Mathers now reports that Iran is trying to smuggle radiological material into the United States."

Hebley paused. The President nodded: *Go on.*

"Mathers reports that the material is aboard a ship that sailed from Dubai more than a week ago. He didn't know its name, but he did provide a few details about its destination and registry. We've focused on several possible candidates, all of which are in the Atlantic Ocean and outside American waters. We have not yet interdicted any of the ships, and, of course, that's one reason I'm here today."

"Do we know the type of material, or what our friends plan to do with it?"

"The type of material is a mystery, sir. As to what they intend, Mathers referred to this as a practice run."

"For—"

"Mathers reports the Iranian stockpile of highly enriched uranium is significantly larger than our previous estimates. He claims that the Iranian government has solved certain unspecified production problems and has now enriched enough material for ten bombs. Depending on the size of the weapons, that would represent one hundred fifty to three hundred kilograms of highly enriched uranium. Further, Mathers claims that the Iranian government intends to transfer HEU to American soil with the aim of building nuclear weapons in the United States."

Not much could shock the people in this room into silence. That last sentence did.

"For an attack?" the President finally said.

"Mathers isn't sure of the intent. But he says his best guess is that Iran wants the weapons here as a deterrent. Without intercontinental ballistic missiles, this would be a low-tech form of mutually assured destruction."

"Blackmail," the Chairman of the Joint Chiefs said.

"One man's terrorist is another man's freedom fighter," Green said.

Tell me this is a practical joke, the President thought. *To get me to pay more attention to foreign policy.* But he had learned that even these men, powerful as they were, looked to him for leadership. Leaders didn't waste time trying to wish away problems.

"Can we trust this source, General?"

"That's the crucial question, Mr. President. The case officer handling him is fairly experienced, speaks good Farsi, has dealt with Iranians for several years. I've spoken to him myself, as have other senior members of my staff. He believes Mathers, and he makes a credible case."

"Do we have any confirmation from anywhere else?"

Hebley cleared his throat. "At the moment, we have no independent confirmation."

"Not one secondary source inside Iran we can ask?"

"Our intel into the Guard is limited, sir. And we have even less visibility into the Quds Force, which is the Guard unit that handles these operations. Not even the Israelis have ever cracked Quds. And their communications infrastructure—"

"Stop telling me what you don't know, General. Tell me what you *do* know."

"What we know, sir, is that this man claims to be a Rev Guard colonel and has given us limited warnings about two terrorist attacks. It may be that this is what the agency calls a false flag operation, that Mathers is working for another intelligence service that wants to provoke us into attacking Iran. But the countries which would benefit the most from a war are our allies. Our analysts don't believe that they would risk angering us this way. An internal power struggle within Tehran could also be driving this. Anti-American elements inside the Iranian government could be trying to hoax us into an attack to bolster their position. Finally, it's possible that our source is real. At the moment, we judge that most likely, though by no means a certainty."

"How likely? Ninety percent?"

"Maybe fifty-one percent at this point, with everything else adding up to forty-nine."

Green caught the President's eye.

"Go ahead, Donna."

"What about a third party? Al-Qaeda, say. If they could find an Iranian to help them, wouldn't they love to trick

304 | ALEX BERENSON

us into this? Get the Crusaders attacking the Shia. Two truck bombs and a hit on a station chief, that seems within their capabilities."

"We've considered nonstate actors such as AQ. We judge the possibility as unlikely. We have excellent intel on AQ and its offshoots and have seen no evidence of their involvement."

"Another terrorist group? One we haven't heard of yet?"

"That's just it. The attacks themselves, I agree, the sophistication was limited. But two weeks have passed since James Veder was killed and we still have no leads. That makes us think we're looking at a national intelligence service, one using high-level encryption to defeat our communications intercepts."

"So we bring this source in, talk to him?" the President said.

"He's absolutely refused to come in for a debrief. We've considered forcing him, snatching him, but we think we'd lose him as an asset. He's provided information only on his own terms."

The President suddenly heard what Hebley wasn't saying. "But at least we know who he is? We've checked him out."

Hebley looked at the door, like he was hoping for a knock to rescue him. It didn't come. "Sir, at the moment we don't even have a photograph of him. He's a very difficult source."

"One reason I like you, General, is you aren't afraid to tell it like it is."

"Thank you, sir."

"That said, you and your entire agency should be embarrassed."

The President generally considered foul language beneath this office, even if some of his predecessors were famous for profanity. Now, however, he decided an F-bomb was warranted.

"It's fucking ridiculous. He's a '*difficult source*.'" The President put air quotes around the phrase. "You sound like a kindergarten teacher. 'Little Johnny is so difficult I can't get him to take a nap.' Do you understand me?"

"Yes, sir."

"I'm not trying to tell you how to do your job. You don't want to snatch him, you think he's more useful to you out there, fine. But get his picture, identify him. You know what? I guess I am telling you how to do your job. Find out if he could access this information. Along the way, maybe you could figure out who killed your station chief. I need more than this if we're going to start scrambling jets. Way more. Fifty-one percent odds, that's worse than nothing."

Hebley nodded.

"Are we clear? I want to hear you say we're clear."

"Yes, Mr. President. We're clear."

Jake Mangiola, the Chairman of the Joint Chiefs, was an Air Force four-star, an old-school fighter jock. Now he gingerly came to Hebley's rescue, one general helping another. "Mr. President, if I may."

"Go ahead."

"I think we all agree that considering offensive action against Iran would be premature. However, given the gravity of this information, it might be prudent for us to undertake a top-to-bottom review of our Iranian APs—"

"AP?"

"Action plan, sir—"

After years of briefings, the President still couldn't get over the way four-stars talked. Like they were reading from invisible PowerPoint presentations, complete with acronyms.

"So you'll have every option if the need arises. We can also move a second carrier group to the edge of the Gulf. We have the *George Washington* south of Sri Lanka now. It'll take three, maybe four days to arrive. Call it an unscheduled training exercise."

"Run your review, get the carrier in close." He had to admit he felt a certain pleasure at snapping his fingers, moving a hundred-thousand-ton aircraft carrier like a kid playing Risk. But his elation passed quickly. The United States hadn't faced a threat this serious since the end of the Cold War. At least.

He looked at Hebley. "Meanwhile, Scott, I assume you want a finding so you and your friends in the Navy can peek at those ships from Dubai. See if they're carrying anything that glows in the dark."

Hebley nodded, obviously glad to be on firmer ground. "We think we have a low-risk option." He explained.

"Anybody object?" the President said when Hebley was finished. No one did. "Good. WHC will get you something this afternoon." White House counsel.

"Yes, sir. We have several days before they're in U.S. territorial waters, but we'd like to make the intercept sooner rather than later."

"Let Donna know when you're ready to move." The President unsubtly glanced at his watch, signaling the meeting's end. Hebley nearly levitated from the couch in his eagerness to leave. The others followed. "Donna, please stay."

Green had worked briefly for the CIA before leaving to go to law school, where she'd met the President. After graduation she had spent a decade on the Hill working for the Senate Select Committee on Intelligence. Profiles usually called her the most hawkish member of the President's inner circle. It was more correct to say she was the champion cynic, believing the worst about every nation's leaders—and usually its people, too. The President had learned not to doubt her judgments, however bitter they seemed. Vladimir Putin *had* turned Russia into a police state. The leaders of China *had* stolen billions of dollars for themselves. The Syrian resistance *was* a bloody jihadi mess.

"We really this clueless about Iran, Donna?"

"Sir, much as I hate to defend Langley, draw up a list of our strategic problems over the last decade, Iran barely makes the top ten. China, Russia, North Korea, Afghanistan, Iraq, Pakistan, Egypt—then Iran. Maybe ahead of Egypt, but you see the point."

"But thousands of people in Tehran and the nuclear facilities must be able to confirm this. Scientists, military—"

"I doubt thousands. A few hundred. But most of them, remember, even the ones who aren't religious, they *want* the bomb. National sovereignty, who are we to say Iran can't have a few nukes when we have thousands. So let's say ninety-five percent would never talk to us, no way, just on principle. The other five percent, maybe they're on the fence, they're scared of what the mullahs might do. Say a couple dozen people fall in that category. Mostly scientists. Literally working in caves. How are they going to reach us? Email nuke@cia.gov? They know if they're caught, they'll be tortured. Killed. Takes courage to make that choice."

"Recklessness, even."

"Yes. At the top, the mullahs have been in charge for thirty-five years. We don't know much about what drives them, how many are genuinely religious, how many just want power. You can say that's our own bad, that after all this time we should have a better picture, but cracking a closed society is tough. And the Guard are really good at what they do—they have to be or the Israelis would eat them for lunch."

"What about the IAEA?" The International Atomic Energy Agency, the Vienna-based group that tracked enrichment programs and reactors worldwide. "All those reports they put out, the monitors, could this really get by them?"

Green didn't smile much, but she was smiling now. "Sir. The way IAEA works is that Iran does what it wants and then lies. I don't mean fibs. I mean they build entire enrichment plants and don't declare them. Then we or the Israelis catch them lying and tell IAEA. Then IAEA goes to Iran and says, *We caught you, tsk-tsk, now let us verify the production of this plant.* The Iranians negotiate for a while. Sometimes they let the inspectors in, and sometimes they don't. Usually they cooperate just enough that we can't say they completely stonewalled us. Even when they do let people in, they delay long enough to have plenty of time to destroy whatever evidence they don't want us to find. I mean, this HEU could literally be coming out of a facility that we don't know exists."

She shook her head. "I know the obvious next question is, 'Why even bother?'"

The President nodded.

"Because the games with IAEA slow them a little, give us a partial picture of what they're doing, how successful they've been. Plus on some level it lets them know that we're watching them. But it's never stopped anyone who really wants a bomb from building one. Not India, not Pakistan, not North Korea."

"So you're saying, yes, we're this clueless. That maybe they have ten bombs done and this guy we're calling Mathers is the only one with the guts to tell us."

"It's possible, sir. I say that with fifty-one percent confidence." Another smile, so the President would know she was joking. Green was a skinny woman, hipless, with short bobbed hair. She was married to a man who could have been her twin. Somehow they'd had one child, a son, though the President couldn't imagine them in bed. He liked her complete sexlessness. He never worried why he wanted her around.

"What if we confront them, tell them what we know? Tell them their choices are the truth or war—"

"The one thing I am sure of, sir, is that that won't work. They will deny. If they aren't doing this and it's a setup, of course they'll deny. But even if they are, they'll deny, because the mere fact that we're asking will show them we're not sure. We need evidence."

"So let's bring this guy in."

"If we can. I was thinking about the material that's on the ship. It depends what it is, though. Low-level material, that wouldn't prove anything. But if it's a chunk of bomb-grade uranium—"

"At least we'd know."

"At least we'd know." Green had been with him long enough to know when their meetings were over. "What can I do now, sir?"

"I want a list of people in the Iranian government who might be open to a back channel. Anybody halfway reasonable. Ambassadors, whoever."

"Yes, sir."

"Never a dull moment, Donna."

"No, sir." She stood, turned for the door.

"By the way, happy birthday." She was fifty today. They both knew that whatever celebration she had planned would be postponed for the foreseeable future. He reached into his desk. "I picked this up special just for you. And by I, I mean the Secret Service."

He pulled out a twin package of Hostess cupcakes and a candle. "Can you believe they almost discontinued these?"

She shook her head. "Thank you, sir." Her voice caught.

"Should we light it now? Wish for no war?"

"I will if you will, sir."

The cupcake was delicious.

19

Reza, Duke, and Salome sat in the kitchen of the safe house in Kadiköy, a quiet district on the Asian side of the Bosphorus. Reza had just finished telling them about his meeting with Brian Taylor.

"Tell me you weren't too queeny, Reza," Salome said.

"Just queeny enough."

Reza's real name was Bijan Parande. He was the only child of an Iranian air force major who had stayed in Tehran after the Shah's fall, betting that the new regime would need professional fighter pilots as much as the old. For a while, the major was right. But as Iran's war against Saddam Hussein sputtered, the ayatollahs decided to purge their military of "counterrevolutionary infidels." In March 1984, Major Parande sent his wife and eleven-year-old son to France. Three months later, the Revolutionary Guard arrested him on charges of treason. He was shot, his corpse dumped in an unmarked grave, his bank accounts seized.

Overnight Bijan and his mother, Afari, were reduced to ungenteel poverty in the northern suburbs of Paris. Afari became a housekeeper. Bijan had been spoiled in Tehran, but he accepted their new life with surprising speed. He had never much liked his father, who had torn out a chunk of his hair when he was seven. Bijan's crime was trying on his mother's shoes.

By twelve, Bijan knew that he preferred men to women. Open homosexuality was neither understood nor tolerated in the *banlieue* where he and his mother lived, so he kept his desires to himself. At seventeen, he fled for London. He wanted to learn English and had the vague idea of becoming an actor. He was almost absurdly handsome, tall and lean with flowing black hair, but his looks far outpaced his skills onstage. To survive, he worked as a busboy and waiter and lived in a cold-water apartment in east London. On his twentieth birthday, a Saudi princeling offered two thousand pounds for a night with him, and his life turned again.

Bijan spent the next fifteen years serving wealthy Arab men in London and Paris. He was expensive and discreet and picked up new clients through word of mouth. He spoke French, English, Farsi, and Arabic, and could easily pass as a business partner for his clients. Sometimes he even visited them on family vacations at their compounds in the south of France. Closeted Arab men took pleasure in such games.

At thirty-five, Bijan found business dwindling. His clients could have what they liked, and they liked young. He could have cut his rates, or accepted men in their seventies with hair growing from their ears. But he had been careful with his money, even bought a small apartment in Paris a few years before. He knew he'd survive, though he feared being bored.

He needn't have worried.

The knock on his apartment door had come almost two years before, a breezy late-spring afternoon in Paris. Salome. She wouldn't tell him her real name, who she was, or how she'd found him. But she knew everything about him, including what the mullahs had done to his father. He wondered if she worked for the DGSE, the French intelligence service. Though she didn't seem French to him. Then again, the French wouldn't consider him French, either, no matter that he'd lived in the country most of his life. When she outlined what she wanted, he agreed immediately.

Don't say yes too soon, she warned. *Think it over. The danger here, it's real. And once you start . . .*

But he didn't need to think it over. He'd enjoyed his youth, but his youth was gone. His mother had died in 2009. Liver cancer. She'd never again seen Tehran. Bijan had no one else. Not a boyfriend, not even a dog. Now Salome wanted him to help make the ayatollahs pay for everything they'd done. *"C'est bon,"* he told her.

Bijan had never stopped speaking Farsi, mainly because his mother had never learned French. Still, his Farsi was rusty,

314 | ALEX BERENSON

his knowledge of Iranian culture even worse. A research trip to Tehran was obviously out. Instead, he moved to Sweden and took a studio apartment in Husby, a poor suburb near Stockholm where tens of thousands of Iranian immigrants lived. He kept to himself, spoke only Farsi. He watched Iranian television in local coffeehouses. He grew a scrubby beard, got a job as a dishwasher. He studiously avoided talking about politics. But after a few weeks, he noticed conversations dying as he walked into stores and restaurants. He'd been pegged as an Iranian spy, or at least a friend of the regime. When he told Salome, she laughed.

Next she sent him to Sofia. Bulgaria. There he shared a basement apartment with roaches and rats. He hadn't been so uncomfortable since his first days in London. When he complained, Salome laughed. *You spent too many nights pillow-biting in hotel suites. Got to toughen you up if you're going to pass for Rev Guard, even a closeted one.* Along the way, her bodyguard—the most terrifying man he'd ever met—taught him basic espionage and self-defense. How to recognize a tail and lose it. How to shoot. How to handle a knife. *Even if you never use any of these tricks, you have to know them. Colonel Reza would.*

Six months in Sofia roughened his skin, put bags under his eyes. *We're getting somewhere,* Salome said. She moved him to Istanbul. There she gave him a tutorial on the Revolutionary Guard and the Quds Force and the first specifics about what she wanted him to do. He was surprised, taken aback. Why would a trained CIA officer accept intelligence from a man whose real name he didn't even know? Why would the officer even respond to his initial effort to make contact? *You're going to tell him a very believable story. Still, you're right, he won't trust you at first,* Salome said. *Maybe ever. But we're going to make what you tell him come true. And he'll have to trust that.*

Reza lived quietly in Istanbul through spring and most of summer. Then Salome told him the time for planning and training had ended. And he became Colonel Reza, an Iranian spy who was having second thoughts about his mission . . .

Now here he was. Twice he had promised Brian Taylor terror attacks. Twice they'd come. He had no idea how Salome and Duke had managed them. He had one job and one job only: to reel in Taylor, make him believe that Iran was about to send highly enriched uranium to the United States.

"Stroke of genius, the gay thing," Duke said. "Taylor thinks he's figured out what makes you tick. Why you're taking this chance. He'll feel like he has an edge. It'll give him more confidence when he goes to his station chief, all the way up the chain."

"Next time he sees me, he's going to take my photo. Even if he has to tie me up himself to do it."

"I promise the agency has snatch-and-grab teams in Istanbul right now," Duke said. "They'll be tailing Taylor, sleeping at his apartment. Langley will have live ears on every phone. They might even have the Turks helping. Only question is whether they'll try to snatch you the next time you meet him. I think we have to assume yes."

"Which is why you're not going to meet him again," Salome said.

Reza was disappointed. He liked playing with Taylor. Reza wondered, too, whether Salome planned to kill him when the job was done. She was a client, and his clients had a habit of discarding him after he'd satisfied their needs. He understood very well the risk he presented to her. He had thought of telling her that he'd left a letter with a friend that was to be opened only in the event of his death. But he had no friends he trusted well enough. Salome probably knew as much.

He supposed as a last resort he could leave the letter in his apartment. Then decided, what's the use? If he died, the property manager would eventually unlock his door. Maybe the manager would find the letter, if Salome's agents hadn't already broken in and taken it. Maybe the manager would view it as something other than the mad ramblings of a dead man, bring it to the local police station. Even then, what would the gendarmes do? How would their investigation help him? He couldn't beat these people who bombed embassies and killed CIA men. He would hope that Salome would trust in his discretion. Anyway, he would be satisfied whatever happened. The last two years had been the most interesting of his life. If he had to trade them for empty decades watching movies alone, so be it.

"So if I'm not to meet him, what happens next?"

"First we need to let them find the material."

"On the ship?" Reza didn't know why he was surprised. Of course Salome would make sure his third tip was as accurate as his first two. He saw where the game was leading, a stepped series of provocations, each more threatening to America than the previous. The sequence had to have one more. He couldn't imagine what that would be. A threat to assassinate the President?

She put a hand on Reza's arm. "Duke and I need to talk." The words spoken in a way that made Reza wonder what Duke had done wrong. "I'll call you. Until then, keep your routine."

"Tell me what you know about Thailand," she said to Duke as soon as Reza was gone.

"My caretaker called. Somebody broke into my house. A Westerner, probably American. I don't know how he found me, but I think he took some papers. Surgery records."

"Photos?"

"I'm not an idiot."

She let that hang.

"I called Singh," Duke said. "The doctor. He told me the guy approached them. At this point, he was trying to pass himself as Saudi. He had some kind of contact at the KSA embassy in Bangkok who vouched for him. Didn't matter. Singh told him to get lost."

"The same man? Went as American and then Saudi?"

Suddenly the pieces fit together. Duke knew who was chasing them. Not a happy thought. "This leak started with Eddie, right? Who knew Montoya. Who knows Vinny Duto from Colombia. Know who else knows Duto?" Duke paused. "John Wells."

She didn't look as surprised as he expected. He wondered

again about her connections inside Langley. "Wells. The retired one who used to work with Duto?"

"He's *trouble*, Salome. He's kept his profile down since the thing in Times Square, but he won't be scared of this. He likes it messy."

"Duto can't help him anymore."

"Senators have a tiny bit of pull."

"So could John Wells have found you through Aesthetic Beauty?"

"I told you, Singh said—"

"Of course Singh said that."

Duke saw she was right. Singh couldn't deny someone had come looking for Duke. The fact that Duke was calling him out of the blue proved Duke knew that much. But Singh would insist he hadn't told Wells anything, even if he had.

"I didn't use my real name, I paid cash, they don't keep pictures."

"You sure?"

"As sure as I can be without looking at their hard drives."

"Do they have current contacts for you?"

"A mobile number and an email address."

"The phone—"

"In my luggage at safe house three. I'll destroy it."

"Let's assume Wells knows your real name, too. Maybe Eddie told Montoya, or maybe they figured it out for themselves." Salome stared at him. Duke wondered if she knew the truth about his link to Veder, why he'd insisted on targeting the man. No matter. They couldn't go back.

"Maybe he does."

"Which means Shafer and Duto do, too. Maybe they're already trying to convince the agency Glenn Mason is involved." Saying it like there was no maybe at all.

"It doesn't matter. Glenn Mason is dead. And I haven't used that name in four years. Never."

"A solid defense. As long as you stay dead."

Not much he could say to that. He didn't exactly trust her, but he knew he was in for the duration. Far too late for him to give himself up. He'd killed a station chief. He'd wind up with a needle in his arm.

"Let's assume John Wells has tracked you to Istanbul. The famous John Wells." Her voice was airy. Almost sarcastic. "What then? What shall we do with him?"

20

ISTANBUL

Wells skipped the cab line at Atatürk Airport. He walked outside the terminal until he spotted a black Toyota compact with a scrape on its bumper and a plastic sign dangling from its mirror. "TAXI," red letters on a white background. The kind of sign that could be pulled down in a moment if the police passed by. A fiftyish man in a blue jacket sat behind the wheel. He smiled as he lowered his window, revealing a mouthful of cracked brown teeth. Wells leaned in, looked for a meter, didn't find one. Good.

"I want to hire you for the day."

The driver raised his caterpillar-sized eyebrows. "Six hundred lira, good price. Plus petrol. My English good, I learn in UK, show you around, tour guide."

Six hundred Turkish lira equaled about three hundred dollars. Hardly cheap for this jalopy, but no matter. "No tour guide."

"Okay, five hundred fifty."

"I may want you to follow someone."

"Chase?"

"Follow. Not too fast."

"Chase who?"

"Whoever."

"For chase one thousand lira. Still plus petrol. To catch, three thousand."

"Long as the jokes are free." Wells stowed his bag in back, folded himself into the seat beside the cabbie. It was covered with the mats of wooden beads that taxi drivers inexplicably liked. He wrenched his seat back, wedged his knees under the dash.

"Big man."

"Small car." The space around his feet was littered with candy wrappers and a water bottle filled with a pale yellow liquid that wasn't Gatorade. "Ever clean this thing?"

"Tomorrow."

Wells gave the cabbie five one-hundred-lira notes. "This to start." About two hundred fifty dollars, more than the guy would make in a week. The driver tucked the bills in his shirt pocket like he couldn't be bothered to count them. He put the Toyota in gear and they merged into the airport traffic.

"This is, what, a one-liter engine?"

"One-point-four."

"I don't think we have to worry about catching anyone." Wells wondered if he could push his legs through the floor, help with acceleration like Fred Flintstone. As an answer, the cabbie downshifted, gunned the engine. The Toyota responded with a surprising burst. Again the cabbie waggled his eyebrows. He seemed inordinately proud of them.

"What your name?"

"Roger." Wells didn't return the question, but he had a feeling the guy wouldn't take the hint.

"I am Kemal. Popular name. For Atatürk." Mustafa Kemal Atatürk, the general who had founded modern Turkey.

"Nice." Wells closed his eyes, hoping to catch up on the sleep he'd missed in Phuket.

"No, too popular. His name all over. This airport, everywhere."

"I'm going to find out a lot about you, aren't I?"

Wells wished he had backup. But back in Thailand, Shafer and Duto had told him that asking the seventh floor for help would be pointless. Another piece of intel had arrived from the Istanbul source. The agency was still confirming it, but Hebley considered it serious enough that he had briefed the President and the National Security Advisor. He was calling it a "direct threat to CONUS." Continental United States.

"What is it?" Wells said.

"They're holding it tight," Shafer said.

"Inside guys who aren't inside anymore. Worse than tits on a bull."

"John—"

"Stop pretending you're pulling your weight."

"Get a photo," Duto said. "Don't have to bring him in, don't even have to talk to him. Just a good-quality photo."

"I got you the surgery. A phone."

"Seventh floor won't even consider the possibility he's alive without a photo."

"They can have Bangkok station send someone to the plastic-surgery place. Singh will confirm Mason was there."

"Forget it, John. They aren't interested."

"How's a photo change that?"

"Because it's easy to understand. It's not a weird theory about some screwy ex–ops officer who changed his identity and is playing dead. And we don't even know who he's working for, but this one doctor in the middle of Thailand might confirm it. You think Hebley wants to hear that craziness? You think the President does? This decision is hard enough. He wants concrete choices. He doesn't want to have to guess at the *facts*. Takes something real to break through that mind-set. A photo's real. I can shove it at them, say, Lookee here, Mason's alive, Mason's in Istanbul, we need to figure out why. Even a general can understand that. Even a *reporter* can understand that."

Wells could hardly argue Duto's authority on how the White House worked.

"You get the picture, John?"

"Fine."

"So get the picture. Call me when you have something not completely useless."

Wells hung up. So he'd have no help in Istanbul. Not unless he brought it himself. He stayed in touch with a couple operators but he trusted only one for a job this sensitive, an ex-Delta named Brett Gaffan. And Gaffan was out of pocket, on his honeymoon. He'd married a twenty-four-year-old named Svetlana, ignoring his buddies' warnings that Russian women were the female equivalent of avalanches: beautiful, destructive, and best viewed from a safe distance.

As a rule, Wells didn't mind operating alone. But here he was caught among Mason, the agency, maybe the Iranian government. Once again he found himself in the uncomfortable position of playing detective in a country where he had no police powers. Plus he didn't speak the language. Having somebody to watch his six would have been nice.

Kemal the cabbie would have to do.

At least Wells had a fix on Mason's phone, and presumably his safe house. It was in Nişantaşı, northeast of Taksim Square. Istanbul's cosmopolitan elite and foreign executives favored the neighborhood, whose narrow streets were lined with boutiques like Louis Vuitton and Chanel. Turkey's government promoted a strict brand of Islam, but most of the country's wealthy remained less observant, and happily lapped up brands that advertised luxury and sex.

Thanks to Shafer, or maybe Duto, the NSA had finally come through on Mason's phone. Mason had been careful with it, using it only three times since Singh gave Wells the number. Even so, the NSA had triangulated it to a couple hundred meters in Nişantaşı. To get closer, Wells would use a handheld sniffer he'd gotten from the agency's

Directorate of Science and Technology. His final freebie before Duto left.

Essentially, the sniffer worked as a homing device, tracking the handset by spoofing the signals from a local cellular tower. As long as the target phone was on, it could be tracked. Best of all, the DST geeks assured him it should work almost everywhere in the world without new software. Telecom companies wanted customers to have access to one another's networks when they traveled internationally, so they used standardized software and routing systems. The sniffer could find a phone in Buenos Aires as easily as Los Angeles.

Istanbul's afternoon traffic gave Kemal time to tell Wells his life story. The cabbie had learned English in Manchester, where he was studying to be an electrical engineer. Back home, he'd worked for the national power company, TEK.

"After nineteen years, they fire me. Wife take daughters back to Izmir. Divorce."

Wells grunted.

"Too much raki. You know raki?" He tipped an imaginary bottle to his mouth. "Like whiskey."

"You still drink?"

"Oh, yes." Kemal said the words almost proudly. "Why stop now?"

"Excellent point."

"What about you, Roger? You have wife?"

Wells wondered what answer would shut Kemal up quickest. "Yes. We're very happy."

That did the trick.

Light snow coated the sidewalks as they turned onto Teşvikiye, a boulevard that gave its name to one of the richest parts of Nişantaşı. Mason's safe house was somewhere in here. "Where now?"

"Just drive."

Kemal piloted the Toyota through the narrow one-way lanes that dominated Teşvikiye. The area sloped steeply toward the Bosphorus. Midrise apartment buildings were packed together, and surveillance cameras common. Wells wondered why Mason had picked the area. Maybe Mason had his main safe house in a cheaper neighborhood, and this was simply an expensive backup. Considering the resources Mason seemed to have, the idea wasn't far-fetched.

Wells realized that finding the handset might be harder than he'd hoped. Dozens of apartment buildings fell within the target area, hundreds of apartments. Mason would have to turn on his phone for several minutes for Wells to have a chance.

Half an hour later, they had exhausted every street in Teşvikiye and were driving slowly along Abdu Ipekçi, which abutted the park on the neighborhood's western edge. A car pulled out from the curb in front of them, leaving an open spot. "Take it."

Kemal looked sulkily at Wells, then pulled in.

"The man you look for, you have picture?"

"An old one."

"Quite a pickle."

"You really were in England."

"I call cousins. Give them picture, we watch."

Wells feared Kemal's cousins would stick out in this fancy nabe even more than he did. "Let's give it time."

As if on cue, a fast electronic beeping sounded from the backseat. The sniffer was designed so it could pass for a phone and be used in public without attracting attention. The top of its screen showed the mobile number it was tracking. In the center, a white dot indicated its current location. A red dot—now in the upper-right corner— showed the target handset's location. In the United States, a street grid would have been programmed in. Here the rest of the screen was blank.

Wells grabbed the Toyota's keys, in case Kemal was thinking about leaving. He pulled on a baseball cap, the cheapest cover possible, and stepped into the dark. He wasn't planning to break into Mason's apartment. Not yet, anyway. Find the guy, then hire a professional photographer for long-lens surveillance shots. Duto and Shafer wanted pictures, Wells would get them a yearbook's worth.

Wells walked up the hill, turned right. The screen blanked out, then came back. Either the hills were blocking the target signal or the device didn't work internationally as seamlessly as the DST claimed. With no grid and no scale, Wells couldn't tell exactly how far away Mason's handset was.

He turned left, edging past two women wearing fur coats more suitable for Moscow. He carried the screen close to his jacket, like a guy trying to watch the playoffs at a wedding. Nothing about this job had been easy. But he was close now. He made another right, onto a two-block street, too small and narrow to attract high-end retailers.

According to the device in his hand, Mason was somewhere on this street. Wells was close. So close—

The dots disappeared. The screen went black.

The phone number went, too. The snooper hadn't lost the signal this time. Mason had finished his call, turned off the handset. Showing decent discipline. Still, the street was short enough for Wells to see every target building. When the phone came back on, Wells should find him.

Wells was slightly surprised that Mason was using an old phone so much. But even the most security-crazed operative needed one permanent number for people who needed to reach him quickly and with certainty. With this new operation coming together, he was rushing, getting sloppy.

Back at the Toyota, Kemal sipped a half-liter bottle of clear liquid.

"Raki." He offered it to Wells.

Wells shook his head. Kemal took another hit from the bottle and turned up the radio, premillennial Britney Spears.

"Can't imagine why your wife left you."

"She likes this even more than me. *Oops I did it again*."

Wells would never understand why the world loved the trashiest parts of American culture the most. Kemal took a long pull off the bottle. His throat thumped like a fish on a line. Great. A drunk wheelman.

"Don't suppose you know where I can find a pistol. A nice nine-millimeter?"

"Gun? No, no."

"You're not that innocent, Kemal."

As an answer, Kemal took another slug.

"Now what?"

Wells was famished. He hadn't eaten since Dubai, twelve hours before. "Dinner."

Kemal steered them to Cumhuriyet, a broad avenue at the edge of Nişantaşı, and much less fancy. They chose a one-room restaurant, pressed-wood walls and plastic chairs, almost a cafeteria. The lamb was cooked to tasteless gray-brown pellets. Wells devoured his plate, ordered another. Kemal claimed he wasn't hungry, but Wells made him choke down a kebab to sop up the raki.

"You don't eat like an American," Kemal said.

"How do I eat?"

"Like a prisoner."

Wells popped a piece of stale pita in his mouth.

"This man we looking for—"

"We're not talking about that."

"One question, then. You come here yourself, to find him. How come no one helps you?"

Words that reminded Wells that he had not even a week before Anne's deadline. He wished she were here. Or at least that he could tell her about everything he'd seen since Miami, the half-drunk man sitting with him now. Of the loneliness that streamed through the winter woods of the world. He reached for his phone. To tell her that he loved her. To tell her that she was right, he would give up this life.

She would tell him to come home.

He would have to tell her he couldn't, not quite yet. Soon, but not quite yet.

What would she say then? Nothing at all, he suspected. And he would be left with the dull aftertaste of cruelty on his tongue. He put away the phone. "Let's go."

The street where Wells had tracked the phone was too narrow for parking, but after circling the neighborhood Kemal found a spot around the corner from its north end. Mason's street ran one way north to south, so if someone was picking him up tonight, the vehicle would have to pass them.

Nişantaşı went to bed early. By nine p.m., the streets emptied. The area took on the buttoned-up feel peculiar to wealthy city neighborhoods at night. Lights flicked on behind curtained windows, the details of life hidden from the commoners below.

A low stream of pop music provided the car's only soundtrack. Kemal sipped from his bottle, nursing it until only drops remained. Just before midnight Wells felt his phone buzzing. Shafer.

"Ellis."

"You in Constantinople?"

"Yes."

"Close to our friend?"

"I think so, yes."

"That threat, it's confirmed. Before you ask, that's all I

know. Whatever game these people are playing, they are not messing around. Get that picture and get gone."

Wells hung up.

A few minutes later, Kemal stirred. "How much longer tonight?"

"Let's say until one. Come back tomorrow."

"You pay five hundred extra."

Wells was about to argue when the sniffer sounded again. The target was maybe fifty meters south. One of the buildings on the two-block street. Headlights lit the back window. Wells ducked low as a BMW sedan rolled past.

"Start the car and wait." Wells jogged to the corner, peeked around. The sedan waited outside an apartment building at the south end of the street. Wells couldn't get a clear look, much less a good photo, without exposing himself. A man in a pea jacket and jeans stepped out of the building, into the back of the BMW. At this distance, Wells couldn't be sure it was Mason.

He ran for the cab, slid in back.

"Follow him. Not too close."

Whatever his love for raki, Kemal piloted the Toyota smoothly. Wells lay on the backseat, head down, staring at his phone, mapping their route. They turned left, right, left again, northeast along the causeway on the shore of the Bosphorus. Wells guessed they were headed for the expressway that ran along the city's northern edge and spanned the Bosphorus at the Sultan Mehmet Bridge. Maybe Mason was headed for a safe house on the Asian side. A few minutes later they accelerated up a ramp. But instead of going over the bridge, they turned west. Away.

After another five minutes, they slowed, turned onto another ramp, accelerated again.

"South now," Kemal said from the front seat. "Back to the city."

The map showed Wells where they were, but he didn't know Istanbul well enough to have any idea whether Mason's route made sense. They'd traveled north on surface roads, west on the expressway, now south on another expressway. This ride stank of a countersurveillance trap.

They turned off the highway. "Beyoglu," Kemal said. They were moving southeast, into the city center. After driving a half hour, they were only a couple kilometers from Mason's apartment.

"Someone following us," Kemal said. "Mercedes, black. We turn, he turn."

Wells wondered if the Mercedes was after him. Or Mason.

The night brightened as they returned to Istanbul's clotted heart. They turned left, stopped at a light, came up a hill. Then a right. Wells lifted his head to see if he could spot the Mercedes. But traffic here was heavy despite the hour, and he couldn't.

"Near Taksim." Another right. "Tarlabaşı. Big street. Big traffic."

After another minute. "Okay. The BM pulling over. Two men getting out. Now the BM going again."

"Pull over." Wells looked through the rear right passenger window. The man in jeans and pea jacket was walking with a second man. He turned his head and Wells saw him in profile. His face was flatter and squarer—more Thai,

336 | ALEX BERENSON

somehow—than the presurgery pictures of Glenn Mason. And he was wearing a hood that shrouded his face. Yet Wells knew. This was Mason.

After three continents, four weeks of searching, Wells had found his man. He felt more relieved than elated. He hadn't wasted his time. He wanted to jump Mason, drag him into Kemal's car. But of course that was impossible. Anyway, as Shafer kept telling him, he didn't need to arrest Mason, just get one good photo.

"The Mercedes," Kemal said.

Too late for Wells to duck. He sat still as the black sedan drove by. It had tinted windows, and he had no hope of getting the plate. Wells had no way to tell whether it was tracking Mason or working with him, but the latter seemed more likely.

On the sidewalk ahead, the two men ducked onto a dark side street that disappeared down a steep hill.

"Very bad there," Kemal said. "No police. Thieves. Drugs."

"Go to Taksim, wait for me." Wells opened the door.

"How long?"

"Two hours. You don't see me, come back here in the morning. But be careful. Watch out for that Mercedes."

"You pay now."

Wells scribbled Shafer's number on a page from his reporter's notebook. "I don't come back, call this man. In America. Tell him what happened. Where we went. He'll pay you."

Kemal shook his head but took the paper. "*Inshallah,* my friend."

"Inshallah."

Wells stepped out, oriented himself. Tarlabaşı was a wide two-way avenue. Wells stood on its western side, with traffic flowing south past him. The commuter hub of Taksim Square marked the avenue's northern end, and million-dollar apartments were only a few hundred meters east.

Yet as Wells walked to the nameless street where Mason had turned, he realized the truth of Kemal's warning. Down the hill he saw not a single streetlight. Not a storefront, open or closed. Fifty meters down, three men huddled around a burning garbage can, shifting against the cold. Tarlabaşı's traffic obviously worked as a barrier between this blighted area and the wealth on higher ground to the east.

As his eyes adjusted to the darkness, Wells saw Mason and his friend maybe a hundred meters ahead. Why had they come here at midnight? Why the long countersurveillance run? The moves stank of setup. Either they were trying to lose a tail, or trap one. But Wells had to take the bait. If Mason knew Wells was after him and Wells didn't bite tonight, Mason would toss his phone and Wells would lose him again. On the other hand, if Mason was really meeting someone down here, Wells could fade into these black streets until he got the picture he needed.

So he told himself. But he knew that logic didn't fully explain his insistence on chasing Mason into this maze without backup or even a pistol. He hadn't come this far to back off now. *You want to play? Think you can take me? Good. Start the clock.*

———————

Wells reached the garbage can. Ahead, Mason stopped walking. Wells stepped close to the can. The sputtering flame inside was as hopeless as the men around it. They had the drawn faces and sallow skin of heroin addicts, dying from the inside out.

Wells counted seven, looked down the hill. Mason and the other man were turning left onto a side street. Wells followed. The smell of sewage grew more insistent. Rats jumped from a trash pile and slipped one by one into a hole in the sidewalk, like soldiers scrambling for cover. Farther down, Wells passed an empty husk of a building, its windows gone, its crumbling bricks covered with posters that warned against trespassing.

He reached the street where Mason had turned left. It ran north-south, parallel to Tarlabaşı. It was narrower than the street where Wells now walked, barely wide enough for a car to pass. Wells peeked around the corner. Mason stood near the end of the block, rapping on a door on the right side of the street, the west side. The door opened, and Mason and his buddy disappeared inside.

Tarlabaşı was maybe two hundred fifty meters away. Even with the hill, at a full run Wells would reach it in less than a minute. He had never felt so imprisoned by his own desire to hunt. He knew the odds he faced a trap were at least fifty-fifty. Yet he walked on.

Six front doors ran down the right side of the street, spaced about every twenty-five feet. But the buildings above them actually formed a single structure, five stories high. One building, split with separate entrances and street numbers, to give the illusion it was six. Mason had walked in the fifth door down.

Wells pulled his autopick and went for the first door. The lock gave so fast that Wells wondered if it had been set at all. The stairs were dark, but Wells chose speed over stealth, hurdling stairs two at a time. If this was a trap, Mason would want to draw Wells as far down the hill as possible before dropping the net. The pursuit would stay loose to keep from tipping Wells off. Still, a couple guys would be behind him. When they came around the corner and didn't see him, they would know something was wrong. So Wells needed to move quickly now. He reached the top floor, kept climbing. Bad as the neighborhood was, basic fire codes still applied. The building had to have a fire door to the roof. Wells figured the door wouldn't have an alarm. It didn't.

The roof was slick with melted sleet. Wells found a chunk of paving stone, jammed open the door to be sure that it wouldn't lock from the inside. He crunched a hypodermic needle under his boot as he stepped around a narrow mattress. He jumped over the half-wall that sectioned the building, landed clean, kept moving. When he reached the fifth section of the building, the section he'd seen Mason enter, he stopped.

On the street beneath him, footsteps. Wells crab-walked to the edge of the building, peeked over. Two men stood below, heads swiveling, pistols loose in their right hands. The front door beneath Wells opened and a third man came out.

So a trap. Mason had known he was coming. Maybe

Singh had told him. *A man came here, he said he was Saudi, he knew all about you . . .* Mason, or whoever was in charge, had laid the crumbs just so. They'd given Wells a taste of Mason's phone to draw him out. They'd run the counter-surveillance to see whether Wells was part of a team or working alone. And Wells had taken the bait like the world's dumbest fish.

At least he wasn't surprised. Furious for his foolishness, but not surprised.

He heard footsteps coming up the stairs below. He scuttled back to the fire door. The high ground was a basic tactical advantage, and Mason's men would want it. They ought to have had someone on the roof already, but they weren't perfect.

The fire stairs were identical to those Wells had taken. They were covered by a half-pyramid that rose from the roof and ended in a door that swung open to the left. Wells crouched on the right side of the pyramid. He was betting the man inside was right-handed. He would push the bar with his left hand, lead with his right. His gun hand. He'd be close to the right edge of the door frame.

The man below ran along the fifth-floor hallway, turned, came up the stairs—

Wells drew his knife. Three seconds, two, one—

The door popped open. With his left hand, Wells grabbed the man's outstretched right wrist. He jerked the man's right arm up so the pistol pointed uselessly into the air. As he did, he spun around the door frame into the man. The guy couldn't stop his momentum, couldn't keep from impaling himself on the knife Wells held. He grunted, too surprised to scream, as Wells worked the blade deep into him. The pistol fell from his hand, and Wells left the knife inside him and shoved him back down the stairs and slammed the door shut as the man tumbled backward, thumping down the stairs, cursing. Wells didn't particularly care whether the man lived or died. He'd needed a pistol and now he had one. He reached down now, grabbed it. A Sig Sauer, which didn't necessarily mean anything either way.

More important was the fact that the guy hadn't been wearing a tac radio. A Delta or SOG team would surely have been miked up. So would elite Israeli, Russian, or European units. Another sign that these guys were private, not government, unless they were so deep undercover that they felt they couldn't carry the proper tactical gear.

A man yelled from deep inside the building, and Wells knew he had to move. The guy he'd stabbed was out of commission, but his friends would be up soon enough. Time to take his new pistol and run. Still, he had a chance. The men coming up the stairs would have to approach cautiously in case Wells was waiting to shoot down at them.

Wells retraced his steps, running north, vaulting the half-walls. As he reached the second section of the building, he heard shouting from the stairwell where he'd stabbed the operative. Then two quick shots, and two more. So Mason's men had given up any hope of taking Wells silently. He was surprised they weren't carrying suppressed pistols. Another tactical error. Maybe they'd figured they wouldn't need them, that they would overpower him before he could respond.

Three more shots echoed from the stairwell as Wells leapt over the final half-wall. If he could get to the first staircase before his pursuers reached the roof, they would have no way of knowing where he'd gone. But he tripped on the edge of the mattress, landed hard on his right shoulder. His momentum carried him to the edge of the sleet-slicked roof. His heels slid over as he swiped at a vent pipe. For a moment his fingers failed to find purchase on the slick metal and he imagined himself tumbling sixty feet to the alley below, bouncing off brick as he fell. He dug in and finally stopped his slide. He picked himself up, ran for the fire door. As he stepped inside, he heard shouting. The stumble had ended his chance for a clean escape. They'd seen him. He shifted the pistol to his left hand and vaulted down the stairs.

Mason's men didn't have radios, but they had phones. Right now they would be calling one another, fixing his position. Five floors of stairs gave them too much time. They would set up outside the front door, gun him down as he tried to leave. But he couldn't go back to the roof, either. They were up there now.

He needed another move.

Each of the six sections of the building was set up in classic tenement style, four apartments per floor, one on each corner. From the roof Wells had seen that the buildings one street west had lower rooflines, because they'd been built shorter and because they were farther down the hill. A narrow alley, no more than three feet, separated Wells's building from the structures that backed it to the west.

On the third floor, Wells stopped. A dim light glowed

under the door to the apartment in the building's back right corner. Wells shoved his automatic pick into the lock. *"Asalaam aleikum,"* he said, loudly enough for anyone inside to hear. He opened the door, slowly. Inside, a naked lightbulb hung above a coffee table crammed with cheap children's toys. A Turkish man in a dirty white T-shirt stood blocking an open hallway. He was small and wiry and held a cleaver high in his right hand.

Wells kicked the door shut. He kept his pistol on the man as he stepped crosswise to the window at the back of the apartment. "I'm not here to hurt you or your family." This in Arabic, his voice low and calm. The man might not know the words. But the language itself, the language of the Quran, would reassure him.

The window was dirty, stuck shut. Wells tugged it up. As he'd hoped, the roofline of the building across the alley was several feet lower than the windowsill. He ought to be able to jump across. Wells pointed out the window, back to himself.

The man nodded.

Wells leaned halfway out the window, then looked over his shoulder at the man. For now Wells still had his right hand free and could cover the guy with his pistol. But to get himself through the window he would have to twist both shoulders through. Wells would be facing away from the man, who could throw the cleaver at him or just run across the apartment and push him out. Wells wouldn't be able to defend himself.

Wells had to trust this civilian whose house he'd invaded. Or shoot him.

"Hamdulillah." Peace be with you. The man nodded again. Wells turned away, squeezed through the window, brought his knees underneath him. He wouldn't have much momentum, but the alley was so narrow that he shouldn't need much.

He jumped. The drop to the opposite roof was only about six feet, but Wells didn't stick the landing cleanly. His knees buckled and he rolled forward onto his right shoulder. A pile of bricks stopped him. He permitted himself one look back. The man with the cleaver stood open-mouthed at the window.

Wells pulled himself upright. He'd come down hard on his left foot, which was permanently tender after an injury years before in Afghanistan. No matter. Mason's men wouldn't know where he'd gone. By the time they realized he was no longer inside the other building, he would be blocks away.

This building made the one across the alley look like a luxury high-rise. It had no interior lights at all. Wells limped down the stairs, plotting his next move. His foot might not get him far, but he could hole up for the night in an abandoned building. He had the pistol. And Mason's team couldn't chase him forever. Even in this neighborhood, multiple shots and a pack of armed men would eventually draw police.

Wells opened the front door, limped out—

And was hit by the four round front headlights of a

Mercedes sedan. After the darkness of the hallway, they were more than enough to blind him. He reflexively raised a hand to shield his eyes. To his left, someone—a *woman*—said, "Drop your weapon."

Wells flicked his head, tried to see her. Couldn't.

"You're pinned." Her voice calm and level.

He had nowhere to go. He couldn't run. If he went back in the building, he'd succeed only in getting himself killed. Along with a bunch of innocent people.

He dropped to his knees. Tossed the pistol to the street. He watched it go with regret, though it had proven as useless for him as its previous owner.

"Lie on your stomach with your hands behind your back."

Wells didn't think she planned to kill him. She could have done that when he stepped out of the door. In any case, when he'd thrown away the pistol he'd given up his choice. He kissed the rough street, more dirt than pavement, and knitted his hands behind his back. He wished he knew how they'd found him. Probably they'd seen him from the other roof.

Mostly he was furious at himself. Too many chances, too many years running alone, too many close calls. Finally, his luck had run out. No one knew where he was. Even if Kemal the taxi driver kept his promise to call Shafer, Wells didn't see how anyone would track him.

Two pairs of footsteps crunched his way. A big man put a knee in his back and flex-cuffed his arms together. A penlight traced his face. "This will pinch," the woman said.

A needle bit into his neck. Wells lifted his head to protest, but the black water inside the syringe filled him. A heartbeat later, it rose to his brain and covered his thoughts. Nothing could stop it, not fury nor willpower nor all the world's desperation.

His mouth fell slack and he slept.

21

Flying flat out, a Black Hawk made the thirteen-mile run from Langley to the White House in eight minutes. Normally, Scott Hebley loved the trip. The helicopter raced low over the Potomac's brown waters, came over the Lincoln Memorial with the Washington Monument ahead. Then turned toward the South Lawn and the great white building where history was made. The feeling of arriving at the absolute center of power couldn't be explained to anyone on the outside.

Today, though, Hebley's stomach grew more unsettled with every spin of the rotors. In Afghanistan, he had overseen the end of a war. The news he was about to present would move the United States close to a new one, against an army far larger than the Taliban. Hebley almost missed the Talibs. For all their bluster and savagery, when they saw they couldn't fight his Marines, they simply retreated into Pakistan. They had never tried anything one-tenth as bold as what Iran was now doing, introducing a new generation to mutually assured destruction. Iran already menaced the entire Persian Gulf. How much more aggressive would the Islamic Republic become if it believed that it had an insurance policy to keep the United States from attacking?

The Black Hawk's turbines whined as the helicopter slowed, descended, and finally touched down on the flat aluminum disks that served as the South Lawn's discreet landing pad. Hebley unbuckled his harness and ignored the outstretched hand of a Secret Service agent as he stepped onto the wet grass. It was just past five p.m., and the sky was fading to black as the sun set behind a thick curtain of clouds.

The agent led Hebley to the door at the edge of the West Wing that was the building's VIP entrance. He passed through a metal detector and his badge was swiped, necessary formalities even for the DCI. Only the President and his immediate family could enter without being checked.

Donna Green's executive assistant waited for him. "The meeting's been moved." He had expected to talk with Green one-on-one before they met the President. Instead, she led him directly to the Oval Office.

Operation CHERRYPICK had gone smoothly, all things considered. The agency had flagged three ships as potential matches for the tip from its Rev Guard source. Its top target was the *Kara Six*, a midsized vessel that carried rugs and clothes from Pakistan to Europe and the United States.

A month before, the *Kara Six* had loaded twenty thousand rugs and fifteen containers of T-shirts in its home port of Karachi. In Dubai, it picked up another six containers of African knickknacks destined for stores like Pier One. The captain of the *Six* was Hassim Sharif, a fifty-one-year-old who had grown up in a Pakistani town on the Gulf of Oman.

After leaving Dubai, the *Six* plugged along at a steady twenty-two knots, covering more than five hundred nautical miles a day. It gave the pirate-choked Somali coast a wide berth and passed without incident through the Suez Canal, the Mediterranean, and the Straits of Gibraltar. Its ultimate destination was the Port of Charleston, which had become increasingly popular for the easy access it offered to Atlanta and the Southeast.

The *Six* was twelve hundred miles east of South Carolina when a carrier battle group led by the USS *Ronald Reagan* found it. The *Reagan* positioned itself one hundred miles south of the *Six*, outside the standard Atlantic commercial shipping lanes. It launched an F-18 carrying two specially modified MK-46 torpedoes. Their warheads had been removed. Instead of exploding, they were designed to ram the ship's propeller and tear off its blades.

MK-46s had been built to chase down and destroy Russian submarines. They had less than no trouble taking care of the *Six*. Thirty-seven minutes after the F-18 launched, the *Reagan*'s Tactical Operations Center reported that the *Six* was floating helplessly in six-foot waves, standard for the winter Atlantic. It had not sent any distress calls, probably because Captain Sharif had no idea why his ship had suddenly turned into a thirty-thousand-ton canoe.

Ten minutes later, the frigate USS *Nicholas*, helmed by Commander Sam Ivory, approached the *Six*. If its captain was surprised at the coincidence, he didn't say so. Via ship-to-ship radio, he accepted Ivory's offer to put divers in the water to check the propeller.

"I'd also like to send a team of engineers to look at your engine, Captain."

"My men can make any necessary repairs."

"I *absolutely* insist."

The four-star admiral who commanded the Atlantic fleet had told Ivory the night before, *We're boarding that ship no matter what. Deniability is important, in case we're wrong, in case we find nothing but a bunch of rugs. The search is more important. Moment comes when you need to put guns on him, you go ahead. The White House and I will back you all the way. You understand, Commander?*

Ivory understood.

"You are saying I have no choice?" Sharif said.

"There's always a choice, Captain."

Half an hour later, Ivory stood on the *Six*'s bridge, along with six very well-armed sailors. The pretense that this was a routine rescue at sea had disappeared. An eight-member Nuclear Emergency Search Team had flown the night before from Andrews Air Force Base to the *Reagan*, then helicoptered to the *Nicholas* aboard two Seahawks. The team was about to board the *Kara*, carrying handheld radiation detectors and two trunks of more exotic equipment.

"Who are these men?" Sharif said.

"Just routine."

"Routine what?"

"Your English is better than I expected."

"We both know this is illegal."

"You let me board voluntarily. My men are here to help get you to shore." Both statements were technically true. If the nuclear search team came up empty, the U.S. Navy would happily tow the *Kara Six* to safety. Sharif and the crew might even get a few thousand dollars each for the inconvenience.

"It's obvious that you disabled my ship."

"I did nothing of the sort." Again, technically true. The F-18 had come from the *Reagan*.

"Now you've blocked my sat phone. It doesn't work since your destroyer appeared."

"I appreciate the promotion, but it's a frigate, Captain."

"Even if you throw me overboard, my whole crew, you can't make my ship vanish. My company knows where we are, half the Atlantic has seen us—"

Sharif was starting to annoy Ivory. "No one's throwing anyone anywhere. I'll be straight with you. If you have contraband on this vessel, you can make your life much easier if you show it to me. We're going to find it."

Like many captains, Sharif was heavy, out of shape. Shipboard cooks weren't known for health food. He rubbed his belly now, as if it might have the answer. Ivory watched him calculate. The boarding might be illegal, but sometimes might made right. Sharif's protest would wait until he docked.

"Let's speak in my quarters."

Ivory commanded ten times as many men as Sharif, but the Pakistani captain's stateroom was twice the size of his. Merchant captains took their privileges seriously, especially when they hailed from caste-conscious developing countries.

Aside from its size, the room was unremarkable. A prayer rug filled one corner, beneath a compasslike device that indicated the direction of Mecca from anywhere in the world. Photos of Sharif and his family dotted the walls. Most notably, a flat-screen television and an expensive stereo system had been mounted beside Sharif's bed.

Ivory had ignored the protests of his SEAL team leader and left his security team behind to come with Sharif. He figured a one-on-one meeting would be the fastest way to convince the captain to give up whatever he was hiding. Now Sharif reached into his desk drawer, and Ivory wondered if trusting him had been a mistake. But instead of a weapon, Sharif came up with a white plastic tube the size of a pen. Ivory's face must have betrayed his ignorance. "E-cigarette," Sharif said.

He put the tube to his lips and dragged. What would have been the lit end of the cigarette glowed red. He sucked for a few seconds and then exhaled a cloud of clear vapor.

"Very healthy."

Ivory's sarcasm seemed to escape Sharif. "Yes." He waved around the tube. The gesture didn't work nearly as well without a trail of smoke. "I don't understand why the U.S. Navy is so interested in my ship. My nephew lives in United States."

"A cabbie in New York."

"An attorney in Dallas. Plus, like everyone, I watch American TV. So I know, you find drugs on my ship this way, it's illegal, no arrest."

"You think this is a *drug* interdict? I look like the Coast Guard? If all you have on this ship is heroin, hash, show me. I give you my word, captain to captain, we will get you to Charleston. Sell it outside police headquarters, no one will say boo." Ivory figured he was telling the truth. The Navy wouldn't want anyone looking at what it had done today.

"Truly?"

Ivory raised his right hand, spoke three words he had never expected would leave his lips. "Swear to Allah."

"I trust you, then."

And you have no choice.

Sharif went to his knees and reached under his bed. He dragged out an unusual-looking suitcase, a hard white plastic shell about the size of a rolling bag. Homing beacons attached to both sides, and a chain was padlocked around it. Sharif grunted as he dumped it on the couch. Ivory picked it up. It was heavy, at least fifty pounds.

"Twenty kilos heroin. You see, Commander. All this, disable my ship, for this."

"Get the key and let's take a look."

"I am only courier."

"Please tell me you've actually seen what's in there."

Along with a half-dozen active and retired Department of Energy engineers, the nuclear team included a bomb expert, Nelson Pearce. Pearce had served two tours as an explosives ordnance disposal technician in Iraq, managing to leave with his fingers and toes intact. He was a wiry black man who wore a perfectly pressed dress shirt and khakis. He walked into Sharif's stateroom and without a word waved a pager-sized device over the suitcase.

"Captain Sharif says it's filled with drugs," Ivory said.

"Good news is I'm not getting unusual alpha or beta or gamma emissions." Pearce looked at Sharif. "Is it trapped? Booby-trapped?"

Sharif shook his head.

"How do you know?"

Another shake.

"Glad we got that out of the way. Commander, I'm going to ask you and the captain to leave the room. Could be anywhere from ten minutes to an hour."

"All the time you need."

While Pearce positioned a portable X-ray scanner over the case, Ivory ordered two SEALs to bring Sharif to an empty maintenance room at the front of the hold. Sharif didn't argue, tacitly acknowledging that he was now a prisoner aboard his own ship.

Twenty minutes later, Pearce called Ivory back to the stateroom. The scan had revealed thirteen brick-shaped objects inside the shell. Twelve were wrapped in plastic. The thirteenth was smaller, five inches long and three inches deep. It glowed red on the scanner's screen like a tumor.

"Red indicates high density. Meaning it's lined with lead to hide emissions. Specifically, gamma radiation."

"So that would be like uranium."

"No, sir. Highly enriched uranium emits almost no gamma radiation. It's more or less safe to handle. Alpha emitters aren't dangerous unless you swallow them. This would be cesium, cobalt. Possibly plutonium. To be sure, we have to open that box. You should talk to the Ph.D.s, but I'm not sure they'd be entirely comfortable doing that here."

"I'll ask."

"One more thing. The density of those bricks didn't match heroin. So I swabbed the case for explosives. We're looking at fifteen kilos of Semtex."

"Please tell me you didn't see any detonators or wires."

"No, sir. I think the case is safe to travel."

"Then you guys can take it back to the *Reagan*, give my boss the good news in person."

Maybe Sharif genuinely believed the case only held drugs. Maybe he had somehow convinced himself that he could talk his way out of this mess. He was wrong either way, but Ivory wanted to keep him cooperating as long as possible. He sat Sharif on a folding chair as the SEALs set up a digital camera.

"I am Commander Samuel Ivory of the USS *Nicholas*. This is Captain Hassim Sharif, of the *Kara Six*, a Pakistani-flagged vessel bound for the Port of Charleston. Captain Sharif has graciously agreed to this voluntary interview to discuss contraband carried aboard his ship. I want to thank him for his cooperation and remind him that the United

States Navy does not interdict narcotics unless specifically requested by the Drug Enforcement Administration. No such request has been made in this case. Therefore, any illegal drugs are of no interest to me or anyone in the USN."

Ivory turned off the camera. "That work for you?"

Sharif nodded. Ivory flicked the camera back on, and Sharif explained that he made the trip from Karachi to the United States three to four times each year. He always stopped in Dubai. There he made a habit of visiting the brothels that catered to the emirate's expatriates. They were illegal, but the police tolerated them as long as they didn't use local women. Sharif favored a place not far from the Burj Khalifa, the world's tallest building. "Six Star Experience. Beautiful girls."

On his previous stopover in Dubai, Sharif was waiting for a taxi outside the Six Star when a man joined him. He, too, had just finished up. "We spoke a few minutes. Then decided to have dinner."

"Just like that?"

"Nothing to do on the ship, waiting to load. I know he's not homosexual, he at Six Star, too. Long night. We have dinner, drink. We both like whiskey. I tell him about my ship. He say he has package he must get to America. Pay sixty thousand dollars."

"Drug smuggling in Dubai—that's punishable by death."

"I see he not from Dubai. Anyway, the port busy, no one care about drugs. And he has very good plan."

Ivory's mother liked to say *If stupid people didn't insist*

on thinking they were smart, the world would be a lot simpler.
He had never fully appreciated what she meant until now.

The arrangement to get the drugs to the *Kara Six* was
simple, if brazen. The smuggler would pose as an electronics installer putting a flat-panel television in Sharif's cabin.
It was his responsibility to get the drugs past Dubai port
security. When he was finished with the installation, he
would leave the case under Sharif's bed. The crew wouldn't
question what was happening. At sea or in port, Sharif was
the unquestioned master of the *Kara Six*. He could have
brought an elephant into the cargo hold and his sailors
wouldn't have peeped. In the unlikely event that Dubai
customs agents ever searched the ship, Sharif would say he
hadn't known about the suitcase. Idiot greed had blinded
him to the fact that the courts in Dubai would find his
story exactly plausible enough to execute him.

"And how do you get it through American customs?"
Ivory said.

"Two hundred kilometers from Charleston, I email.
Then, exactly one hundred kilometers, I turn on beacons,
throw case overboard."

"So if you didn't open the case, how did you know it
was drugs?"

"He tell me heroin. What else would it be?"

"Tell me about this man."

"He called himself Ahmad, but I don't think that's his
name."

"Where was he from?"

"I don't know. Not Dubai."

"This man gave you sixty thousand dollars to smuggle

358 | ALEX BERENSON

drugs. You must have looked him over. Could he have been Pakistani? Iranian?"

"No. Not Iran or the Gulf. Maybe Lebanese, Syrian."

"He speak Arabic?"

"We talked in English. I don't speak Arabic."

"Height? Weight?"

"Maybe one meter eighty. Eighty kilos." About six feet, one-seventy-five pounds.

"I don't suppose you have a picture of him?"

Sharif shook his head.

"Okay, that was last time. Tell me about this time."

"Two days after I throw the case overboard, I get email from him. Everything fine, I should tell him next time I'm going to America."

"You have a phone for him? Email?"

"Only email. So six weeks ago, I tell him, we make same deal."

Ivory thought of Sharif's stateroom. "This time he installed the stereo."

"Yes."

"Okay, Captain. I have to talk to my bosses. You may be here a while. Can I get you some water, something to eat?" Just keep him talking.

Sharif patted his pockets. "Just my cigarette."

"Of course."

An encrypted feed of the interview quickly made its way up the chain from the *Nicholas* to the *Reagan* to Atlantic fleet headquarters in Norfolk to the Pentagon and Langley.

Meanwhile, NEST's scientists opened the box in one of the lead-shielded emergency rooms near the *Reagan*'s nuclear reactor. Inside they found three hundred grams of cesium, enough for a nasty dirty bomb.

Now Hebley had the job of telling the President and the National Security Advisor what they'd found.

"Big day," the President said when he was finished.

"Yes, sir. About the only good news was that we found cesium and not HEU or plutonium. Cesium isn't impossible to come by. If this is some plot to suck us into war with Iran, the fact that we still don't have direct evidence of bomb-grade material is comforting."

"That what your analysts think? That this is a hoax?"

"No, sir. The agency now judges that this is a genuine plot. Eighty percent certainty."

"Just like Saddam's weapons of mass destruction?" Donna Green said.

Hebley ignored her. "Sir. If I may speak frankly. You put me at Langley because you felt it was ungovernable and unaccountable. From what I've seen, a lot of that's true. Three case officers tell four different stories about an op, and they're all lying. They spend their whole lives using other people. I mean, at least the Marines shoot you in the face."

The President's face tightened, and Hebley saw he'd overstepped. Only people who'd known him for decades could treat him as a human being. Everyone else served the office, not the man.

"The reason I mention all this is that I don't want you to think I'm naïve. The CIA's a snake pit. But what I'm

seeing now transcends turf wars. Everyone's trying to figure this out, why we can't get SIGINT confirmation, why
the Brits and the Mossad don't know anything. Our best
guess is that the Iranians know the risks they're running,
and that knowledge of this program is limited to a small
number of senior regime officials. We think only a dozen
people may really know what's going on, including only a
couple of the top scientists. Everyone else, in the dark."

"Would they compartmentalize that way—"

"Think about our own nuclear program during World
War Two, we had a great advantage, huge country, we
didn't have to worry about satellites or spy planes. Even so,
we basically imprisoned our own physicists until the war
was done. The Iranians know we're looking at everything
they do. The idea that the Rev Guard would go out of its
way to try to create deniability here makes sense."

"And the fact that over the last few months they've been
so positive in public, opened negotiations?"

"Putting Mathers aside, and the ship. Our analysts believe, and I agree, that what they say in public, whether it's
at the UN or on Twitter or wherever, doesn't mean anything. Either they let us into their plants or they don't. And
they're still not."

"So you believe they're cynical enough to have agreed
to negotiate just to buy time for this scheme?"

"Sir, in the 1980s, they sent close to a million of their
own men to die in a war. I don't think they'd have a problem lying to the United States."

"But we have this source," Green said. "This magic
source. If we didn't have him, we'd blame the embassy

bombings and Veder on al-Qaeda. We wouldn't even know about the cesium. We'd be whistling our way over a cliff like everyone else."

"Mathers is real."

"I wish I shared your conviction."

"We know they have a program. Mathers has simply told us it's further along than we thought."

"He's done more than that, General. He's suggested a very specific threat. The kind that starts a war. And, correct me if I'm wrong, it's not just that we don't have any confirmation of this, none of our allies have picked anything up, either—"

"The Mossad has warned something like this is a possibility."

"That was war-game bull out of Tel Aviv. Not relevant."

Hebley stared at Donna Green. In Sangin, Afghanistan, a full-bird Marine colonel had once thrown up during a briefing under the weight of that stare. The guy had been running sick, but even so. Green didn't throw up. Green stared right back.

"You are correct," Hebley finally said. "We've got no other confirmation."

"Thank you."

"I thought you had bigger balls than this, Donna. If we're going to war, let's do it *before* they put the nuke on our soil—"

"Nothing's happening today," the President said. "I agree with Donna. We need more than this before I'll consider military action."

"Scott, there's a plane waiting for you at Andrews,"

362 | ALEX BERENSON

Green said. "Have somebody pick up your go-bag, make sure it's got a fresh suit. You're going to Paris, to see Hamad Assefi." The Iranian ambassador.

"He knows I'm coming?"

"Not yet," Green said. "The DGSE can set it up, yes?"

"Probably. We're going to have to tell them something."

"Tell them we've found that the Iranian nuclear program is more advanced than we believed. We need to start raising the curtain on this anyway."

"You're going to tell Assefi we know what they're doing," the President said. "Without specifics. Just that they're on a very dangerous path."

"I doubt he'll know anything."

"That's why we want you to talk to him," Donna said. "If the mullahs and the Rev Guard have made an end run here, let's at least make sure the rational folks know."

Hebley feared the mission would be a waste of time at best, but he saw the President was done hearing objections from him on this day.

"Good luck, Scott."

Hebley offered the President his crispest salute and received the briefest of nods in return. He couldn't get out the door fast enough. Least now he knew how that colonel in Sangin felt.

22

Wells was gone.

Twenty-four hours since he'd last checked in. He hadn't called or emailed. He hadn't sent a telegraph or a semaphore or a pigeon. He'd dissolved like a spoonful of sugar in a hot cuppa tea. Shafer wanted to believe he was in the weeds, about to take the photo of Glenn Mason that would turn everything around. But Wells had said the day before that he was close. By now he would have gotten the shot, or realized he was chasing a false lead. Either way, he'd want to talk to Shafer. He had no reason to go silent. Ergo, he hadn't gone silent by choice.

Shafer wanted to be surprised. In truth, he had expected this moment for a long time. Maybe as long as he'd known Wells. Certainly since Wells had left Exley. Adrenaline was a drug, and Wells was a junkie. Only Exley and Anne wanted him clean. Everyone else enabled him. Like all junkies, he chased bigger and bigger fixes. Now he'd put himself in so much danger that all his skills couldn't save him—

His phone buzzed. The burner handset reserved specifically for Wells.

Shafer grabbed it. It slipped through his gristled hands, bounced off the floor, stopped buzzing. Shafer's eyes filled with tears.

He was getting too old for this. Age hadn't just taken his knees or his eyes. It had blunted his mind, made him a mawkish fool. Crying would do no one any good, least of all Wells. Shafer checked to be sure no one was outside his office. Then closed his fist, smacked himself in the forehead hard enough to hurt. He felt much better.

The phone buzzed again. He went to his knees, grabbed it like a prize pearl. "John."

"Do I speak to Mr. Ellis?"

Not Wells. Not an American. "Ellis Shafer, yes."

"Roger Bishop give me number. Say you pay me."

"We'll pay. You have him?"

"Not me."

"Who are you?"

"My name Kemal. I drive him. From airport."

Over the next fifteen minutes, Kemal detailed what he'd seen. He had locations and times but no details. He hadn't written down the BMW's plate. "Before he go, he tell me, wait for him at Taksim, so I do. Two hours. He don't come."

"Did you see the man he was after?"

"Not really, no."

"Are you home, Kemal?" Late afternoon in Langley, so past midnight in Istanbul.

"My taxi my home."

"If you say so. Find a Western Union, call me again. I'll send you money."

"Yes."

"Be careful. These people are dangerous."

"You think I don't know?"

Shafer wondered if Mason had killed Wells. Most likely. If not, he was being kept alive for a specific reason, and it wasn't his winning personality. Maybe Mason feared that if Wells was found dead in Istanbul, Shafer and Duto could convince the seventh floor that the connection Wells had chased was real. Right now Wells had been missing for barely twenty-four hours, not enough to matter. Kemal's version of events proved only that Wells had shown lousy judgment, racing into a terrible neighborhood alone in the middle of the night.

Shafer called Duto, told him what Kemal had said.

"Think our friends upstairs will care?"

"No."

For the first time in his life, he and Duto agreed on everything.

"I'm going to Istanbul, Vinny."

"By yourself."

"Stake out the apartment."

"You think you can do better than the best field guy ever."

"They were waiting for him. They won't be waiting for me."

"They will catch you in five minutes, Ellis. If Wells is alive, he'll get himself out of there. Your job is to make the connections. So *make them*."

Duto was right. A fact that only made Shafer feel worse.

"Anything new from our adventure on the high seas?" Duto said.

"From what I hear, not much. Captain's in isolation on the *Reagan*. They haven't decided what to do with him. He's sticking to his story. NEST has gone over the ship, hasn't found anything else. Crew remembers a guy installing a television on the stopover in Dubai before this one, then the stereo system this time, so that backs up. But Sharif said leave him alone, so nobody talked to him. He did his thing and left. We've asked them about nationality, they don't think Iranian, maybe Turkish, Lebanese. But none of them are Arab, they're all Filipino or Pakistani, so what do they know? And plenty of Iranians are lighter-skinned."

"Sharif—"

"No AQ connections as far as we can tell, doesn't show up in the databases. Family's in Lahore, we and the ISI have already sweated them. Not religious. Drinks, known to gamble, money problems, only two kids, only went to the mosque on Fridays."

Shafer was bugged by something he'd just said, but he wasn't sure what.

"Could be a cover."

"Anything could be anything. Most of the time you back-trace a guy like this, the story you get is the truth.

Meantime, we've talked to the company that owns the *Kara Six*. Cover story is a drug interdict, we found a thousand kilos of heroin, we're bringing the ship to Miami. According to what the captain said, he was supposed to drop the package and send the email for the pickup two days from now. So we have a little time. NSA's chased the email and the number, but so far nothing."

"We're buying his story."

"Until we get a better one."

"This mysterious electronics installer, anything on him?"

"Good news is the Dubai port has three thousand surveillance cams. But ninety-five percent are live only. The entry gates have sixty-day recording, but only the customs warehouses, the refiners, and the fuel storage require a permit or a badge. Rest of it, show a passport, local ID, you're in. The ships themselves are responsible for their own security, keeping out stowaways. Long story short, the guy could have driven up in a sedan, the television in the trunk, and we'd have no way of knowing who he is. But we have six case officers in Dubai looking. We're trying to track the television and stereo equipment, too, see if we can figure out who bought it."

"Smart."

"Yeah. But Dubai has huge used electronics markets so it may not go anywhere. Meantime, most of SOG is in Istanbul. No one's told me explicitly, but I think we've decided if the source pops up again, we're taking him."

"It strike you these people are going to a lot of trouble

to make sure we never see them, Ellis? Rev Guard officers have DI"—diplomatic immunity. "And even some of Quds Force."

In other words, if the Iranians really were running this operation, why were they going to so much trouble to stay hidden? "You know what Hebley'll say to that. That when you're thinking about starting a war with the United States, you take extra precautions. He might even be right."

They were silent for a while.

"You thought I was pigheaded when I ran the place," Duto finally said.

"I think this is a ball that wants to roll. If that makes sense."

"To be continued." Meaning Duto understood what Shafer was saying, that the seventh floor *wanted* to believe in the story coming out of Istanbul. And that they should have the conversation when Shafer wasn't at headquarters.

"I'll let you know if I hear from Wells."

"He's fine, Ellis. Boy's a survivor. When the apocalypse comes, it'll be him and the cockroaches."

Shafer knew that Duto was just soothing him, but he was desperate to believe.

"Reporting to you, King Rat."

"*Inshallah.* Figure out who's paying for this, Ellis, before we start dropping bombs."

Shafer tried. He saw now that he faced the reverse of the typical detective's problem. Instead of a deep pool of suspects, he had only a handful. But he had too few clues to eliminate them. He was stuck guessing, not analyzing. Again and again, he considered the agencies that might have the communications and money and operatives to run a false flag plot targeting the United States. The FSB. The Mossad. Maybe the DGSE. But he kept running aground on motive. Whatever country had done this hated Iran, but it was willing to risk its relationship with the United States.

Yet Shafer had the maddening feeling that he already knew the answer, that if he only twisted the kaleidoscope once more around, the pieces would slip into place. An Iranian exile group was out. They hated the regime, but they gossiped so much that they could barely sneak anyone over the border without the Guard hearing.

Reverse engineer. Find the piece that's sticking out, doesn't fit. Pull on that until the whole machine comes apart.

The timing. The Israeli embassy attacks were less than six months old. Before that, the source known as Mathers hadn't existed, as far as the agency knew. Yet Glenn Mason had worked on this operation at least since he'd faked his own death close to four years ago. What had Mason been doing all that time?

Assuming Shafer and Wells and Duto weren't crazy, this false flag was meant to stampede the United States into attacking Iran. To use American firepower to do what the plotters couldn't. Maybe Mason and his group had spent those first two years trying to stop Iran directly, before realizing they couldn't.

Shafer remembered now, a half-dozen or more assassinations in Europe and Asia, all related to the enrichment program, Iranian scientists and foreign nationals, too.

None of the murders had been solved, as far as Shafer knew. They looked a lot like James Veder's killing, professional, but not high-tech. No drones or remotely detonated bombs. Hands-on work. The world had naturally blamed Israel, the Mossad.

Shafer called Duto. "Remember, maybe three years ago, bunch of guys connected with the Iranian program got hit?"

"Sure."

"You talk to Tel Aviv about that?" Home of the Mossad's headquarters.

"Rudi always denied it." Ari Rudin, known as Rudi, had run the Mossad for a decade before leaving for reasons similar to Duto's. Elected leaders didn't like their spy chiefs to be too powerful.

"You believed him?"

"There were a couple things that made me think he wasn't lying. I didn't see the Israelis killing EU nationals in Europe."

"They've operated there before."

"Against Arabs, yes." The Mossad had famously carried out reprisal killings all over Europe against the Palestinian terrorists who assassinated the Israeli Olympic team. "And if they caught a European in Tehran, I don't think they'd care. But the blowback from the EU if Israel got caught smoking a host-country national would be big. It'd have to be a very high-value target, I mean someone whom the Iranians couldn't afford to lose. And none of these guys fell in that category. They were little fish."

"So why risk it?"

"Correct. Plus Rudi said something else, too. I said,

Okay, not you, who, then? He said, I don't know, I don't want to know. This is a *mitzvah*."

"Mitzvah?" Mitzvah was a Hebrew word that meant good deed.

"What he said. From his point of view, it was scaring these Eurotrash helping Iran, plus if whoever was behind it went down, he wouldn't have any blowback because the Mossad wasn't involved."

"But he didn't tell you who."

"Like I said, he insisted he didn't know."

"It would have to be privately run, though."

"If it wasn't him, and it wasn't us, who else could it be?" Duto paused. "And you're asking because you think maybe this is the same people?"

"Just guessing."

"And nobody put it together because who's going to connect anti-Iran assassinations from three years ago with an op that starts with hits on two Israeli embassies. Not bad. See, your boyfriend gets lost, you put that big brain in gear."

"Heng dikh oyf a tsikershtrikl, vestu hobn a zisn toyt." A Yiddish curse Shafer hadn't heard since his childhood: *Hang yourself with a sugar rope, you'll have a sweet death.*

"I love it when you go ethnic on me, Ellis—"

Shafer didn't expect trouble getting a look at the files on the Iranian assassinations. As Duto had said, no one had connected them with the current crop of killings. He called Dave Hikett, the guy who had told him what had happened on the *Kara Six*. They'd served together in Warsaw in the late eighties. Hikett was now the deputy director of Counterproliferation, which theoretically oversaw the agency's efforts to stop the spread of nuclear weapons, but in reality spent most of its time stuck in turf battles with the Pakistani, Iranian, and North Korean desks. A couple months before, Hikett had told Shafer he was sick of the infighting, ready to retire. Hikett, Lucy Joyner, a couple guys in the DST—Shafer could count his real friends inside on one hand. Live too long, no one comes to your funeral.

"Ellis."

"Dave. Question for you—"

"Now's not a good time, Ellis. Lot going on. Call you back."

"Dave—"

But Hikett was gone.

Everyone at Langley consented to being monitored on the house phones as a condition of employment. The unwritten rule was that the agency listened only for good reason. But Hikett had as much as told Shafer he was under surveillance.

Shafer wondered how much trouble he might be in. Plenty. He talked to Duto and Wells on burners, but those wouldn't matter if they had his office bugged. He had revealed classified information to Duto twice today. The fact that Duto was a United States senator and former DCI would save Shafer from criminal prosecution, but not from losing his job, his pension, any connection with this place.

He had to admit Carcetti had warned him.

Shafer picked up the phone to call Hikett again, then stopped himself. He would only get the man in more trouble. Hikett lived on the Hill, a divorcé with two cats and a girlfriend Shafer had never met and suspected might not exist. Maybe he'd go by tonight and they'd figure out some place in Southeast to meet, somewhere where they'd stand out but the agency's internal security guys would stand out even more. Or maybe Hikett just wanted to retire with his pension intact, and, even more important, his clearance, so he could work for Booz Allen for a couple hundred grand a year. In that case, he wouldn't call at all.

Shafer *believed* in this lead. Hikett's files would have police work and intel tips from a half-dozen countries. Forensic evidence. Maybe Mason had even let a surveillance camera take his photo. But Shafer wouldn't be getting a look at those files tonight.

Shafer had tacked into headwinds for most of his career. This was different. He had assumed that Hebley and his inner circle had fallen hard for this Rev Guard source. It happened. Somebody walked in with great intelligence and was right a couple times, the questions just melted away.

Now for the first time, Shafer wondered whether someone on the seventh floor was actively aiding the conspiracy. A senior CIA official steering the United States into war. The idea was implausible at best. But no longer impossible.

If he couldn't get a look at Hikett's files, he'd find the answer somewhere else. He had the clues already. He just needed to see them. He put his face in his palms and closed his eyes and tried to *see*.

23

Two days now.

Or maybe not. Maybe one and a half. Maybe three. Time was elastic. Wells had no windows, no way of telling day from night. He could hear the faint hum of highway traffic through his bricked-up cell, but he didn't recognize any pattern in the noise. The knockout drug hadn't fully cleared yet. Smog pickled his mind, and his stomach felt tight and tender, like he'd swallowed a half-dozen golf balls. He suspected he'd been hit with a near-fatal dose of Rohypnol.

James Thompson would have appreciated the irony. Thompson, his old buddy from Dadaab. Now serving thirty-two years in a max-security federal prison in North Carolina for kidnapping and fraud. With his sentence shortened for good behavior, he'd be paroled at about sixty-five. Wells would have locked him up for life, but the decision hadn't been his.

He expected his own sentence to be shorter but harsher. A few more days as an unperson in this unplace. A bullet in the back of the head. Then what? Probably they'd carve up his corpse, throw it in a trunk, dump it in the Black Sea. They weren't sentimental, these people. Even through his haze he understood that much.

Good news was that his foot wasn't broken. The swelling was coming down. He'd tested it, found it bore his weight. In another day or two, he expected to be able to run on it. If he could just get free.

At first he had thought his kidnappers let him live because they wanted to know who was helping him. He'd readied himself for torture. An episode in Beijing years before had shown Wells how much punishment rough guys could inflict even without electricity or knives or any other depravity. Pain broke everyone, and it broke most people quickly. Ironically, the best way to fight was not to imagine the agony ending, but instead to slow time, break it into the smallest fractions possible. A second. Then another. Anyone could stay quiet for a single second.

Sooner or later, that illusion crumbled. Getting a break from the agony became absolutely necessary. Wells planned to give up the tiniest fragments possible, lying along the way, forcing the torturers to unscramble the mess. He didn't look forward to this game. It would end with his death. Along the way, the pain would be impossible to imagine, even as it happened. Yet he wasn't exactly afraid, either. He would make them sweat for every bit of him.

Now Wells wondered if they planned to torture him at all. They'd stuffed him in a crude cell, eight feet square, twelve feet high. The room smelled faintly of tobacco. Maybe his guards were holed up nearby and smoking. Maybe the place had once been a cigarette warehouse. Turkey still exported cigarettes all over the world. A sixty-watt bulb on the ceiling provided the only light, and it never went off.

They had cuffed Wells's right hand to a post in the wall with a four-foot chain. His toilet was a bucket. A surveillance camera was mounted over the door, a cheap fish-eye lens available at any electronics store, its red light steady.

Still, they were feeding him, a basket of pita bread and a liter of water twice a day. His legs were free. The cell was unheated, but they'd given him a blanket. He even had fresh underwear and shorts. Basic comforts, to create the illusion they cared about him, so he wouldn't resist.

He hadn't seen Mason or the woman who had drugged him. The only people who'd come into the cell were two guards. He always asked them the same questions: *Where am I? When can I see Mason?* They never answered. In other words, his captors were basically ignoring him. Not in a *we're-isolating-you-to-soften-you-up* way. In a *we're-busy-and-don't-have-time-for-you* way.

The realization didn't improve his mood. The only reason that they wouldn't bother to ask him questions was if they already had the answers. They knew who he was, they knew he was working with Shafer, and probably Duto, too. And they knew he hadn't found enough to stop them. Again, Wells wondered why they hadn't shot him. If they didn't need information, most likely they were holding him as leverage, a way to slow down Shafer and Duto. But they had to know that he would never ask Shafer to keep quiet. If they ordered him to do that, Wells would tell them to put him down like a dog instead.

Wells looked around the cell, noticing pipes on the ceiling he hadn't seen before, flecked white paint and rusted iron. Maybe his body was finally breaking down the sedative. Minute by minute he felt sharper, more perceptive. He examined the room's bricks for cracks or crevices, found none. The chain that held him was padlocked to a ring in the wall. He tugged on it, testing it. But it had been hammered in and had no give. He leaned against the wall and listened for anything that would give him the rhythm of the city. Distant diesel engines, what might have been a foghorn, a long, eerie sound. No voices.

He turned his attention to the handcuff, but the guards had locked it tight around his wrist. Theoretically, with enough motivation, a prisoner could "deglove" a cuff, using the metal itself to tear away flesh until he could pull it over the bones of his hand. But Wells couldn't believe anyone had ever managed a real-world degloving, even if the alternative was dying in a locked cell. He imagined his wrist bloody and raw as he tore the cuff into his bones.

Did he have any tools at all? *The bucket.* Blue plastic, with a plastic handle, the kind kids used at the beach. His toilet. His captors emptied it every morning. Wells looked at it, wondered—

The door opened. Glenn Mason.

Medium height, his arms middle-aged and slack. His

face strange. Wide and puffy, like someone had inflated a balloon under his skin. Like he'd overdosed on human growth hormone. Barry Bonds syndrome. His nose squarer and flatter than it had been. His eyes smaller in his face. Even his ears different. Wells saw why the face-recognition software had failed.

Mason wore a T-shirt, jeans, boots, and a Taser strapped on his belt. He stepped inside the cell but left the door open. "The famous John Wells. You can call me Duke."

Duke. His fake name at the clinic.

"Aesthetic Beauty did you right."

"You want me to admit it, John? Sure. Isn't this where you tell me I can't get away with it? That if I just tell you who's behind all this, maybe you can cut me a deal?"

Wells lifted his cuffed right hand. "Not sure I'm in a position to make ultimatums."

"Love to know how you found me in Thailand."

"Luck. And a lot of time in Patpong."

"I figured. Speaking of. I made that run strictly to shake you out. See how many guys you had with you. Didn't think you could be stupid enough to follow me alone down that hill. I guess the folks at Langley who always said you were lucky, a cowboy, they were right?"

"You have nothing better to do than trash talk?"

Mason put a smartphone on the ground, kicked it gently to Wells.

"Turn it on."

Wells did. On the home screen, a picture of Evan. Sitting on the bench in his San Diego State uniform, hands on his knees, leaning forward, desperate to get in the game. *No.*

"Taken two days ago. At Colorado State."

How had they found him? Heather had given Evan his stepfather's last name when he was only five. Very few people knew that Wells had ever been married, much less that he'd had a son.

"Played ten minutes, five points and an assist. Good-looking kid. Not surprising, your ex is pretty hot."

This man, suffocating Wells with his own powerlessness, torture worse than any waterboarding. Making a joke of *threatening his son*. Wells wanted to tear the chain from the wall and throttle the man until his eyes bulged dead from his reconditioned face. But now more than ever he had to control his temper. Keep Mason happy. Make him believe his plan had worked. So he could get out of here. Then he would kill the man and everyone helping him. Burn their houses, salt their land, a plague of locusts. All of it.

"Leave them alone." His voice even. "Whatever you want."

Mason dug another phone from his pocket, held it up. The burner Wells used to call Shafer. The phone he'd been carrying when Mason's team caught him.

"Your friend Shafer has called you a bunch of times. You need to talk to him, tell him you were wrong. Figure out what's new on his side."

"Glenn—"

"Duke."

"Duke. I don't want to argue, but he won't buy it. It'll make him more suspicious."

"What, then?"

"How long have I been here?"

"Two, two and a half days."

Afternoon in Istanbul, morning in D.C. A chance for Wells to get some sense of day and night. "I'll tell him I thought I was close, but it was a trap, you guys set me up. I took off, a car hit me, knocked me out. I had no ID, and I just got let out of the hospital. I'm still after you, but you've gone to ground and the phone we used to track you isn't working and you obviously know I'm here, so I have to start again."

Mason hesitated. Like he wanted to clear the new plan with his boss. But didn't want to have to tell Wells he wasn't in charge. Again Wells thought of the woman who'd knocked him out. That cool, commanding voice.

"Okay. Tell him they took you to Kasımpaşa hospital."

"Kasımpaşa."

"And find out what he knows. If he has anything more."

"He'll probably want to check back tomorrow. You okay with that?"

"Tomorrow's tomorrow. Send back that phone."

Wells slid back the smartphone as Mason unlocked the burner, cued Shafer's number. Wells didn't ask how he'd beaten the passcode. Whoever was running this could afford a good tech team.

"You push the green button, do your thing. I see you try to call anyone else, I Tase you, take the phone. Then we kill your kid. I hear you tell Shafer anything but what we agreed on, I Tase you, take the phone. Then we kill your kid. You with me?"

Wells nodded. Mason unbelted the Taser, kicked the burner across the cell. Wells reached for it. Rehearsed what he'd say. This call he'd play completely straight. Buy time to figure a way out.

He pushed the button. One ring, then voice mail. Wells nearly hung up. Shafer always answered this phone. But maybe he was one step ahead, maybe he realized that Wells might be calling under duress and they would be better off not talking.

"Ellis. Sorry I haven't called. Been stuck in the hospital. Mason set me up, I didn't get the picture, a car took me. I was unconscious for a whole day, they held me for observation for one more. But I'm out now, and I need to talk. Call me."

He hung up. The message seemed lame to him, but Mason seemed pleased. He waved his fingers, come hither. Wells tossed him the phone. "He'll call back in not too long."

"He knows you're alive, he won't freak, do anything stupid. You do the same." Mason stepped into the hallway. "Like those drunk-driving public-service announcements. The life you save may be Evan's."

This guy couldn't lay off. His girlfriend had told Wells he didn't talk much, but maybe he'd dropped that persona, too, when he'd gotten his new face.

"See you soon." Mason shut the door, leaving Wells by himself, nothing but his self-hatred for company.

Anne had been more right than she knew. How could he have imagined that being married or having kids was compatible with this life? Especially now that he didn't work for the agency. He didn't have the protections of a regular CIA officer. Or even an off-the-books operative, a so-called NOC, under nonofficial cover. The NOCs ran mostly on their own, but when missions went bad, at least they knew the agency would try to help. Not Wells. Shafer or Duto wouldn't come for him. He would get out of this mess on his own or die. Either way, he would leave Anne behind, let her find a man who could love her as she deserved.

Then what? He didn't know. If Mason and his people could make the connection, anyone could. Between him and Evan, Wells couldn't see any solution to the problem. Maybe there was no solution. But before he could do anything about it, he had an even more basic problem to solve.

Escape.

24

Snatch-and-grab
Of a foreign national.
In a megalopolis.
Without the permission
Of the host country.

Brian Taylor ran the sentences through his mind, an International Criminal Court haiku. Officially, the agency planned to "detain" Reza. No one wanted to say *kidnap, abduct,* or *imprison. Extraordinary rendition* was even worse, a phrase bagged and burned years before.

The risks of the plan were hard to overstate. What if they had to take Reza off a crowded street? How many Turks would see? How quickly would the police show? A clean grab wouldn't end the potential for disaster. Reza might refuse to work with the agency afterward. Or the Iranians might be watching. Then Reza would be worse than dead after the agency kicked him loose.

Taylor wanted to object. Reza was *his* asset. But the choice wasn't his anymore. The agency could no longer tolerate Reza's anonymity. It had to know who he was, where he'd grown up, gone to school, why he had decided to betray his country, his history with the Guard, the names of his bosses. All the questions he had refused to answer.

It had to know if he was real.

And if Reza became so angry that he refused to talk? Even with Guantánamo off the table, the CIA had plenty of leverage. It could tell Reza that it would slip his name and photo to the Iranians if he didn't cooperate. The Guard's revenge would be swift and brutal, whether or not Reza worked for it.

But again Reza had confounded them. Since his late-night meeting with Taylor, he had vanished. Three SOG teams were searching. Martha Hunt had told Langley they were wasting their time. Istanbul was as big as New York City, and no one had an idea where Reza might be. The operatives should stay close to the consulate, wait for Reza to call. But they were bored with their hotel rooms. They wanted to feel useful.

Meantime, FBI had detached four specialists in missing-persons cases. NSA had sent a team of its own. In other words, even more guys in khakis were roaming around than usual. And no one had much to do. Taylor felt certain that despite their efforts, Reza would beat them. The man knew that they would have the dogs out, and he'd outquicked them three times already. Nothing for Taylor to do but keep his phone charged and wait.

The call came as he sat at his desk at 5:15 p.m., another gray day come and gone.

"Reza?"

"Seventy-four Gonca. Number six. In Bahçelievler." A fast-growing, densely packed neighborhood northeast of the airport.

"It's time to come in."

"A present there. It speaks for itself. Bring a Geiger."

"Did you check your account?" After the *Kara Six* intercept, the CIA had moved another three hundred thousand dollars into Reza's UBS account. The money remained untouched.

Reza didn't answer. Brian watched the little digital timer on the phone tick away . . . Forty-two, forty-three . . . Not long enough. Keep him talking. "What about your friend? Your family?"

"Pray for me, Brian. Even if neither of us believes in Allah."

"You need our protection, Reza, you need—" But Taylor was talking to an empty line.

Hunt walked into his office. "NSA says he's in Fatih, possibly on Vatan."

Not good enough to find him, as they both knew. Vatan was a boulevard that ran through Fatih, a poor, densely packed neighborhood in the Old City. If Reza was in a taxi, he could step out and vanish into Fatih's back alleys. If he was walking, he could get on a tram. If he was driving himself, he would reach the inner ring highway in minutes. He would be long gone before the first operative reached Vatan.

"I'm going to Bahçelievler," Taylor said.

"Trap."

"I'm going."

"I'll get two detectors."

She was already walking to the locked closet where the station kept its pager-sized radiation detectors. Taylor stuffed his pistol in his waistband holster. "You really do care," he shouted down the hall.

"Keep telling yourself that."

Without debate, they took a taxi directly from the front consulate gate. Not great tradecraft—terrible tradecraft, in fact. But they both wanted to get there as fast as possible. They barely spoke along the way. Taylor didn't think he'd ever see Reza again. Either the man was one of the greatest sources in the agency's history or a dangerous fraud. Taylor wanted to believe, but he was losing confidence. More cesium wouldn't convince anyone, either. According to the Counterproliferation desk, that stuff was available. Hard to get, but not impossible.

Seventy-four Gonca stood in the center of a row of identical six-story apartment buildings, concrete and painted a bright lemon yellow, with sliding glass doors that opened onto small smoking balconies.

Taylor pulled on gloves and Hunt did the same. He reached for his pistol, but she tapped his arm. "Not yet.

Too many kids." She took an autopick from her pocket. "Ready?"

"As I'll ever be," Taylor said, and wished he hadn't.

Ten seconds later, they were inside. The first floor smelled of dinner, lamb with plenty of garlic. The building had two apartments per floor. Number six was on the right side of the third floor. Its front window had been dark from the street, Taylor remembered. He didn't see any light under the door.

He motioned Hunt to the left side of the door and pulled his pistol. He pointed to the lock: *You pick, I'll open.* He half expected that Reza would have doped the lock with Krazy Glue, one last hurdle. Instead it clicked smoothly. Taylor held the pistol low in his right hand, reached for the knob with his left. Reza could easily have rigged a shotgun behind the door. If Taylor had been alone, he might have hesitated. But not with Hunt looking him over with her ice-blue eyes. He grabbed the knob, shoved open the door, ducked inside.

No shotgun.

Behind him, Hunt closed the door. They left the lights off, let their eyes adjust to the light trickling through the front window. The apartment had one big front room, a combination living area and galley kitchen. It was sparsely furnished, only a futon and a coffee table. It gave off a distinct hotel feeling.

Hunt pointed to the radiation detector on her belt. The single light on the side was a steady green, meaning that it wasn't picking up emissions. Yellow for alpha, orange for beta, red for gamma. Red meant *get out.*

Hunt pulled open the door beside the kitchen. Behind it, a corridor ran past two more doors, ended at a third. Hunt went to the end. Taylor took the first door on the right, found an empty room. Not even a bed. In the closet, a prayer rug that looked like it had never been used. Maybe it had come with the place.

Behind the second door, a narrow bathroom, basic toiletries, an unopened pack of L&M cigarettes under the sink. Reza's brand. Taylor picked them up with his gloved hands, put them in his jacket. The techs would test everything for prints, though Taylor couldn't imagine Reza making that mistake. All along, the radiation detector stayed green. He walked out of the bathroom just as Hunt emerged from the third door, shaking her head.

Back in the kitchen, Taylor pulled open the cabinets. Cooking oil, rice, bags of pita bread. A Quran tucked next to a spice rack. And a tall brown bottle of Amarula, a milky South African liqueur, instantly recognizable by the elephant on its label. An old girlfriend of Taylor's had liked the stuff. Strange to see it here. He put it on the counter.

In the living area, Hunt checked under the futon's cushions. Her BlackBerry buzzed. "SOG got to Vatan. Nothing. Your friend's jerking us around."

But Taylor didn't think so. Reza hadn't lied to him. Played him endlessly, but never lied. He tried the refrigerator, found it empty aside from a pomegranate and two water bottles. In the freezer, a frozen rack of lamb angled against the back wall. Taylor started to close the door. Then stopped. He pushed the lamb aside. He found a letter-sized envelope. Behind that, a plastic-wrapped tube, four inches tall, an inch-plus around, the size of a stack of half-dollars. He pulled the tube out with his fingertips, gingerly, like he was afraid of freezer burn—

His detector alerted. A steady beeping, the light flashing yellow. Alpha. Safe to hold, at least that's what the Counterproliferation guys had told them in their briefing. Which had lasted all of forty-five minutes.

"Martha." He held up his detector. Hunt joined him. For a moment, they stood stupidly in front of the open freezer door, looking at the tube like a couple of stoners trying to figure out which ice cream to eat next.

"Whatever it is, let's get it back to the station." He dropped the tube and envelope in her purse and reached for the Amarula.

He held up the bottle. A chunk of glass in the base had been cut out, replaced with a brown plastic plug. A dime-sized slot on the plug's face allowed it to be tightened or loosened. Taylor pulled the plastic-wrapped cylinder out of Hunt's purse, checked it against the hole. The cylinder was slightly smaller.

"Unscrew it, pour out some booze, drop the thing in," Hunt said.

"*Thing* being the technical term."

"But won't the weight be wrong? The density?"

"Pack the bottle in a suitcase, who's checking? Especially because the bottle and whatever's inside must be enough to hide the radiation. Then you fly anywhere. One bottle of liqueur, no customs agent in the world will care."

"How did you know?"

"Reza's weird, but Amarula didn't make sense even for

him." He checked the other cabinets, just to be sure. Nothing else.

Hunt spun a finger in the air. *Time.* Taylor put the Amarula bottle in a plastic bag, took one last look at the kitchen, and followed her out, keeping his pistol unholstered. No chances now.

At the consulate, they went for the coms center, ignoring the questions from the SOG team leader and everyone else. In what now seemed like a major mistake, a nuclear emergency team hadn't been sent to Istanbul. The Air Force was sending radiation experts from its base at Incirlik, but they would need hours to arrive. Hunt had already asked the Turkish Interior Ministry if police could find the apartment's owner, interview everyone in the building. As a cover story, she said the FBI had connected the apartment to an al-Qaeda operative in Chicago.

Meantime, the DOE nuke experts had warned them not to unwrap the tube. Taylor figured that was one piece of advice they wouldn't follow. He pulled the Amarula bottle from the bag. "Drink?"

"Funny." Hunt extracted the plastic-wrapped tube and the envelope from her purse, slid him the envelope. "This first."

Inside, two sheets of paper. First, a handwritten itinerary. Turkish Airlines from Istanbul to Kinshasa, Democratic Republic of the Congo. Kinshasa to Luanda, Angola, on TAAG, Angola's national airline. Then Luanda to Havana, again on TAAG. Several dates were listed for each flight.

"I hope he's flying first class," Hunt said.

"Only airport on that list that would have radiation-detection equipment is Atatürk. He gets out of here, he's good."

"So he lands in Havana. Ninety miles from Key West. Then what?"

"Goes out into the Gulf and leaves it for whoever made the pickup from the *Kara Six*. Same way, a homing device."

"Or he just hands it off, ship to ship." Reza could easily find a Cuban fishing crew to help make the transfer for a few thousand *dinero*. "Or even brings it to Florida himself."

"Not clear from this if he actually made the reservations," Taylor said.

"That is a checkable fact. What else does he have for us?" Taylor looked over the second page:

1.3 kilos Uranium. Bomb-grade. Come over border two days ago. We change plan with ship because other ship doesn't get through. ☺

Did not expect material so quickly. Please don't blame apartment man. I pay cash, he know nothing. Best for everyone if I disappear.

Khodafez
"Reza"

He slid the letter to Hunt.

"A smiley face? He's giving us a kilogram of what he says

is weapons-grade uranium and running with the hell-hounds after him, and he throws in a smiley face."

"That's him. His way of taking credit for the interdiction. I wish you could have met him."

"*Khodafez?*"

"Good-bye."

"He must know we'll do anything to find him."

"How's that been working out for us?"

"I need to call Langley," she said. "But first things first. One-point-three kilos is about three pounds. How much HEU in a bomb?" she said.

"More than this."

They both knew the stuff couldn't blow up just sitting on the table. No doubt it was safer than regular explosive. But that truth couldn't close the pit in Taylor's stomach. They were looking at the seed of a million nightmares.

She fished through her purse, came out with a Swiss Army knife. "Should we?"

"A Swiss Army knife? Thought you were cooler than that."

"My ex-boyfriend gave it to me."

Taylor wondered if he was hearing things, or if she had just put a not-so-subtle emphasis on *ex*. If this piece of metal really was what Reza said, the world had moved much closer to nuclear midnight. But if he'd impressed Hunt today, the news wasn't all bad.

He reached for the knife.

25

The Oval Office had six visitors this time. The Four Horsemen. The National Security Advisor. And James Shaham, director of the Global Security and Nonproliferation Program at the Oak Ridge National Laboratory, in Tennessee. Shaham was a nuclear physicist from his square wire-framed glasses to his scuffed black oxfords. He was there for a technical briefing, but he was suffering a severe case of OOFS—Oval Office Fright Syndrome. His face was slick with sweat, and he squeezed his hands together so tightly the President worried he would break a finger.

"When you're ready, Dr. Shaham."

Shaham untwisted his hands long enough to mop his forehead. A cloud of white flakes snowed out of his curly gray hair. "Little nervous, sir."

"I hadn't noticed." The President smiled and Shaham seemed to relax.

"The situation, Mr. President. Seven hours ago, a CIA

team delivered an ingot of one-point-three kilograms of uranium to Oak Ridge for review. The agency reported this material is believed to be a product of the Iranian nuclear program and was recovered in Turkey. I have no further details on where or how it was found. For my purposes, those facts are largely irrelevant. A preliminary on-site analysis of the ingot found it to be weapons-grade enriched uranium, approximately ninety-four percent U-235. Our task was to confirm the analysis, which we did, and then to match the ingot to known repositories of fissile material. Meaning, did it come from a national stockpile, whether ours, Russia's, or another country's."

So far Shaham hadn't said anything that the President and everyone else in the room didn't already know. "How does that matching work?"

"After the end of the Cold War, the major nuclear powers shared samples of their fissile material, highly enriched uranium and weapons-grade plutonium. The feeling was that if a piece like this turned up, everyone would want to know where it came from. The physical samples were sent to the International Atomic Energy Agency in Vienna to be assayed by scientists there. The data was then shared with the contributing countries. I assume you're not interested in the technical details, but everyone's HEU looks different. Impurities, enrichment levels, radioactive signature, levels of tertiary uranium isotopes. Plutonium has similar differences, though that's not at issue in this case."

"And every country with weapons has joined?"

"Except North Korea, sir. That includes Israel, even

though it isn't a declared power, as well as Pakistan after its first nuclear test."

"Can we be sure they're providing representative material?" Donna Green said.

"Excellent question, ma'am. We can't. As a condition of joining, every country agrees to let IAEA inspectors sample their stockpiles every three years. Even so, it is possible that a country could try to fool the program by de-enriching and then re-enriching material. There might be some similarities with the existing samples, but our scientists can't say for sure that they would prove a match. That's an interesting technical question we're looking at right now. But this material, as best we can tell, is fresh. That is to say, it doesn't share a signature with any existing samples."

The room was silent. The President had known this, too. The answer had come back a couple hours before. But hearing Shaham saying it was a different matter. He came off as the opposite of a warmonger. Everything about him broadcast precision, caution, professionalism.

"Two hours ago, we put out a Yellow Alert through IAEA. That means we're asking the other nuclear powers to check their stockpiles. We don't have to explain why. Just, as a courtesy, please let us know if you've had significant losses since your last report. We'll get answers in the next forty-eight hours, but I'm not optimistic. A loss of this size would surely have been reported already."

"But you can't say for sure that the material's Iranian," Green said.

"That's correct, ma'am. We don't have an Iranian

sample. We're not even sure the Iranians have reached this level of enrichment. All I can tell you for certain is that we haven't seen material like this ingot before."

"Could a private group have done this?" Hebley said.

"General, I never say never to anything except perpetual-motion machines. But enriching a kilogram-plus of uranium to this level requires large facilities that can't be hidden. Hundreds of scientists. Billions of dollars—tens of billions, if they're going to be put underground."

"So no?"

"It's very unlikely."

"What about North Korea?" the President said.

"That's a possibility, but we believe this grade of enrichment is beyond them."

"Next question. How close is this to a bomb?"

"Depends on the size of the bomb, and the skill of the scientists putting it together. Our own scientists can build a one-kiloton nuclear bomb with two and a half kilograms of HEU."

"That's only two of these."

"Correct, sir. A bomb that size is tiny by nuclear standards, the equivalent of a thousand tons of TNT. Fifty tractor-trailer loads. During the Cold War, we regularly detonated bombs with ten thousand times as much power. Even so, a one-kiloton bomb explosion in midtown Manhattan would kill tens of thousands of people. More realistically, assuming a cruder bomb design, a bomb like that would require four to seven kilos of HEU. A bomb ten times as big, ten kilotons, would require six to twelve kilos. That's Hiroshima-sized. It means a half-square-mile hole."

"Five of these ingots could do *that*?"

"Between five and ten, sir."

"And how hard is it to build the actual bomb?"

"Compared to enriching the uranium, easy. The basic designs have been public for decades. An engineer and a machinist could put one together in a couple weeks, especially if they had access to the right explosives."

The right explosives. Shaham didn't know about the Semtex that Commander Ivory had found on the *Kara Six*, but everyone else in the room did.

"Thank you, Dr. Shaham," the President said. "If we have any questions—"

"Mr. President, sir. If I might make one last comment."

No one interrupted the President in this room. He cleared his throat, and Shaham suddenly took great interest in his shoes.

"Sorry, sir."

"Go ahead."

"I would only point out that an ingot of this quality, this, whoever did this, it's not their first time at the rodeo."

"You say this from personal experience?" the President said. James Shaham made a singularly unlikely cowboy.

If Shaham knew he was being mocked, he didn't reveal it. "This feels like they've had several runs. Four or five at least."

"So what you're telling us is that there's more HEU out there."

"I don't know how to define *out there*, sir, but produced. Of course, I could be wrong, sir. This is based on instinct, not evidence. I always prefer evidence."

"Thank you, Doctor. If you wouldn't mind waiting outside."

Shaham walked out on shaky legs.

As the door shut behind him, Green murmured, "Rawhide." Nothing more. The report hadn't put anyone in a joking mood.

The President looked at Hebley. "General. Let's save Shaham for a minute. I haven't seen you since your trip to Paris. I'd like to hear firsthand what you thought about Assefi." The Iranian ambassador to France.

"Sir. These conversations are always difficult. With the translators present. But as best as I could tell, he had no idea what I was talking about. He asked me more than once for more information. It was a short conversation, no more than twenty minutes."

"What did you think of him personally?"

"Assefi's polished. No beard. Hand-tailored suit. More Persian, less Iranian, is how I'd put it. Best we can tell, they figure they need a couple guys like him to give the Europeans cover to keep doing business with them. As I said, he seemed perplexed."

"Did that change your overall view of the situation?"

"No, sir. Both when I was at the Pentagon and now, I believed that the Iran power structure is highly concentrated. It's hard for us to understand. We have so many different constituencies, power is genuinely diffuse. You, Congress, lobbying groups, Pentagon bureaucracies, multinationals, et cetera. In Iraq, Afghanistan, I saw it up close, in the end a handful of people make the decisions. Assefi, Rouhani, they're useful as front men, doesn't mean they know what's really happening, much less can change it." Rouhani was Hassan Rouhani, the president of Iran.

"So how would you reach the men who can?"

"We need to get their attention. We've seen it again and again, especially since Syria, these regimes believe we're not going to act. They think they can bluff us."

"Just to review." The President tented his hands together. "We have an unknown source of weapons-grade uranium. The man who tipped us, the agent you called Mathers, supposedly a Revolutionary Guard colonel, he's disappeared."

"Yes, sir."

"We don't have any independent corroboration. No signals intelligence, no human source, nothing from our allies. Nothing. We don't even know this man's real name. Nor do we have a photo."

"That's correct, sir."

"But this source has provided us with four major pieces of intelligence, and they've all proven correct. Including, today, bomb-grade uranium that our own experts say doesn't seem to have come from any known nuclear program."

"Yes, sir."

"Mr. President." This from Jake Mangiola, the Chairman of the Joint Chiefs. "If I may. The Iranians can easily allay our suspicions if they let us inspect Natanz and the other plants."

"Hadn't thought of that," the President said drily. Mangiola flushed. "Just so you know, tomorrow morning Donna is going to call Rouhani to see if he wants to talk to me directly. If he will, I'm going to tell him that we have direct evidence that his government is trying to move nuclear material to American soil, and he must allow the United States directly to inspect his enrichment plants. I have to try." The President paused. "Assuming the Iranians choose not to pull down their pants for us, what do you have for me, Jake?"

For the next twenty-five minutes, Mangiola and Kenneth Belk, the Secretary of Defense, offered a menu of choices with steadily increasing casualty counts, from cyberattacks to missile strikes on enrichment plants to a sustained bombing campaign against military and even civilian targets. The President remained impassive throughout, hidden behind his hands.

"We're presuming for now that a full-scale invasion is off the table, though the planners have spent some time on that, too," Belk finally said.

The President pushed his chair away from his desk. He wanted a cigarette, but he wouldn't let these generals see him smoke. Smoking was weakness.

The silence in the room stretched.

"No," the President finally said. "None of it's right. What do we have? Three pounds of uranium."

"It came from somewhere," Hebley said.

"I agree. I'll even buy it's Iranian. But we have to start with something that tells the world this is a crisis without killing a lot of people. I want awe, not shock. Nobody's forgotten Iraq, WMD. I want room to escalate. A lot of room."

"What about a blockade?"

"I don't mean to joke," the President said, "but it sounds so Cuban Missile Crisis. The cyber stuff is worse. *I will destroy your Internet*. I know it's real, but it seems silly. I want something they'll see in Tehran."

"Like a drone strike," Belk said.

"Except the opposite," Green said. "Drone drops one bomb, kills a bunch of people." She leaned forward, hands on her skirt. "But maybe—" She broke off.

"Donna?" the President said.

"I might have something."

26

In 1971, a psychology professor at Stanford University chose seventy-five students to play prisoners or guards in a mock jail in a campus basement. By the second day, the guards were spraying prisoners with fire extinguishers, keeping them naked, locking them in closets. The experiment was supposed to last two weeks, but the abuse became so severe that the professor ended it after six days. More than forty years later, the Stanford Prison Experiment remained a milestone, proof that power corrupted.

But Wells saw a second moral, one more relevant to him at this moment. After a single day, the amateur guards at Stanford had defined prisoners as defiant or compliant. They focused on the troublemakers and ignored the rest. Full-time corrections officers never let down their guard, even around supposedly model prisoners. But the men watching Wells were soldiers-turned-mercenaries, not jailers. They knew Wells was dangerous. But he'd given

THE COUNTERFEIT AGENT | 403

them no reason to mistrust him. He hadn't resisted in any way. On the contrary, he'd followed their orders without complaint.

The guards still took plenty of precautions. They made him face the wall when they entered the cell, so they could check the cuff on his right hand. They'd never unlocked him. And they never brought firearms into the cell. Instead, they wore Tasers, single-shot stun guns. Even if Wells could grab a Taser, he could disable only one guard. The backup would disarm him.

But—even after only six days—the guards had become slightly less vigilant. They put food directly in front of Wells. They came within arm's reach when they took his waste bucket. Most important, they no longer watched him in pairs. A single guard entered, leaving the door open, his buddy down the hall. Sloppy. Lazy.

Wells would make them pay.

The day before, Mason had come back. "Why did Shafer stop calling?"

Wells shook his head.

"He's gone to ground. You signaled him."

"You heard the message I left. It sound like code?"

"Tell me how you got involved with this."

Wells didn't argue. He wanted to keep Mason happy, and he suspected Mason already knew most of the story. He explained, skipping only his trip to Panama. Montoya and Singh would have to look out for themselves. Sophia Ramos was innocent.

Mason didn't look surprised at anything Wells said. "Langley help?" he said.

"Not as far as I saw."

"Seventh floor didn't want to hear."

"I wasn't there, but Shafer said they actively pushed back. I had to guess, I'd say Shafer's figured out you grabbed me, decided his best play is laying low. That with the juice you have at Langley, he can't stop this, and if he tries, he'll only get me killed."

"From what I know, that's not Shafer's style. Or yours."

So Mason wasn't even bothering to deny that the group he worked for had some connection inside. Wells decided to let the thread lie. Better if Mason didn't realize the importance of what he'd admitted.

"Guards tell me you've been a good boy," Mason said.

"I just want my family safe. It's not about me anymore." Wells knew they both understood the implication.

Mason dug Wells's burner phone from his pocket. "So let Shafer know he's doing the right thing. Elliptical. Obviously, don't say 'hostage.' Nothing like that. Nothing he can take to anyone."

"Your theory is correct, something like that."

"Ad-lib it. I trust you. Circumstances being what they are." Mason dialed, slid Wells the phone.

The call went straight to voice mail. "Ellis. Just want you to know the target's practically in my sights. Stay cool, keep doing what you're doing. I'll handle it. Talk soon." Wells clicked off, tossed Mason the burner.

"Just what the doctor ordered."

"Don't suppose you want to explain what this is really about." *Since I'm dead anyway.*

Mason shook his head.

"Or should we call your boss? Ask her if you're allowed to talk?"

Mason's silicone lips tightened, all the answer Wells needed. "It's about the truth, John—you don't mind if I call you John? Doing what we should have done already."

"From over here, it looks like tricking the United States into war. Killing a station chief."

"Tell me you've never shot an American."

But of course Wells couldn't.

"You knew the whole story, you might even help. Too bad." Mason walked out.

Mason had the swagger of Usain Bolt three strides from the finish line. Wells knew his own sell-by date was close. For now, the scales still tilted in favor of keeping him alive, leverage to keep Shafer quiet. But Mason or whoever was in charge would decide soon enough Wells was more trouble than he was worth.

So. Time to go. Or die trying.

Wells had to trust that if he failed, they wouldn't hurt Evan. He didn't see why they would. Dead, Wells was no threat. Evan would be in greater danger in the short run if Wells escaped. Soon as he got free, Wells would call Shafer, have him ask the FBI to cover Evan and Heather and Anne.

He spent the first part of the night putting together his plan, the second half crafting the weapon he needed. He had learned the rhythm of his captivity, could distinguish day from night. He had seen only the two guards, one in his late twenties, the other close to forty. He doubted there were others. Anyone else who was here would have given in to the temptation to look him over. The older guard was in charge. The younger did the scut work, removing his slop bucket each morning for cleaning.

They looked in on him four times a day, every six hours. The younger guard brought him breakfast and dinner. The older checked Wells at lunch and in the late evening, around midnight. Otherwise they left him alone, his cell door deadbolted from the outside. Theoretically, they could be watching him constantly through the spy cam. Wells guessed it fed a laptop nearby, wherever they lived and slept. He doubted they bothered. The chain binding Wells was so short that he could take only a single step in any direction. Watching him in here would be nearly as boring as *being* him.

With no toilet, and the bucket washed only once a day, the cell smelled fierce by the time the younger guard arrived each morning. They hadn't allowed Wells to shower or shave. He had toilet paper and a few wet wipes, but he couldn't imagine how he smelled and looked. Even in Afghanistan, he'd never felt as filthy as he did now, with only stale air and flies for company. He wasn't sure how the flies got in, but they did.

On the other side of the bricks, the highway noise picked up. Wells hadn't slept, but he felt stronger than he had in years. This time he wasn't facing a raggedy Somali militia, or a Delta sniper who'd snapped after too many tours. Mason was a traitor. And Mason had threatened his son.

The Quran's first verse flashed through Wells:

You alone do we worship, and You alone we seek for help.
Guide us to the Straight Path.
The path of those whom You bless, not of those whom
You have cursed nor of those who have gone astray.

He didn't know how to find Mecca in here, so he decided to face the door, his own mihrab. He closed his eyes, knelt, offered the regular dawn prayer. When he was done, he raised his head and imagined Anne, in North Conway, her deadline to him irrelevant now. He hoped she was sleeping peacefully. Not thinking of him. She'd made the right choice. And he knew what she'd say to him now, if she saw him here. Nothing from the Quran. Four words. Her state's motto. Taken from a letter a Revolutionary War general had written in 1809:

Live free or die.

The slop bucket was between his legs. Wells wrinkled his nose against the smell, pushed down his shorts, crouched over it. In case anyone peeked on the monitor before coming to check on him. In this unpromising but necessary posture, he waited for dawn.

The footsteps came minutes later. The deadbolt popped back. The door creaked open. Still squatting above the bucket, Wells leaned forward to cover himself. The young jailer stood in the doorway. He was wiry, ropy muscles, no fat at all. Nearly as tall as Wells. Like a tennis player. Wells imagined he'd have tennis-quick reflexes, too. He moved on the balls of his feet. The Taser rested on his right hip. Wells would have to move decisively, without hesitation, to have any hope of surprising him.

"Good morning." His voice was low, marbly. Eastern European. He frowned as he realized he'd interrupted Wells over the bucket.

"Stomachache."

The jailer stepped back into the hallway, locked the door. He returned with toilet paper and a bottle of water. By now Wells had his shorts up. The guard tossed him the roll and the bottle. *Good.* Already he thought of Wells as sick. Weak. Walking in on a stranger on the toilet was inevitably distracting. Most important, Wells had a reason that the bucket was at his feet instead of its usual spot in the middle of the cell.

"Thank you." Wells cleaned himself as best he could, tossed the paper in the bucket.

The guard twirled his finger. Wells faced the wall, pressed his left palm against the bricks, lifted his right arm out and away. The guard came wide to his right side and tugged hard on the chain that held the handcuff. Wells grunted as the steel bit his wrist.

The guard stepped away. "Turn."

Wells turned around, facing out.

"Sick."

"No, I'm fine." But Wells knew he didn't look fine, or smell fine. Not after six days in this room and twenty-four hours without sleep. He nudged the bucket with his toe. "Please, can you clean it—"

The guard stepped toward Wells, reached down for the bucket, pulled it up—

And the filthy mixture inside poured out the bottom. The guard looked down in shock as the stuff cascaded around his shoes—

Wells wrapped his left arm around the man's waist, hugged him close. With his right hand, Wells reached into his shorts and pulled the five-inch pie-shaped piece of plastic that he had broken from the base of the bucket. He had spent hours whittling the plastic against his handcuffs, making a homemade shiv, its sides letter-opener sharp. The four-foot chain gave Wells room to drive his right arm forward. The guard tried to spin out, but Wells held him firm and forced the knife into him, above the hipbone, aiming for the liver. The plastic blade didn't cut as smoothly as a real knife, but the guy's skinny frame left him unprotected. Wells sawed through skin and muscle until he reached the viscera underneath.

The guard screamed. Wells shoved in the blade as far as he could, then pulled it out. Bright red blood followed. The guard reached for the Taser on his belt. Wells let go of the knife, wrapped his right hand around the guard's head. He drove forward with the crown of his skull and connected with the guard's forehead, bone on bone. The world went white. But Wells stayed upright and conscious as the guard moaned and collapsed at his feet.

Wells grunted, breathed deep against the pain. At his feet the guard rustled, semiconscious. Wells turned the man's head so the back of his skull lay against the floor. He lifted his heel and brought it down on the small bones of the man's throat, firm, driving through, crushing his windpipe. A killing strike. The guard thrashed hopelessly.

Footsteps pounded down the corridor outside. Wells reached for the Taser. He came up with it as the second guard, the older man, arrived in the doorway, shouting. The guard turned and raised his pistol. Wells aimed the Taser for his chest and pulled the trigger.

Twin black wires exploded from the Taser. Powered by compressed nitrogen, the wires covered the fifteen feet between Wells and the guard in a fraction of a second. When they made contact, the metal barbs at their tips cut through the guard's T-shirt and into his skin, completing an electrical circuit that ran across his chest. Fifty thousand volts passed through him. He dropped the pistol and went to his knees, yelling.

The company that made Tasers had once claimed they were nonlethal. No more. After hundreds of deaths, Tasers now carried prominent warnings of their potential to kill. They worked by causing muscles to clench uncontrollably. Every muscle. Even the diaphragm. Pulling a Taser's trigger produced a five-second shock, nineteen pulses per second of electricity. A five-second hit was painful but not hugely dangerous unless the person being shocked was already close to cardiac arrest. But what most people didn't know was that Tasers would pump out electricity as long as the shooter held the trigger. They had no override. And until the shock ended, the person being Tased couldn't breathe.

Wells didn't let go.

The next three minutes were the worst of his life. But he knew if he stopped, the guard would pull off the barbs. He would be free, with Wells defenseless, still locked to the wall. Wells couldn't even stop at leaving the man unconscious, because he didn't know how long he would need to get the cuff off his wrist.

For sixty seconds, the guard shrieked. Then the pain and fury on his face turned into empty panic. His mouth fell open. His face reddened. A cyanotic blue crept into his skin. His hands trembled, and the twitch spread up his arms. His tongue lolled. A faint white froth cupped his lips. He toppled forward, landed face-first against the concrete floor of the cell. Blood poured from his shattered nose and pooled around the twin wires of the Taser. Yet the barbs didn't lose their grip. The electricity still flowed.

The noises coming from him faded to a low grunt. His eyes rolled back and the shaking in his arms and hands slowed until only a single finger twitched. The middle finger, a coincidence, surely. The puddle of blood lapped toward Wells like a poisonous lake overflowing its banks. It stained the man's face, coated his tongue.

Wells couldn't watch anymore. He squeezed his eyes shut. He had killed so many men in so many ways, yet this death was both the most savage and the most cowardly. He felt like a child burning an ant under a magnifying glass.

This was murder, not combat. As though the Taser was drawing its charge from what was left of his soul.

Still he squeezed the trigger. When he opened his eyes the guard wasn't twitching anymore. Wells had added another corpse to his pile of sin. He held on another thirty seconds. When finally he did let go, the Taser fell from his hand and clattered on the cell floor like a cheap plastic toy. Wells wiped his hand across his mouth, whimpered, leaned against the wall.

He didn't want to move. He wanted to close his eyes and imagine anything but this place. But then Mason would arrive, and Wells would have murdered two men for less than nothing. The thought broke his stasis. He shook his head, quickly, almost a spasm, like he was cleaning an Etch A Sketch.

He had killed the guards knowing that he still didn't have a plan for what came next. He hoped the younger guard would be carrying something that would let him pop the handcuffs, a pocketknife or a pen. He'd learned the trick during his training at the Farm, and after realizing a couple years before that he'd forgotten it, he'd made a habit of practicing.

Wells squatted beside the dead man. And felt a key in his right front pocket. A handcuff key. Never argue with good luck. Seconds later, he was free. He wanted to run. He didn't. Don't move. *Think*. He looked like a mental patient. He'd be a target for any cop who saw him. He had no passport or visa, no identification at all. He couldn't call the consulate for help. His name would ring alarms at Langley, and whoever was working with Mason would hear. Wells had to ensure the Turkish authorities ignored him until he found a safe route out of the country. He might be here awhile anyway. He wasn't leaving until he knew Mason was dead.

So. Find a phone. Call Shafer, get his family protected. Then shower, shave, find clothes and shoes. The younger guard's stuff should fit.

Wells went to the door, pulled down the security camera. If Mason had remote access to the feed, Wells would rather he see a blank screen and wonder what was happening than see a dead guard and know. Wells knelt next to the second guard, wetting his knees in blood. The dead man wore white briefs, a T-shirt, a fake Rolex. Wells eyed the time. Seven-fifteen. No reason for Mason or anyone else to show this early. He picked up the pistol and stepped into the hall, his legs stronger with each step.

He found himself at the end of a corridor maybe seventy-five feet long, naked bulbs overhead. The air stank of cigarettes, but even so, it felt cooler and fresher than his cell. After a few feet, the wall on his right ended. A railing replaced it, turning the hallway into a kind of catwalk, with doors on the left. Wells walked along, found himself looking down at a factory floor, empty except for a few scattered sewing machines. An abandoned textile factory. Poor countries made clothes. Turkey wasn't poor anymore. This strip of rooms had no doubt belonged to management, watching over the paid-by-the-piece stitchers below.

A metal staircase at the end of the catwalk connected

the floors. To the left, an open door. Inside, Wells found the office where his guards had lived. Two narrow cots were shoved against the back wall. A hot plate sat on an aged wooden desk. The cigarette smell was Eastern European, tobacco with a hint of formaldehyde. A laptop sat on the floor, silently playing porn. Wells clicked off the website, flipped down the screen. He'd take the computer. Maybe its browser history would have some clues.

First, a phone. A pile of dirty clothes lay between the cots. Wells grabbed the jeans that lay on top, found a mobile phone, a burner. He called Shafer. Home, cell, office. But Mason had spoken true. Shafer wasn't answering. Wells had wanted to be sure he had protection arranged before calling his son or ex-wife. Instead, it looked like he'd have to call them first, tell them to go to ground. They'd be terrified. And furious.

Then he thought of Duto. For a few anxious seconds Wells couldn't remember the man's number. At last he did. Two rings, then—

"Who's this?"

"John."

"You're not dead." There was a touch of something like irony in Duto's voice, a late-night radio host talking to a regular caller.

"Don't sound so happy. Where's Ellis?"

"He called three days ago. Said he knew who was behind this, but he had no proof, no one would believe him. I told him to tell me, we'd figure out a play. He said he couldn't because they were holding you and he was sure they'd kill you if he told anyone. But now you're out."

"I'm out. You know who it is?"

"No. I'm walking into the White House, but when I'm out I'll call Shafer, tell him you're okay, make him tell me, assuming he actually knows and this isn't a slow-motion breakdown—"

"First you have to get the FBI to put Evan and Heather in protective custody, and make sure Anne knows there's a threat."

"Immediate threat?"

"My *family*."

"The President's briefing a bunch of us, and I think he's hitting Iran, I mean within the hour, I'm not sure how, but this could be our last chance to stop this thing—"

"Vinny, listen to me—" Wells gripped the phone so tightly he feared he might crack the housing. "I don't care if you're about to meet God Himself. Something happens to Evan, you don't have to worry about cancer, a heart attack, a jihadi coming for you. I will slice you up—" He felt his anger running away and didn't care. He meant every word.

"Take a breath, John, I get it—"

Wells imagined Duto blinking his heavy eyelids the way he did when he wanted to convey that he understood. "Don't John me—"

"*I get it.* Tell me where to find them."

Wells gave Duto their addresses, phone numbers.

"You have my word."

"All right. Text me when Evan's okay. And tell Shafer to call."

"Yes, sir. Any other orders, sir?"

Wells hung up, called Evan. Who didn't answer. Not entirely surprising, considering what the number must have looked like on his caller ID.

"It's your dad," Wells said. "I think it's around eight-thirty where you are." Eleven hours behind. "Next hour or two, the FBI is going to get in touch, ask you to come with them. Please don't argue. It's for your own safety, I promise, and it won't be too long. Just trust me, okay? I'll explain later."

He hung up, called Heather. He was almost glad when she didn't answer. Whether the threat was real or fake, she'd be furious with him. He left a message like the one he'd left for Evan and clicked off. He would leave Duto to call Anne. Mason hadn't threatened her directly, and he needed to move. And part of him didn't feel ready to talk to her, not from this place.

Beside the cots, a door opened into the plant manager's private bathroom, a grubby toilet and a narrow shower. Wells turned the plastic knob. He was pleasantly surprised when the showerhead blasted a jet of water, doubly surprised to find it hot. He pulled off his spattered T-shirt and underwear and stepped in. The blood sloughed off his legs and reddened the shower's plastic floor. Wells scrubbed himself down with a bar of soap that smelled like it had been marinated in cheap perfume, forced himself out after three minutes. No shave.

The younger guard had kept his clothes neatly folded in a powder-blue Adidas gym bag under his cot. His jeans and windbreaker were slightly small, but Wells could walk the world now without catching a cop's eye. The sneakers were okay, too, a size small but they'd do. Wells shoved the pistol in the waistband of his jeans. Inside the desk drawer, he found a keyless car fob, two passports, a rubber-banded stack of Turkish lira, a lighter, another phone. All a boy could want.

Suddenly the phone in the drawer rang, its screen lighting up with a local number. Then the phone in his pocket began to buzz. Maybe Mason had noticed that the webcam wasn't working anymore. Someone would be over here soon. Wells tossed the laptop and everything from the desk drawer into the guard's blue bag. He slung the bag over his shoulder as he left the office behind.

The factory's main floor was unlit. But the pallid winter sun threw enough light through the barred windows for Wells to realize it had been cleaned recently. He didn't see piles of trash or puddles of grease. This building wasn't a squat. Someone maintained it. Someone paid for the phones, hired the guards, registered the cars. No matter how good they were, they had to have left a trail. Now Shafer knew where that trail led, or so he'd told Duto. Wells wondered why Shafer felt so boxed, so sure no one would believe him.

Wells reached the front door. Chained shut. He turned around, wondering how much time he had. At the back, in the center of the building, a fire door was unlocked. Wells pushed it open, stepped outside for the first time in nearly a week.

He found himself in a weedy parking lot surrounded by a fence. It sat atop a low-rise, the land around it semi-rural, semi-industrial. Maybe five hundred meters away, four new prefab buildings were stacked close together. Past them was a row of high-voltage electric power lines and a four-lane highway. There was no sign of the Bosphorus or any of Istanbul's landmarks. Wells could have been anywhere.

The guards' ride, a four-door Nissan, was tucked behind two Dumpsters. Wells unlocked the doors, slid inside, pushed the starter button. The car hummed alive, the screen in the center console lighting up with a map of Turkey. The GPS showed he was on the Asian side of the Bosphorus, maybe thirty miles east of central Istanbul. Wells figured his best bet was to head back to the city center, the street where he'd first tracked Mason. He was sure the man had an apartment there, though maybe not in the building Wells had seen him exit. Then the guard's phone rang again. And Wells realized that he didn't need to go anywhere, didn't need to hunt. Soon enough Mason would come to him.

27

The drones came from every direction, all at once.

One, two, a dozen. Gray against the gray morning sky, but so low they couldn't be missed. They flew slowly over the wide city, over avenues, markets, highways, and parks, all heading for the same target, Imam Khomeini Square, the heart of Tehran. Their engines filled the air with a high whine, an unsettling sound, a mosquito that couldn't be slapped. On the streets below, men and women tilted their heads up to see the bombs hanging from the drones' long skinny wings.

Then they ran.

The air-raid sirens came too late. The network that connected Iran's radar installations had failed minutes before the Predators crossed into the country's airspace. By the time air defense commanders in Tehran sorted out the frantic phone calls from Kohkilooyeh and Lengeh and the other stations, they no longer needed radar to know what was happening. They could step out of their reinforced concrete shelter to see for themselves.

As they frantically tried to scramble the fighter pilots at Mehrabad, the sonic booms began. Seven streaks appeared in the west, a V formation, not even two hundred meters above the earth. One lucky photographer, a film student at the University of Tehran, managed two clear shots. They revealed a fighter with a split tail, no visible weapons, twin rear winglets. An F-22A Raptor, the most advanced fighter ever built.

The Raptors left a trail of shattered windows and howling dogs. Children shouted as their parents tugged them inside. Not everyone ran. The pious went to their knees, bowed their heads, trusting Allah would protect them.

At the eastern edge of the city, the jets turned in a tight semicircle and retraced their path, creating a second wave of panic. Three minutes later, they were gone. Meanwhile, the drones were dropping their bombs, aiming at the runways of Mehrabad, putting the airport out of commission. The Iranian fighters were now grounded, and the missile arrays around the city couldn't fire without working radar. The city was defenseless.

Then the attack ended.

The drones turned north. Barely half an hour after they first appeared, they reached the Caspian Sea. Five kilometers offshore, they tipped their noses down and followed one another into the sea, a series of spinning suicide dives that would have pleased the original kamikazes.

Their operators were unhurt.

It was nearly midnight on the East Coast, but the major media outlets were staffed and ready. Two hours before, the White House Press Office had warned bureau chiefs at the networks and the big papers that it would release a statement from the President just after midnight. *Remember when we killed bin Laden? Like that. Only bigger.* No details.

The newsroom cynics assumed a sex scandal involving the President and his National Security Advisor. Maybe the indictment of a senior cabinet member. A soon-to-be-fired producer at MSNBC speculated over Twitter that the President had lung cancer. When the White House didn't bother to rebut the report, it echoed across the Internet's peanut gallery, picking up details.

Then, at 11:56 p.m., even before the F-22s cleared Iranian airspace, the first reports of the strike on Tehran arrived from the official Iranian news service. Five minutes later, the President's press secretary appeared in the White House pressroom to release a speech that the President had just recorded in the Oval Office. *No questions tonight. Just this. He'll have a full press conference tomorrow.*

"My fellow Americans, a few minutes ago I ordered our Air Force to carry out a mission over Tehran, Iran's capital city. I authorized this operation because we have recently learned that the Iranian government is much closer to producing nuclear weapons than previously believed. To be specific, in the last few days the United States has seized more than a kilogram of weapons-grade uranium, which we have concluded was produced by the Iranian nuclear program. Our intelligence agencies now believe that Iran may have produced enough highly enriched uranium to build several nuclear bombs."

The President wore a charcoal-gray suit with an American flag on the lapel, a white shirt, a blue tie. His face was relaxed, his tone low and confident, the voice of a man certain in his decision.

"For more than a decade, the government of Iran has misled the United States and the international community about its efforts to create a nuclear arsenal. This most recent deception is the most serious yet. We can no longer tolerate these lies, especially since we have indications that Iran may ultimately try to bring nuclear weapons onto American soil. Let me be clear. The United States would view such an action as an act of war.

"Our attack today was precise and calibrated. We aimed only at infrastructure and minimized any loss of life. In fact, the Secretary of Defense informs me that we did not kill a single Iranian, soldier or civilian, with our action. But the Iranian government must know that our planes and drones can overwhelm its defenses and destroy its military. The Iranian people must know that our forces can quickly bring their economy to its knees."

The camera pushed in toward his face, a touch of showmanship. "We know that not everyone in Iran agrees with this nuclear program. In fact, our intelligence community believes that its existence may have been kept secret even from senior Iranian government officials. We want peace, not war. But we can no longer allow Iran to pretend to negotiate with us or the international community while it builds a dangerous nuclear stockpile. Tonight I call upon the government of Iran to end for all time its efforts to build nuclear weapons. As a first step, I demand that Iran open all its nuclear facilities and the records of its weaponization programs to United States inspectors. These demands are not negotiable. Based on what I have learned in the last few weeks, I can no longer outsource American safety to the International Atomic Energy Agency. The IAEA's inspectors are hardworking, but Iran has obstructed and mocked them at every turn. I am setting a deadline of two weeks from today for the Iranian government to respond to my demand."

The President pursed his lips, nodded.

"Two weeks is plenty of time if the Iranian government cooperates. No time at all if it doesn't. In case the regime doubts my resolve, tomorrow morning, I will ask the House and Senate to approve a broad military campaign against Iran. Air and missile strikes will be its first wave. But make no mistake. I will also ask for authorization for an invasion as a last resort if necessary. I have already discussed the evidence with selected senior members of Congress, as well as the leaders of Britain and France. They agree it's convincing. They agree it demands a response. Tomorrow, the Secretaries of State and Defense will make a broader presentation to Congress. We will publicize as much evidence as possible. I want the American people and the world community to see why we must take action. However, I will not ask for United Nations approval for military action. This threat is to the United States, and it demands an American response.

"Ultimately, the choice for war or peace will be made

in Tehran. If the Iranian government drops its nuclear programs and opens its doors to inspection, the United States will gladly end the threat of military action. Our goal is not regime change. It is only to ensure that the American people do not face a new threat from weapons of mass destruction."

The President had hardly moved during his speech. Now he leaned toward the camera.

"But if Iran is unwilling to cooperate, rest assured that I will do everything necessary to protect our homeland. Other nations have mistaken America's resolve before. They have always regretted the error.

"May God bless the United States of America. Thank you, and good night."

28

Wells watched from the back left corner of the textile factory as two BMW sedans stopped at the factory's rear gate, a hundred meters away. A man stepped out from the lead BMW, pulled open the gate, slipped back into the car as it came through. He didn't bother closing the gate. These guys obviously didn't plan to stay long.

The sedans raced past an empty guard shack and across the trash-strewn lot. They stopped hard about ten meters from the factory's rear fire exit. They parked side by side, the width of a car between them. Not too close, so the guys could cover each other if they came out under fire. Four front doors swung open. Four men stepped out. Three were compact and muscular and carried Heckler & Koch UMPs, fat, stubby machine pistols favored by Special Forces soldiers.

The fourth was the man Wells had desperately hoped to see. The fourth was Mason.

Wells edged backward, into the alley along the left side of the factory. They couldn't see him unless they came for him, and he'd see them first. He had hidden the guards' Nissan in the smaller parking lot at the factory's front end. He'd correctly figured that Mason and his men would use the gate in back rather than the one in front, which was chained and padlocked.

On top of the dead spy cam and unanswered calls, the missing Nissan would lead Mason to fear the worst. He would have no choice but to take his guys inside. Wells had walked the building's perimeter, seen for himself that the fire exit was the only unlocked door. Once Mason went in, Wells would have him pinned.

Wells had a Glock 19 and two spare mags he'd taken from the guardroom. He also had improvised a Molotov cocktail from a T-shirt, an empty bottle of raki, and gasoline he'd siphoned from the Nissan. Molotovs were poor man's grenades, more messy than deadly. But at the right moment, they could be devastating.

The Nissan had proven useful in one final way. Wells had broken off the car's right-side mirror with a tire iron and bashed the plastic housing until the glass inside was free. He'd propped the mirror against the fence that marked the factory's property line, about ten feet from the corner where he hid. The resulting view wasn't exactly high-definition, but it let him see the men without having to poke his head out.

Wells watched as Mason pointed at the roof and spoke to his men. Then he and two mercs ran for the back door, weapons drawn. They disappeared from Wells's view as the door creaked open, then slammed shut. The third merc stood alone between the cars.

So Mason had seen that Wells might be trying to trap him. Even so, Wells thought he had made the wrong play. He should either have left two men outside or risked bringing everyone inside. A lone guard couldn't do much but get himself killed. Mason's close-combat inexperience was showing. A twitch of a lyric passed through Wells: *It was a small mistake/Sometimes that's all it takes.*

He couldn't remember the singer's name. After he killed Mason, he'd look it up.

On the other hand . . . Wells had wound up chained to a wall the last time he'd gone after Mason. Underestimating your opponent was the biggest mistake of all.

The guard tracked the edges of the building with his H&K, starting at the left corner, up and across the roofline, down to the right corner. When he was finished, he swung the muzzle across the front of the building and repeated himself. He looked like a pro to Wells, a combat veteran who would open up without hesitation.

Wells counted twenty-four Mississippis as the guy made two passes. By now Mason and his men would have reached the second floor. Wells wanted them to be near the cell when he made his move. He needed as much time as possible to deal with the guy out here before the others came back.

Wells imagined Mason would stay behind as the mercenaries cleared the catwalk. He'd watch for movement on the empty first floor, nervously tapping the phone in his pocket as he wondered what to tell his boss. In their short acquaintance, she hadn't struck Wells as the type to tolerate mistakes. *Fool me once, shame on you, fool me twice, bullet in your head . . .*

Even as he pictured what was happening inside, Wells watched the mirror. The guard swept his machine pistol over the roof of the building for the third time. Wells slid to the corner, peeked out. The guard was a hundred feet from Wells, maybe one-twenty. Back in Kenya this distance had given him problems, but he'd spent a lot of time practicing his shooting since then. Plus the H&K wasn't as big an edge as it seemed. Short-barrel, short-stock machine pistols tended to bounce. Shooting accurately with them took years of practice. Wells would find out soon enough how well this guy was trained.

The guard looked at the top-right corner of the factory now, as far from Wells as he would be. Wells stepped out, pistol high in his hands, took a quiet step. The guy stood at a slight angle to him. He extended his arms, a shooter's stance, squeezed the trigger twice. Two loud cracks echoed off the factory behind him. The shots thumped true—

Too late Wells realized the guy was wearing a bullet-resistant vest. Not the ceramic plates that infantry wore, those would have been obvious. A thin Kevlar vest like the ones cops hid under their uniforms. They weren't much use against an assault rifle, but Wells didn't have an assault rifle. The Glock fired a medium-velocity 9-millimeter round, and Kevlar could stop those. Wells knew what had happened because the guy didn't crumple when the round hit, didn't go down all at once with blood spurting. Instead, the impact of the rounds pushed him sideways and he stumbled back against the BMW farther from Wells.

Wells put himself in the mercenary's position. He would feel like he'd been punched hard. He might even have a broken rib. But he'd realize quickly that he wasn't seriously injured and that he had a huge tactical edge. He had the vest. He had a better weapon. He had reinforcements coming. He'd see that all he needed was to hold Wells at bay until his buddies got out of the building.

Wells had two choices. Both lousy. Run for the front of the building, where he'd left the guards' Nissan, and hope he could drive out before Mason's men trapped him. Or kill this guy before the others showed up.

He'd never much liked to run.

Wells raised the Glock, fired three times more, aiming high on the chest. If he was lucky he'd catch the guy with a head shot, but he didn't expect to be lucky. He wanted to force the guy down, make him go to ground between the sedans. One round hit the guy square in the chest and knocked him backward off the second BMW. All those hours at the range had paid off. Too bad Wells had picked a target he couldn't kill.

The merc dove out of sight. He'd gather himself, decide to quit playing defense. He'd crawl or crab-walk toward the BMW that was nearer Wells, use the hood for cover while he lit Wells up. That's what Wells would do, anyway. He hoped the guard was reading from the same playbook.

Wells jammed his pistol in his waistband. He pulled the lighter he'd stolen and the Molotov. Making a Molotov was art, not science. Wells had torn a thin strip of cotton from a T-shirt, doused it in gas, and stuffed one end in the bottle, which was three-quarters full of fuel. If the T-shirt was too soaked, the bottle would explode before Wells could throw it. Too dry, and the flame would die in midair.

Wells flicked the lighter alive, touched flame to fabric. The fire roared instantly. Wells threw the Molotov in a high slow spiral like he was looking for a receiver on a fade route. The BMWs were parked maybe eighty feet away. Wells figured if he landed the Molotov within five or six feet of the merc, he'd have a chance. The pavement would shatter the bottle, spread burning gas in every direction. As the bottle left his hand, Wells grabbed his pistol and angled toward the back of the BMW. He wanted the merc to look at him, not the Molotov. He hoped that the merc had been so focused on getting into position to counterattack that he hadn't even seen Wells throwing it.

Wells took three steps. He looked over his shoulder just as the Molotov landed on the edge of the nearer BMW's front hood. It struck on the passenger side, close to the windshield, and exploded in a ball of fire that seemed half gas, half liquid. A river of flaming gasoline poured off the hood—

The merc screamed and jumped to escape the flames engulfing him. The sweater he wore over his vest burned wildly. The vest itself was fire-resistant, but it couldn't protect the merc's head or arms from the flames coming off his clothes. Worse, glass from the exploding bottle had raked his face. He screamed and clawed at his eyes. If he had been thinking clearly, he would have realized his facial injuries were agonizing but not life-threatening. He would have run to dry pavement and rolled to put out the flames. But of course he wasn't thinking clearly. He was desperate, half blind, and in shock, his hair and skin burning with an acrid choking scent.

The moment screamed for mercy, but Wells only had a pistol. He fired, moved. Two shots, two steps. He needed to end this before the others came through the fire door for him. Two more shots. Two more steps. Wells was working his way through this magazine in a hurry. No matter. With two spares, his biggest concern right now was a tired trigger finger. *Out of ammo*, an instructor at Ranger school had told him once. *The three saddest words in the English language. You know what's worse? Dying with left-over magazines on your belt.* Two more shots. Wells was hoping to manage a head shot through sheer repetition.

He did. The guard stopped screaming as suddenly as he'd started. His body dropped like a marionette free of its strings and thumped down insensate. Nothing left of him but flesh already cremating. Maybe Wells had been merciful after all.

How many seconds since his first shot? Twenty? Wells ran for the BMW. As he reached it, the fire door swung open. Mason. Wells fired twice. Mason disappeared like a groundhog who'd misread the calendar. The door slammed shut behind him. Just in time, too, because the Glock's slide snapped open to reveal an empty chamber.

Wells thumbed the release. He shook out the empty mag

as he grabbed the replacement in his pocket. In one smooth motion, he slipped the fresh mag into the well. It clicked home and Wells released the slide. He fired off two quick shots to be sure the door would stay closed long enough for him to consider his next move. If he could consider anything over the smell of a slow-cooking corpse.

He could keep the guys pinned inside for a few minutes, but they'd find a way out. If nothing else, one of them would shoot his way through the factory's front door. Wells couldn't depend on the police to arrive in time, either. The plant was far enough from the nearest occupied building that anyone who heard the shots might mistake them for engine backfires, at least at first. And Wells didn't necessarily want to be at the factory when the cops showed. They would stick him in custody for days or weeks, until they sorted out what had happened. By then, the war might already have started.

Wells poked his head into the BMW to see if Mason's men had left a key in the ignition, then realized his mistake. Like many new cars, the BMW didn't use an actual key. It had a push-button starter that worked when its sensors detected a fob with the correct encryption. Maybe Mason or his men had left the key in the center console for a quick escape. Nope.

Then Wells realized. If the dead merc on the other side of the sedan was carrying the key in his pocket, it would be close enough to trigger the BMW's sensors. If the heat from the fire hadn't cooked it. Wells slid inside, pressed the starter.

The car hummed alive.

Wells set the seat back as far as it would go and crouched behind the steering wheel, getting as low as he could. Even if the tires were ruined, he was sure the rims were all right. The fire hadn't burned long enough to melt steel.

For his purposes, running on rims would be fine. He put the car in drive, rested his foot on the brake pedal. Ten seconds passed.

The door swung open. A burst of fire followed, an H&K on full auto. Covering fire, the guys inside trying to figure out if Wells had run for the gate or disappeared around the side of the factory. Wells guessed Mason and one merc were back here, as the other tried to shoot his way out the front door. A second burst, this one from the far end of the factory, confirmed the theory.

Another covering burst, and then Mason stepped into the doorway. He fired twice in the general direction of the sedan, then turned toward the Dumpsters and fired twice more. The merc stepped out from the door behind him and moved toward the corner where Wells had first hidden, firing a five-shot burst.

They were shooting blind, spraying rounds in the broadest possible arc. Not the best strategy, but then they were a wee bit jumpy after seeing what Wells had done to the others. They hadn't figured out yet that he was directly in front of them. The BMW's engine was nearly silent at idle, and the puddle of gasoline was still smoking, providing extra cover. Even so, Wells knew they'd see him soon enough.

And then the merc looked at the BMW. He turned, swinging the H&K around—

Wells twisted the steering wheel with his left hand, raised the Glock with his right. He stamped the gas and the sedan roared ahead. The merc got the machine pistol up and shattered the windshield with a half-dozen rounds. But Wells kept coming until the BMW slammed him against the wall and tossed the H&K out of his hands.

The brick behind the merc propped him up and channeled the blow into his lower body. His hips and the big bones in his legs shattered. Only the fact that the BMW was pinning him kept him upright.

Wells wasn't wearing his seat belt. He flew at the steering wheel, but its airbag exploded out and smothered him. He had expected the crash. Even so, he was disoriented. In television commercials, airbag inflation looked pillow soft. In reality the bag came out hard enough to snap a toddler's neck, the reason that child seats were always put in the rear. Two seconds passed before Wells pushed himself away from the bag wrapped around his face. He looked up—and saw the merc leaning forward, his face white and stretched in agony. He clawed at the BMW's hood like he wanted to tear the car apart. Wells followed the merc's eyes down to the hood and the Heckler & Koch. It had landed close to the windshield. The merc got a hand on it—

Wells raised his Glock, fired through the windshield, again, again, until the back of the merc's head exploded. The machine pistol fell from his hands and clattered against the hood. His corpse sagged off the wall, his upper body leaning forward, his legs still pinned. Wells shoved the BMW into reverse, feathered the gas. And went nowhere. He reached for the starter and then remembered that deploying airbags automatically killed a car's battery and cut its engine. He was stuck in a dead car.

The front and back passenger-side windows exploded almost simultaneously, kicking glass through the car like a burst piñata. Mason. Wells had forgotten him. He couldn't be more than twenty feet away.

Get out. Wells popped open his door and twisted his body onto the pavement so that he faced the BMW. Mason was somewhere on the other side, though Wells couldn't see him. The driver's-side window exploded in a rain of glass over Wells's head.

He grabbed the machine pistol, lifted it sideways, squeezed the trigger, firing blindly across the car, five shots and then five more, anything to force Mason away. Wells didn't know how big a magazine the H&K had, probably thirty- or forty-round. Most of them had to be gone. He still couldn't see Mason, but he heard a grunt and wondered if he'd scored. Then footsteps backing off, and more shots.

Wells edged to the back of his ruined BMW and peeked out over the trunk. Mason was crouched maybe fifty feet away behind the other BMW. Wells wondered why he hadn't simply taken off and then realized he must not have the key.

Mason saw him peeking. And waved.

In answer, Wells popped off a single shot with the Glock. He felt like one of those dumbass jihadis he'd trained beside in Afghanistan, pistol in one hand, H&K in the other. All he needed was a sword strapped to his belt.

Mason appeared content to wait. He crouched silently,

his pistol propped on the trunk, almost daring Wells to come at him. He raised his head long enough for Wells to see that he was smiling. *Enjoying* himself. Somehow the smirk made Wells think of Evan and Heather. Maybe Duto had messaged him. Maybe they were safe. But Wells couldn't afford to take his eyes off Mason long enough to find out. The thought of the phone in his pocket maddened him. He forced himself to forget it, focus on the problem at hand.

Mason's grin widened. Like he knew exactly what Wells had just done. Like he'd read Wells's mind. "What now?" Mason said.

"Put the pistol on the ground, walk out where I can see you, and lie prone. It's over."

"Please."

Shots echoed from the front of the building.

"He's out now," Mason said. "Coming around the building. He comes up my side, we'll get in this car and drive away. He's got the key. He comes up your side, he'll be behind you and we'll have you."

"Whatever happens to me, this game you're running, it's done."

"You don't know what happened today in Tehran."

"Tell me."

"You don't have me in custody, you don't have anything—"

As if on cue, the first siren sounded, European-style, *woo-oo, woo-oo,* a long way off—

Mason's head cocked toward the sound. It was a small mistake.

Wells left the H&K on the trunk and stood with the Glock in both hands and sighted Mason's head and locked in and squeezed the trigger three times, *one two three,* the pistol solid in his hands. Mason raised his own pistol and managed to get one round off before Wells's second shot caught him in the jaw and tore through his throat. He dropped the pistol and sat on his ass on the cracked pavement. Wells ran for him, ready to put him down if he managed to raise the pistol. But every time he lifted it off the ground, it slipped through his fingers like it weighed a thousand pounds.

Wells knelt beside him, put the Glock to Mason's forehead. The blood leaked out of his mouth and half his jaw lay on the pavement next to him.

"Month ago, I didn't even know you existed."

Mason grunted.

"We were both better off. Any last words?"

"Go fuck yourself," Mason whispered.

Wells shoved the gun in what was left of Mason's mouth and put the pistol against his soft palate and pulled the trigger.

He ran back to the second merc he'd killed, the one he'd pinned against the wall. The guy's pants were soaked with blood, but Wells sifted through his pockets until he found a BMW key fob. Mason and the first guy he'd killed had carried keys to the car Wells had wrecked, so this fob must belong to the undamaged sedan.

Once the police arrived and found these corpses, the

game would be over. It would have to be. Whatever Mason had meant about Tehran, the fact that his body was here would prove beyond doubt that he'd faked his own death. Everything else would follow. The obvious conclusion would be that he'd killed James Veder and that he'd been running an op here. The agency and White House would have to throw out the evidence the mole had given them.

Wells slipped into the undamaged BMW, pushed the starter. The engine came to life. As it did, the phone he'd taken from the guards buzzed. He pulled it, looked down. A text from Duto. Two words. *Everyone safe.*

He put the car in reverse, swung around, cruised for the gate. He put down the windows and let the winter air rush in. Outside the gate he found a paved two-lane road. He turned right, toward the power lines and highway, already thinking of his next move. He'd have to call Duto, arrange to get out of Turkey.

He had driven halfway to the power lines when he saw two cars speeding toward him. Another BMW, followed by a Mercedes, two men in the front seats of each. As the cars blew past, the drivers looked at him like they recognized him but couldn't figure out why. Wells had the same eerie feeling. Then he saw the woman sitting in the backseat of the Mercedes. The woman who'd captured him, who'd put the needle in his neck.

Good. Let her go to the factory, see what he'd done. The police would take care of her, too.

Only later—much too late—would Wells realize he'd made a mistake. And not a small one.

29

WASHINGTON, D.C.

H ow often have I said to you that when you eliminate the impossible, whatever remains, however improbable, must be the truth?"

Shafer and Duto sat in Duto's suite in the Dirksen Senate Office Building, the curtains open to a glimpse of the Capitol dome. It was nearly two a.m. Normally the Capitol complex would be empty at this hour. Tonight the echoing footfalls outside were constant, as aides scurried to their offices to put out press releases and figure out what their bosses should think and say about the attack.

Real surprises were even rarer in Washington than anywhere else. The never-ending war between congressional Democrats and Republicans was as tightly choreographed as a Hollywood fight scene, with the same goal: milking maximum audience response at minimum risk to the players. The White House used focus groups, polls, and trial balloons disguised as leaks to test public reaction to every move the President might make.

But tonight's attack counted as a real surprise. Now CNN played silently on a television beside Duto's desk, drones flying, men and women running along a broad boulevard. The words crawling below announced the arrival of a new global crisis: *PRESIDENT SETS ULTIMATUM OVER NUCLEAR PROGRAM . . . THREATENS WAR . . . DRONES STRIKE TEHRAN AIRPORT . . . IRAN FOREIGN MINISTER: ATTACK "CRUEL, COWARDLY, UNPROVOKED" . . .*

Duto flicked off the television. "What are you talking about, Ellis?"

"Sherlock Holmes to Watson. Eliminate the impossible, whatever remains must be the truth? Good enough for a fictional nineteenth-century detective, good enough for me."

"Point?"

"Motive is the key. Always. But we keep tripping on the same rock, the countries that want Iran's nuclear program stopped bad enough to try this are our *allies*."

Duto roused himself, rummaged in his bottom desk drawer for a bottle of Dewar's and one glass.

"I would have thought Dewar's beneath a connoisseur such as yourself."

"Notice I'm not offering you any." Duto poured an inch into the glass. "Wells gets out and you come right back to life with the sassy talk and everything else. It's worse than a crush. You're a groupie. Groupies don't get to drink. And even worse, you're repeating yourself. You've been talking about motive for two weeks. When do we get to the part I don't know?"

"Eliminate the Mossad, every other national intelligence service that could do this as a false flag, who's left?"

"Iran. Trying to get under our skin."

"Makes even *less* sense. Why now? They have every reason to want to get the bombs here in secret."

"So you're telling me what? That Langley's right, Reza's real? After all this."

"No. Reza tipped us to the Veder assassination, which Mason pulled. If Reza's real, he and Mason aren't on the same team. So why would Mason be in Istanbul now? Why kidnap Wells? Only possible explanation is that Mason and Reza are working together, Mason and his guys ran the earlier ops that Reza leaked. Now they're watching Reza's back. Ergo, Reza's not real."

Duto sipped his scotch. "So Reza's fake, it's not Iran, it's not Israel, it's nobody."

"What's left?"

"Remember at Langley, I tried to brain you with that depth gauge?"

"You weren't actually hoping to *hit* me."

Duto nodded.

"Okay, not Iran, not another intel service—"

"It's us?"

Shafer was momentarily stumped. He had to admit he had never seriously considered that possibility. He turned the pieces to see if they fit. "Interesting idea . . . but no. Unless *us* is actually you, given how long ago it started.

And who else would it be? Too complicated for DOD. State isn't interested in starting wars."

"NPR."

Shafer laughed.

"Just tell me, Ellis."

"If it's not a national service, the only possibility left is a private group."

"No. Way too expensive. Not just the ops, but the way they've covered their tracks. Coms, logistics, SOG-class operators. Low nine figures, minimum."

"That's my point. The money makes it improbable. Not impossible. Look at the evidence. A small team, and as far as we can tell, Mason did all the recruiting himself. They've gone to incredible lengths to make sure we never get pictures. Like they know that if a single thread unravels, it's all over, because they've got no government protection. And the ops are medium-tech, not high."

"Tell me who has two hundred million to spend on this. And don't say a Saudi prince. Abdullah isn't putting up with that nonsense anymore. Moving that much money is a problem, too. You gotta have a clean source."

"Like a casino."

Duto put down his scotch, closed his eyes, massaged his temples like he'd come down with the world's worst migraine. "Are you saying what I think you're saying?"

Shafer took advantage of Duto's momentary blindness to grab his glass.

Duto opened his eyes. "Aaron Duberman. Am I right?"

Shafer raised the tumbler. "Salud, Vinny."

"Gimme back my scotch."

Aaron Duberman was a billionaire twenty-five times over, according to *Forbes*. In the nineties, he had turned around his failing casino company by rebranding it as the sci-fi-themed 88 Gamma and aggressively courting young Asian players. But it was Macao that had made Duberman one of the wealthiest men in the world. Along with Sheldon Adelson, Duberman had expanded into the former Chinese colony when more-established casino companies stayed away.

Now Duberman's 88 Gamma dwarfed its competitors. The company ran casinos on six continents, an empire that reached from Sydney to Buenos Aires. Duberman's fortune defied the imagination.

Two years before, he had married an Israeli model who at the time was precisely half his age, twenty-eight to fifty-six. The wedding was held in the Bahamas, on Gamma Key, Duberman's private island. To entertain the eight hundred guests, he'd hired The Rolling Stones, The Who, Kanye West, and Jay-Z. He and his wife now had twin one-year-old boys. Besides Gamma Key, they divided their time between estates in Los Angeles, Las Vegas, New York, London, Cannes, Tel Aviv, Jerusalem, and Hong Kong.

In the last election, Duberman had given $196 million to support the President's campaign. No one had ever spent more. Political analysts still argued whether the President could have won without it. Yet Duberman had never publicly discussed what, if anything, he wanted in return.

During 88 Gamma's first few years in Macao, Duberman had spent tens of millions of dollars to promote a better relationship between the United States and China.

News organizations had questioned the spending, and human rights groups accused him of being a pawn of a totalitarian government and letting greed cloud his judgment. Duberman called them fools. "I'll make just as much money in Macao even if there's a new Cold War," he said. He'd spent even more money to promote Israel's ties to the United States, and been even more vocal.

But about five years ago, he had suddenly slashed his spending on both causes. And while he donated more money than ever to presidential and congressional campaigns, he refused to discuss politics.

"People come to my casinos to have a good time, they don't care what I think about legalizing pot or the West Bank or health care," he told the *Wall Street Journal* in his last interview, eighteen months before. "For every customer who likes what I say, I risk losing two more. So I decided to shut my mouth."

"Okay, make the case," Duto said.

"One. He can spare the money. Man spent forty million dollars on his wedding."

"One."

"Two. He has endless untraceable cash. Macao alone must handle millions of dollars in paper currency every day. The company as a whole has to be wiring hundreds of millions of dollars a week. Even if we were looking we couldn't find the problem transfers."

"Two."

"Three. He's got an open line to the President. Not saying the man does whatever he says, just that Duberman has a chance to push his views quietly."

"Three."

"Four. Doesn't it strike you as odd that he's gone totally quiet about Israel? I found an op-ed he wrote for *Haaretz* six years back, he called Iran the greatest threat to both the Middle East and the United States and said America had to stand with Israel. He was so vocal, and now nothing? He cut off his China funding, too. Like he's trying to keep anyone from wondering what he's doing, why he's spending all that money to get close to the President."

"I'm not sure that'll convince anyone. It's too easy to say the guy just changed his mind, realized politics and casinos don't mix."

"Nobody changes their mind about anything past fifty."

"Give me *something* that's not open-source."

"Five. When Mason went off the rails in Hong Kong, you know where he spent most of his time? None other than the 88 Gamma Macao, according to his file."

"Thought he was fired for failing a drug test."

"He also lost at least two and a half million dollars playing blackjack."

"Nobody investigated?"

"There was no point. The money was his, an inheritance, and he hadn't done enough work in HK to know anything anybody would pay for. Hassim Sharif, the captain of the *Kara Six*, he had a gambling jones, too. How much you want to bet the 88 Gamma Corporation got some of his cash?"

Duto reached for the Dewar's bottle and tipped it to his mouth. He drew a long slug, nearly coughed it back, but sputtered it down.

"Nicely done," Shafer said.

"Accusing the President's biggest donor of treason. Next best thing to the man himself."

"I'm right, Vinny."

"I don't disagree. In terms of actual evidence. We have a connection from Mason, who's dead, as far as the seventh floor is concerned, to 88 Gamma Macao. Anything else?"

They sat in silence, Shafer sipping his glass, Duto sipping his bottle.

"Least you see why I didn't tell you before," Shafer said finally. "Why I said we were beat. Especially with Wells in the tank."

"Maybe your boy got that picture of Mason on the way out."

"Let's hope so." Shafer looked at his watch. "Wells called, what, two hours ago?"

"Yeah. I didn't tell you yet, but he said Mason threatened his kid. And the ex, Heather. He made me promise to call the Feds, get them protected."

"Tell me you did, Vinny."

"Of course I did. Threatened to cut me up if I didn't."

"At least now I know why he rolled for them," Shafer said.

"Point is, if Wells finds Mason, I seriously doubt the man will be alive for a debrief."

"A body would do just fine."

30

S alome mumbled under her breath, the filthiest curses she knew. Directed at herself.

She was a fool. The proof was the corpse leaking blood all over the trunk of her Mercedes. This day should have been the sweetest of her life, the finish of everything she had worked toward for a half-decade and more.

Instead, she was forced to wonder if John Wells knew enough, could prove enough, to undo what she'd done. Wells. A man she'd already caught, a man who should already be dead. The threat to his family had been fake, a bluff. She wished it were real. At this moment, she would gladly kill his son, everyone he cared about.

She shifted her curses to Glenn Mason. Why had she let him convince her that keeping Wells was a good idea? *A few days,* he'd said. *Just to tie Shafer up until this moves past the point of no return. Plus we might have questions for him.*

As a rule, she didn't like keeping prisoners. They had to

be hidden, fed, guarded. There was always a risk they'd escape. They could ask Wells whatever they needed to know when he woke up, then shoot him, dump his body into the Black Sea. Mason told her not to worry. *We'll chain him to a wall, won't even unlock him for the toilet. The guy's tough, he's not Houdini. And he won't want to risk his kid. A week at most, then I watch him beg for mercy, put a bullet in his head like he deserves.* Those last words should have told her what Mason was doing. So desperate to prove he was a hard case, a killer.

Until today, when Wells showed Mason what a killer really looked like. Now all the king's horses and all the king's money couldn't put Mason's brain back together again. Salome was short on sympathy. *Duke.* Over the years he'd proven more skilled at running ops than she'd expected. Somehow she'd forgotten that he was a broken toy. Stupid.

She went back to cursing herself.

The morning could have been much worse. By the time she and her men reached the factory, the sirens were close, only a couple minutes out. She stepped out of her car and looked at the bloody mess around her, the corpses and wrecked car. Nothing would explain it away.

She wondered if she should just bundle Mason's body in the trunk and take off. But even without Mason, the factory offered plenty of evidence to support the story Wells would tell once he reached safety. She and her men needed to make the bodies disappear, empty the office where the guards lived, even rip out the post where Wells had been chained. At least she had been smart enough to have tarps and tools stored in the trunks of her cars. When she realized that the feed from the camera in Wells's cell had gone dead, she'd feared the worst. So the cleanup job wouldn't take long, an hour at most. But they didn't have an hour.

A fire wouldn't work, either. It would just attract more attention. She needed to make sure the cops didn't come inside. Otherwise she might as well just lock herself in, go down shooting.

Lock herself in—

The answer came to her.

"Ari." Her bodyguard, the man she trusted more than anyone. He spoke some Turkish, not much, but enough for her purposes. She told him what she wanted. "Just be sure you wait until they're out of their cars—"

He nodded.

"Your clothes. You can't look like that."

He tossed off his suit jacket, pulled off his tie, tore a hole in his shirt, swabbed his arms and legs in the gasoline residue on the pavement. From well dressed to vagrant in seconds. He grabbed the machine pistol lying on the pavement, ran for the gate.

She turned to the others. "We move the burned BMW behind there"—she nodded at the Dumpster—"so no one outside the gate can see it. We wrap the bodies in the tarps, throw them in the trunks. We move the cars into the alley. Then we hide there, too. When the cops get to the back gate, they won't have anything to see. Let's go."

Two sets of sirens were howling close by, *oo-ooo, oo-ooo.*

But as Salome had hoped, they were headed for the front gate, the natural first choice. And the front gate was chained, padlocked, and rusting. It obviously hadn't been opened in months. The cops would poke at it for a minute or two before they realized they needed to try the back.

The BMW took the most time. It wouldn't start. The men had to push it while Salome steered. By the time they were done hiding it behind the Dumpster, the cops had already reached the front gate, spent several minutes yelling in Turkish, and left. The sirens screamed away. But she knew where they were headed, to a cross street about two kilometers away that offered access to the road behind the factory.

Salome and her men covered themselves in blood and brains and charred flesh shoving the corpses into the cars. No one spoke, but she knew her men wondered how Wells had done all this by himself. She did, too.

They finished and hid in the alley alongside the building just as the sirens rolled to the back gate. Someone shouted angrily through a megaphone in Turkish.

What she'd feared. Ari had locked the gate from the outside, once he was through. But unlike the reinforced front gate, the back had a single chain holding it shut. It would easily give if the cops rammed it. And if they got inside they would see the cars. The game would be up.

Everything rested on Ari.

Suddenly, the cop began shouting even more loudly, but not at them.

Yes.

She'd ordered Ari to come around the corner of the

factory just after the police arrived. An H&K in his hands. Not to shoot. A firefight would only make matters worse. He was to play dumb, a barely functional Syrian refugee who had found his way to Istanbul. He was wandering around *outside* the factory when he stumbled on the H&K. He decided to shoot off a few rounds. He was sorry for any trouble he'd caused. He had no identification, no money. He was very sorry.

The cops would take the H&K. Maybe they'd arrest him. She didn't know what charges he'd face. But ultimately he hadn't done anything terrible. He'd work his way through the system and be released. Or maybe they wouldn't bother bringing him back to the station. They'd beat him, drive him back to the highway, tell him to get out of Istanbul. No matter. Ari could handle himself.

As long as they believed that the shots had come from outside, they'd have no reason to bother coming inside. Whoever had called 155, the Turkish police emergency number, had obviously been too far away to know what was really happening. If the caller had reported anything more than hearing shots, a dozen police cars would have shown up. And they wouldn't have stopped at the gate, they would have driven through.

Low voices.

Just go. We'll clean this mess up like it never existed. John Wells can tell whoever he likes whatever he likes. He'll sound even crazier than he is.

A minute passed. Another. Then the sirens flicked off. The police cruisers turned away from the gate, crunched down the road, their engines fading into the distance.

Forty-nine minutes later, she and her men rolled away. She would wrap the bodies in chains and dump them in the Black Sea. As she should have done with Wells. She should have believed the stories she'd heard. Unarmed, chained to a wall, he'd broken free, killed five of her operatives. Now she had to decide whether to go after Wells with what was left of her team, or disappear and hope that nothing he or Shafer did could stop the war. What the President had done in Tehran this morning couldn't be undone. The Iranians *knew* the uranium wasn't theirs. They wouldn't understand why the United States had said it was, or why it had attacked them. They would believe the White House and CIA were faking evidence to support an invasion. They would be frightened. And furious. They would never agree to negotiate, much less to open their doors. Their refusal would further inflame the United States. The situation would spiral. By the end of the President's two-week deadline, the two sides would be headed for war.

Could Wells or Shafer find her by then? Could they find the man behind her?

Duberman had given her carte blanche. But she couldn't make this decision herself. She reached for a burner phone, punched in a number that began with an 852 prefix. Hong Kong. "We need to talk. I'm coming to Olympus."

Olympus was Duberman's mansion on Victoria Peak, which overlooked Hong Kong Harbor. The world's most expensive real estate. A house near the top of the Peak had recently sold for $230 million. Duberman's had a better view.

Salome flicked off the phone, tossed it onto the highway.

She had hundreds more. She wished she could replace her men as easily. But even with her team crippled, she had to hunt Wells down. She couldn't just hope he would go away. He knew too much.

She would kill him. The sooner, the better.

EPILOGUE

His life fit in the back of a Subaru, with room to spare. A suitcase of clothes. Books, a few framed photos, his pistols and gear. All he'd accumulated in more than forty years. A blessing, maybe, but at the moment it felt like a curse.

It was the coldest night of the year in New Hampshire, fifteen below. Old snow crushed the earth, but above the sky was clear, the stars bright and impossibly close, the air itself frozen to death.

Anne and Tonka stood a few feet away. Tonka whined and looked from Wells to the door and back: *Why did you bring me out here?* Even so, when Wells opened his door, the dog forced its way between him and the driver's seat, teeth bared, trying to keep him from the car. Wells pulled a hand from a glove and ran it over Tonka's back and knelt low until the dog stopped growling and licked his face.

"One day—"

"Don't say that."

Anne's face was tight.

"Sorry—"

"Or that."

Wells reached for her.

"No." But she closed her eyes and opened her arms and hugged him through her thick down jacket.

"You're in there somewhere," he said.

She tilted her head up to him. When she opened her eyes, the tears came. Then Wells was crying, too, the tears shocking and hot against his frozen cheeks.

"I didn't know you could cry."

"Maybe I'm in there somewhere, too." He broke away. "Wish me luck?"

She shook her head. He wanted to tell her he loved her. That one day, sooner or later, he'd find the strength to give up the game and come back. But he knew the words would only hurt her more.

He leaned forward, kissed the tears from her cheeks. And silent as the air, he went.

Two days since his escape. On the afternoon he'd broken out, a Turkish-flagged fishing ship had picked him up at Sife, a Black Sea resort forty miles from central Istanbul. Wells sat in the ship's cabin for the next eight hours. He wondered what had happened at the factory, why the police hadn't found the bodies. At an Internet café, he scanned English-language Turkish news websites.

There should have been dozens of articles. But somehow she—whoever *she* was—had escaped. Had she paid off the cops?

He had no problem finding articles about the drone attack on Tehran, though. Iran's supreme leader, His Eminence Ayatollah Ali Khamenei, had called the bombing "a Zionist-Satanist plot" a few hours before. "The Islamic Republic will never negotiate. The United States must know it will not escape the consequences of this unprovoked attack."

In Washington, congressional leaders from both parties announced their support for a hard-line stance. "This danger transcends partisanship," the Speaker of the House said. "Iran must understand it cannot hold the United States hostage." Oil was up twenty-seven dollars a barrel, the biggest one-day rise ever. European stock markets had fallen seven percent, and American stocks were expected to plunge even further when they opened.

Wells knew he should call Evan and Heather, give them some idea what had happened. But the escape had left him exhausted beyond measure. He couldn't face those conversations. He settled for tapping out a short email, apologizing and promising to explain further in a day or two.

When the ship came, no one spoke to him. He was grateful.

The ship ran west-northwest, along the curve of the coast, one more trawler in the Black Sea's crowded waters. Just past midnight, it turned toward the dim lights of the coast. After another half hour, it angled into a narrow cove and stopped twenty meters from a narrow beach. Two cars waited on a low bluff above. A man standing between them waved a flashlight to the ship. The captain hitched an aluminum ladder to the railing.

"You swim?"

Wells made his way down the ladder, flopped off in the world's worst racing dive. The frigid water shocked him, but he forced his way to shore. The man with the flashlight walked down to meet him.

"Welcome to Bulgaria."

"You have no idea how happy I am to hear that."

The man led Wells to the backseat of the second sedan. A gray-haired man looked him over as the two-car convoy rolled off, silently flashing the blue lights used by secret police across Eastern Europe and Russia.

"Mr. Wells. I am Director Kirkov of the NIS." The Bulgarian National Intelligence Service.

"Guess Vinny still has some friends."

"He said to tell you you owe him another favor."

"I think I owe *you*."

Kirkov smiled. "You look like you could use a night's sleep, Mr. Wells. You will stay at my house. Tomorrow morning, a Bulgarian passport and a flight through Warsaw to New York. I'm sorry, no nonstop from Sofia. You arrive in the afternoon."

"Thank you for this."

"I don't suppose you'd like to tell me what happened?"

"After it's over."

Kirkov put out a fleshy hand. "Let's shake on it, then."

From Kirkov's mansion, he called Evan and Heather. The FBI was watching them at a safe house in Utah. They weren't happy, to say the least. Heather: *Provo? Anybody consider the threat of death from boredom?* Evan: *I hope this was real. Because you ruined my season.* Both insisted that they hadn't seen anyone or anything unusual in the days before the FBI came. Wells wondered if Mason had been bluffing. Even so, he asked them to wait a few days, and they both agreed.

From JFK, he went straight to North Conway. He owed Anne that much, at least. Himself, too. One last good-bye. One last look at the house where he'd spent the best part of the last four years, in every sense. Some part of him was foolish enough to believe the words he hadn't had the strength to say, that one day he would retire and come back to her.

Now he was in Duto's office in Philadelphia, where everything had begun a month before. Again Duto and Shafer sat side by side on the couch. This time they were drinking coffee, not beer.

"Trying to stop a war and you think it's a good time to visit your girlfriend," Duto said. "Tearful bye-bye."

Wells thought of the cell, what he'd done to get free. "Come with me next time, Vinny. See how long you last."

"Problem with you, you want points for fixing your own mistakes."

Shafer and Duto were all he had. An exhausting thought.

"You win, Vinny. I'm done arguing." Wells reached for a Dunkin' Donuts cup big enough to fuel an airplane. Normally he drank his coffee black, but now he salted it with milk and sugar until it could have passed for a Frappuccino. Anything to take the bitterness away. "Can we talk about the matter at hand? Who's behind this? Who's the woman? And how do we stop it?"

"Don't know about the woman," Shafer said. "But I can tell you who's paying the bills." For the next ten minutes, he outlined his theory.

"You agree?" Wells said to Duto when Shafer was done.

"It makes more sense than anything else."

"Fits with what I saw. Money no object and yet it felt like they had no backup."

"So Duberman hired this woman," Shafer said. "She brought in Mason. Got the HEU."

"Do we have any evidence?" Wells said.

"Not without Mason," Duto said.

"Can't you go to Hebley, man to man, DCI to DCI, get him to see reason?"

"Before the drones, maybe. Not now. Now it's all public."

Duto was right, Wells saw. At this point, without absolute proof the plot was fake, Langley, the Pentagon, and the White House couldn't back off the narrative they'd created.

"And you haven't come up with anything, Ellis? Not a single lead?"

They sat in silence.

"Twelve days," Duto said finally. "That's what we have. Assuming the President sticks to what he outlined in his speech."

"HEU's the key," Shafer said. "They got it from somewhere. We figure that out, we can unravel the chain. Maybe."

"So all we have to do is find a supplier of highly enriched uranium nobody else in the world knows about. So we can take down a guy with twenty-five billion dollars in the bank. The President's richest donor."

"Tell me that smile means you have an idea," Duto said.

I'm smiling because I'm not tired anymore. Because right or wrong, I live for the chance to play this game. I know what it costs and I don't care.

And the higher the stakes, the better.

"Twelve days," Wells said. "Twelve days."

ACKNOWLEDGMENTS

Without Putnam, these pages would only be a Word file. Neil Nyren hasn't made a bad edit yet, and Ivan Held and his team are the best in the business. Thanks also to Heather Schroder, who knew John Wells when he was just a gleam in my eye, and Tom Young and Matthew Snyder (your faith will be rewarded, I promise).

Most of all, to Jackie, who juggles being a doctor, wife, and mother more dexterously every day. The best is still ahead.

This is the greatest job in the world, and I wouldn't have it without you. As always, I welcome comments and suggestions at alexberensonauthor@gmail.com. I read every email, and so far I've kept my promise to respond to each one personally. I hope to continue that practice. If you want more frequent updates, feel free to follow me on Facebook and Twitter.

Now, back to work . . .

TURN THE PAGE FOR A SPECIAL PREVIEW
OF ALEX BERENSON'S NEXT THRILLER

TWELVE DAYS

AVAILABLE IN HARDCOVER
FROM G. P. PUTNAM'S SONS

PROLOGUE

For as long as he could remember, Vikosh Jain had wanted to see India. His family's homeland for a hundred generations. The world's largest democracy. The birthplace of his religion.

While his friends moved into their own apartments after college, he lived at home, paying off his student loans and saving money for what he knew would be an epic adventure. The trip became an obsession for him. He mapped every train ride across the subcontinent, from Mumbai to Delhi, Kashmir to Madras. Finally, when he'd saved the eleven thousand dollars he'd budgeted for a ten-week trip, he bought his ticket.

What a fool he'd been.

After a month, he couldn't wait to get home. He was sick of India. Sick *with* India, too. Despite following all the rules, avoiding street food and drinking bottled water, he'd found himself glued to a toilet a week after he arrived. The cheekier travel websites called what had happened to him *the Delhi diet*. It sounded like a joke, but it wasn't. By the time the doxycycline kicked in, he'd lost ten pounds. He could hardly walk a flight of stairs. His skin might let him pass for local, but his gut was suburban New Jersey through and through.

Not just his gut. Coming here had taught him how American he really was. Every time he stepped into the streets he was overwhelmed. By the dust that coated his mouth. The shouting, honking, hawking crowds. The pushing and shoving and relentless begging. By the way the men openly pawed women on buses and streetcars. He felt disconnected from all of them, even the ones who had money. He'd planned to spend a week with his father's family in Delhi, but he left after two days. He hated the way his aunt screeched at her maids and gardeners. Like they weren't people at all.

Before the trip his parents had warned him that his expectations were unrealistic. When he emailed home to complain, long paragraphs of frustration, his father had answered in one sentence, *You need to accept it for what it is.* And after another long screed: *Don't you see? This is why we left.*

Even as Vik read those words his stomach pulled a 720-degree spin, like a reckless snowboarder had taken up residence in his gut. He wondered what he'd eaten this time. He wasn't scheduled to fly home for another six weeks. But enough. Enough was enough. He went online and found that for only two hundred dollars he could change his flight. He could leave this very night. For a few seconds he tried to convince himself to stay, that he would be quitting, betraying his heritage. But India wasn't his country. Never had been. Never would be.

He reached for his credit card.

Now, after an endless taxi ride to Chhratrapati Shivaji International Airport, an hour-long wait to enter the terminal, four bag searches, three X-rays, and a barking immigration officer, Vik was almost free. He had what might have been the worst seat on the plane, the end of the cabin's last row. So be it. He'd be close to the toilets. He settled himself into a chair and waited to board.

Nick Cuse had captained nonstops to Mumbai and Delhi for two years. After twenty-eight years at Continental—as he would always think of CAL as his employer, never mind the merger or the name on the side of the jet—he could choose his runs. Most captains at his seniority preferred Hong Kong or Tokyo, well-run airports that weren't surrounded by slums like the one in Mumbai. But Cuse had started as a Navy pilot, landing F-14s on carrier decks. He was keenly aware that every year commercial aircraft became more automated. Every year pilots had less to do. He wanted to end his career as something other than a glorified bus driver. Mumbai was a lot of things, but it was rarely boring. Twice he'd had to abort landings for slum kids running across the runway, airport cops chasing them like something out of a bad movie.

His copilot for this trip, Henry Franklin, was also former Navy, just young enough to have flown sorties in the first

Gulf War. They'd shared the cockpit three days earlier, and Cuse was happy to have Franklin with him for the ride back. Ninety-nine times out of a hundred, a civilian with a week of training could have done what they were about to do. But the hundredth time defined the job. A good pilot felt a crisis coming before his instruments did, and defused it before it became serious enough to take down his plane. Cuse had that sixth sense, and he saw it in Franklin. Though the guy was a little bit sharp to the crew.

Now they sat side by side in the cockpit making final preflight checks. Their Boeing 777 was just about full, making weight and balance calculations easy. Two hundred and sixty-one passengers, seventeen crew members. Two-seven-eight human souls traveling eight thousand miles, over the Hindu Kush, the Alps, the Atlantic. They would fly in darkness from takeoff to landing, the sun chasing them west but never catching them.

Every time you leave the earth, it's a miracle, Cuse's first instructor at Pensacola had told him. *You come back down, that's another. A miracle of human invention, human ingenuity, human cunning. Never forget that, no matter how routine it may eventually seem. Always respect it.*

"Captain," Franklin said. "We're topped up." An eight-thousand-mile flight into the jetstream required the 777 to leave Mumbai with full tanks, forty-five thousand gallons of aviation-grade kerosene. The fuel itself weighed more than three hundred thousand pounds, accounting for almost half the jet's takeoff weight. They were carrying fuel to carry fuel, an inherent problem with long-range flights.

Cuse glanced at his watch, a platinum Rolex that had been his wife's present to him on the day they signed their divorce papers. Nine years later, he still didn't know why she'd given it to him. Or why he'd kept it. 11:36 p.m. Four minutes before scheduled departure. They'd leave on time. By Mumbai standards they had a good night to fly, seventy degrees, a breeze coming off the Indian Ocean to push away smog from trash fires and diesel-spewing minibuses. He looked over his displays one more time. Perfect.

Cuse liked to keep the cockpit door open as long as possible, a throwback to the days when pilots didn't regard every passenger as a potential terrorist. He nodded through the doorway to the purser.

"Green across the board here, ready to push as soon as everyone's down. Tell 'em sixteen flat and smooth."

"Yes, sir."

Franklin reached for the door. "Lock and arm, Captain?"

"Lock and arm."

"Greetings, United Flight 49. I'm Carl Fisher, your purser. We've closed the cabin door and are making final preparations for our flight to Newark. At this point, United requires you to put your cell phone on airplane mode. To make the flight more relaxing for you and everyone around you, we don't allow in-flight calls. But you are free to use approved electronic devices once we've taken off. The captain has informed me that he's expecting our flight time to be sixteen hours, with very little turbulence. We do recommend that you keep your seat belt fastened for the duration of the flight in case we run into any unexpected rough air . . ."

Vik thumbed in one last text to his mother—*On the plane, see you tomorrow*—and then turned off his phone. Even if his stomach settled down, he doubted he'd sleep. He was caught between the cabin wall and a chubby twentysomething woman wearing a Smith College sweatshirt and hemp pants. She smelled of onion chutney and positive thinking.

She caught him looking at her and extended a hand, exposing a dirty Livestrong bracelet. "We're going to be neighbors for sixteen hours, we ought to know each other's names. I'm Jessica."

Vik awkwardly extended his own hand. "Vik. Let me guess. Yoga retreat?"

"Am I that obvious? How about you?"

"I came to visit family."

"That's so wonderful. Getting to see the place where you're from."

"Yeah. Sure is." Despite himself, Vik liked this woman. He wished he could have seen the country through her eyes instead of his own.

It was only 11:50 p.m. by Cuse's Rolex when Franklin swung the jet onto 09/27. For years, the airport here had tried to operate a second, intersecting runway, a prescription for disaster. Complaints from pilots and its own controllers had finally forced it to stop. Now 09/27 was the airport's sole runway. At this moment, it was entirely

empty, two miles of concrete that ran west toward the
Indian Ocean.

"United Airlines four-nine heavy, you are cleared for
takeoff on runway oh-nine right. Wind one-two-zero, ten
knots." The air-traffic controllers here had call-center English, clear and precise.

"Forty-nine heavy, cleared for takeoff oh-nine right."
Cuse clicked off. "Thrust check?"

"Thrust check complete," Franklin said.

"Flaps? Final takeoff check?"

"Final takeoff complete."

"Full thrust."

Like all new-generation jets, the 777-200 was fly-by-
wire. Computers controlled its engines, wings, and flaps.
But Boeing had designed the cockpit to preserve the comforting illusion that pilots physically operated the plane.
Instead of dialing a knob or pushing a joystick, Franklin
pushed the twin white handles of throttle as far forward as
he could. The response was immediate. The General Electric engines on the wings spooled up, sending a shiver
through the airframe.

"You have throttle," Franklin said, officially giving Cuse
control of the plane for takeoff. He dropped the brakes and
the three-hundred-fifty-ton jet rolled forward, at first
slowly, then with an accelerating surge. He felt as though
he were wearing blinders. The city, the terminal, even the
traffic control tower no longer existed. Only the runway
before him and the metal skin that surrounded him.

"One hundred knots. V1 is one-five-five." At one hundred fifty-five knots, the 777 would reach what pilots called

V1, the point at which safety rules dictated going ahead with takeoff even with a blown engine. Cuse named the figure with every takeoff, a formality. He knew it as well as his own name.

"One-five-five," Franklin repeated, a secular *Amen*.

Cuse's gut and the instruments agreed: V1 would be no problem. The engines were running perfectly. The runway markers clipped by. They passed one hundred thirty knots, one forty, one fifty, nearly race-car speed, though the jet was so big and stable that Cuse wouldn't have known without the gauges to tell him—

"V1." And only a second later. "V2." Now the Triple-7 had reached one hundred sixty knots, almost one hundred eighty-five miles an hour. As soon as Cuse pulled up its nose, the lift under its wings would send it soaring. Cuse felt himself tense and relax simultaneously, as he always did at this moment. Boeing's engineers and United's mechanics and everyone else on the ground had done all they could. The responsibility was his.

"V2 plus ten. Rotate." Cuse pulled back the yoke. The jet's nose rose smoothly and it leapt into the sky. *A miracle of human invention*.

"Positive climb. Gear up." Cuse pushed a button to retract the landing gear. They were gaining altitude smartly now, almost forty feet a second. In less than a minute they would be higher than the world's tallest building. In five they would be able to clear a good-sized mountain range.

"United four-nine heavy, you are clear. Continue heading two-seven-zero—"

"Continue two-seven-zero, good-bye—" That last word not strictly necessary, but Cuse liked to include it as long as takeoff was copacetic, a single touch of humanity in the middle of the engineering. *Good-bye, au revoir, adios amigos, but no worries, I'll be back.*

They topped four hundred feet and the city bloomed around them.

"Flaps," Franklin said.

"Flaps up. Climb power."

Vik pressed his nose against the window, looking down at the terminal's bright lights. He felt an unexpected regret. Maybe he should have stayed longer, given the place another chance. He might see it again. Once he married, had children, a trip like this one would be impossible. Unless he married a wannabe yogi like Jessica and got stuck taking trips to India for all eternity.

"I miss it already," she said, as if reading his mind.

"Yeah, what's not to love?" He wondered if she knew he was being sarcastic.

Second by second, the jumbled neighborhoods around the airport came into view. At ground level, Mumbai hid its massive slums behind concrete walls and elevated highways. But from above, they were obvious, dark blotches in the electrical grid, the city's missing teeth. Some of the largest surrounded the airport. Vik had read a book about them. He imagined rows of rat-infested mud-bricked huts, children and adults jumbled together on straw mattresses, trying to sleep, plotting their next dollar, their next meal.

So much desperation, so much bad luck and trouble. Yet they pushed on. But then what else could they do?

Then, from the edge of the slum nearest the airport, Vik saw something he didn't expect.

Twin red streaks cutting through the night. Fireworks. Maybe someone down there had something to celebrate for a change. But they didn't peter out like normal fireworks. They kept coming, arcing upwards—

Not fireworks. *Missiles.*

"No. No—"

Jessica leaned over, put a hand on his arm. "Everything okay?"

Following a failed al-Qaeda effort to shoot down an Israeli passenger jet in Kenya in 2002, the Federal Aviation Administration seriously considered making American airlines retrofit their fleets with antimissile equipment. But installing thousands of jets with chaff and flare dispensers, along with radar systems to warn pilots of incoming missiles, would have been hugely expensive. Estimates ranged from five to fifty billion dollars. Worse, the engineers who designed the countermeasures couldn't say for sure that they would allow a passenger jet to escape. Passenger planes were far less maneuverable than fighter jets, and their engines gave off big, obvious heat signatures. And major airports were so congested that some experts said the systems ultimately cause jets to fire flares in each other's paths.

The seriousness of the threat was also unclear. Despite their easy-to-use reputation, surface-to-air missiles required substantial training. After a few months of memos, the FAA shelved the idea of a retrofit.

And so American jets remained unprotected from surface-to-air attack.

From the cockpit, Cuse felt the missiles before he saw them. Something far below that didn't belong. He looked down, saw the streaks. They had just cleared the airport's western boundary. Unlike Vik Jain, he knew immediately what they were.

"Max power." He shoved the throttle forward and the turbines whined in response. "Nose down—" He dropped the yoke.

"Captain—"

"Look out your window." Cuse toggled Mumbai air traffic control. "Mumbai tower, four nine heavy has an emergency. Two missiles—"

"Repeat, United—" the controller said.

"Two SAMs. Look out your window—" He flicked off. The tower couldn't help him now.

"Man oh man," Franklin said.

Cuse snuck another look. In the five seconds since he'd first spotted them, the missiles had closed almost half the gap with the jet. They had to be deep in the supersonic range, twelve hundred miles an hour or more. A mile every three seconds. Of course the Boeing was moving too, at three hundred miles an hour and accelerating, with a two-mile horizontal lead and a thousand feet of vertical. If the SAMs were Russian, they probably had a range of three to four miles. At three miles they'd probably escape. At four they wouldn't.

The world's deadliest math problem. Those beautiful deadly streaks would either reach him or not, and the worst part was he'd already played his only card. He couldn't outmaneuver the missiles, or hide from them. He could only try to outrun them.

"Gonna be close," Cuse said.

In 44A, Vik had felt the surge of the engines. Then the plane leveled off, more than leveled off, started to drop. *They know. They'll do whatever they do to beat these things and we'll be fine.* But the missiles kept coming, closing the gap shockingly fast, homing in on the jet, arrows from the bow of the Devil himself.

He grabbed Jessica's hand.

"Whoever you pray to, pray. *Pray.*"

"Hail Mary, full of grace, the Lord is with thee—" The words tumbled out of her. Vik just had time to realize he was surprised. He'd expected a Yogic chant. Then one of the streaks flared out, fell away.

"Yes—"

But the other didn't.

The Russians referred to the missile as the Igla-S—Igla being the Russian word for *needle*. NATO called it the SA-24 Grinch. The Russian military had first put it into service in 2004, updating the original Igla, which was more than thirty years old. They'd invested heavily in the re-design, knowing that it would have a wide export market. Armies all over the world depended on surface-to-air missiles to neutralize close air support. A single SAM could take out a twenty-million-dollar fighter. Russians more than doubled the size of the Igla's warhead. They improved its propellant to allow it to catch even the fastest supersonic fighter. They added a secondary guidance system.

And they lengthened its range. To six kilometers.

The 777 never had a chance.

Twelve seconds after its launch, the Igla crashed into the Boeing's left engine. The warhead didn't explode right away. Its delayed fuse gave it time to burrow inside the casing of the turbine.

A tenth of a second later, five and a half pounds of high explosive detonated.

In movies, missile strikes inevitably produced giant mid-air fireballs. But military jets had Kevlar-lined fuel tanks. In the real world, missiles destroyed planes by shearing off their engines and wings. They crashed, rather than exploding.

This time, though, the Hollywood myth was accurate. The 777's fuel tanks weren't designed to survive a missile strike. And the plane carried far more fuel than a fighter jet. It was a flying bomb, fifty times as big as the one that had blown up the Alfred P. Murrah Federal Building in Oklahoma City.

The explosion started in the fuel tanks under the left

478 | ALEX BERENSON

wing. It almost instantly created a superheated cloud of burning kerosene that tore apart the cabin in less than two seconds. From Nick Cuse, in the cockpit, to Vikosh Jain, in the last row, all 278 people on board were simultaneously incinerated. They didn't die as much as *evaporate*, their physical existence denied.

Despite his immediate action, Cuse was unable to save his jet. Even so, he proved himself a hero of sorts. By getting the Boeing offshore—barely—before the missile struck, he saved the city from the worst of the fireball. If the explosion had happened over the slums, hundreds of people would have burned to death. Instead, Mumbai's residents lifted their heads and watched as night turned to day. Buildings more than a hundred feet high were the most severely damaged, so for once the rich rather than the poor suffered most.

The fireball lasted a full thirty seconds before fading, replaced with an unnatural blackness, a cloud of smoke that didn't dissipate until the morning. By then, the toll of the attack would be clear. Besides the 278 people on the plane, two people on the ground died, and 365 more had second- and third-degree burns. Planes all over the world were grounded.

And the United States and Iran were much closer to war.

1

The images were horrific. A man's legs, brown skin sloughed off, exposing the yellow-red meat underneath. A layer of jet fuel burning on top of the ocean, charring a chunk of bone. Worst of all, bits of a stuffed toy, blood smearing its white fur.

The first reports of an explosion in Mumbai showed up on Twitter ninety seconds after the jet was hit. A half hour later, 12:30 a.m. in India, 2 p.m. in Washington, the Associated Press and Reuters confirmed a plane crash. The Indian Navy was sending ships to search the waters west of the city, Reuters said. Two hours later, a bleary-eyed spokesman for the Indian Ministry of Civil Aviation identified the jet as a United Airlines flight bound for Newark. "The situation is difficult," he said. "At this point we cannot expect survivors."

Almost immediately, Reuters broke the news that the jet's captain had reported seeing missiles in the air seconds before the plane exploded. Then an Indian news agency reported that airport authorities had surveillance video that showed a missile striking the jet. By 8 p.m. Eastern, CNN and Fox and everyone else had the video. The anchors murmured somberly, *Disturbing, we want to warn you so you can have your children leave the room . . .*

The video was silent, not even a minute long. The camera was fixed and faced west from the airport's control tower. It didn't capture the actual launch of the missiles. They were already airborne when they entered the frame. From left to right, twin red streaks rose toward an invisible target. After five or six seconds they faded, apparently too far away for the camera to catch. But they hadn't stopped their chase. The proof came with the explosion, a white flash tearing open the night, resolving into a mushroom cloud. The shock wave hit seconds later, rattling the camera as the cloud in the distance grew.

HORROR IN THE SKIES, the crawl under the video said, and this time CNN wasn't exaggerating. India's navy would surely call off its search by morning. No one could possibly have survived.

The inevitable next act would be assigning blame.

The video ended. CNN cut to a serious-looking man in a gray suit with a white shirt. *Fred Yount, Terrorism Analyst at RAND Institute*—

John Wells flicked off the screen before he had to hear

Yount. A man squeezed a trigger somewhere in the dark. A few seconds later almost three hundred people were dead. Whatever Yount had to say wouldn't change those bare facts.

Wells had quit the Central Intelligence Agency years before. But he'd never escaped the secret world. He knew now he never would. He felt like a swimmer fighting a whirlpool. He was strong enough to avoid being sucked down, but not to reach land. He could only tread water, knowing that one day his body would fail.

He was in his early forties, but his chin was still sturdy, his shoulders still thick with muscle. Only the patches of gray hair at his temples and the permanent wariness in his brown eyes betrayed his age, and his too-close acquaintance with the world's sins.

Wells lay back on his bed, stared at the ceiling. He was in room 319 in the Courtyard Marriott at the Washington Navy Yard, a hotel favored by randy congressmen for its nearness to their offices. More than anything, Wells wanted to close his eyes. Sleep. But he had a plane to catch in less than four hours. He had arrived in the United States only the night before. Now he was going back the way he'd come, over the Atlantic, bound for London and then Zurich. To meet with a man who didn't much want to see him. Then, maybe, to Mumbai.

Wells understood. He didn't want to see himself either. Not at the moment. He was carrying himself around like a rain-soaked cardboard box about to burst. Too many miles. And too much death. Wells blamed himself for the downing of the jet. A few days before, he'd discovered the truth about a plot to maneuver the United States into war with Iran. He'd nearly found a way to stop it. But his enemies had outplayed him.

He'd failed.

Wells turned out the bedside light. He closed his eyes and for sixty seconds thought of the jet's passengers. Then he made himself forget them. Nothing else to do.

He wasn't sure if he'd fallen asleep, but a light knock stirred him. The room door swung open. "Nice opsec." Ellis Shafer's gravelly, mumbly voice. The lights flicked on.

"If it came to that I could kill you in my sleep, Ellis."

"Hitting you hard?"

"I'm all right." Wells pushed himself up.

"Of course you are." Shafer sat on the bed next to Wells. "They probably didn't even know what hit them. Except the captain. Obviously."

"I feel much better."

"Should I tell you they're in heaven with seventy-two million virgins each?"

"Ellis—"

"Too soon?"

Wells had been raised Christian but converted to Islam more than a decade before, in the mountains of Pakistan. Shafer was a Jew who had declared his atheism at his bar mitzvah more than fifty years earlier. Unlike Wells, he still worked for the CIA. Barely. Until one of the new director's new men got around to dropping off a letter of resignation for him to sign.

Over the years Wells and Shafer had worked together on a half dozen operations.

But they had never faced a mission as tricky as this one.

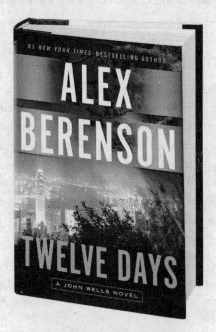

THE NIGHT RANGER

A JOHN WELLS NOVEL

When four young volunteers in Kenya decide to take a break from working at a Somali refugee camp, they pile into a Land Cruiser for an adventure. But they get more than they bargained for when they are kidnapped. John Wells is asked to try to find them, but he does so reluctantly. East Africa isn't his usual playing field. And when he arrives, he finds that the truth behind the kidnappings is far more complex than he imagined.

"Berenson gives readers top-notch, fast-paced excitement…John Wells is a worthy hero readers can count on."
                                                —*Kirkus Reviews*

alexberenson.com
facebook.com/alexbersonauthor
penguin.com

M1563T0914